Welcome to the adventure

Where loyalty matters, magic runs deep,
and nobody stands alone.

1

LISA CASSIDY

THE NAMELESS THRONE

THE INKWEAVER ARCHIVE

BOOK 1

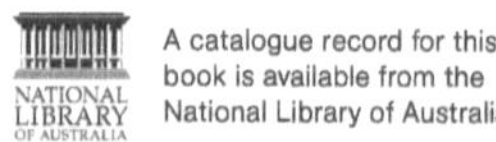

A catalogue record for this book is available from the National Library of Australia

National Library of Australia Cataloguing-in-Publication entry

Creator: Cassidy, Lisa, 2023 - author.

Title: *The Nameless Throne*

ISBN (paperback): 978-1-922533-11-1

Subjects: Epic fantasy fiction

Series: *The Inkweaver Archive*

First published in 2023 by Tate House

Cover artwork and design by J Caleb Designs

Map artwork by Chaim Holtjer

Also by me

The Mage Chronicles

DarkSkull Hall

Taliath

Darkmage

Heartfire

~

Heir to the Darkmage

Heir to the Darkmage

Mark of the Huntress

Whisper of the Darksong

Rise of the Shadowcouncil

~

A Tale of Stars and Shadow

A Tale of Stars and Shadow

A Prince of Song and Shade

A King of Masks and Magic

A Duet of Sword and Song

~

The Inkweaver Archive

The Nameless Throne

The Dreadwater Gate

The Wyvern's Cry

The Unleashed Storm

Contents

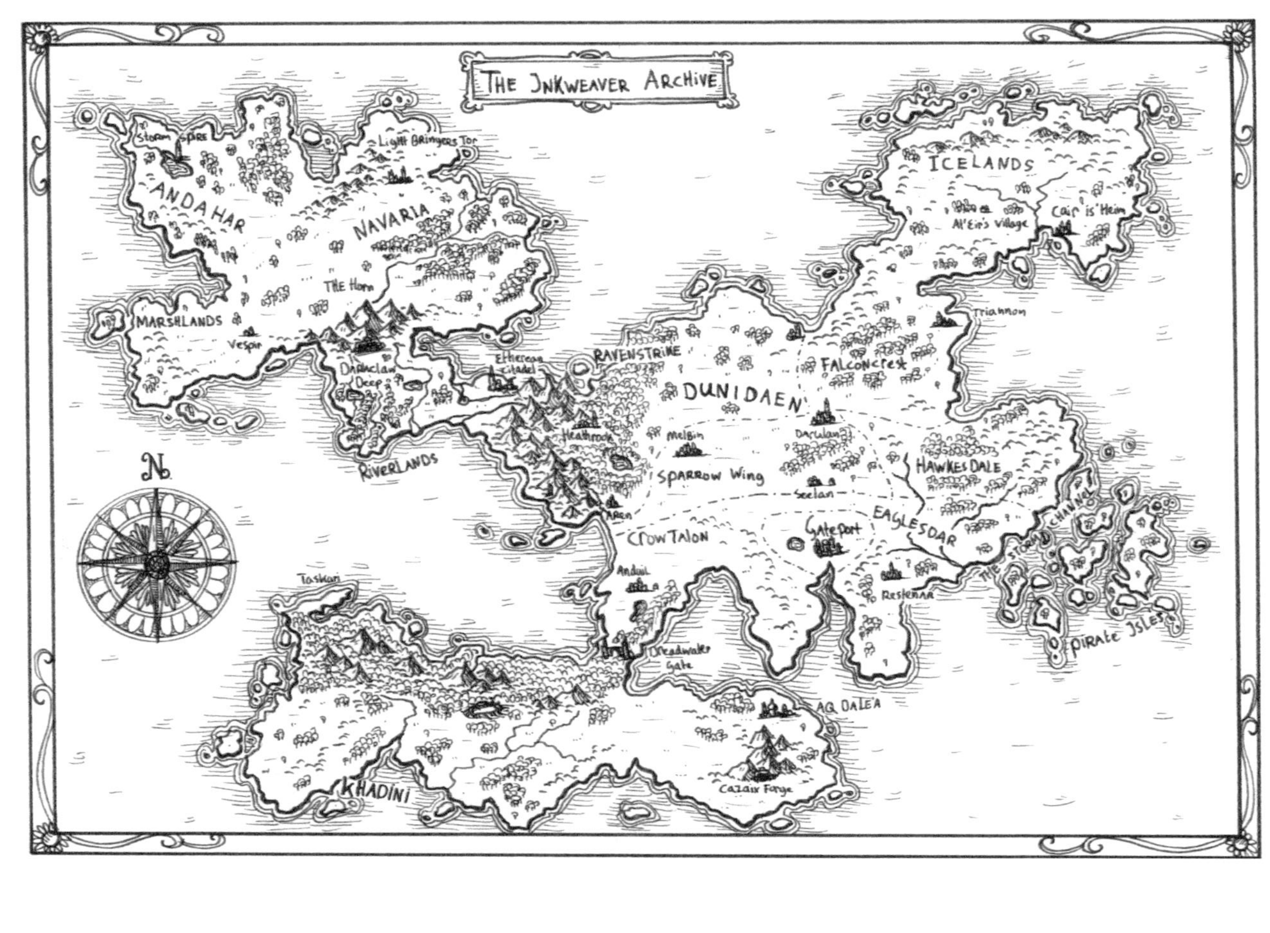

The Inkweaver Archive
N.
Storm Spire
Light Bringers Tor
ANDAHAR
NAVARIA
The Horn
MARSHLANDS
Vespir
Drakclaw Deep
Ethereon Citadel
RAVENSTRIKE
Heathrock
Melgin
DUNIDAEN
RIVERLANDS
SPARROW WING
Aren
CROW TALON
Anduil
Seelan
Gate Port
EAGLESDAR
Daculan
FALCONCREST
HAWKES DALE
ICELANDS
Al'Ein's Village
Cair is'Hein
Triannon
Resterar
THE STORM CHANNEL
PIRATE ISLES
Toshan
Dreadwater Gate
AG DALE'A
Cazaix Forge
KHADINI

PART 1

Chapter 1

T he danger came in the journey, not the destination.

That critical piece of patrol lore whispered through Arya Nameless' thoughts as she rode behind Captain Narran at the top of their shield of twenty Raiders. Her gaze was in constant movement, scanning the snow-covered ground, the trees, the step of the horse ahead of her. Down the column, her shield-mates did the same.

An icy wind blew, tugging at their cloaks, gloved hands, and the heavy cowls drawn up over their heads. The sheer weight of the layers they wore in addition to their weapons required impressive physical stamina, but it was a necessity. An improperly dressed Raider was a dead Raider in the heights of the Diamondfang Mountains.

Today Arya was glad of the intense focus required on patrol. It was a welcome distraction from the simmering anger that tensed her shoulders so tightly they ached. Her mare tossed her head uneasily, sensing her mood.

Or maybe it was something else the animal sensed.

Arya's wariness ratcheted up another notch.

Her shield was over halfway through the journey from their base, Icecliff Fort, to undertake a welfare check at the distant SheerRock Fort. The regular status update from their sister fort was several days overdue. It wasn't an unusual occurrence—messenger birds were vulnerable to all sorts of things in this icy corner of the world—but Icecliff and SheerRock guarded the only two paths across the mountains from Dunidaen into the neighbouring kingdom of Andahar. Those paths had lain blocked and unused for decades, thanks to the Nightstalker, but still, it was Raider duty to make sure the border remained secure.

The trail they were on wound into a patch of thick forest, and the silence took on a tension that was almost palpable. Hands slid towards sword hilts. Horses caught the mood and snorted, tossing their heads. Weather and terrain were only two of the dangers Raiders faced on patrol. Predators, particularly bears, wolves, and snow leopards, were another.

And, most dangerous of all, the threat of—

A shout ripped open the stillness around them. The sound cut off as quickly as it had come. Without thought, Arya drew her sword with a clear ringing sound that echoed down the line as the rest of the shield followed suit.

She'd recognised Torsen's voice in that cry. He and Charlin were the shield's outriders—their job to circle the main column as it moved to forestall an ambush. Worry flared hot and bright in Arya's chest, and she was hard pressed to hold and wait for orders.

"Halt." Captain Narran's voice rang out. "Arya, Laskin, go check on Torsen and Charlin. Everyone else hold here, stay alert, and be ready to fight."

Without hesitation, Arya urged her mare off the trail in the direction of Torsen's cry. Laskin came close behind, watching her back. Within a few strides, they found their path blocked by a thicket of trees and brush. Behind them, their shield had already vanished from sight.

Around them all was silence. No cries had followed the first.

She let out two short, sharp, whistles—a Raider signal that requested an echoing whistle to acknowledge and report location. Narran whistled back from the main column, and Arya waited for Charlin or Torsen to follow suit.

Only silence answered.

Shit. She tried again.

Nothing from either Charlin or Torsen.

Arya glanced back at Laskin, breath frosting in the cold. "They might have decided to try and go around the copse to make sure nothing was hiding beyond it. It's what I would have done."

"Agreed." Laskin scanned their surroundings. There were no hoofprints in the snow, nothing to show passage of two mounted Raiders. His worry was evident in the way he clenched his gloved hands on his reins.

Arya dismounted, reaching for her bow and quiver of arrows. "Let's split up. I'll try and push straight through the thicket in case one of them dismounted, you circle it and see if you can ride around. We don't go any further than whistle distance without the full shield as backup."

He flicked a glance at her before turning his horse. "Be careful."

Arya gripped her bow in her left hand, an arrow ready in her right, and moved forward into the trees. Branches scraped at her face and arms. Fresh snow crunched under her boots despite her attempts to step quietly. As the copse began to thin out, she spotted tracks breaking the white surface ahead. She knelt to take a closer look. They were human.

Either Torsen or Charlin had dismounted for some reason, or somebody else was out here with them.

A Shadeweaver.

Fear thrilled through Arya's blood, and when she rose to her feet, she moved with new caution, bow nocked and raised. If a Shadeweaver ambush lurked nearby, she was starkly aware of how alone she was and how long it would take the shield to reach her.

But if Torsen was hurt, she wanted to get to him as quickly as possible.

The distant bubbling of flowing water teased her senses, but there were no other sounds in the deathly quiet afternoon, just that of her own breathing and the soft crunch of her boots in the snow. But there was *something...*

Arya froze.

It was almost winter. Any water in this forest should be frozen over.

Unease gripped her, and she quickened her pace. The source of the water came into sight as she stepped through a narrow space between two trees and emerged near the banks of a stream.

Arya's gaze went instantly to the figure lying prone on the ground—Torsen—and the man crouched over him. Torsen was dead, his throat cut open, his body half sprawled in the shallows. They must have fought, the heavy weight of Torsen's body cracking the ice sheet covering the surface of the stream.

The kill was fresh. The crouching man held a knife that still dripped, red splashes against stark white. He was young, probably only a few years older than Arya, wearing ragged layers and a thick woollen hat pulled down low over his forehead. Dark brown eyes watched her with faint amusement, as if the sight of her holding a drawn bow wasn't threatening in the least. "Hello, Raider."

She aimed her arrow at the man she had absolutely no doubt was a Shadeweaver. A snarl in the back of her throat ripped through the quiet. "Step away from him."

The killer rose lithely to his feet, keeping loose hold of the knife. From that angle, he could throw it at her in a blink. She kept her breathing steady, confident she could loose her arrow before he could throw the knife.

He cocked his head. "Do you think you can kill me?"

The smugness in his expression burned her, and she loosed her arrow right at his heart. But just as her muscles bunched on the draw—in that briefest of moments before releasing the tension—Arya's vision blurred. It was for a fraction of a second only, but when her vision cleared, it was to watch her arrow thud into the tree directly behind where the Shadeweaver had been standing.

She swore, stance shifting as she searched for him. He'd moved off to her right, his smile widening in a flash of white teeth against his brown skin. Quick as she could, she drew another arrow, loosed it. But her vision blurred again, and the arrow flew uselessly through the trees. Arya swore, drew and nocked another arrow, but this time the Shadeweaver had vanished.

Her heartbeat thudded in her ears as she continued to turn, gaze frantically searching the snow-covered trees, certain he must be hidden nearby and poised to attack with that knife.

But he was gone as if he'd never been there.

"Raven's balls!" she swore furiously. How had he moved so quickly?

The sound of hoofbeats had her lifting the bow again, but it was only Laskin, Charlin close behind him. "You're all right?" Arya asked them in relief.

"Fine," Charlin said. "Torsen and I got separated checking out a noise he heard, and I—" Charlin came abruptly to a halt, turning white as his gaze fell on Torsen's body. "Raven's balls. Another Shadeweaver attack? How many were there?"

"Just one that I saw," she said grimly, beginning to pace the edges of the clearing, looking for the Shadeweaver's tracks to follow. There was nothing. Just hers and Torsen's boot prints in the snow. "I got a couple of shots off, but he moved faster than anything I've ever seen. It was like he was toying with me. Then he just vanished. Dammit, where did the bastard *go*?"

"One Shadeweaver attacked a pair of fully armed outriders?" Laskin's jaw was set.

Arya nodded. "And he took Torsen down with ease."

"He separated us first, too," Charlin said.

She didn't have to say aloud how concerning that was. Shadeweaver ambushes usually involved multiple attackers and a cleverly laid trap, using the terrain and their knowledge of it to overcome the Raiders' superior training and numbers.

"Could be Ranier is changing up his tactics," Laskin said thoughtfully.

The name rang through her, eliciting a faint shiver. Raider gossip claimed that Ranier, the notorious leader of the Shadeweavers, sported a jagged scar down his face from eye to mouth, had eyes dark as coals, and breathed violence with every word. Not that anyone knew that for certain. Only the Shadeweaver inner circle knew what Ranier looked like or where he was at any given time.

Laskin dismounted and knelt beside Torsen's body, reaching out to close his eyes. When he stood, the sadness on his face was replaced by focus. "We'd best get back to the shield. There could be more of them out here."

"You two go back. I'll track him," Arya said, frustrated anger bubbling away inside her. It was easier to feel that than grief. She wanted to wipe that smug smile off the killer's face. "He killed Torsen, we can't let that go."

"Captain Narran would never allow you to track him alone, and nor should she," Laskin said. "Our priority is making sure all is well at Sheer-Rock Fort. If it is, we'll report this there, and they can send a patrol out to look for the killer and recover Torsen's body for burial."

"By then his trail will be cold," she snapped.

"Laskin is right." Charlin's gaze was still on Torsen, but he tore it away. "Look what he did to Torsen. Besides, there *are* no tracks to follow."

Her jaw clenched so hard pain snapped through her teeth. "Fine."

As they turned to leave, Arya gave the forest around them one last sweeping glance. He was out there, close by, she could *feel* him on the cold air that swept through the trees.

"I'll come for you," she promised the empty forest.

And then she turned and ran after the others.

Chapter 2

Unsurprisingly, Captain Narran echoed Laskin's sentiments. "I'm not compromising our patrol for a revenge mission. We can't be sure the Shadeweaver didn't set up the kill to draw us after him and into an ambush," she said firmly, then lifted her voice so the whole column could hear. "No outriders. We push on for SheerRock."

Nerves taut, each Raider rode with one gloved hand on the reins and the other resting on the hilts of their swords. With their faces and hair almost entirely obscured by the cowls they wore drawn over their heads, Arya and her shield-mates were almost indistinguishable from one another. But the striking raven emblazoned in black on their dark red cloaks marked them as Raiders, soldiers belonging to Warlord Ravenstrike, ruler of the northern-most State of Dunidaen.

Occasionally, a clump of snow would slide off an overhanging branch, and one of the horses would skitter in fright. There was no way to know for sure whether more Shadeweavers lurked nearby. They knew this ground even better than the Raiders, and they were masters of concealment.

A violent criminal organisation, the Shadeweavers had their stronghold in the Diamondfang and the Wraith Forest—thick forest spreading from the eastern edge of the mountains and into Dunidaen. The group was active throughout the country, but without the mountains and forest that gave them a place to hide and build strength and resources, they'd have been wiped out by the Dunidae warlords decades earlier.

Eventually the shield left the forest and wound their way up the eastern face of a looming mountainside. The pace slowed as the horses navigated the trail, wary of verglas. The thin ice sheets that formed after freezing rain or frozen-over meltwater could be found on hard, smooth surfaces like rock and were almost impossible to see.

Laskin spoke suddenly at her side. "Are you excited to meet our new warlord?"

She shot a scowl his way. "We can gossip later when we're safely inside SheerRock. The Shadeweavers could be planning another attack."

Laskin's expression tightened briefly, grief shining in his eyes. But he shook it off like the rest of them had. There would be time for mourning Torsen later. "I doubt it, not now we're on alert. Plus, those clouds coming down from the west mean we're in for bad weather tonight. Any self-respecting Shadeweaver will be hunkering down to ride it out. We're safe for the moment."

He was right. But Torsen's death had only worsened the black mood Arya had been nursing since leaving Icecliff and she didn't want to give him the satisfaction of agreeing. Instead she answered his question in a way she knew would annoy him, complete with a dismissive shrug. "One warlord is the same as any other."

The State of Ravenstrike's warlord had died suddenly and unexpectedly four months past, his heir along with him. Word had come to Icecliff Fort only days earlier to announce that his eldest daughter, Thiara Ravenstrike, had been confirmed by the Dunidaen Council of warlords as the new Warlord Ravenstrike. Not only that, but she intended to make an official visit to the fort.

This news had initially intrigued Arya just as much as any other Raider. Right now though, she was mad at everything and everyone, and the business of Dunidaen's States and warlords were far down her list of things she gave two shits about.

Laskin levelled a look at her that spoke volumes. She gave him a mutinous glare. He didn't wilt in the slightest. She dialled up the glare. He smirked.

Arya conceded. "Fine. Pretend I'm mildly interested. What have you heard from your suspiciously good gossip network?"

Laskin glanced around, a practiced sweep to confirm all was clear, before speaking. "The State Council didn't really have a choice but to confirm her, given her father had no other living sons. Although from what I hear, they came dangerously close to appointing his fourteen-year-old grandson."

"They considered making a *boy* warlord?"

"There's never been a female warlord before. No State outside Raven-strike even allows women in their armies. Our new warlord is an unknown entity, and presumably that made the other warlords uncomfortable—worse than that, I'd guess. Scared. Rulers set in their traditions don't like change."

Arya's anger seeped back in. She'd just lost a shield-mate, a man who'd shared his allotment of sweetcake with her two nights earlier because he knew it was her favourite. What did warlord politics matter when they couldn't help Torsen or make her shield-mates any safer. "Interesting gossip I suppose, but it doesn't make a difference to anything for us."

"On the contrary," he said. "For example, if our new warlord's views on magic-wielders are less relaxed than her father's—and more aligned with most of the other warlords—then she'll want more done about the Shadeweavers, irrespective of the fact they count only a small number of magic-wielders among them. It will be us Raiders sent in to do it."

"They just killed Torsen, Laskin." The words ripped from her in a snarl. "Shadeweavers think they can act as they like, no matter the laws, and they kill us without remorse. They *should* be hunted down, magic or no magic. I hope our new warlord *does* do more about them than her father did."

"That's rather narrow thinking," he observed, but flashed her a smile when she scowled at him. This was typical Laskin, teasing to rile her and distract her from grief. "Do you want to talk about what's actually eating at you yet?"

"No," she said shortly. "I want to survive this patrol by concentrating properly on our surroundings rather than indulging in idle chatter."

"Right you are." He huffed a breath that sounded suspiciously like a swallowed laugh, and they fell into silence.

***

Dusk was falling by the time they approached their destination. Narran didn't have to tell them to be extra vigilant as they rounded a bend to see SheerRock Fort looming high on the rocky mountainside above them.

Arya's gaze swept the battlements, quickly picking out the usual complement of Raiders on guard. Nothing seemed amiss.

The sharp pealing of a bell cut through the dusk. Two long notes that hung in the icy air before falling silent. That ring pattern was a warning to everyone inside SheerRock that the gates were about to be opened for a shield of Raiders arriving or departing on patrol.

Into the silence left by the bells, a groan sounded, followed by a high-pitched shriek as the two steel entry gates slowly swung inward. Soon the gap widened enough to reveal the entrance courtyard inside. Snow drifted from the sky, dusting the grim stone surface.

Within minutes, the gates stood fully open, the only time the fort was vulnerable to attack. When closed, nothing short of a full-on magical assault could breach its high stone walls. And that kind of magic no longer threatened Dunidaen.

As soon as they were through, the winch started up again behind them. Usually, when departing on patrol, the final clang of the gates closing behind them echoed like a warning. A reminder that the only true place of safety in these mountains had just closed them out. But tonight it meant they could relax the focused vigilance they'd been maintaining for two days straight. Arya let out a long breath. They were safe now.

All was well at SheerRock Fort.

Once they'd settled the horses into the stables, Captain Narran dismissed Arya's shield before going to report to the fort commander. Their mood was glum. Having reached the safety of the fort, they now had time to grieve Torsen's death. It had been more than a year since their shield had lost a member and this loss felt fresh, cutting.

Arya felt the grief just as heavily, the emotion worsened by having been unable to *do* anything about it, to avenge Torsen in any way. She loved each and every one of her shield-mates, was proud to stand with them, despite their differences and the small frictions that arose from day-to-day life in an isolated fort. More, she felt responsible for them. Even though she wasn't their captain, they were *hers*.

Still, she didn't follow them as they trailed inside for dinner in the mess. Instead, she lingered at the doorway of the stables, idly watching snow drifting from the darkening sky, and wondering what was happening in Narran's conversation with the commander. She hated not being a part of it.

Footsteps sounded, heralding Laskin's approach. Short and stocky, with dark brown skin and short-cropped black hair that was beginning to show spots of grey, he moved with an assured calm that she envied. He had a good twenty years on her, but Laskin was her favourite shield-mate.

"What are you staring at?" he asked.

"I was keeping an eye out for the Etherean," she joked.

Laskin snorted. "Nobody's seen an Etherean since the borders closed forty-odd years ago and they retreated to the highest peaks of the Diamondfang. What makes you think one is going to pop in for a late supper?"

"Don't you ever wonder about what's beyond the Diamondfang, Laskin?"

He gave her a look. "Unlike you, I *can* read a map. What's beyond the Diamondfang is why Dunidaen is so terrified of magic-wielders. You ever wonder why they seek refuge with the Shadeweavers? We shun and harass them to the point they have little choice if they want to have any kind of a life."

She glanced at him curiously. "That's your disapproving tone. I know Andahar has been quiet since the borders closed, but you don't think there's merit in the fear that the Nightstalker might get restive one day ... decide to recruit our magic-wielders to help him expand Andahar's territory by taking Dunidaen?"

Laskin sighed. "What makes you assume that any magic-wielder in Dunidaen would want anything to do with the Nightstalker? Besides, he's not only Andahar's king, he's the only living Sky Lord. His magic is exponentially more destructive than the abilities the occasional Dunidae is born with. If the Nightstalker decided he wanted to have another go at us, he doesn't need them." He gave her a look. "And that is why Captain Narran made the right decision to continue on to SheerRock today instead of hunting down Torsen's killer."

Arya huffed a breath, crossed her arms, and grumbled. "Yes, yes, I know."

The job of the Raiders stationed at Icecliff, SheerRock, and Windfall Forts—the last sitting at the southern end of the Diamondfang just outside the largest port city on the west coast of Dunidaen, Aren—was twofold.

Maintain a watch over Dunidaen's north-western border with Andahar.

And try to contain the activities of the Shadeweavers.

In Arya's mind, the first task was mostly ceremonial these days. Sheer-Rock guarded the underground road—the only entrance into Dunidaen from Andahar aside from the pass over the Diamondfang, which ran through Icecliff Fort further to the north. The two roads that had been blocked up for *decades*. That nobody had tried to get through for *decades*.

Still, Ravenstrike State's duty to Dunidaen was more important than a single Raider's life. She knew that. But it rankled anyway.

She sighed. "I think I'm just going to quit."

"You're not going to quit."

"Don't be so sure," she muttered.

"If you act like a petulant child when things don't go your way," he said with insufferable calm, "you'll simply prove to them that you don't have the maturity to be a shield captain."

"Thanks for the support." She glared at him. Laskin had obviously stopped waiting for Arya to bring up the real reason she was so angry.

Three days previously, one of the shield captains stationed at Icecliff had retired. Arya had fully expected to be promoted into the vacant position. She was one of the most capable fighters at the fort and had successfully acted as temporary captain of their shield the previous month after Narran had badly injured her ankle in a training drill.

Instead, Commander Lerin—the battalion commander in charge of the fort—had promoted someone else. Arya liked the new captain well enough, but Arya was better. It was infuriating to have the position handed to someone else. More than that, it was humiliating.

"You're barely seventeen. There's plenty of time for promotion."

She scoffed. "Ravenstrike takes Raiders as young as thirteen, even twelve sometimes. If we're old enough to risk our lives tangling with Shadeweavers and keeping the border safe, we're old enough to be promoted."

"They take children because it's the only way to keep the army manned," he said with increasingly annoying patience. "That doesn't mean children should be leading armies."

"Do *you* think I can do it?" Arya turned to catch his gaze, arms crossed.

He didn't shy away from her look. "If you'd been our captain today, you would have led us all madly hunting down that Shadeweaver. Even if he *wasn't* attempting to draw us into an ambush, you'd have delayed our arrival at SheerRock—our mission. What if the attack on Torsen had been a deliberate ploy to keep us away from SheerRock while the Shadeweavers launched an attack on it?"

She shifted uncomfortably. "That's a little farfetched."

"You have good instincts for leadership; it comes naturally to you. But too often you let your temper rule you and override those instincts. That's something you can work on, and a little more experience under Narran will only help."

She sighed. "Sometimes I literally *itch* to take control, or to implement a better strategy."

"That's because you're a control freak. You had to survive as a child on the streets of Aren, and to do that, you had to be in control, of yourself and your surroundings," he said.

"That's what it means to be a Nameless," she said simply. "Dunidaen calls us that because we have no parents, no family, but it also means we have only ourselves to rely on. And yes, I want that control still, because it keeps my shield-mates safe. The Raiders took me in, Laskin, gave me a life."

"And what makes you think the decisions *you* make are always the right ones for your shield-mates?"

Her jaw tensed. "I just do." It was a knowing inside her, part instinct, part need, part something she couldn't name.

He huffed a breath. "Even as a shield captain you would still have to follow orders, you know?"

She smiled briefly, finally cracking under his relentless reasonableness. "Will you at least give me a few more hours to wallow in my self-pity?"

"I can do that." He grinned. "Now come and eat. You know they'll all be feeling maudlin, and you're the one that can cheer them up when something like this happens."

She pushed off the barn door and followed him. "A game of cups, do you think, or a rendition of '*Molly's sweeping brush*'?"

"Definitely the latter. The sound of your voice raised in song won't fail to make them forget their sadness and run screaming from the room."

"You're a laugh riot, old man."

"Watch who you're calling old, young upstart."

***

Captain Narran appeared in the mess much later, crossing to a table where some of the shield captains based at SheerRock were enjoying a mug of warm mead. Ignoring Laskin's warning look, Arya excused herself from her shield—still sad but somewhat cheered after a hot meal and some laughs—and crossed the mess.

"Captain?" She saluted.

Narran looked up. "Arya, what do you need?"

"I wanted to ask if there was any issue with the overdue messenger bird?" Arya kept her voice deferential—demanding answers of a higher ranked soldier was a guaranteed way of getting told to mind one's own business.

"Apparently something got into the coop a week ago and killed the birds. Commander Marik knew a shield from Icecliff would be dispatched when he failed to check in, so he's asked me to take a request back for a new batch of messenger birds to be sent here."

Arya felt an inexplicable shiver down her spine. "Something killed *all* the birds?"

Narran nodded. "The commander thinks it was probably a wolf or fox that got inside the walls."

"Were any of the other animals inside the fort attacked?"

"Just the birds." Narran gave her an odd look. "It's not like a stray wolf is going to go after horses in guarded and well-lit stables."

Right. Arya pushed aside her disquiet at the news. "What about Torsen. Will Commander Marik send out a patrol to retrieve his body and hunt down his killer?"

"I made the request, but he's the commander of this fort, Arya, so it's up to him."

"But Captain—"

"Enough," Narran snapped. "We're heading back to Icecliff at first light, so make sure the shield knows they're to be mounted and at the gates on time. Dismissed."

She *barely* held back from telling Narran to give the orders herself, and instead saluted stiffly and walked off. Back at her shield's table, she expelled a breath of frustration and summoned a lighter tone. "Captain wants to be gone at first light, so it's an early start tomorrow, lads and ladies."

Charlin sighed heavily. "Another false alarm with the messenger birds, I take it? Losing a good Raider for no reason. Again."

"Yes," she said. "And before you ask, the captain made a request of Commander Marik to send a shield after Torsen's killer."

Laskin's glance spoke volumes, but he didn't say anything. A fission of relief went through the rest of the shield at her reassurance that something would be done about Torsen. Arya smiled at them and lifted an eyebrow. "A final round of mead before bed? In Torsen's honour, of course."

***

That night, Arya dreamed.

It was the same dream she'd been having on and off for nearly a year, since just after she'd turned sixteen. It began as they always did. She stood in a dim hallway, with high, arching windows lining the wall to her left. They were open to the air, and a night breeze billowed the sheer curtains inwards. Faint moonlight was the only source of light. The sky beyond was clearer, sharper, than she'd ever seen it in reality. The stars looked like pinpricks of glittering diamonds.

At the end of the hall, the dim shape of a man was visible, something bulky hanging over his shoulders. He stood at the last window, staring outwards, his expression intense and focused.

As always, Arya walked slowly down the hall towards him. Her hand fell unconsciously to the hilt of her sword, only to find it wasn't there. It never was. And, as always, the man seemed to sense her presence as she approached.

He turned.

Arya couldn't stifle her gasp. Until now, the dream had always ended here, before she saw the man's face. Something about his movement had always catapulted her to wakefulness. This time it didn't.

He was unlike anyone she'd ever seen before; lean—*skinny*—and with a shock of silver-white hair. His features were fey, with high, arched cheekbones, thin lips, and a narrow, almost pointed jaw. He took a step towards her, and what she'd assumed was a bulky pack over his shoulders spread out into massive wings that almost reached the walls on either side of the hall.

He was one of the Etherean.

Relief filled his expression, and he opened his mouth and said something. She blinked, her thoughts feeling as if they were trapped in a mire as she tried to make a response. But even as her mouth opened, the dream ended, and she woke with a start, as abruptly as she always had after these dreams. And like each one before, it left her with a faint throbbing at her temples.

Arya lay there on her pallet in the barracks' dormitory, blinking, the details of the dream already fading. Had her conversation with Laskin earlier made her dream of the Etherean? One thing remained starkly clear, though, resonating through her mind over and over. The word the Etherean man had spoken when he'd seen her, the relief in it.

"Finally."

Chapter 3

The two-day journey back to Icecliff was uneventful, but the attack on Torsen left every moment of it laden with tension as they braced for another. By the time the high walls of the fort grew visible in the distance, they were exhausted. The main road they were on, once a major thoroughfare, divided the fort in two, passing under a high stone bridge that connected the two halves of Icecliff.

Habit had Arya glancing farther down the road to make sure it was clear. West of the fort, the road wound upwards for miles towards the pass over the Diamondfang Mountains. Today, snow covered its surface, and nothing stirred in the trees lining the road.

Empty, deserted, as it always was.

They rode through the gates into Icecliff to find Commander Lerin waiting for them, Arya and her shield were all exhausted. Captain Narran spurred her horse over to him, and the two shared a few words.

"We've orders to dismount and let the grooms see to the horses," the captain said when she returned. "The new warlord has arrived and wants to meet us."

"Captain, what about Torsen?" Charlin asked.

Narran let out a sigh. "I informed the commander of his death. A farewell ceremony will be held as soon as it can be arranged, like always."

"What about sending out a patrol to look for his killer?" Arya pushed. "If we sent a shield from here, I could show them where—"

"Warlord Ravenstrike wants to see all of us now." Her captain's mouth tightened as she cut Arya off. "Those are our orders." When nobody instantly responded, her voice carried an edge as she snapped, "Why are you all still mounted?"

Arya shared a frustrated glance with Laskin before dismounting along with the rest of the shield. They mingled for a few moments in the armoury, putting swords and bows away and allowing themselves to start relaxing after the tension of a patrol. It was a feeling Arya knew she'd never forget—the intense sense of warmth and security soaking into her bones after hours outside the walls exposed to multiple dangers. Today, though, it was tainted by grief and frustration, and their usual post-patrol banter was absent.

Narran soon appeared to hurry them up, and they followed her through the fort, climbing levels until they reached the bridge over the road. On the opposite side were more stone buildings inside equally high stone walls. They'd once been the trading and border administration offices when the road functioned as the main trading route between Dunidaen and Andahar. Now Raiders used the entire fort, although there were quarters set aside in this section for when the warlord or members of the Ravenstrike family visited.

Captain Narran led them through into a large room on the top floor. Arya took a seat towards the back of the room. She was weary and longing for a hot meal and shot of rum. Hopefully this wouldn't take too long.

"Attention!" Narran barked suddenly.

Arya rose along with the rest of her shield and saluted sharply. A woman entered, moving briskly to stand at the head of the room. She was perhaps in her mid-thirties, and tiny, only reaching Arya's shoulder. Light blond hair and sharp blue eyes framed a face that was a classic, cool beauty; features only enhanced by her assured presence.

Laskin's words about how tenuous Thiara Ravenstrike's position was came back to Arya, and despite her weariness and grief, curiosity roused inside her.

"Good evening, and please sit down." The new warlord spoke crisply. She waited a moment as they took their seats, before continuing. "You are the last of the shields stationed at Icecliff I have met, and I understand that you've just returned from patrol so I won't keep you long." She paused. "Raider Kait, am I boring you so quickly?"Arya shifted in her seat, impressed. It seemed those eyes missed nothing, not to mention the warlord had learned the names of the shield. It had to have been an educated guess to pick which of the three female Raiders was Kait, but it had been the correct one. Kait stopped whispering to Charlin and straightened, turning red. "I'm sorry, Warlord."

Thiara shifted her gaze to their captain. "Shield Captain Narran, I presume Commander Marik was able to give you a reason for missing his check-in?"

"Yes, Warlord. All is well at SheerRock. Something got into their bird coop and killed the birds."

Thiara raised a single eyebrow. "All of them?"

Arya felt a little leap of satisfaction. At least she wasn't the only one who thought it odd.

"Yes. He requested delivery of new birds. I have already spoken with Commander Lerin, and his intention was to send a Raider down to Heathrock city first thing tomorrow to purchase new birds."

Arya raised her hand. The warlord's faded blue eyes turned to her instantly, sharp as knives. "Raider Arya, isn't it?"

She stood, saluted. "Yes, Warlord."

The warlord's gaze rested on her a moment longer, unreadable, before she spoke. "What is it?"

"I find it strange that every bird was killed, yet all the other animals inside SheerRock Fort were left alone."

Thiara Ravenstrike turned to Narran. "Does Commander Marik keep any other animals inside the fort that would be of interest to a fox, or a wolf?"

"No, Warlord. Just horses, some cows for milk, and a couple of goats."

The warlord's face tightened, impatience already settling in, so Arya spoke quickly, before she could be told to sit down. "Warlord, can I also point out that until new birds are purchased and delivered, Commander Marik has no way to contact anyone outside SheerRock Fort with any speed?"

"While that is true, I don't see a good reason for concern," the warlord said. The spark of satisfaction Arya had felt earlier died as quickly as it had come. "The circumstances of the attack make sense, and there has been no other threat to SheerRock Fort. We are at peace."

"Yes, Warlord." Arya sat without another word.

Thiara turned back to Captain Narran. "Why do I only count nineteen Raiders in this room? Is your shield not at full strength?"

Arya shared a look with Laskin—another impressive pickup. Whatever else she was, their new warlord was sharp.

"One of my shield was killed by a Shadeweaver on our way to SheerRock, Warlord. These types of attacks occur frequently while Raiders are on patrol."

Thiara Ravenstrike frowned. "I've been briefed on the losses you suffer while conducting patrols, and the numbers are far too high. I intend to do something about that."

Arya flicked another glance at Laskin, who wore a little frown. He might have been right about the new warlord changing things up. She still didn't understand why expending more effort on wiping out Shadeweavers bothered him, though.

"I'm glad to have met you all," Warlord Ravenstrike finished. "I will remain at the fort for a few days so that I can gain a thorough understanding of how things work here. Thank you for your time this evening."

"Attention!" Narran called.

They rose as one and saluted, holding until the warlord had swept from the room.

"Dismissed," Narran told them then. "Get yourselves to the mess for a hot meal. Tomorrow you're all off duty. I'll see you the morning after for drill."

"She's no different than any of them," Charlin muttered as they walked out. "Remote and high and mighty. Doesn't matter whether she's a woman or a man."

"I bet that'll be the last time we ever see her up here too," Kait noted.

Arya wasn't sure how she felt about the new warlord, or how much she cared. Thiara Ravenstrike was clever, certainly, but when it came down to it,

Arya doubted that anything at Icecliff would substantially change because of her.

Besides, Kait was right. The warlord would be gone soon, and Arya was unlikely to ever see her again.

***

Arya spent her day off braving the cold to practice in the archery range. It ate at her that she'd missed the Shadeweaver killer on both her shots. The taunting expression on his face was seared into her memory. She held that look fixed in her mind as she loosed arrow after arrow into the targets, pushing through the burn of tired muscles and sore fingers.

That night, they held the farewell ceremony for Torsen, and all Raiders not on duty filed into the mess to raise a mug of ale in his honour while each took turns speaking aloud what they'd miss most about him.

She woke with a sore head the following day and had to run to make drill on time. It was barely light outside, and an icy flurry of snow whipped up, dusting the grey stone at Arya's feet with white.

She joined the warmup laps of the drill yard, and soon she was covered in a layer of sweat, the skin of her cheeks and nose numb from cold, but everything else too warm. The run was quieter than usual today, Torsen's absence starkly obvious—he'd hated running and always lagged at the back, subject to a constant stream of good-natured ribbing.

"Enough!" Narran called a halt. "Grab a training sword and form partners for sparring. Quickly, now! It's so cold out here that if we stop for too long the sweat will freeze on our skin."

"Hell no." Charlin shook his curly head when Arya approached him. "I'm not sparring with you when you have that black look on your face. I don't fancy being beaten to a pulp this morning."

Laskin's voice cut in. "Not afraid of a girl, are you, Charlin?"

"Don't give me that bullshit," Charlin barked. "Girls are just as good as boys, no matter what the other armies in Dunidaen tell you. I'd take Arya at my back over you any day. I'm just not offering myself up to her for a beating."

With that he strode off, calling for Taze to join him. The youngest Raider in their shield nodded equably, and they squared off in the yard.

Laskin unsuccessfully tried to hide his grin of amusement "Don't worry, Arya, I'm not afraid of you."

She scowled.

"I said *quickly*." Narran's voice cut across their chatter. "Not tomorrow!"

Narran disappeared halfway into the session, leaving them to spar for longer than usual, but Arya didn't mind. The physical exertion helped work off more of her anger and grief. Soon she felt better than she had since leaving on patrol, although Laskin was wincing from the new bruises scattered around his body.

"Eyes up!" Captain Narran shouted as she reappeared in the yard, bringing them to a halt. Seamlessly, they turned to face her and stood straight, training swords loose at their sides.

"The new birds for SheerRock have arrived, and we've been tasked with delivering them," Narran said. "Once that's done, we're to undertake a routine patrol of the Wraith Forest and clear out any lurking Shadeweavers from the area where Torsen was killed. Gather your weapons and be at the main gates as soon as possible."

"Why us?" Charlin asked. "We just got back from patrol, plus we're a man down."

"Orders are orders. Get to it."

Grumbling broke out as the shield put their training swords away and headed to the armoury. Nobody wanted to be away from the shelter of Icecliff so soon after returning from patrol, and with winter approaching. Arya was more sanguine about it. Maybe, despite the time that had passed, they'd be able to find enough traces of Torsen's killer to track him down. At the least they'd be able to bring his body back for a proper burial.

In the armoury, she tugged on her thick, fur-lined Raider cloak and buttoned the cowl around her neck. Once that was done, she buckled her sword at her hip and grabbed two quivers of arrows from the nearby stacks. She slid a knife into her belt and reached for her bow, then followed the others outside.

Having already cooled down from sparring, Arya immediately felt the bite of icy air as she exited the armoury. The other members of her shield walked out to their horses, hugging themselves and shivering with cold, faces hidden as deep inside their cowls as they could get.

"Hurry up," Narran snapped. "I know it's cold, there's no need to make a big song and dance about it for my benefit."

It wasn't long before the shield was mounted and ready. Those riding in the middle of the column carried six new messenger birds, securely stored in two cages, properly padded and protected against the cold.

Arya glanced up, catching sight of their new warlord watching from a higher walkway. Despite her warlord's features being obscured by her winter layers, Arya fancied that the woman's penetrating gaze was focused entirely on her. She almost lifted her hand in a wave, before realising how silly that was.

The bells rang to signal the opening of the gate, drawing Arya sharply from her thoughts. She tore her gaze from the warlord and stared ahead, preparing herself for the focus that was required the moment they left the safety of the walls.

The gates slowly opened, Narran called the order, and they were off.

Warlord Thiara Ravenstrike became a distant memory.

Chapter 4

T he weather remained clear for the first day of the journey to Sheer-Rock, but not long after they set out on the second morning, a strong wind whipped up, bringing with it icy snowflakes that pelted the shield as they rode.

Narran had taken one of the outrider positions, and when visibility began dropping, Arya cast a worried glance at the sky. That *knowing* instinct tugged at her. When she glanced down the column, the driving snow was already obscuring those at the back from view. She turned to Taze and Kait, riding behind her and Laskin. "Let's slow the pace a bit. I don't like how the light is fading, and I'd prefer to stay in visual contact."

Kait passed the directive down the column and soon the shield was bunched together nicely. Arya's shoulders relaxed.

"We should start looking for shelter," Laskin said. "We won't survive a proper storm out in the open, and that's where this weather is heading."

Arya nodded agreement. "We'd be better off pushing the pace and making for SheerRock. Captain Narran knows what an oncoming storm looks like as well as we do. She'll be back soon to give the order."

As if on cue, two faint whistles sounded over the stiffening wind—the outriders checking in. Arya whistled back the all-clear, then glanced uneasily at the sky again. The shield was quiet, each Raider huddled into their cloaks and cowls to conserve what heat they could. None of those layers would save them if they ended up exposed in the middle of a blizzard.

The path they were on narrowed where it cut between two thickly forested mountain slopes, the light dimming from the thick canopy overhead. Essentially a chokepoint, this section of the trail had been a Shadeweaver ambush point in the past, so all were on high alert. Hoofprints in the snow showed Narran and the outriders had already gone through.

With a burst of extra caution, Arya let out two sharp whistles, wanting to be sure their outriders hadn't run into trouble passing through the narrow trail.

The wind cut the sounds into shreds, and they all listened hard for a response. Initially, Arya thought nothing of the rustling branches above her, given the blowy weather. But her trained wariness had her glancing up anyway, and when she did, her breath froze in her throat.

"ATTACK!" she screamed, reaching for her sword.

Before the word had left her mouth, a writhing, hissing creature dropped towards her. Arya managed to get her sword clear of its sheath before it hit her, but the blade cut uselessly through what seemed like insubstantial smoke, doing no damage. A line of fire opened up on her right bicep as something sharp—claws?—raked down her arm.

What the—

Another hiss sounded so close to her ear that fear rippled down her spine. Claws swiped perilously close to her face. She jerked backwards to avoid them, and then Laskin was there, leaning over to bury his dagger right through one of the thing's two red eyes. It screeched in agony, and Arya winced as the high-pitched sound tore through her ears. Then it exploded in a puff of inky ash.

"Thanks," she managed breathlessly. "What the hell are these—watch it!" Another creature swooped into sight, claws raking at Laskin's exposed face this time. He ducked violently to the side, almost falling out of the saddle. Arya made another lunge with her sword, and it was enough to drive the thing away from Laskin until he recovered his seat.

A sword was too unwieldy in such tight quarters.

She had a single instant for that thought before she was jerking to the side to avoid a slashing swipe from another creature's claws. In the same breath, she sheathed her sword with her right hand and drew her dagger with the left. Straightening, she drove the smaller blade into the thing's eye and this time felt pressure and a pop under her strike—akin to driving a knife into a grape or overripe berry. The eyes and claws seemed to be the only substantial parts of the creature. It died with another loud screech and exploded into ash that coated her face and went into her mouth. She spat out its foul taste, stomach heaving.

Into the echoes of the creature's death scream came other shouts; cries of pain and fear, mixed inextricably with piercing hisses and shrieks. Momentarily clear, Arya glanced over to make sure Laskin was managing before pressing her calves into her terrified mare's side and pushing her into a jerky canter down the column. She rode hunched over, swiping at what seemed like a cloud of hissing shadows determined to feast on any patch of bared skin.

"Keep together!" she shouted. If the shield scattered in panic, they'd be picked off one by one. "Stay on the trail! Use your daggers and aim for the eyes. Aim for the eyes!"

At the rear of the column, Arya turned her mare with a quick press of her calf and leaned over to slash at a creature clinging to Taze's left side while he tried to fight off a second that curled around his head. Its wraithlike form was almost entirely blinding him, and even though he clawed desperately at it, his fingers slid through insubstantial shadow. Blood dripped down his neck, splattering on his jerkin. It took her two tries, but Arya eventually skewered the creature through the eyes. More ash exploded on a deafening scream.

Freed from distraction, Taze was able to kill the one attempting to claw through his jerkin layers. "What are these things?" he demanded, breathing heavily.

"Use your dagger, go for the eyes, and stay together," she shouted, kicking her horse forward.

The fighting was fiercest in the middle of the column, where the creatures had centred their attack. Two Raiders lay prone on the ground. Their horses had bolted. Allicen was hanging half out of her saddle, blood saturating the sleeve of her Raider jerkin and slicking her hand. Every time she tried to straighten up, a creature swooped at her.

It was impossible to count the exact number of the things, but it seemed like they were everywhere. The shield was struggling to regain the upper hand. They were seconds away from being overwhelmed—that was if they didn't lose control of the horses first.

Arya swiped at another swooping creature, desperately trying to think of … a flash of an idea came to her.

"Taze, Laskin, can you cover me?" she called out. "Bring the column in close so they can't pick us off at the ends."

Both Raiders hefted their daggers and manoeuvred their horses closer, simultaneously trying to watch the treetops in case one tried to drop on her and keep the things lunging at them at bay. "Whatever you're doing, hurry up," Laskin bellowed.

Arya hastily sheathed her dagger and reached out to snap off a tree branch hanging over the trail. Then, fingers fumbling with urgency, she pulled the flint from a pouch at her waist, wrapped together with a small vial of Khadini oil. After dousing the end of the branch in drops of the oil, she sparked the flint and flames roared into life, so blisteringly hot she could feel the burn through her gloves.

She waited a few seconds to ensure the makeshift brand was burning steadily, then stood up in her stirrups and swept it through the densest clump of creatures, shouting a warning at the same time. "Get clear! Khadini flame!"

It worked even better than Arya could have hoped. Raiders dropped from the saddle and dragged their horses clear while the wraith creatures screamed in unison. The fire spread rapidly through the pack, the flames catching unbelievably easily to their insubstantial forms. For a moment they were a seething mass of burning darkness, then as one, those that hadn't caught fire fled back into the shadows between the trees. The rest drifted to the ground as ashes. Flames rippled along the ground before burning out.

Arya stared, chest heaving, arm throbbing, thrown by the sudden silence.

The shield froze too, uncertain as to whether the creatures would resume their attack.

"Wattin, you'd better get over here," Allicen's voice cut into the silence, calling for the shield's healer, ignoring her savaged arm. "Jime and Etan are down."

It wasn't just them. A quick sweep of the column showed almost every Raider bleeding from somewhere. And those things could come back at any moment. Arya thought quickly, "Everyone who can still fight keep your eyes peeled and daggers out," she ordered. "Form a protective circle around the injured so Wattin can work."

They hurried to follow her orders while Wattin knelt by the fallen, rapidly unpacking his saddleback of supplies. It wasn't until Arya was comfortable that they were in a solid defensive position that she belatedly realised that Captain Narran and the outriders hadn't returned at the sounds of fighting.

"Quiet!" she called, then whistled as loud as she could—the two short, sharp, whistles that requested an echoing whistle to acknowledge and report location.

Silence came back.

Arya tried again, the mood of her shield turning grim and fearful as silence reigned. She swore under her breath, then glanced at Wattin frantically working on the injured. They couldn't stay here. Those things might return, not to mention the oncoming storm. Her gaze sought out Laskin. "What in raven's balls were those things?"

"Wraiths, I think," he said grimly, tightening his reins as his horse scented the ashes and promptly tried to bolt.

Arya's gaze shot to him. "What?"

"The only way to kill them is to stab them through the eyes," he spoke quickly, loud enough for the shield to hear. "Their claws are razor sharp, and they'll kill a person by inflicting a hundred wounds until they bleed to death. Attacking their bodies is useless. They're completely insubstantial apart from the eyes and claws. They survive on blood. Their bodies absorb it somehow."

"Do you think Arya got them all with that fire?" Charlin asked, looking all around as if a wraith could jump out at him at any second.

"More like scared them off, I think," Laskin said.

Arya tossed her still-burning brand to Laskin and dismounted to join Wattin where he knelt by Etan. "How are you doing?"

"Jime's gone," Wattin said, jaw clenched. "Etan is badly hurt but I can probably stabilise him. We're going to have to stop the bleeding in Allicen's arm too. She's pretending she's fine, but it looks to me like one of the gashes might have nicked a vein."

"Allicen!" Arya snapped. "Dismount and get over here." As soon as the Raider moved, gingerly sliding from the saddle, Arya turned her attention back to Wattin. "What can I do to help?" she tried to keep the urgency from her tone. "We can't linger much longer."

"We need to get them somewhere warm and dry, and where we can boil water to clean the deeper gashes before stitching them. Otherwise what I do here won't matter." He briefly looked up and around. "Can you make sure nobody else has wounds deep enough to worry about blood loss?"

Arya clapped him on the back. She trusted Wattin and his steady competence implicitly. "Do what you can. I'll figure out the rest." She stood and faced the shield, speaking loud and firm. "As soon as Wattin has stabilised Etan and Allicen, we move. Those creatures could be back at any minute, and that storm is still blowing in." Even as she spoke, another icy gust blew along the trail, bringing more snow.

"You're taking command?" Kait looked uncertain. Her face was deathly pale as she watched Wattin buckle his belt around Allicen's upper arm in place of a tourniquet.

Arya looked at Laskin, willing to defer to him and his experience and knowledge. But he gave her a little smile and looked at the shield. "Damn right she is," Laskin bellowed. "Someone needs to take command, and there's no time to sit around arguing over who that will be!"

His support and trust in her warmed her, giving her the surge of energy she needed to push past weariness and fear and focus her determination on achieving a single goal—she was going to get them all to safety, no matter what. "First, if anyone has a wound deeper than a finger's width, or you're losing blood at more than a trickle, put your hand up now."

Those with shallower gashes had already been strapping the bandaging from their packs around wounds, and as Arya met their gazes, one by one, they all gave her a reassuring nod.

"Right, we're going to make for SheerRock. It's the closest shelter and we need their healing supplies. Kait, Taze, get over here and help Wattin settle Etan and Allicen on your horses. Your job is to keep them safe and stable while we ride. Everyone else, you watch their backs. Any questions?"

"Should we look for Captain Narran and the others?" Charlin asked.

"No," she said regretfully. "If they're alive, they're out of whistle range. We can't afford to waste the time it would take to go looking for them, and I don't want to split our strength in case those things attack again."

Forestalling further objections, Arya swung herself back into the saddle and reined her mare around to address the shield. "We ride together, and as fast as the horses can go in this terrain. Laskin, you take point. Let's go!"

The storm hit while they were still on the trail.

The light vanished almost entirely, until Arya had to shout instructions for the shield to bunch even more closely together. A screaming wind whipped falling snow into blizzard conditions, reducing visibility until she couldn't see more than a metre or so ahead of her.

Laskin was half out of his saddle in an effort to keep the trail visible beneath his horse's hooves; if they diverged off into the mountains and got lost, it would be a death sentence.

Numerous times, they attempted to light a brand to illuminate the way, but each time the icy wind blew it out. Raiders shivered violently as wind and snow cut through their jerkins and cloaks. She couldn't imagine how Etan and Allicen were coping.

The best she could do was ride up and down the column, ensuring nobody got separated, shouting words of encouragement to keep them going. It was exhausting, her voice turning hoarse and sore, but she persisted, determined to see them safe.

As they left the forest and began to pick their way up towards SheerRock, the wind grew wilder, tearing at their cloaks and cowls, and the horses' pace slowed on the incline. The air was so cold that it burned a path down into Arya's lungs, making her feel as if she were being turned into an ice statue from the inside out. Snow drove into her face and eyes and every bit of the exposed skin on her face had turned numb. She'd lost feeling in her fingertips and toes.

The walls of the fort appeared out of the storm, so abruptly Laskin almost rode straight into the gates. He rang the bell vigorously, but the sound was torn to shreds by the whistling wind of the blizzard.

The gates remained firmly shut.

Arya swore, gaze scanning the battlements above, looking for a guard to get their attention. They needed to get out of this weather fast. But she couldn't even see the tops of the walls clearly—any torchlight had probably been blown out—and that meant the guards probably couldn't see them either.

She slid out of the saddle, almost falling as cold-stiffened limbs refused to cooperate. "Keep ringing the bell!" she shouted hoarsely to Laskin. "Hopefully someone will hear it."

She slugged through the deep snow until she reached the base of the fort's wall. Once there, she stared up at it towering over her, trying to think clearly despite the fierce cold sapping her strength and will. She just wanted to sit down and rest.

Her shield. She had to get her shield out of this.

Arya staggered back to her horse, pulled the rope from her saddlebag, fashioned a loop at one end, then hurled it up towards the top of the gates, where spikes punched high into the air. Her first throw wasn't nearly strong enough, and the wind tossed the rope aside so it fell back at her feet.

Exhausted, sobbing with the effort, she picked it up and threw with every shred of strength she had left. A gust swept over them at the same moment, carrying the rope higher, so that the loop dropped over one of the spikes.

Arya tugged at the rope, slumping in relief when it caught firmly. She looked over at Laskin. "I'll be as quick as I can."

He nodded and turned his horse, the words he shouted at the shield torn apart by the wind.

It was a nightmare climb. Her natural agility and balance did no more than keep her from falling as relentless gusts of wind tore at her with every inch she climbed, and her arms and fingers were so stiff with cold she could barely move them enough to grip the rope and pull herself up. Every inch of progress was a fierce battle against the storm and her fading strength.

She was only halfway up when her frozen fingers didn't grip the rope properly and she slid down several metres before she could re-establish her hold. Her arms burned in agony and it was all she could do to simply hang there. At that moment, a particularly strong gust wrapped around her, pulling at her.

Arya gritted her teeth, expression set in a snarl. She was *not* going to let this storm beat her.

She took a breath, reached up with her right hand, forced her fingers to close around the rope, then dragged herself up. Then she did it again, breath rasping, agony with every pull. It was clumsy, brutal, but she got to the top. Manoeuvring around the spikes was almost harder than the climb, but eventually she was sliding down the rope into the snow on the other side of the gates.

Staggering on wobbly legs, she made for the gatehouse. The interior was dark and empty, and she cursed Commander Marik for not keeping it manned, even in a storm like this. Operating the winch was nearly beyond her—and in the end, she could only manage three turns of the wheel, enough for a narrow opening.

It was enough. Raiders immediately began filing through one by one. Wattin was first, leading those carrying the injured Raiders.

"The gatehouse is empty," she shouted over the wind. And visibility was so low she couldn't even see the other buildings of the fort. Her mind blanked then, cold and exhaustion finally having its way with her.

"Stables," Wattin shouted back. "The horses need to get out of the weather to survive as much as we do, and it's the closest shelter."

She nodded, forcing her groggy thoughts in order. It was a good idea; the stables for visiting patrols were located right by the entry gates for convenience. "Lead them there."

While Wattin led the Raiders the short distance to the stables, Arya waited, slumped wearily against the winch, to make sure everyone made it through the gates. Laskin and Charlin were last, and Laskin brought her mare with him. Once through, he dismounted and slogged through the snow to help her with the winch.

The gates closed quickly with his help, and then the two of them led their horses after the others. The stable door stood open, welcome flamelight beckoning through the darkness. Kait was busy lighting lamps throughout the main barn when Arya and Laskin stumbled in.

Laskin took the reins from Arya's frozen hands. "Here, let me take her."

"Thanks," she said gratefully, turning her attention to the space. Everything in her wanted to curl up on the straw and sleep, but she couldn't. Her shield was her responsibility now. So she let herself take a few steadying breaths, then forced her thoughts into order.

Wattin had lain Allicen and Etan out in one of the empty stalls and organised someone else to gather spare horse blankets while Taze started a fire to boil water. The rest of the shield were unsaddling the horses in spare stalls and getting them rubbed down and settled. Relief slumped Arya's shoulders as she did a headcount and ascertained they'd all made it inside. She couldn't rest yet though.

"How are they?" she asked Wattin. He kneeled beside Etan, his healing pack open beside him, preparing a needle and sutures. Bandaging was packed tightly into the gash across Etan's abdomen, keeping the bleeding to a trickle.

"As soon as the water is boiled, I'll clean out both their wounds properly then stitch them up. I'm doing my best to get their body temperature up with these blankets," he replied, pausing in his stitching to look at her. "Hypothermia helped slow their bleeding and probably kept them alive, but now we need to raise their core temperature. A hot drink should help?"

"Consider it done." Arya stood, heading for the fire that Taze had successfully gotten going in the middle of the open space between rows of stalls. Having a fire in a barn was dangerous, but necessary.

"How's that neck?" she asked him. With clear olive skin, dark eyes, and a skinny frame that drowned in his uniform layers, her youngest Raider seemed more boy than man, even with his black hair cut Raider short. The two deep scratches on his neck looked angry and painful, yet he'd kept his cool impressively during the fight. She wondered if that was because he was a Nameless too, and knew that things could always get worse, so it didn't pay to panic.

"The cuts are shallow. No treatment necessary," he assured her.

"At least clean them out with some fresh snow," she said, "and bring in a bucket of the stuff while you're at it so we can keep boiling more water. Wattin says Etan and Allicen need a hot drink once the wounds are cleaned out."

The storm gusted wildly outside, rattling the walls and doors, but inside it was growing noticeably warmer. Arya stripped off her gloves and rubbed her icy hands to restore the feeling in them, wincing at the sharp pins and needles that resulted. Charlin appeared with a blanket, and she took it with thanks, taking off her snow-soaked cowl and cloak and wrapping the blanket around her shoulders. She felt better now, the weariness something she could ignore until she was able to rest.

Laskin appeared at her side. "The horses are resting comfortably. I don't think any are in danger of illness or injury."

That sounded like good news, but …

"What is it?" she asked, noting his hesitation.

His voice lowered. "None of the birds survived. They were lost back at the attack sight."

A little tremor of unease rippled down her spine. "You think that was deliberate?"

"Impossible to tell. In one way, it's not surprising wraiths killed defence-less birds in the middle of a frantic fight. But…"

"Yeah. It doesn't feel good." She sighed, then ran her gaze over the shield. These were hardy men and women, accustomed to the harsh reality of life at a border fort, but they'd lost another shield-mate and two others were missing in the middle of a life-threatening storm. Not to mention how exhausted they had to be after fighting off vicious creatures they'd never encountered before. She didn't miss the sunken shoulders, the lack of energy in the air, the way their eyes kept flicking fearfully towards the door.

Arya clapped her hands, loud enough to catch everyone's attention. Once they were all looking her way, she spoke, keeping her voice brisk and confident. "We're going to sit tight in here and wait out the storm. It's been a shitty day, and we'll mourn Jime properly, but the way you all fought earlier makes me proud to be part of this shield. Now, we're safe for the moment, so it's time to bunker down and get some rest."

The Raiders gratefully dug out their blankets and curled up around the fire. As soon as Wattin got a mug of hot willow bark tea into Allicen and Etan, colour returned to their skin, and some of the pain in their jagged expressions eased.

"Thanks for getting us out of the storm, Arya," Etan said, his teeth still chattering a little. "You saved our lives."

She grinned. "I can't let you die, or else who's going to watch my back? Wattin, you need to get some rest too."

"I want to look at that wound on your arm first," he said pointedly.

"It's fine," she said with a wave.

"Your sleeve is caked with dried blood, Arya. I'm not resting until I look at it, so if you want me to rest..."

Arya capitulated with a sigh. "Go on then. Do your worst."

"Laskin, you said those things earlier were wraiths?" Taze asked while Wattin worked on cleaning and stitching Arya's arm by the light of the fire. At his question, most of the others shifted, opening their eyes. It didn't seem like any of them had been able to fall asleep.

"I'm pretty sure," Laskin said, waving a hand to forestall all the questions about to spill out. "My father was a Raider back in the day, stationed at SheerRock for a time. He told stories about them. Before the border closure, they were a real problem—slipping over from Andahar and feasting on livestock and Raiders alike." Laskin paused, looking like he was digging for what else he could remember. "He said you couldn't hear them coming if they didn't want you to, but despite the tales about them, they can't just appear out of thin air, either. While mostly incorporeal, they move through space. Fast, though, very fast."

"So they're from Andahar? You don't think that—" Charlin asked, but Arya cut him off.

"Let's concentrate on getting some rest. At first light we rouse the fort and Commander Marik can send a few shields after the surviving wraiths. I'm pretty sure my flame got most of them." She wanted them to focus on the present, not uneasy possibilities.

"What about the captain and Giana?" Kait asked after the missing outriders, her voice reflecting the worry on all their faces.

"We'll go in search of them first thing when it's safe." The chances of any them still being alive if they hadn't found shelter were minimal, but they were trained Raiders and they knew how to find or build a makeshift shelter.

It wasn't a lost cause, not yet.

But as the Raiders settled, closing their eyes again, Arya's thoughts lingered on the question she hadn't let Charlin finish asking. Creatures from Andahar attacking a Raider patrol when none had been seen in over fifty years and the border was supposedly closed? Worse, that was twice now that SheerRock's messenger birds had been killed.

Someone didn't want this fort to be able to communicate with the outside world with any speed. Arya was sure of it now. And SheerRock stood watch over the underground road.

After all these years, was Andahar stirring?

Chapter 5

Arya woke groggily as someone shook her shoulder, eyes reluctantly blinking open to see Taze crouched beside her. "Something wrong?" she mumbled.

"You asked us to wake you when the weather calmed."

She yawned and sat up, wincing as she knocked her bandaged arm against her knee. The blanket fell from her shoulders, and cold air immediately drifted in, making her shiver. Taze had been on last watch, she recalled. "Has day broken?"

"About a half hour ago, I think, maybe less. It's hard to tell; the storm only just blew itself out."

She heard only a blustery breeze rattling at the doors of the barn. The screaming winds of the night before had gone, and a watery light filtered through the windows high in the walls.

Taze continued, "I haven't heard anyone moving about outside, although I would have thought one of the shields here would be saddling up for a patrol after that storm. They probably still need to dig through the snow drifts."

Yawning again, Arya rose to her feet and stretched out cramped muscles, swearing when the gash on her right arm made itself known once again. "Get everyone awake and tacking up the horses. I'll go and report to Commander Marik, but as soon as that's done, I want to ride out to look for Captain Narran and Giana."

Concern shadowed Taze's dark eyes. "Do you think they're still alive?"

"If they are, we'll find them," she promised.

He rose to his feet. "Thanks, Arya."

"Laskin?" Arya called him over while buckling on her weapons' belt and shrugging on her partially dried cloak. "Come with me to visit the commander?" An older Raider would probably get a quicker reception by a fort commander, much as it galled her.

He nodded and grabbed his cloak too. "How's that arm?"

"Fine. I'll have some nice new scars soon." She buttoned her cowl around her neck. "Let's go."

Laskin slid the door aside and they emerged into the fort's entrance yard, blinking at the brightness of the white snow under a clear morning sky. The ground was layered inches deep in the stuff, its surface completely unmarked.

Arya frowned. "I can't believe nobody has been sent out to man the gatehouse yet."

"It shouldn't have been empty last night either," Laskin said.

"Not even a magic-wielding Shadeweaver would have been able to mount an attack in last night's storm. Better to keep everyone safe inside." Arya set off, making slow progress as her boots sank deep into the snow.

Laskin stepped in her tracks, and when she turned to glare at him, he gave her an innocent look. "We old men have to conserve our energy."

She snorted. Eventually, they reached the double entrance doors and Arya banged her gloved fist on the wood a few times, then stepped back to wait. When nobody answered, Laskin tried the same thing, only harder.

Silence.

"You're kidding me?" Arya said in disgust. "They'd better not all be asleep in there."

Laskin looked neither amused nor disgusted.

"What?" she asked.

He ignored her, stomping back down the steps so he could walk along the building until reaching a window. There, he scraped away the frost that had collected on the glass and peered inside. "I can't see anyone," he called out.

"What do you mean, you can't see anyone?" She walked over to join him, staring just as uselessly through the window. The hallway inside was empty. "There should be *some* movement in there. It's breakfast time. No Raider misses mealtime."

Laskin's expression was grim. "Exactly."

The first stirrings of alarm began seeping through her. Sharing a look, she and Laskin headed around the side of the building towards the kitchen entrance, their progress more urgent now.

Here, too, the snow was unmarked. Nobody had been outside since the snow had stopped falling.

Yet the kitchen entrance stood ajar.

Arya drew her sword, using the tip of it to push the door open wider. It creaked, the sound rippling loudly in the still morning air. When nothing moved, Arya took a step inside, sword ready, Laskin a step behind her. "Hello?" she called out.

The kitchens were empty. A congealed pot of stew perched on an unlit cookfire, while a half-sliced loaf of bread sat on the central table. Flour scattered one bench, with a rolling pin lying in the midst of it. Snow had blown in through the open doorway.

"Kitchen staff would never leave such a mess before retiring for the night," Laskin murmured. "And there should be multiple cookfires lit with breakfast preparations in full swing."

"So where the hell are they?" The ominous feeling in the pit of Arya's stomach intensified. Something was very, very, wrong. She looked around, then pointed to the internal door leading into the fort. "You search here and the storage cellars. I'll take a look through there, see if I can find someone."

He nodded. "Stay within shouting distance."

Sword held ready, Arya stepped into the main corridor leading off the kitchens. It, too, was empty, with a deserted air about it. The skin on the back of her neck prickled, and she slowed her pace. It was only a short distance down to the mess. The doors stood open, the large rectangular space inside just as empty as the kitchen had been.

Arya stood staring at the rows and rows of empty tables and benches. They were tidy, table surfaces clear of plates and cutlery, which meant dinner the previous night had been cleaned away. So wherever everyone had gone, they'd done it sometime overnight.

They hadn't gone out the gates, because those had been winched shut when Arya's shield had arrived, and even with the sounds of the storm they'd surely have heard the squealing of the winch from the stables so close by. Not to mention nobody in their right mind would have ventured into that storm.

She took a long, steadying breath. Which meant—

"Arya!"

Laskin's shout made her jump, heart almost thudding out of her chest. She swore, loudly and profusely. Leaving the empty mess behind, she jogged back down the hall to the kitchens. He wasn't there, so she walked through and found him at the top of the steps leading down into the storage cellars. "What is it? You damn near gave me a heart attack."

He pointed wordlessly. Arya looked down and froze. Two servants lay sprawled brokenly at the bottom of the stairs. Dried blood covered their clothes and skin and splattered the walls and floor around them, making it hard to tell what they'd died from. Arya's stomach turned.

"I had a good look," Laskin said. His dark skin was pale, and there was a look in his eyes she'd never seen before. Shock. "They're all down there, I think, all the kitchen staff. Cooks, servers, everyone. All dead."

"Raven's balls," Arya cursed weakly. She'd seen death before, but this ... she was glad she hadn't yet eaten anything that morning. "What did this?"

"They're pretty torn up." He swallowed. "But the pools of blood that should be under the bodies with wounds like that ..."

He trailed off, and she looked—no pools of blood. He'd said wraiths fed off blood. Something crawled up the back of Arya's neck, and she spun, expecting an enemy to be sneaking up behind them, but the kitchen remained empty, deserted. "The mess was empty, but someone cleaned up after dinner last night. Where the bleeding balls are the Raiders stationed here?"

"I'm starting to think we might not want to know the answer to that," Laskin said.

She nodded slowly. "If they all had dinner as usual, then the next place they would have gone ... check the barracks first?"

Laskin led the way back out of the kitchens. They tramped through the snow, leaving a line of prints between the main building and the barracks. The front doors were closed, but not locked, yielding easily to Laskin's gloved hand.

Arya's dread grew as they moved inside, tightening in her chest like a steadily closing vice. She already knew what they were going to find and part of her just wanted to turn and run away and never look back.

Laskin stopped at the threshold of the first dormitory they came to, expelling a long, expletive-laden breath. Arya forced herself to step up beside him.

The Raiders lay prone on their bunks, killed the same way as the kitchen staff. Blood dried on wounds all over their bodies, but again, there was none pooling around the corpses. Most of them would be unrecognisable, she thought, even to those that had known them well.

"We have to check them all." Her voice came out flat, empty, but her heart was beating too fast in her chest.

Laskin didn't say anything, but he turned to follow her. His hand was curled so tightly around the hilt of his sword she could hear the leather of his gloves creaking.

A faint trembling set into her muscles as they walked through room after room of dead Raiders. A handful had fallen in the doorways or corridors—maybe they'd been awake and on their way to the privy at the time of the attack.

Five shields, one hundred Raiders, all dead in their barracks.

The rasp of their breathing was too loud in the silent hallways as they finished checking every dormitory room and returned the way they'd come, not speaking until they were back out in the snow before the barracks.

Arya swallowed, took a deep breath, let the icy air on her skin shock her senses back into some kind of calm. But she remained trembling inside, sick with what she'd just seen. "Wraiths?" she asked aloud.

"That would be my guess," Laskin's voice was distant, and he was squinting up into the sky. "I think the weather is closing in again."

Arya's head snapped up, and her stomach sank at the sight of heavy grey clouds drifting in from the north. "It can't. We have to get out of here. What if whatever killed everyone comes back, or is still here?"

Laskin started at her words, as if he hadn't even thought of that, and he turned in a circle, searching their surroundings intently. As he did so, a light snow began falling. A breeze kicked up along with it, sending snowflakes whirling around her head.

Fear thrilled in her stomach, combining with the still-there nausea to threaten expelling her empty stomach contents into the pristine snow. She swallowed, tried once again for calm. "How close do you think it is?"

Laskin squinted up at the sky again. "No more than an hour away is my guess."

"Shit, shit, shit." Not long enough to ride clear of it and make a stab at getting back to Icecliff, not without risking all their lives. "Come on, let's get back inside. We're vulnerable out here alone."

"You'll get no argument from me."

Struggling against the strengthening wind and deep snow, they trudged back to the stables. Arya knocked and slid open the door, waving Laskin in before entering and closing it behind her.

The rest of the shield immediately gathered, fidgety and shuffling. They'd clearly noticed something was up. It was Charlin who spoke first. "What did Commander Marik say? And where is everyone? Nobody has come to the stables, or to man the gates, since you left. There are no Raiders up on the walls either."

Arya looked at Laskin. He shook his head and made a gesture as if to say, *No thanks, you can be the one to tell them what we found.* She scowled at him.

"What is it?" Wattin asked, no fool.

Shit. Arya turned away from Laskin and addressed the group. "There's no easy way to say this. The Raiders and servants in the fort have been killed. The deaths were … brutal. There's not enough blood to marry up with the wounds we saw, so it's looking like wraiths were responsible."

There was a long silence, fifteen men and women staring at her as they processed what she'd said, clearly hoping she was making some kind of morbid joke. And when it became clear she *wasn't*, the fear that began creeping through the room was palpable in its intensity.

"*Every* Raider in this fort is dead?" Kait clarified, face white.

"Yes."

Panic threatened. She could see it in their frozen stances and widened eyes. And if it caught hold, and those wraiths came back again, they'd be lost. She glanced sideways at Laskin, but he gave a little shrug.

She had to give them a plan. A sense of control. Something to do that would make them feel safer. Arya's thoughts raced, fighting to put aside her own fear. Small steps. They were trained soldiers, experienced in battle, even if they hadn't faced this particular adversary before.

She forced herself to sound brisk and confident. "Another storm is closing in, so we'll hunker down here until it passes. Kait, Charlin, you'll take watch at the back entrance. Taze, Wattin, you two are on guard on the front. Everyone else, split into pairs and start boarding up all the windows. Wraiths can't get in if we don't leave them any space to do so." Or at least, she hoped they couldn't. Laskin didn't speak up, so she assumed he didn't know any different.

"Should a couple of us go out to look for Captain Narran and Giana before the storm closes in?" Taze asked. "I'm willing to volunteer."

Arya hesitated. It was a courageous offer, and part of her desperately wanted to accept it. If her shield-mate and captain *were* somehow still alive out there, it made her sick to her stomach to leave them to another storm and possibly wraiths. But that would mean risking more of their lives, and she wasn't confident it was worth it. She shook her head. "No. After what Laskin and I just saw, I don't want Raiders riding alone outside these walls. We stick together."

They looked at each other, the impending panic not entirely dispelled, even with a clear set of instructions.

But then Laskin clapped his hands loudly, startling them into focus. "You heard Arya, get moving. We'll scavenge wood from the unused stable doors, and there are nails and hammers in the storeroom where Charlin found the blankets last night."

They did begin moving then, and Arya sent Laskin a grateful look. Charlin called out as he was halfway towards the storeroom. "Arya, should we stockpile some planks close to hand we could use as brands? Your torch worked pretty well to repel the wraiths yesterday."

"Good idea," Arya said. "We don't want to be wielding open flame in here unless we're forced into it, but it would be good to have a failsafe."

"Do you think it will be enough?" Laskin asked her in an undertone.

She watched her shield-mates busy themselves with her orders, the fear in the room fading now they had something to focus on. She reached out, clapped Laskin's shoulder. "We'll make damn sure it is, Laskin. No wraith is taking any more of my shield-mates."

***

Inside the stables, with the windows boarded, it grew almost completely dark, and the Raiders lit a handful of lamps. They'd doused the main fire in the interest of rationing their wood supplies for brands and wrapped themselves in their cloaks and horse blankets to stay warm.

The hours passed slowly. Arya rotated the watch on front and back doors in two-hour shifts, while the rest of the shield sat around playing cards or talking. Etan had recovered enough to join them, which gave them all some heart despite the fear looming at the edges of the room, tugging constantly at their calm.

Arya went on watch with Laskin at roughly midnight. They sat facing each other on opposite sides of the back entrance. A narrow corridor led back to the main stables, far enough that Arya couldn't see the shield and could only barely catch their soft conversation.

They sat in a comfortable silence for some time, lulled by the flickering lamplight and the late hour. When a sudden gust of wind rattled the door, Arya jumped halfway to her feet, hand on her sword.

"It's just the wind," Laskin said, then smiled. "I hope."

"Those bodies…" She sat back down. "If wraiths could do that to a fort full of Raiders, how would we survive if they come back? They obviously didn't have any trouble getting over these walls."

"If they attacked at night, the guards on the battlements wouldn't have seen them coming," Laskin said. "And once they were in, they could have overwhelmed sleeping Raiders very quickly. You remember what it was like out on the road when they attacked us. It was chaotic."

She nodded. "And we were armed and mounted and had room to move. Inside the barracks, it would have been dark and cramped. Many of them probably wouldn't have even realised what was happening—and wouldn't have had weapons nearby." Arya shuddered at the thought. "It would have been horrific."

"Like a nightmare come to life," Laskin agreed.

"Do you think Captain Narran and Giana are still alive?"

"No," he said bluntly. "If they were, they would have heard the fighting and yelling when the wraiths attacked our column and come to help."

Arya let out a sigh. It was what she'd already figured, deep down. "You think they were killed first, to prevent them warning us of the attack?"

"Don't you?" He shook his head. "The wraiths must have overwhelmed them so quickly they couldn't get a warning whistle off, but if you hadn't looked up right at the moment you did, the same might have happened to us."

"This conversation is not making me feel any better," she grumbled.

"If you want to feel worse, think on this," he said grimly. "Wild creatures don't attack large groupings of humans inside thick stone walls when there is much easier prey out in the forest."

She stared at him. "You're suggesting the wraiths attacked the fort with some kind of purpose in mind?"

Laskin shifted, as if his thoughts were making him uncomfortable. "Or someone directed them to. My father told me the Raiders used to wonder if the wraiths were controlled or created by one of the Andahari Sky Lords with their magic. They didn't behave like normal predators."

The Nightstalker.

Their eyes met. His name had been hovering silently between them ever since discovering those bodies.

Lucius Nightstalker, the Sky Lord who'd turned on his fellow Sky Lords and murdered them all in a coup to take the Andahari throne. Who'd then turned his attention to Dunidaen and Khadini when the warlords and Khadini emperor had vociferously protested his assassination of the true king and their ally. Only their combined force of arms had forced the Nightstalker into an agreement to remain behind his borders in return for Dunidaen and Khadini recognising his right to rule Andahar. Or at least, that's how Arya had always heard it.

Now her mind sparked, jumping from thought to thought. "There's only one reason someone might want to take out an entire fort—this *particular* fort. And if you put that together with the messenger birds being killed so that nobody here could send word out ... or a request for help..."

Laskin watched her steadily, waiting for her to reach the same conclusion he clearly already had.

Arya sighed and rubbed tiredly at her eyes as all her relief dissipated. "We need to go into the underground road. Make sure it's still blocked up."

"Are you sure that's a good idea?" Laskin asked. "The shield is down to sixteen, and two of us are hurt. We'll be a lot more vulnerable outside these walls."

"It's our duty. SheerRock exists to protect the underground road into Dunidaen from the west. If that's been breached..."

"Yeah," he said, letting out a heavy breath. "Ravenstrike will be the first place hit."

That grim prospect had them both fading into silence, and they passed the rest of their watch listening to the sounds of the storm outside. Every time something banged or tapped or rustled, she strained to try and make out if it was just the storm or a pack of bloodthirsty wraiths trying to get in.

But nothing came for them. Yet.

Arya took a steadying breath and told herself to stay calm and get some rest. She and her shield-mates might be the only ones standing between an invader and the defence of Dunidaen. And if that was the case...

Something *would* come for them.

Chapter 6

A s the storm blew itself out near dawn, the Raiders—none of whom had really slept—gathered for a meagre breakfast of bread and cheese. Huddled together, they were an unshaven and tired-looking lot, with dried blood spattered on their uniforms and streaks of wraith ash on their skin. Arya shuddered as she remembered the fetid taste of it in her mouth.

Still, they were ready for what came next, and Arya took heart from that. She cleared her throat, "I know this won't be ideal news, but we have to address the possibility that SheerRock Fort was taken out so that something or someone could come through the underground road from Andahar un-detected. If that's the case, Icecliff and Windfall Forts need to be warned as quickly as possible."

Charlin snorted. "Even at full strength, SheerRock wouldn't notice a troupe of elephants and troubadours coming through the underground road these days unless they were stupid enough to march all the way down to the actual fort."

"Andahar doesn't know that we've grown lax in watching the border entries," Allicen pointed out. "The whole purpose of SheerRock is to guard that road."

"The birds, too," Wattin said quietly. "First all the birds here were killed, then *we* were attacked bringing fresh birds. Not to mention, if Laskin is right, the wraiths that attacked us are *from* Andahar."

A grim silence fell over the group as Wattin's words sunk in.

Etan said bluntly, "Arya, are you suggesting that *we* go and have a look at the rockfall blocking up the underground road?"

Protests began forming on multiple faces at this idea. Arya considered her next words carefully. She didn't have any official authority over them. If she tried issuing a direct order, there was a chance they'd just ignore her. She would have to convince them instead. "By the time we ride back to Icecliff and get another patrol out here, that's four days minimum, more if the bad weather continues. That's far too long to leave the border undefended."

"If memory serves, it's not a long ride to the underground road's entrance," Laskin offered, backing her up. "We could be there and back in a day, shelter here overnight, then head straight back to Icecliff."

"It's our duty," Arya added simply.

None of them looked thrilled at the idea of spending another night in SheerRock, but nobody protested out loud, either. Arya's shoulders relaxed.

"What about Allicen and Etan?" Taze asked.

"I'll take your advice on that." Arya turned to Wattin. "I'd rather not leave them here and divide our strength, but I will if you think it would worsen their injuries for them to ride."

"If we're attacked—" Wattin started, but was drowned out by both Raiders speaking at once.

"I can still lift a sword if needed." Etan insisted.

Allicen snapped, "It's my off arm hurt. My sword arm is fine."

Arya gave a crisp nod. "I take your word on it. You ride with us."

Wattin lifted his hands in capitulation.

"It will be risky," she said soberly, seeking out and meeting each of their gazes in turn. "The wraiths are presumably still out there, and if something *has* come underneath the Diamondfang, we risk running right into them. But we'll be better prepared this time. We take brands, as many as we can carry, and we share out our remaining vials of Khadini oil. If the wraiths hit us again, those with the oil will light brands, and the others will cover them with our daggers. We chased them off before, we can do it again."

This seemed to reassure them, and she got a series of nods in return. She smiled, rose to her feet. "Collect your brands and go get the horses tacked up. We ride now."

When Arya drew her sword and cautiously slid the stable door open, it was to the faint blue light of pre-dawn. Snow had piled up even higher along the stable walls, but it had stopped falling, and the sky was clear.

Weather in the mountains could change quickly and without warning, but usually a clear sky presaged at least a few hours of calm. Arya carefully scanned the white snow covering the yard, feeling slightly reassured when she saw the surface remained unbroken.

Not that wraiths would leave footprints.

Supressing a shiver, Arya hauled the doors all the way open for the first Raider to lead his horse out. "Come on, Taze, let's go get those gates winched open."

Arya led the column with Taze at her right shoulder, Laskin bringing up the rear with Charlin, their steadiest hands at top and tail. Allicen and Etan rode in the centre, protected on both sides and watched carefully by Wattin. The dark smudges under their eyes and the stiff way they held themselves betrayed the pain they must be feeling, but they rode straight-backed and determined. The sight of them gave Arya a flicker of pride.

If something was trying to get through into Dunidaen, they were going to find their hands full facing the Raiders from Icecliff Fort.

The old road headed west of SheerRock—though the snowfall meant the only way they could tell they were *on* the road was by the even line of trees on each side. It made hard going for the horses, and Arya was glad they'd had a full day and two nights' rest.

There was no chatter. Each Raider's attention remained on high alert. Being on the road meant wraiths couldn't drop on them from the tree canopy above, at least, but all were uneasily aware that if something *had* broken through the underground road, they were heading straight towards it.

Not long after the walls of the fort vanished from sight behind them, the road became a slow incline winding its way between rugged mountain slopes. After an hour or so, they rounded a corner onto a straight stretch of road.

Arya straightened in the saddle. Directly ahead was a high stone archway set into the rocky face of a mountainside. The opening towered over them as they came closer, hooves thudding into the snow. Beyond the archway loomed utter darkness.

The entrance to the underground road.

Arya reined in. "Taze, Charlin, Kait, light the torches."

The column waited, tense with wariness, while the three Raiders dug out flint and oil and got their brands lit. Everywhere they looked, the snow was unbroken. There was no sign of people or horses having passed through. The mountains were quiet, even the winds having ceased their endless whistling. An eagle soared high above, taking advantage of the good weather to hunt.

Arya studied the archway. The workmanship was exquisite. There were no gaps that she could discern between the blocks of stone. Engraved lettering graced the top of the arch. It was hard to read because the surface was so weathered, and she squinted, trying to make it out.

"*Unleash the Storm,*" Taze murmured, freshly lit brand lifted in his free hand, held carefully clear of his body. Khadini oil was both highly flammable and burned extraordinarily hot. "I can't decide whether that's ominous or impressive."

"Whatever it was, it doesn't mean anything anymore." Instead, she focused on the darkness beyond the arch. Wondering if something was waiting in there for them.

"Good to go, Arya!" Charlin called out.

She lifted a hand for them to proceed but kept her horse at a walk, hand ready on the hilt of her sword. Darkness enclosed them as they passed under the archway, broken only by the flickering flame of their torches. The walls of the tunnel were so wide that the torchlight barely reached the walls on either side. The air had a faint musty taint but seemed fresh enough. The cold sank deep into their bones.

Taze shifted, reaching out his torch. "Look, some sections of the wall have images carved into them."

"Let's take a look," she murmured. "But quickly."

The column moved over to the road's edge, the torch bearers holding the flames close to the wall so they could all see it. Arya raised a hand to run her fingers over the faded surface. The section Taze had found looked like it depicted a battle scene, though a lot of it was concealed by weathering and patches of moss.

"What are these?" Kait's voice was bright with eagerness.

"Voice down!" Arya snapped.

"Sorry," she whispered. "But take a look here."

Charlin drew his belt knife and scraped away all the lichen from the image Kait was pointing to. She helped, brushing off the debris as he scraped.

They all stared at the cleared section in amazement.

It was a beautifully depicted scene that reached halfway up the wall. In the centre, a man sat on a throne. A simple crown rested on his head. Around him sat four others, two women and two men. Behind the seated humans was a wyvern, rising high above their heads, wings spread as if ready for flight.

"It looks like a portrait," Kait breathed, reaching out to touch the king's face. "They're Sky Lords, aren't they?"

"Something tells me that's not the Nightstalker," Allicen said.

"No," Laskin murmured. "It would be the king he killed to steal the throne, or one of his ancestors."

Arya found herself staring at the image with as much fascination as the others—what must it have been like, to see a wyvern sweeping through the skies above? To *ride* one? And what a weapon to have against your enemies.

"How did the Nightstalker manage to kill four other Sky Lords and their wyverns?" Etan asked, eyes alight in curiosity.

"The answer to that is why Dunidaen fears him and his magic so much," Charlin grunted. "Nobody knows."

A rustle sounded in the distance, probably nothing, but it snapped Arya out of her daze. "Enough gawking," she said sharply, wheeling her mare around. "We keep going. Be ready for attack."

They were back in their column and moving onward in moments. As they continued along the abandoned highway, encountering nothing but echoes, Arya found her eyes drawn towards the images depicted on the walls, but each time she wrenched her gaze away.

Distractions here could mean her death or that of her shield-mates.

They'd been riding for roughly a half hour—it was hard to tell with any confidence in such endless darkness—when Taze's torch illuminated a blockage in the road ahead.

"We're here," Arya announced. "Everyone halt. Kait, bring your torch up. Laskin, Charlin, keep close watch on our rear."

Arya rode forward with Taze and Kait, the light from their torches illuminating the entirety of the blockage. Chunks of stone, rock, and dirt filled the gap from wall to wall and floor to rocky ceiling. It was packed in, crawling with the same moss that dotted the walls, and looked like it hadn't been touched in decades … except…

"Raven's balls," Arya muttered, dismounting. "Taze, with me."

The two of them walked over to the far-right side of the rockfall, where it met the tunnel wall. Arya's sharp eyes had spotted a patch of darkness that didn't match the surrounding area. Taze whistled under his breath when he illuminated it with his torch.

A gap had been tunnelled though the rockfall. Not large enough for a horse to fit, but big enough for a human to scramble through.

Or wraiths.

"It appears pretty fresh," he murmured, pointing at the lack of weathering on the rock and dirt that had been dug through to make the gap.

Arya swore again, then unbuckled her sword belt and shrugged off her thick cloak and cowl. "Get that light as close as you can to the opening. I'm going to make sure it goes all the way through and that this isn't the work of some animal building a den."

He looked dubious. "I doubt an animal did this. It looks to me like it's been carefully done so as not to destabilise the rest of the rockfall."

"Given the potential consequences, we need to make sure."

He nodded. "If anything happens, yell out, and I'll be after you in a second."

"If I yell, you get the shield out of here immediately and go straight back to Icecliff with a warning that something has come through the Diamond-fang," she said. "That's an order, Taze."

Not staying to dispute it further, Arya leaned forward and scrambled into the gap. Darkness enveloped her quickly, her body filling most of the makeshift tunnel and blocking the light from Taze's torch.

Everything went black, and she froze, terror flaring through her at the thought of being stuck under a mountain of rock and stone. She'd never been good in enclosed spaces—couldn't bear them for longer than a few minutes at a time. Her chest was already closing over, making it impossible to draw in a full breath. She swallowed, fighting the urge to back out. Sweat slicked her skin despite the cold. Her heart was beating too fast, she couldn't—

If she didn't do this, Taze would. And if there was danger on the other side, he could be hurt or worse. With a snarl of determination, she forced herself to keep going.

The rockfall to block the road had been thoroughly done, and even in her panic-induced speed, it took Arya longer than she'd expected to scramble through and reach the other side. She clambered out into pitch-black darkness, stumbling, chest heaving, relief flooding her in waves.

Once she had a modicum of calm back, she waved her arms around and took a few steps in a circle to be sure she *was* in an open space. Then, she forced herself back into the hole before there was time to think about it.

By the time she reached the other end her breath was coming in short gasps of escalating panic, and her skin was slick with sweat. Taze hovered anxiously, relief cascading over his features when she crawled out. She stayed low for a long moment, trying to regain control of her breathing, looking away from the light of the flame, not wanting him to see how terrified she'd been. Slowly, the panic receded, the relief a cool balm spreading through her.

As soon as she was confident she had herself under control, she stood and brushed dirt from her uniform, reaching down to grab sword and cloak to put back on. "It goes all the way through." She pitched her voice loud enough for the whole shield to hear. "We ride, now, as fast as we can. Icecliff needs to be warned."

Chapter 7

Urgency gripped Arya and her shield as they made their way back along the road at a canter, the torches burning low. It would be midday at the earliest by the time they got back to SheerRock, which meant pushing hard to get to the halfway point of the return trek to Icecliff before nightfall. Doable if the weather was good. Impossible—and dangerous—if not.

The Raiders emerged from the archway, blinking rapidly, vision blurring as their eyes adjusted to the bright white of the snowy landscape. Arya's gaze went immediately to the hoofprints left in the snow from their journey in. They were undisturbed, and no new tracks had been—

An unearthly howl pierced the morning air, the echoes of it still fading when more howls rang out. The sounds were triumphant, hunters who'd found their prey, and shockingly loud in the snow-dampened silence.

"Ware!" Charlin shouted a warning from the back of the column.

Arya wheeled her mare to see a large grey shape leap from a fallen tree by the northern side of the road and snap at a Raider's neck with deadly-looking fangs. Her shield-mate leaned back just far enough to avoid having his throat torn out, but his horse was not so lucky. Another creature had slunk onto the road underneath the horse and ripped its claws down the horse's withers. It screamed, rearing, and the Raider tumbled to the ground, only barely managing not to be crushed.

"Shadowhounds!" Laskin shouted, drawing his sword.

Arya drew her own sword, and bellowed, "Keep together! Stay on the road. Stay calm."

Even as she spoke, more grey shapes leaped from the trees around them. They were far bigger than any hound Arya had seen before, standing almost as tall as her ribs, muscled yet wiry, a pair of long fangs dripping with saliva emerging from a long snout. Their coat was a mottled grey and the claws they wielded appeared razor sharp.

Wattin yelled as he desperately tried to fight off a pair of slashing claws, and Kait urged her horse over to help him, the two of them barely managing to keep it at bay. Charlin turned his horse towards them.

A snarling shadowhound came straight at Arya, snapping at her leg. She lifted her foot out of the stirrup just in time and swung her sword at the thing. It ducked away and came at her again. This time she let it get in close, leaned back at the last second, then stabbed it in the neck with her dagger. Dark, ichor-like blood sprayed, burning where it spattered on the narrow band of bare skin between her gloves and jerkin sleeve.

Momentarily distracted—her attention on trying to locate Allicen and Etan amidst the fighting to make sure they were all right—Arya didn't see the next attack coming. A burning pain tore down her left leg, and she swore and stabbed frantically at the shadowhound that had come up on her other side, its jaws closing on her calf. It took three stabs into the thing's neck before it let go. By then her mare was completely panicked. She fought Arya bitterly, rearing and trying to bolt. Pain was a live creature in her leg, her black breeches already soaking with blood.

Arya shoved all the distractions away. There was no time for them. While swinging her sword at a hound leaping at her right side, she felt pressure on her left boot and looked down to see another one digging its claws into the leather to try and gain enough leverage to leap at her throat. Arya struck angrily at the thing, managing to graze her blade along its ribs as it twisted away. And then another came at her, eyes glowing with something feral and triumphant. She swung her sword again and again until her arm burned with the effort.

A loud snarling came from the trees to the south of the road. Arya wrenched her mare around, sword lifted, to see another shadowhound streak from the shadows. Only this one was inky black in colour, so dark any light around it seemed to bleed away.

Still fighting to keep her horse under control, Arya watched, confused as it attacked the shadowhound nearest her, closing its jaws around the thing's throat and shaking it violently until it died. The black shadowhound then launched itself at a grey one slinking towards her horse, which she hadn't seen.

Was it *helping* them?

She turned her attention back to her shield. The centre was buckling, with panicked horses fracturing the shield into smaller groups that would be even more vulnerable. Arya was too far away to get there, not with her attention needed on the hounds circling her mare—somehow, they'd separated her out from the end of the column. But even as she began to panic, the black shadowhound launched itself into the middle of the creatures massing around the centre of the shield, sowing confusion with every snap of its jaws.

When Arya had a spare moment to glance back, it was to see the centre holding, the shield re-forming despite the fierce onslaught. Relief flooded her. If she could just get back to them, they could go on the offensive—

Arrows began hissing from within the trees lining the southern side of the road, a deadly rain that pounded the attacking shadowhounds. They started falling, and the pack of creatures surrounding Arya thinned out. She shifted in the saddle, dagger raised in position to bury it in the remaining hound leaping at her...

...but as she turned, something caught her attention—the black shadowhound, focused on worrying the neck of a creature trying to get at Taze's horse, hadn't noticed another shadowhound leaping for its neck, jaws open.

Without thought or reason Arya threw the dagger in her hand instead of using it to defend herself. With the split second she had left, she jerked backwards so that bared fangs missed her throat, but then the full weight of the shadowhound hit her and she flew out of the saddle, hitting the snow hard. She grunted, the sword falling from her other hand. Desperately, she reached up to close her hands around a furry throat, needing all her strength to hold the snapping jaws away from her face. Its claws scrabbled at her chest, tearing rents into her quilted jerkin. The scent of rot filled her senses.

She found herself staring into rabid eyes, such a dark blue they were almost violet, and to her utter shock she read *recognition* there. The shadowhound snapped at her throat again, but propelled by sheer panic and survival instinct, she wrestled with it, managing to get it off her. Then, she reached for her sword and brought it slashing around as the thing leaped back towards her. The blade bit deep into its neck and it let out a whine before collapsing, dead, into the snow.

She staggered back to her feet, breathing hard, spattered in blood. The column was almost clear of shadowhounds now, the remaining creatures fleeing into the forest with a series of frustrated howls and leaving their dead behind. She couldn't see the black shadowhound anywhere.

"Form up into defensive posture!" Arya bellowed, limping after her frightened mare and pulling herself back into the saddle. Those arrows had come from humans, not creatures. "Quickly now! Weapons out. Be ready."

Her shield, battered and bleeding, did their best to follow her orders. Three of their horses were down, but all Raiders were alive. Arya's calf burned where the hound had bitten her, but she gritted her teeth and ignored the pain. They couldn't rest yet.

They'd barely gotten themselves sorted when two hooded figures stepped onto the snowy road behind Charlin and Laskin. A glance over her shoulder revealed two more moving onto the road behind her, effectively blocking them in. She recognised the motley clothing and dark hoods instantly.

Shadeweavers.

"Our archers are in the trees surrounding you, and you just witnessed how accurate they are," one of them called out. "I would advise you not to make any hasty moves."

Her chest heaved after the exertion of the fight, her thoughts racing while she caught her breath. Without knowing the numbers of Shadeweavers that surrounded them, they were at a distinct disadvantage. "What do you want?"

The man who'd spoken glanced towards the trees, gave an almost indiscernible nod, and another Shadeweaver walked onto the road. He continued past his companions and came to a halt in the space halfway between them and Arya's shield. In one smooth movement, he pushed back his hood.

Arya stiffened. Behind her, several Raiders hissed. Tack jangled as horses grew edgy again. She'd never seen the elusive leader of the Shadeweavers in the flesh before, none of them had, but they'd all heard the stories. The jagged scar from eyebrow to mouth, the shaved head, the dark eyes that shone with repressed violence. The tattoos that crawled over every inch of his skin apart from his face.

This was Ranier standing before her.

Her first instinct was to shout the order to capture him. She'd even opened her mouth to issue it … until she remembered the archers in the trees. They were surrounded.

Her shield had to survive so that they could carry a warning back to Icecliff.

"Greetings, Raider," Ranier said, sardonic, hands folded loosely in front of him. "I take it you know who I am?"

Laskin came up on Arya's side, watching her back as always. Without a word, he handed her the dagger she'd thrown. Its metal blade was covered in drying black blood.

"What do you want?" she asked, voice cold.

"Who is your leader?"

"I am."

"You're not old enough to lead a shield of Raiders," he sneered. "You're still a child."

She didn't flinch from his gaze. "I am in charge. Whether you accept that or not is frankly not my problem. Leave us to continue on our way, unharmed, or we will fight our way through."

In the silence that followed, Ranier studied her. It was an old trick, waiting for the other to fill the uncomfortable silence, and Arya had no intention of falling for it. She was entirely happy to sit in awkward silence for as long as he wanted.

Eventually he gave a slight nod, as if she'd passed a test. "I admit, I genuinely didn't think any of you Raiders would be bright enough to check, but I take it you've also just learned that the rockfall blocking the road into Dunidaen has been … disturbed?"

Arya said nothing. She had no intention of sharing information with the enemy. What if all their worst fears were coming true—the Nightstalker stirring, and rousing the magic-wielders of Dunidaen to his service? As quickly as that thought came, she dismissed it. If he'd intended them harm, Ranier would have let the shadowhounds eat them.

A faint smile crossed the man's face. "I wish to speak with you, Raider. I promise a temporary truce—no harm will come to your Raiders if you agree the same."

She shook her head, glancing down the road. They needed to move. "We don't have time for a cosy chat. How about this instead—let us go on our way and we won't attack?"

"Hasn't our assistance just now earned me a few moments of your time? I offer information on the creatures that just attacked you."

Her gaze narrowed. "You know what those creatures are?"

"I'm willing to tell you everything I know." He cocked his head. "For a price."

Arya considered that. They were taking a warning back to Icecliff but had scarcely any information on what the threat actually was. A short delay might be worth having more information to take with them.

"Ranier is an honest man, despite being a Shadeweaver," Laskin murmured in her ear. "He has invoked a temporary truce. He will not betray us."

"How do you know so much about everything?" she muttered, then sighed. "You'd better be right."

In an abrupt movement, she dismounted, biting down on the pain that stabbed through her injured leg as it took her weight, and turned to face her shield. "Laskin, you're with me. Everyone else—keep a watch on the perimeter. I don't want any surprises." She paused. "Nobody makes a move unless they're attacked first. Is that clear?"

A series of nods went down the column, though none of them looked happy about it. Ranier turned and walked a short distance farther down the road to where the other two hooded Shadeweavers waited. Arya and Laskin followed.

Both Shadeweavers pushed back their hoods at a quiet word from their leader. As the second man did so, he gave Arya a familiar, mocking smile.

Torsen's killer.

Arya lunged at the man with a snarl, sword halfway out of its sheath, only pulling up short when Ranier stepped in her path, quick as a flash. "Stand down, Raider."

"*You* back off. He murdered one of my shield-mates."

"He was attacked," Ranier said calmly.

"No," Arya said, meeting his eyes. "Torsen was murdered."

"He was a Raider, and we kill Raiders before they can kill us. It is the way of things in this part of the world, which you well know." That shimmering violence—it seemed barely restrained—flashed in Ranier's eyes. "You agreed to a temporary truce. Leanir stays."

"Arya," Laskin said quietly.

Laskin's voice wasn't enough to take the edge off her rage, but remembering what was at stake did. Survival to carry a warning back to Icecliff. Teeth gritted, she stepped back, though her fingers curled around the hilt of her sword with a strangling grip.

The triumphant smugness in Leanir's expression was enough to set her off again, so she tore her gaze from him and studied the other Shadeweaver. This was no grown man, but a boy, a year or two younger than her. Fine raven hair fell across his face, obscuring some of his features, and he regarded her with expressionless light grey eyes, meeting her gaze without hesitation. There was defiance in that gaze, and a touch of wildness too. Whatever it was, it resonated strongly with something inside her.

Ranier gestured to the boy. His sleeve slid back when he did, revealing the intricate tattoo on his forearm. It was beautiful, the ink dark and gleaming, but she couldn't quite make out what it depicted in the brief flash she saw. "This is Darmanin. May we have the honour of your names?"

So formal, this bloodthirsty and merciless Shadeweaver leader.

Arya shifted her attention back to him. "You can call me Raider Nameless. With me is Raider Laskin. What do you want?"

"A simple exchange. We help you in return for your cooperation."

"Help us? With what?"

"As you have already learned, the border has been compromised," Ranier began. "Wraiths and shadowhounds have entered Dunidaen for the first time in fifty years. We must address the possibility that the Nightstalker rouses from his decades-long slumber."

"The mountains are full of predators," Arya said. "That's nothing new."

Ranier's face twisted into a snarl and Arya was abruptly reminded of how dangerous this man was. "I'm not interested in playing games. We know everyone in SheerRock Fort is dead."

She stilled. "How could you know that?"

Ranier didn't seem any more interested in sharing details with her than she was with him. "The shadowhounds you encountered this morning, the wraiths that attacked you yesterday—they are not normal predators, Raider. Surely you have come to the same conclusion as I, that SheerRock was attacked so that these creatures could come through the underground road undetected."

"For what purpose?"

"I do not know. Yet I cannot think of any good reasons." He lifted an eyebrow. "Can you?"

Arya studied him, glanced at Leanir and Darmanin, then the trees surrounding them on either side of the road. Ranier hadn't set his Shadeweavers to aiding them just now without a very good reason.

A little smile flickered at her mouth. It wasn't only Raiders who moved through these mountains and the Wraith Forest. "You're losing people too," she said. "You need our help. That's why you're talking to me."

Ranier's eyes narrowed on hers, measuring. "A quick mind."

"And an increasingly impatient one. You say you don't know why the creatures are here, but you wouldn't be offering a deal unless you had a pretty good idea. Quit holding out and tell me what you want from us."

"I believe the creatures were sent to test the strength of Dunidaen's border defences."

Arya scoffed. "I grant you the attack on SheerRock seems strategic, but it was also the largest concentration of warm bodies in this area of the mountains. If packs of wraiths *have* migrated across the Diamondfang, what makes you think they weren't just hungry?"

Ranier smiled grimly. "The fact that *someone* had to dig through the roadblock to let them through." At Arya's silence, Ranier continued. "We don't know exactly how many came through, yet, but Darmanin has been working hard to track their numbers. We estimate hundreds."

"Darmanin?" Arya shifted her gaze to the dark-haired youth. "Is he your only scout?"

"He can get into areas that the rest of us cannot," Ranier said.

"Which means he has magic," she said flatly.

"That's irrelevant," Ranier said. "Whether you believe these creatures are being directed for a purpose or not, Icecliff is crucial to the defence of Dunidaen's north. If the wraiths do there what they did at SheerRock—"

"I understand the consequences, Ranier," she snapped at the condescension in his voice. "But now that we're warned, we can make sure that doesn't happen. I'm still not clear on what you want out of this, beyond wasting my time."

His face tightened, that menace leaping out again, as if he were barely holding himself in check. "I told you we could help. We—"

"What makes you think we need it? Icecliff Fort has never been breached. I'm sure we can deal capably with any attack, be it from Shadeweavers or packs of wraiths and shadowhounds."

"You talk big, Raider, but SheerRock has already been taken without any casualties to the enemy," Ranier said. "This is not the same adversary that you are accustomed to dealing with. This enemy comes at you through snow and darkness and strikes terror and panic into its prey. Your disciplined Raiders will turn into a panicked mob when facing wraiths coming at them through every crack in those big stone walls of yours.”

“The Raiders at SheerRock weren’t warned,” she countered. “Icecliff and Windfall will be. And why would we risk our safety further by trusting anything you say?”

“These creatures are moving through our home too. If they drive us out, we have nowhere to go,” Ranier said, anger threading his voice. “It is in our interests to help you. A common enemy makes us allies, even if only temporarily.”

That was true enough. “What help are you proposing, exactly?”

He paused. “We are tracking the creatures. We can provide you with early warning if they approach Icecliff so that you’re not taken by surprise. In addition, our warriors can help you defend the walls.”

She studied him for a moment. Everything in her warned her against trusting a Shadeweaver, despite Ranier’s rational arguments. Still, what had happened at SheerRock had shaken her. If wraiths made a similar attack on Icecliff … they would need all the help they could get.

“I’m not the right person to be talking to,” she said eventually. “I don’t have the authority to agree to an alliance.”

“All I’m asking is that you to carry our offer of help back to Icecliff. To demonstrate our good faith, we will escort you back via a faster route to ensure your warning arrives quickly.”

Arya turned to Laskin. “What do you think?” she asked in an undertone.

“I think we could use help, if what he suspects is true,” Laskin said. “Either way, there’s no harm in doing what Ranier asks and presenting his offer to Commander Lerin.”

“You don’t think it could be some elaborate trap?”

Laskin scratched his jaw. “It’s hard to see what that could be. And we saw with our own eyes that the rockfall has been compromised.”

“What if *they* did that?”

“To what end? I can’t see it.”

Arya nodded and turned back to Ranier. "You make sure my shield makes it safely back to Icecliff, and I promise to deliver your message. That's the only deal I'm willing to make."

"Accepted, Raider." Ranier gave her one final look. "I'll leave you in Darmanin's hands."

With that, he turned and strode off the road, vanishing quickly into the dim light between the trees.

As soon as he was gone, Arya's gaze shifted to Leanir. "Don't think this will stop me from killing you one day soon."

He sneered. "You're more than welcome to try."

"Leanir, please fetch my horse," Darmanin spoke softly.

Leanir's face tightened at the command, but he did as asked, stalking off the road. When Darmanin was the only one left standing there, Arya turned and walked back to her shield, Laskin close behind. Those who'd lost their horses in the shadowhound attack now rode double with lighter shield-mates.

"Etan, Allicen, how are we doing?" she called out once mounted.

"Arm's still attached," Allicen said cheerfully.

"Sore but still in the saddle." Etan's voice was weaker than Allicen's hearty shout, and Arya sent a concerned glance Wattin's way, but the healer gave her a reassuring nod; Etan was okay to ride.

"Glad to hear it." Without further preamble, she quickly outlined the discussion with Ranier, then pointed down the road to where Darmanin was mounting a bay gelding. "That's our escort back to Icecliff, so keep your swords ready but follow his lead. I'll answer any question you have once we're safely back. Let's go!"

Arya took one final sweeping look of their surroundings as the shield lurched into movement, trying to dispel the disquiet tightening her stomach. It was still daylight and everything was quiet and calm. But it was a long journey back to Icecliff, with a new menace now lurking in the deep forest and shadowy places.

And they had to trust a Shadeweaver to get them there.

Chapter 8

I nstead of taking the Raider trail from SheerRock up to Icecliff, Darmanin led them on an unmarked route that plunged through thick forest along the western slope of a looming mountainside before winding up through a narrow ravine.

It was a silent, tension-filled ride. Darmanin was uncommunicative and none of the Raiders were able to relax with their lives in the hands of a Shadeweaver guide, despite the temporary truce. They started violently at every moving shadow, froze every time a sound drifted on the icy breeze.

No doubt it weighed heavily on all their minds that they were Icecliff's only hope of receiving warning in time to prepare for a potential attack, and that their enemy knew that as well as they did.

With the long ride to think it over, Arya wasn't as sure. Ranier's suspicions were ominous, but if the Nightstalker was looking to invade Dunidaen after all this time, she doubted he would begin by digging a narrow tunnel through which to sneak wraiths and shadowhounds. Why do that when he could just fly his wyvern over the mountains and reduce Icecliff and SheerRock to rubble with his magic?

But Ranier was right that wraiths and shadowhounds hadn't dug that tunnel themselves. So who had, and why? And why take out SheerRock if not to hide the breach in the underground road? Her thoughts chased themselves around and around until her head ached and she gave up trying to puzzle it out.

It was just after midnight when the familiar cliff path that led across the mountainside to join the main road to Icecliff came into sight ahead, moonlight glinting off white snow. The sky was clear enough that the myriad pinpricks of light depicting Heathrock city were visible miles below.

Before turning onto the trail, Darmanin reined in, his gaze searching out Arya, breath frosting in the icy night air. "You know the way from here?"

She nodded.

"Be careful. Two shadowhounds have followed us the entire way."

"What?" She straightened, immediately looking down the column.

"They're well back," he reassured her, "but following our scent. I don't know why. I doubt their intention is to attack, there's not enough of them, but keep an eye out until you're inside those walls of yours."

"How do you know that?" she asked suspiciously.

He ignored her. "Once your commander has decided whether to accept our help, signal from your western wall—a single torch burning for one hour. We'll be watching for it and send a bird to pick up any message you have for us."

"How will you direct an untrained messenger bird to our western wall? And how will we get messages back from you?"

"I think we'll all be happier if I don't answer those questions." He paused as he turned to leave. "You should be more careful of the threats you throw around. Leanir is a very dangerous man."

"Leanir doesn't scare me, Darmanin."

"He should."

The boy was gone before she could reply or even ask how he planned to protect himself if the trailing shadowhounds attacked him, vanishing into the shadows between the trees. She shook herself—weariness was beginning to take over, not to mention the throbbing pain of her wounds. "Almost there!" she called out bracingly. "Quicker we get back, quicker we can get some warm mead into us. Charlin, Laskin, keep an extra close watch on our rear until we're inside those walls."

A ragged cheer went through the shield, and they moved into the trail.

The horses were as weary as their riders, but even they perked up once they realised they were approaching the Icecliff stables. They picked their way carefully across the mountainside trail, then pushed the pace up the road to the fort. Arya glanced back frequently but saw no sign of the tracking shadowhounds. Maybe they'd gone after Darmanin.

Shouts of surprise came from the walls when they were spotted, and the familiar screeching of the gate winch shattered the night-time quiet. By the time Arya and her shield rode through, the shield captain on guard duty was halfway down the steps from the battlements and then hurrying over to them.

"You're back three days early," she called, gaze searching out and then stopping on Arya. "Where's Captain Narran?"

"Captain Sapontis!" Arya saluted, even as the last remains of her hope drained away. "We were attacked and got separated. She hasn't made it back here?"

Sapontis shook her head grimly.

Her heart sank. Around her, the mood of their shield plummeted too; from relief at having made it back safely to grief.

"Why the double guard on the walls?" Arya asked. She'd noticed it riding in.

"A patrol shield sent out three days ago never returned. A shield sent out looking for them this morning couldn't find any trace of them," Sapontis replied. "Commander Lerin has still had no word from SheerRock, even though you were scheduled to have delivered the birds two days ago. He decided to put us on defensive footing."

"Good call," Arya muttered. She dropped out of the saddle, wincing as pain radiated up her left leg. The bleeding had stopped but the wounds stung badly. "I need to see Commander Lerin at once. I've got urgent news."

"You look like you should go to the healers, and so does your shield." Sapontis' expression deepened to shock as she got a good look at them. "What happened to you?"

"Lerin. Where is he?" Arya insisted.

"He's in council with Warlord Ravenstrike and the other shield captains. They're trying to decide whether to send more patrols out to figure out what's going on."

The warlord was still here? That wasn't good news, not if they were about to come under attack. Arya turned to her shield. "Dismount, see to your horses, then get to healers, food, and rest, in that order. I'm going straight to speak with Commander Lerin." She lifted her hand. "Not a word about our patrol to anyone. I don't want us causing a panic before Commander Lerin decides on a plan of action. One of you breathes a word about it, and I'll beat you black and blue."

"Got it, Arya." Charlin barely hid a smirk. "No gossiping or we end up like Laskin after the other morning's drill."

Sniggers and chuckles went through the group and Arya relaxed. "Go on, get out of here. We meet tomorrow to raise a mug for our fallen shield-mates."

"What happened was that bad?" Sapontis asked in an undertone.

She hesitated. "If your shield can spare you for a short time, Captain, it's worth you coming with me and hearing my report."

The two headed indoors, Arya almost groaning as the relative warmth of the fort interior swept over her. She hadn't been properly warm for days.

Sapontis halted outside the door, tilting her head at Arya. "For what it's worth, I'm glad you made it back, Arya."

"So am I." She nodded at Sapontis before pushing the door open so they both could walk through.

The windowless room hummed with a comforting melody of conversation, crackling flames, and parchment rustling. Arya's sweeping glance took in the warlord, Commander Lerin, and the rest of the fort's shield captains. The roaring hearth filled the room with a smoky haze, wreathed with the scent of mead. Arya's stomach woke up suddenly and let out a loud grumble. Sapontis gave her a quick amused look before they both saluted.

"Raider Nameless." Commander Lerin rose from his seat at the head of the table in surprise. "Wasn't your shield scheduled to be away another few days at least? Where is your captain?"

Arya stood at attention. "Commander, I've come with urgent news. We—"

"Why isn't Captain Narran here reporting it, then?" he demanded. His face was flushed in the firelight, eyes bloodshot as if he'd been awake too long.

"We were ambushed on the way to SheerRock. Captain Narran and our second outrider became separated from the shield in the attack. A storm hit and we were forced to seek shelter at SheerRock." She swallowed, burying the grief that wanted to rise. "We have to assume they're lost, sir."

Lerin's mouth tightened. "You didn't go looking for them?"

Stung by the accusation in his voice, Arya's temper flared, but Thiara Ravenstrike's voice cut through the room before she could say something unwise.

"Attacked by Shadeweavers?"

"No, Warlord. By wraiths. Creatures from Andahar, as I understand it." Arya ploughed ahead quickly to forestall questions. "There's worse news. Every Raider and servant at SheerRock is dead, killed by wraiths, we think. Given SheerRock's purpose, we rode up to the underground road. The border rockfall has been compromised, and there's now a clear path through from Andahar into Dunidaen."

Stunned silence filled the room. Just one piece of her news would have been shocking enough. But all of it together...

Thiara Ravenstrike spoke into the ensuing silence. "You say *wraiths* killed everyone in SheerRock?" There was something in the woman's eyes that Arya thought curious, though she couldn't quite pin down what it was. It wasn't fear, but something close to dread.

"Yes, Warlord. Not only wraiths. After ascertaining the underground road was compromised, we were attacked by shadowhounds on the road back to SheerRock. It felt like an ambush—the creatures trying to prevent us bringing a warning back here."

"Inconceivable." Lerin shook his head. "I remember the stories my father used to tell. He said small numbers of them used to slip over the border—terrorising the villages nearest the Diamondfang and our Raider patrols—back when the trade routes were open, but that stopped once the border was closed."

"It sounds like it's not closed any more, Commander," Thiara Ravenstrike said.

He huffed. "How large was this opening, Raider?"

"Large enough for me to scramble through on hands and knees."

"So small, then."

Gritting her teeth at his dismissive tone, she pushed on. "Sir, Warlord, there's more. Shadeweavers helped us fight off the shadowhounds when we were ambushed. Ranier was there and spoke to me afterwards under a temporary truce." She summarised the conversation for them, including Ranier's suspicions.

Someone muttered the Nightstalker's name under their breath, others turned to each other in alarm.

Lerin opened his mouth, a blustering response written all over his face, but Thiara Ravenstrike held up a hand to stop him, instead fixing her pale blue eyes on Arya and asking, "And you believed him?"

"I don't trust anything Ranier says, Warlord," Arya said. "But I cannot deny that he saved Raider lives today. The Shadeweavers are far more vulnerable than we are behind these walls, and therefore he has a vested interest in helping us destroy these creatures."

"That's if we assume he speaks the truth about the creatures and their purpose," Thiara pointed out.

"Warlord," Lerin broke in, "the Shadeweavers are immaterial. If what Raider Nameless claims is true, then SheerRock is down and the Diamond-fang is infested with creatures from the west who might come for Icecliff next. We don't have full operational strength, which means we can't hold the north-western border. We'll have to retreat."

Arya's mouth dropped open. He wanted to *what*? A nudge from Sapontis had her closing her mouth in a snap before anyone noticed.

Thiara Ravenstrike gave him a withering look. "We're not retreating any-where just yet, Commander. What of Windfall Fort?"

"As of yesterday, they are still active," Lerin admitted. "Their bird arrived on schedule. But they are a week's ride away and cannot reinforce us in time, even if it were smart to deplete their strength to bolster ours."

"I'm not giving up my fort without a fight," Thiara said. Of everyone in the room, she was the one person yet to look shocked, stunned, or afraid. Arya found herself impressed by the woman's composure. "Ravenstrike's duty is to watch for any signs of the Nightstalker stirring and hold our borders if it comes to it, not to run scared the moment we suspect danger is coming."

She held Lerin's gaze for a moment, as if making sure he understood her message, then continued, "If the Nightstalker intended invasion, why bother testing our defences instead of flying his wyvern over the Diamond-fang? And why now after years of peace? I'd say chances are good that this situation is very much one we can manage with the resources at our disposal."

Her words echoed Arya's thoughts almost identically, giving her a start of surprise.

A brief silence followed, and one of the older shield captains spoke hesitantly into it, "Warlord, as powerful as the Nightstalker and his wyvern are believed to be, he'd need an army if he wanted to hold any territory he captured. And we shouldn't forget that fifty years ago he only agreed to retreat into Andahar because he hadn't yet consolidated his rule and feared Dunidaen and Khadini's powerful armies joining together to dislodge him from his new throne and restore the rightful ruling family."

This emboldened another captain to speak, "He might be stronger now. Not to mention, our alliance with Khadini is nowhere near as strong as it once was. He might see us as more vulnerable."

"Point taken," Thiara Ravenstrike conceded. "But I assume as trained soldiers, all of you would agree that what we're seeing here does not bear any of the hallmarks of an invasion—of either armies or a Sky Lord and his wyvern?"

Silence met her words. It was hard to tell whether the captains agreed or just weren't brave enough to speak any further. Arya was unsure where she sat—the warlord's logic was sound, but at the same time, the unease lying in her gut ever since the wraith attack hadn't gone away.

Lerin was still shaking his head. "I'm sorry, Warlord, but in my experienced opinion, we cannot hold Icecliff with the numbers we have here. We must retreat. If General Desomer were here, he would no doubt agree that—"

"Like you, General Desomer reports to *me*, Commander, irrespective of whether he is here or not," the warlord said sharply. Lerin turned a deep red. Arya had to bite back a smile at his thwarted fury. "I'm not retreating, and I don't like repeating myself." Then she swung her gaze to Arya. "How were you able to fight off the wraiths when they first attacked?"

"I used my vial of Khadini oil to light a brand—when I threw it into a cluster of them, the flame spread quickly. Their only other point of vulnerability seemed to be their eyes, but they're quite small and a hard target to hit while their claws are raking at you."

"What sort of help is Ranier proposing to give us?"

"He indicated he would put his fighters at our disposal, and his scouts will warn us of the approach of the creatures so that we're not taken by surprise."

The warlord waved a dismissive hand. "We can scout for ourselves and certainly don't need half-starved criminals to fight when we have trained Raiders. No, I quite like the idea of allowing the wraiths and shadowhounds to wipe out the Shadeweavers on our behalf. Commander Lerin, would you agree that our priority is confirming the numbers of these creatures and determining whether they do, indeed, intend to attack Icecliff?"

"Yes, Warlord." Lerin bit the words out.

"Then let's discuss how best to do that." The warlord's gaze lifted to Arya. "Well done on getting this information to us, Raider Nameless. Please pass on my thanks to your shield. You're dismissed."

Lerin waved a hand, already turning away from them. "Captain Sapontis, get back to your guard shift. We can ill afford to have fewer eyes up on the wall right now."

Arya saluted, turned on her heel, and left, Sapontis right behind her.

As the door closed behind them, she began to feel the exhaustion and pain that had been tugging at her for hours settle like a weight on her shoulders. She'd done her duty, made it back to Icecliff with the warning. Further decisions were now in hands other than hers. Normally that would rankle so badly she'd be unable to sit still, but tonight she was glad to be able to eat and rest.

"You look like you're about to fall over," Sapontis said. "Get that leg looked at then get some rest, Arya. You deserve it."

***

She woke to bells ringing through the fort.

As soon as her brain processed that it wasn't the once-off ring pattern that signalled the front gates opening, but was still pealing out, she shoved her blankets off and sat up, wincing when the movement tugged painfully at the new stiches in her leg.

"General alert." Kait was scrambling out of her blankets in the cot across from Arya. "Best move quick."

General alert meant all Raiders who heard it and weren't on duty should dress, arm themselves, and report to the mess. Arya's muscles had stiffened up overnight, and all her wounds ached abominably as she dragged on the several layers of her Raider uniform. She groaned all the way through it, scowling at Kait's obvious amusement at her dramatics.

Both women buckled on their weapons' belt last, then grabbed their cloaks from hooks lining the wall on their way out. The majority of the fort wasn't heated, and particularly in winter, all layers were needed even just to head down to the mess for meals.

The members of their shield were milling about in the corridor outside. At Arya's appearance, they headed down the hall. They'd barely made it to the end of their dormitory corridor when Shield Captain Sapontis appeared. Her grim expression cleared when she saw they were up and dressed. "We need your shield active. Wraiths and shadowhounds have been spotted near the walls."

"How many?" Arya asked.

"It's unclear—we haven't sent any scouts out yet, but the Raiders on the eastern walls spotted them at first light, gathering in the forested slope to the south and east and cutting off the road down to Heathrock. Commander Lerin has ordered a full five shields deployed along the walls with four in reserve. Yours is assigned to the bridge." She paused. "Arya, you're good to keep temporary command of your shield?"

Arya nodded, saluted. "Yes, Captain. We'll weapon up and head straight out. Do you know when the commander will send the scouts out? It would be good to have a better sense of what we're facing."

"I'll let you know as soon as I do," Sapontis said, then left, harried strides carrying her quickly away.

Air so cold it burned their lungs with every breath greeted Arya and her shield as they emerged onto the high, arching bridge that linked the two sections of Icecliff. She stared westward, up the forested mountainside looming over the fort. Winter sunshine shone over the Diamondfang peaks, setting alight their characteristic sparkle. Today, the usually stunning sight served only to put her in mind of the shadowhound fangs snapping inches from her throat the day before.

Below them, the main road up to the pass headed west for a couple hundred metres before disappearing out of sight around the mountain. The layer of snow covering it from an overnight fall was unbroken.

"I can't see anything," she called.

"Me either," Charlin reported from where he and the others stood at the eastern side of the bridge, staring down the road towards Heathrock city.

"I'm no wraith expert," Laskin said, "but I'd be highly surprised if they're willing or able to move around in direct sunlight. They'll be maintaining the cover of the trees along the south walls where the light is dim."

Arya glanced uselessly in that direction—the southern side of the fort was obscured by the buildings inside the walls. They needed to get scouts out while the weather was good.

The doors at the base of the bridge opened and Etan appeared, Allicen with him, her arm bulky with bandaging but otherwise looking well. Despite being on his feet, though, Etan was pale and drawn. Arya went straight to him, giving Allicen a brisk nod as she passed to join the others, then said quietly, "Are you up for this?"

He straightened his shoulders. "I can stand and fight if it comes to it."

"You were pretty cut up, Etan, and you lost a lot of blood. There's no shame in resting a bit longer before joining us."

"Our shield is undermanned already, Arya. I'm good to go, I promise. Besides, all we're doing right now is standing and watching, right?"

Reading the determination in his eyes, Arya conceded. "Stick close to me. If we come under attack, I'll cover you."

"I'd appreciate that." He smiled.

Arya swung to face the rest of the shield gathered at the top of the bridge. "Listen up! Allicen, Kait, you'll take position on the eastern entrance to the bridge. Taze and Wattin, take the western entrance. Everyone else, split yourselves between the north and south sides of the bridge. Keep alert watch—if you see *anything,* sound the alarm at once."

"Why haven't they attacked yet?" Charlin asked as the Raiders dispersed to their assigned positions.

Arya forced a light-hearted smile and said loudly enough for them all to hear, "I don't know, Charlin, probably because they caught a look at your terrifying face the other day and are too scared to come anywhere near it."

Laughter followed her comment, and the tension eased.

For now.

She wondered how long the calm would hold once night fell or a storm blew in and hundreds of those horrifying creatures came at them.

Chapter 9

Dusk fell, and unease began creeping through the ranks, slow and insidious. Commander Lerin switched the four fresh shields onto duty and rested others. The air grew heavy with an increasing sense of threat, but it wasn't one that they could see or defend themselves against.

Arya sent someone to update the commander every hour or so and receive updates in turn. Each update left her increasingly frustrated. The creatures had been spotted north of the fort walls, which meant they were now probably surrounded on at least three sides, although it was impossible to confirm that. Commander Lerin still hadn't sent out any scouts.

As if reading her mind, Laskin broke the comfortable silence they'd been sharing. "Standing around inside these walls watching and letting them prepare is a tactical error," he grumbled. "As is not accepting Shadeweaver help. At least we'd have an idea of what was out there if they scouted for us."

Arya felt a flicker of that remembered anger returning. "A Shadeweaver murdered Torsen in cold blood just a week ago. I don't want them anywhere near us."

"Even so." It seemed like he was going to leave it there, but after a pause, he kept going. "There's something you should know. About Darmanin in particular. His last name is Crowtalon."

Arya spun to stare at him. "As in...?"

"As in Warlord Mathas Crowtalon's younger son, yes. It took me a while to place him because he looks older, but I spent several years with the Crowtalon Lances and was assigned to the household guard for a time when the boy was young. Darmanin was always ... unusual. The warlord threw him out of the household when he was eleven or so. The reason he gave at the time was wild behaviour not befitting a warlord's son, but seeing Darmanin with the Shadeweavers ... I wonder now if the warlord suspected his son had magic."

Arya shrugged, turning her attention back to the fort's surroundings. "Darmanin is a Shadeweaver now. His name makes no difference to anything."

She could feel the scowl Laskin gave her without looking. "He was a child with no home, no resources, and was potentially a magic-wielder. He had nowhere else to go *but* the Shadeweavers, not if he wanted to survive."

"That might be true, but he's been with them for several years now. He's one of them, and we need to treat him as such." Arya shook her head. "I have no desire to compromise the safety of my shield-mates by fighting alongside murderers who've already killed mine."

"And if fighting alongside them could save your shield-mates' lives?"

She had no good answer for that.

"The Shadeweavers aren't all assassins and criminals, you know. Nor are they all magic-wielders." Laskin was relentless. "There are children, elderly, innocents among them. They'll be slaughtered by these creatures, too, alongside the ones you hate."

"It was the warlord's order to spurn their offer of help, not mine, Laskin," she snapped, unsettled by his poking, by how true it was.

The bridge door opened before Laskin could respond, and Captain Sapontis emerged to summon Arya to a meeting the warlord had requested. She left Laskin in charge and followed Sapontis, instantly appreciating the relative warmth of the interior of the fort. With relief, she shoved the cowl off her head and took off her gloves, stretching cold-numbed fingers. She'd lost feeling in her nose and ears so long ago she wasn't even sure they were still attached to her face.

"Still nothing to the west?" Sapontis asked peremptorily.

"No, Captain. Why hasn't Commander Lerin sent out any scouts to find out exactly what kind of numbers we're facing?"

"No idea." Sapontis was brisk, not inviting further questions, so Arya shut up.

Flickering wall sconces lit the meeting room, illuminating those present in a warm glow. The hearth crackled merrily and Arya shed her cloak before taking a seat, thrilled for once to be able to participate in a strategy discussion. She'd wanted to be part of these for so long, it felt incredibly good to finally be here.

"We need to provoke these creatures into attacking, if indeed that's what they intend," Lerin was saying as Arya sat. "Morale is already wavering as fear sets in. I don't want Raiders to start deserting."

"That's unlikely," Thiara said witheringly. "They have nowhere to desert *to*, Commander."

Arya stifled a smile at the warlord's verbal slap, but she quickly looked away when those ice-blue eyes turned towards her, as if sensing Arya's amusement.

The warlord continued, "However, I agree that fear *will* become a problem if we let a siege drag on. We want Raiders clear-headed and able to fight, not unmanned by panic. What is your assessment of the situation—what have our scouts told you?"

"I judged it too risky to send scouts out and possibly deplete our numbers further," Lerin said. "My assessment is that the creatures haven't attacked because they don't have the numbers for it. Ranier was no doubt lying or exaggerating, or Raider Nameless got his information wrong. I'd say we're simply dealing with a few wraiths and shadowhounds in search of prey—when they get too hungry, they'll move on, and we are in a stronger position behind the walls." The longer he'd spoken, the more Thiara Ravenstrike's disapproval was clear, and even Lerin seemed to realise this, because he finished with a gritted, "You were right to caution me against retreating, Warlord."

Throughout his report, Arya had veered from incomprehension of his failure to send scouts out, to fury at his implied insult, to shock that an assessment from a battalion commander could be so wrong. She shifted in her chair and searched the faces at the table, waiting for someone to speak up and point it out.

No takers.

"How are you assessing *anything* with confidence if you haven't sent scouts to ascertain how many creatures there are and where they're positioned?" The warlord's voice was ice old.

"I concede the attack on SheerRock was a blow, but they were unprepared," Lerin blustered. "Now that Icecliff has been warned, the creatures have not tried to attack."

That didn't answer the warlord's question. A few places down the table, Captain Sapontis shifted in her seat but stayed quiet. Nobody seemed inclined to point out the obvious.

Arya sat up straighter. "Respectfully, sir, I disagree. If they do not intend to attack, why are they coalescing here, instead of dispersing to hunt easier prey, like Shadeweavers or mountain animals? I consider it more likely that they are waiting for the right conditions. They attacked SheerRock at night, under the cover of darkness and during bad weather."

"Raider Nameless has a point." Thiara spoke before Lerin could, cutting him off once again.

Lerin's jaw tightened. "Warlord."

His agreement was delivered in a sharp tone, as if forced out. Arya wondered how long the commander of Icecliff Fort would keep doing as his warlord ordered.

Captain Sapontis spoke into the stiff silence that followed. "Irrespective of the creatures' intentions, we need to take the offensive before fear and exhaustion set in."

"Clear weather like we had today rarely holds for more than two days during winter," another captain agreed. "As early as tomorrow we could be facing worsening snowfalls or a storm, which, if Raider Nameless is correct, means that's when the creatures will attack."

"Reserves from Heathrock should arrive within two days, as soon as General Desomer receives my bird and deploys them," Thiara Ravenstrike said crisply. "We only need to hold out that long. I've also sent word to the

High Warlord and all other warlords about the breach of our border. If we need further reinforcements, we'll get them."

Nobody responded to that immediately, but multiple shared looks went around the table. On this one, Arya was with the shield captains. If they were truly facing an attack, two days could be far too long, even if fresh shields from Heathrock were able to fight through the creatures cutting off the road to get to them.

"Warlord, if the fort is attacked, then we should expect that any shields deployed from Heathrock will face resistance in reaching us," Sapontis said eventually.

"Acknowledged, Captain." Thiara Ravenstrike inclined her head, thought for a moment, then said, "So we go on the offensive before we're pushed into a corner. Ideas for that?"

Conversation started up again as Lerin and the captains discussed options, while the warlord interjected occasionally with a question or clarification. Arya grew increasingly irritated when it became apparent that most of the shield captains cared more about having their views heard than finding a workable solution. Not that it was easy to come up with a plan when they had so little information to work from.

Her thoughts turned to Laskin's words earlier that day about the Shadeweavers. As little as she'd wanted to hear them, he'd had a point. The beginnings of an idea came to her.

"Sir, if I may?" Arya spoke into the next available silence. The table turned to stare at her, so she forged ahead. "I have an idea."

"Raider—" Commander Lerin started, but the warlord spoke over him.

"Tell us," Thiara said, utterly uncaring of the fact her words had Lerin's cheeks flushing in the firelight, brows drawing close together.

Arya sat forward. "My shield could ride west along the road—our goal to provoke the wraiths and shadowhounds into attacking us. If we can draw enough of them in, it would open up a gap in their lines surrounding the fort. It should also make quite clear how many creatures we're facing. It's possible we could clean them up alone. If not, and we're overwhelmed, you could exploit the breach we create by sending a larger force of Raiders out to attack. If all goes well, we could mop them all up here and make sure they never get anywhere near Heathrock or Ravenstrike State."

"What you're suggesting is highly risky for your shield. You're already undermanned." One captain spoke up, doubt written all over his face. "If there are the hundreds of creatures out there Ranier warned of, you could be wiped out before the second force of Raiders hits the breach and breaks through—if you're even able to create one in the first place."

"Understood, sir. But my shield-mates and I have fought these creatures before, successfully, and that gives us an advantage. We'll retreat inside the walls if we become overwhelmed, but even in that worst-case scenario we'll have a better sense of the numbers we're facing. How they respond to our attack will also tell us whether they're a rational fighting force or hungry predators just looking for prey."

Captain Sapontis nodded. "I think it's worth a try. Commander?"

"I think provoking an attack is a foolish idea when we've got a fort with impregnable walls designed to *defend* against anything," Lerin said heavily. "I do not support this plan. We should wait the creatures out. They'll either attack and spend themselves against our walls when they grow too hungry or disperse to find easier prey."

Thiara Ravenstrike considered for a long moment, nails tapping idly on the wooden surface of the table. Everyone else waited, sipping at their mead or casting sidelong glances at Lerin, who had his arms crossed over his chest and wore an expression that was somewhere mixed between petulant toddler who'd had his toys taken away and superior condescension.

Then the warlord spoke. "I have weighed the risks and made my decision." Thiara held his gaze. "We will enact Raider Nameless' plan."

A tense silence enveloped the room. From where it rested on the tabletop, Lerin's hand curled into a fist. After a moment, the commander gave a jerky nod. "Yes, Warlord."

"Then we proceed," Thiara said. "I would suggest a dawn attack, if we can be ready for it? Let's not give any bad weather time to roll in."

"We can be ready, Warlord," Arya promised.

Lerin turned to her. "You and your shield need to get a few hours of sleep if we're moving at dawn. Captain Sapontis, your shield will replace them on the bridge. Both of you are dismissed."

Arya pushed her chair back, saluted, and left the room. Sapontis caught up to her after a few strides. "Your plan is a brave one. But highly risky."

"We'll retreat if it becomes too dangerous, Captain."

"*If* you have an opportunity to do so," she pointed out.

Arya acknowledged that with a nod.

There was a silence, and then Sapontis said, "None of them will admit it out loud, but we need to break this stalemate for more reasons than the obvious."

Arya lifted an eyebrow. "You mean like the fact Commander Lerin is about two seconds away from outright refusing to follow our new warlord's orders?"

Sapontis glanced around the empty corridor around them, then lowered her voice. "Be careful of what you say out loud. You're on enough thin ice as it is."

Arya shrugged. She didn't much care what Lerin thought of her.

"Good luck tomorrow." Sapontis stopped at the junction where they were to part ways. "We'll all be with you in spirit."

"Appreciate that, Captain."

Arya pushed open the double doors to the bridge, and Sapontis left to go and gather her shield.

"Listen up!" she spoke loudly enough for her voice to carry. "We're off duty until dawn. Back to barracks and sleep."

"What happens at dawn?" Charlin asked as they left their posts with sighs of relief and gathered around her.

She straightened her shoulders, let the fierceness she felt shine through her eyes and expression. "You're getting your wish, Charlin. At dawn tomorrow, our shield is going monster hunting."

Chapter 10

In the dark pre-dawn of the following morning, Arya's shield gathered at the fort's gates. No bells would ring today to signal their departure, and Raiders had spent the night hours oiling the hinges of the gate winch.

Hopefully they'd take the creatures by surprise.

Arya hadn't slept. Instead, she'd spent the time thinking about how to give her shield the best chance of success. As weary as she was, the joy she got from having command, to be able to plan and deploy her shield as *she* saw fit … she thrived on that feeling. Better yet, if she succeeded today, then Lerin would have no choice but to promote her. Her thoughts wandered down that track, thinking of the improvements she'd start making to their patrols, how she'd use her shield-mates in different ways to maximise their strengths, how...

A soft rumbling came from their left, breaking her from her thoughts: two Raiders rolling a barrel of Khadini oil across the cobblestones. They stopped, righted it, then opened it up before stepping away. A little squirm of guilt went through Arya. Her shield captain, a woman she'd respected and liked if sometimes chafed against, was dead, and Arya was already planning how she'd do her job better.

She should be focusing on getting her shield-mates out of this coming battle alive.

"Torch bearers, one at a time," Arya told her shield quietly. "Douse them thoroughly, but make sure not to get any drops on your clothes."

One by one, they rode up to the barrel and dripped a cloth-wrapped torch into its contents. The fort had a limited supply, so they were careful not to waste a single drop.

A whinny came from the stables, and Arya glanced over her shoulder. More Raiders were appearing now, the five shields that would wait here, ready to ride out and attack the gap in the lines surrounding the fort that Arya's shield would hopefully create.

Arya doused her torch last, waited until the material had soaked in and all extra liquid had dripped back into the barrel, then urged her horse forward to the head of their column. Dawn light crept across the sky. A breeze had kicked up, but the air was cold and clear; for the moment, the weather was on their side. "Ready?" she asked the shield.

A series of firm nods went down the column. She could read from their postures, the focus in their expressions, that they were prepared. A fierce smile crept across her face.

"Light us up," Arya said to the Raiders standing near the barrel.

One by one, the two Raiders moved down the column, lighting the brands. At the same time, the guards on the gates began winching them open, the lack of screeching disconcerting.

Arya's torch lit up with a *whoosh* as the Raider set it alight, and she held it carefully away from her body. The heat was so intense she could feel it even through the multiple layers she wore. Khadini oil was flammable enough to light up even damp wood, and it burned hotter than any other source.

As soon as the gates were opened wide enough to ride through, Arya didn't hesitate. She gave the order and urged her mare into a canter. Her shield fell in seamlessly behind her, and they burst through the gate, thundering down the main road and turning west, under the bridge and up into the Diamondfang.

"Close in!" Arya shouted.

At her order, those carrying torches broke wide, giving space for the others to move into the centre of the column. The torch bearers then closed around them. The oil-fed flames flared bright in the dim light.

"Faster!" She urged her mare on. Her plan relied on building up enough speed and momentum that the creatures were forced into a quick decision to attack them en masse.

They made it a few hundred metres.

A long howl broke out, followed by another. Then a sibilant hiss, spreading through the trees to either side of the road. As the fort grew farther behind them, the forested slopes closing in over the road, creatures surged out of the trees.

The numbers gave Arya a jolt—they looked much closer to Ranier's estimation than Lerin's assessment—but she quickly recovered. She hadn't been sure what they would face, but she had a plan to manage larger numbers.

"Stay tight, keep moving forward!" Arya bellowed.

They made it another fifty metres before the creatures cut them off, boiling onto the road ahead.

"Here it comes!" she shouted.

And then the creatures enveloped them, a dark cloud of hissing and snarls, the stench of rank fur filling the air and clogging her mouth and nose.

Arya swept her torch at the wraiths that dived for her, and they screamed, dodging away from the flames. Fire crackled and spit as it spread through those pressed too close together. More high-pitched screams echoed behind her, deafening in their intensity. The shadowhounds were less afraid of the fire, but the scent of burned fur soon filled the air as they tried and failed to break through the circle of burning brands.

"Fire at will!" Arya roared.

The Raiders riding on the periphery held the creatures at bay with their flaming torches while those in the centre drew arrows and loosed them, quick and accurate. Arya pushed the shield onwards, even as the wraith pack became denser and shadowhounds snapped at her mare's fetlocks. Their place slowed to a crawl, but they kept moving. She wielded her torch like a sword, not able to let up for a second for fear of letting a wraith or shadowhound through.

If the integrity of the fire circle was broken, they'd be lost.

Arrows hissed from the protected centre, dropping one hound after another. Any wraith that got close enough to the torches burst into flame, screaming, the fire spreading to any others that made the mistake of getting too close. The noise was shrill enough that it became hard to focus.

A glance backward to check on her shield-mates proved a costly mistake. A wraith dived at Arya's neck, hissing. She jerked violently backwards, almost toppling off her horse. The wraith changed direction quickly, and she was forced to let go of the reins so she could pull her dagger and stab it through the eyes. Its death shriek rang through her ears for several moments afterward. Ash spattered her cowl and jerkin, the foul scent filling her nose.

The noise and fire soon proved too much for even their well-trained mounts, and the shield's forward momentum faltered as horses fought their riders and tried to flee. Concentration split between fighting and maintaining the integrity of their formation.

They fought desperately, utterly beset. Arya couldn't see anything but writhing blackness, snapping jaws, and rippling bright flame. She swung her torch ceaselessly, barely managing to keep the things off her. Shield-mates flashed in and out of sight. Somehow, they were staying together and holding formation.

But for each creature they killed, another took its place. There were too many. If they stayed still, they'd be overwhelmed.

"Forward!" she shouted above the chaos, making a quick decision to push forward instead of retreat—if they could break clear of this pack, then they could turn back and trap the creatures between her shield and the second force that should be emerging from Icecliff any moment. "Let's try and get clear!"

Dragging her mare's head around, Arya loosened the reins and allowed the horse the panicked canter that she wanted, hoping her shield would be able to follow. They did, slowly, but surely. Her arm burned with the effort of swinging the torch, sweat slicked her skin, and breath burned in her chest. The screeching of dying wraiths pounded in her brain, making it almost impossible to think straight.

And then they were through.

Open road lay ahead of them, the layer of snow over its surface unbroken, winding ever higher into the mountains. Arya wheeled her horse around, lifting her torch high, and swore aloud at what she saw.

They'd succeeded beyond her expectations. An unbelievable number of wraiths and shadowhounds had been drawn out of the surrounding forest to attack Arya's shield, and they massed on the road between her shield and the fort.

Ranier had been right about their numbers.

But the backup force of Raiders wasn't exiting the fort quickly enough, and the creatures were already coalescing to surge after Arya's shield. Shit. Shit. Shit. She thought quickly, then opened her mouth to call the order to flee down the road. Maybe they could ride fast enough to get clear, then double back around to...

Movement blurred at the top of the escarpment to the south, right above where the monsters were massing on the road—a small number of hooded fighters scrambling down the rocky surface, armed to the teeth. They moved as a loose group, no formation, no structure, just determined purpose.

The Shadeweavers had come.

At first Arya panicked, assuming they were joining the attack in retaliation for their truce offer being ignored.

But then the first of the Shadeweavers hit the road's surface and a shadowhound leaping towards her died mid-leap, an arrow through its throat. Arya looked up, her gaze falling on Leanir's now familiar figure. He stood atop the escarpment, coolly firing arrow after arrow. Not one single one missed its target that she could see.

"Hold!" she roared to her shield, who, like Arya, had been turning their horses in preparation to flee. "Contain them here!"

With the Shadeweavers hitting the creatures on the southern flank, if Arya's shield could contain them from fleeing west along the road, they could break the siege.

Instantly, her shield turned, torch bearers re-forming around the archers, who were busy unhooking their spare quiver of arrows and tossing the empty ones aside. She thought her heart would burn with pride.

"Not one creature gets past us!" she ordered. "ATTACK!"

And then they slammed into the seething mass of wraiths and shadowhounds and all was chaos again. She did her best to keep to the edge of the cluster, snapping off orders to make sure her shield contained the creatures from fleeing west and wading in to help when a side was vulnerable or a back uncovered.

At some point she heard a rumble in the distance, over the sound of snarling and hissing and cries of battle. She looked down the road, hope building in her.

The second force of five shields from Icecliff came into sight, bloodred uniforms bright against white snow, riding out to attack the now-diluted force of wraiths and shadowhounds remaining near the walls of the fort. As they did, many of the creatures attacking Arya and the Shadeweavers peeled away, streaking down the road to attack the new force.

Finally.

A wraith swiped at her, and Arya turned her attention back to the fight, renewed energy flooding her tired muscles. "We've got this!" she bellowed to her shield. "The second force is out. Just a little longer and we'll be sipping celebratory rum over the corpses of these things."

It was bitter and fierce, but the Shadeweavers entering the fray made the difference. A frantic, exhausting half hour later, and Raiders and Shadeweavers alike stood on the cleared road, splattered with gore, staring at over a hundred shadowhound carcasses scattered across the snowy road darkened with blood and piles of greasy ash.

There were no Raider or Shadeweaver bodies among them.

Arya blinked, lifted a sleeve to wipe the gore and sweat from her face, then did a headcount of her shield. All fifteen still sat their horses. Next, she stared down the road towards Icecliff. Large numbers of mounted Raiders were visible in the trees around the fort, but it seemed the fight there was almost over too.

She let out a shuddering gasp of relief. They'd made it. Triumph surged in the wake of relief, rushing through her in a heady wave. Her plan had worked. A grin stretched across her face, and she was about to turn to her shield and promise two extra shots of rum after dinner, when Taze murmured beside her, gesturing to the Shadeweavers, "They saved us just now."

Even as he spoke, Darmanin set out towards them with quick strides. Arya immediately refocused, hand falling to the hilt of her sword. His companions—no more than fifteen or so in number—lingered by the edge of the road, but now they held the reins of their mounts. Leanir was not among them.

"You helped us," Arya greeted him, wary. "Why would Ranier do that after—?"

"He didn't. I chose to help," he cut her off. "We don't have time to demand answers of each other if we're going to chase down and destroy what remains of those creatures. Your Raiders dealt with a large part of their force, but stragglers have fled west, deeper into the Diamondfang."

"How do you—" Arya cut herself off. Better not to know. "You're suggesting we join forces?"

"I want to keep my people safe, and you presumably want the same for your Raiders." He cast his gaze over them. "I've seen how you look out for them. A brief and strategic alliance until the creatures are all dead is what I offer."

"Without Ranier's approval?"

Impatience flashed over his face, a look that made him seem nothing like a child. "We need to move now if we're going to do this, Raider."

Her instinct was to refuse any Shadeweaver help, but she'd just watched them battle wraiths and shadowhounds as fiercely as her Raiders had. And having their support meant they could go after the creatures now, rather than waiting for Lerin to approve sending backup shields from Icecliff.

And she wanted every one of those things dead so they could never threaten her shield-mates again.

Arya met Darmanin's fey-grey eyes and nodded. "Offer accepted. We'll ride along the road at speed, cut them off before they can reach the pass over the Diamondfang."

Darmanin shook his head. "That's not how they came through."

"We don't know that the roadblock up at the pass hasn't been compromised too. You said they were heading west—there's a good chance they're looking to flee back over the border."

"They didn't come here just to run back home so quickly," he said decidedly. "I can find them faster. Look for me."

Before she could say anything else, he stalked off, muttering something to the nearest Shadeweaver as he went.

"Arya, we need to report in," Laskin said at her shoulder. "We don't have authority to—"

"If we waste time reporting in, the creatures will have too much of a head start and we might never find them all. They'll remain a threat to us and Ravenstrike." She turned her horse. "Who's up for chasing down what's left of those creatures and wiping them out for good?"

A series of nods and calls signalled her weary shield was up for a chase. She grinned at them, then searched out Etan with her gaze. He was bone white and barely able to sit straight in the saddle. "Etan, ride back to Icecliff and let Commander Lerin know what we're doing."

"Arya—"

"That's an order. Your courage is not in doubt, Etan, but I won't risk your life on this. You need rest," she said firmly. "Everyone else, we ride at the canter. I want to catch those things before they get back over the border."

"What about them?" Charlin pointed at the Shadeweavers who'd been with Darmanin. They were sitting their horses a short distance off, a surly lot, but clearly waiting.

"You let me worry about them. Come on, now, we're already losing too much ground. Let's go!"

They lurched into movement immediately, but Arya held her mare in. Some instinct—a prickling under her skin—making her pause and stare into the trees where Darmanin had disappeared.

She could just make out where he'd stopped a few metres into the brush. Arya squinted, trying to see better into the gloom. It looked like the boy closed his eyes in concentration, then his hands—which had been closed into fists—relaxed and opened. A shudder went through him, and he tossed his head back, the entire line of his body turning rigid.

Then, he changed.

It was impossible to describe better than that. But one by one, human limbs became something unhuman.

Within moments, a black shadowhound stood where a human boy once had.

Chapter 11

A rya stared.

Darmanin shook himself, almost as if letting tension out of his body, then he loped off deeper into the trees, soon vanishing from sight.

Yet Arya continued to stare after him. The black shadowhound who'd helped them when they'd been ambushed. The shadowhound she'd risked her life to save in the heat of that battle. It had been Darmanin. A magic-wielder.

"Nice trick."

She spun, only then realising that Laskin had remained while the rest of the column and the Shadeweavers cantered down the road, almost out of sight now.

He smiled at her look. "I've always got your back."

She huffed. "Thanks, Laskin."

"That's an interesting magical ability, and one that helped save all our lives the other day," Laskin said, glancing back into the trees. "A shame having it means he'll be exiled and shunned for the rest of his life."

"We'd best hurry." Arya ignored his pointed comment and pressed her calves to her mare's side, pushing her into a gallop after the others.

Once they caught up, Arya moved into the gap between the Raiders and trailing Shadeweavers, a lone buffer between the two groups, which would hopefully forestall any trouble. She sent Laskin ahead to lead the shield.

As they rode, the sun rose higher into the sky, turning the snowy line of the Diamondfang into a fiery explosion of pink and gold colour. The light illuminated the way as the road narrowed into an icy gorge. Little shivers danced over Arya's skin. It was an eerie experience, riding along a deserted highway with only the high gorge walls surrounding them.

The road wound upwards through the gorge for a few miles until emerging onto a wide plateau. The Diamondfang peaks spread out for miles around them, the tallest ones wreathed in cloud and hidden from sight. The Raider column slowed to an almost halt, staring around in wonder, and Arya found herself doing the same.

She'd never seen anything so stunning in her life.

"The home of the Etherean," Kait murmured, her words echoing across the plateau. "I wish I could meet one."

"You never will, if the warlords have any say in it," Laskin said. "They don't want any more to do with Etherean magic than they do Sky Lord magic. The Khadini too. And the Etherean know it. They'll stay safe up here in their mountain home as they have for decades."

"What magic?" Kait asked.

"Healing," Wattin said, a note of wistfulness in his voice. "They are masters of it."

"What is there to hate about healing magic? Or any kind of magic, really." Taze frowned.

"Those with magic have tools that the rest of us have no defence against, and there are no boundaries or rules that govern how they're used. It's unfair and dangerous," Allicen said.

Taze said, "I disagree. Sure, magic is an extra ability, but it's not that different from being stronger than others, or having better eyesight, or being born incredibly clever. Isn't it how you choose to use those things that matters?"

Everyone stared at him. Arya had never heard it put like that, but now that she had, she turned it around in her mind, then tucked it away for further thinking about when not on a dangerous mission.

Charlin snorted. "Magic is shunned in Dunidaen because it's feared by the warlords—it's a direct threat to their power and authority. Andahar and their Sky Lords were all fine and dandy as allies when they were benevolent rulers, but when the Nightstalker turned on his own and killed them all, he demonstrated what magic could do if turned against us."

"Enough chatter!" Arya had given them a moment to enjoy the sight, but every second they wasted the creatures could be getting farther away. "We keep moving, eyes alert. Faster, now."

The pass was barely a mile farther along. The road widened, then flattened out for a short distance until it hit a massive rockfall reaching a quarter-mile or so high, covered in a layer of ice and snow. The trading post that had once been one of the busiest buildings on the continent stood on the north-facing mountainside, rambling and in severe disrepair.

"Let's take a closer look," Arya ordered. "Make sure it hasn't been compromised."

They crawled all over the lower parts of the rockfall, but there was no sign anybody had touched it in decades. Ice had frozen most of it into place, and the thick layer of snow over it was untouched.

The Shadeweavers hunkered down a good distance away, silent as they watched the Raiders clamber over the rockfall. Arya was sure she wasn't imagining the amusement in the looks they shot each other, though.

"Wraiths could probably get over that, but not shadowhounds," Laskin offered once they were done. "And humans couldn't without climbing gear and expertise. I don't think anything has come this way in a very long time."

"Agreed." She let out a breath. "So this part of the border isn't breached, and the creatures don't seem to be trying to flee home this way. That's two pieces of useful information."

"It begs the question of where they *are* going, though."

"Back to the underground road? Gathering somewhere for another attack?"

"Maybe. If it's the first, they're probably too far ahead of us now to catch them."

"Why'd they head west instead of south for SheerRock if they intended to cross the border that way, though?"

Laskin shrugged. "It might be time to turn back, report in. Commander Lerin can decide the best way to send out patrols to sweep the Wraith Forest and Diamondfang for the remaining creatures."

Arya snorted. "It's become quite clear to me that Lerin can't strategise his way out of a bowl of oatmeal. No, we need to get them now, Laskin, while they're on the back foot and fleeing. Not when they've had time to get stronger and re-position."

"We're undermanned, Arya, not to mention bloodied and tired. We—"

"Arya's right. We should keep going," Charlin called across. "We're all good to go."

Laskin glanced between her and the rest of the shield, who clearly agreed with Charlin and Arya, then let out a resigned sigh. "Fine. Far be it from me to insert some sense into this unapproved and risky mission."

Darmanin chose that moment to return, simply walking onto the road and ignoring all the puzzled looks coming his way from the Raiders. The Shadeweavers rose silently to their feet, and one handed Darmanin the reins of his horse.

Arya clapped her hands at the sight of the boy's nod. He'd found the creatures. "Mount up, quickly now. We've got their trail."

***

By nightfall, both riders and horses were exhausted. They'd followed Darmanin all afternoon, over rough, tricky terrain that taxed all of them to their limits.

The wraiths and shadowhounds had dispersed into smaller groups rather than staying together, which confused Arya to no end. They pushed hard, catching up to the groups one by one. Each encounter led to intense, vicious fighting, but the smaller numbers meant the combined force of Raiders and Shadeweavers had the advantage each time. And while the Raiders had superior arms and fighting style, Arya was quickly forced to admit that the Shadeweaver knowledge of the terrain had them moving faster and safer than her shield would have otherwise.

As the sun grew low, Arya ordered a halt. "Going on in the dark will only risk lives," she said when Darmanin protested. "It doesn't look like the creatures are trying to flee back over the border or head down into Ravenstrike State, so we can pick this up at first light after everyone has rested."

"And what about Shadeweaver camps?" he demanded.

"We haven't come across a single one of those today, either. The creatures are on the run. They're not attacking anything." Arya spoke firmly. "We rest for the night."

He took this with ill grace but presumably accepted her words, because he communicated her orders to the Shadeweavers. Then he disappeared back into the trees.

Their Shadeweaver companions found the ideal spot to make camp in a lee in the rock of the mountainside, with a clear view around them that would forestall a sneak attack. The horses they left tethered on a section of the slope above, where they could paw through the snow to graze.

The Shadeweavers remained uncommunicative as they chose a corner of the space and organised themselves, while the Raiders settled down opposite them.

"We're not going to have any problems, right?" Arya addressed them bluntly.

One of the women bared her teeth. "Sleep tight, little Raider. You have nothing to fear from us tonight."

Even so, Arya set a guard rotation and noticed the Shadeweavers doing the same.

She had to stifle a laugh. So much trust.

Arya, the last to curl up on the hard ground after making sure her shield were all settled, was still awake when Darmanin returned. He stepped lightly over the sleeping bodies and crouched beside her to murmur, "There's nothing nearby that could pose a danger to us."

"Do you have a sense of where the creatures are going, what their intentions are?"

"If I had to guess, I'd say all they're trying to do is get clear of pursuit." He frowned. "They don't seem to be trying to make it to a central location or join their strength. It's almost like…"

"Like what?"

"Like they have individual purposes … no, more like … whatever it is they're trying to do, it doesn't need all of them." He sounded frustrated, like he couldn't articulate it the way he wanted to.

"Or they're just wild animals who managed to get across the border and are now behaving just like any snow leopard or bear. Looking for prey." Except for the whole digging through the roadblock and taking out an entire fort thing. She sighed.

"I doubt it," he murmured, mostly to himself.

Arya almost left it there, but curiosity prompted her to say, "Contravening Ranier's orders," she said, "I imagine that's a dangerous thing to do."

Quicksilver grey eyes flashed in her direction. "I make my own choices, Raider. I am beholden to nobody."

Those words rang with sincerity, not immature arrogance. It resonated so strongly with Arya's sense of herself—that she was capable, just as capable, if not more so, than any adult or man, despite her age—that it took her a moment before she said, "I doubt that's how Ranier sees those under his command. Why would you even want to help us?"

"Ranier has his pride too, and it was infringed upon when your commanders refused to accept his help. But that did not change how vulnerable we Shadeweavers are to these creatures. So I left with those who felt the same, and we waited near Icecliff in case we could be of help. When I saw you were close to being overwhelmed, we acted."

"So it wasn't because I saved your life the other day?" she challenged softly.

There was a brief, still silence. But all he said was, "That is a debt still to be repaid, Raider." He rose to his feet.

"Darmanin?"

He turned back, eyes glimmering.

"You're really Warlord Crowtalon's son?"

He nodded once, his expression betraying no surprise that she knew this. She met his gaze, seeing in those depths a boy who was as fierce and desperate for strength and autonomy as she was. A Shadeweaver, but in some ways a kindred spirit.

"My name is Arya."

His mouth curled in a slight smile, and then he turned away, disappearing into the shadows of night.

Chapter 12

Arya took over watch in the early hours. After sending Taze to his blankets, she settled against a nearby tree, staring out into the night, entranced by the silvery glitter of moonlight on snow.

There'd been too many clear days in a row. More bad weather would hit them soon.

That was the last thought she remembered having before she fell asleep, her exhausted body finally giving in.

The hum of voices drifted into her dreams.

"She embodies all of their worst traits," one voice said, unhappy.

"In addition to some of their better ones," a different one added. This voice sounded familiar, but she couldn't quite place it. *"Cerilla said her Raiders fought like soldiers led by a strong leader."*

"Perhaps," the first voice conceded. *"But I am concerned about what we could be letting loose on the world. Perhaps it is best to let things lie, Elder."*

"Letting things lie could lead to our end. The closing of borders and trade is increasingly impacting our ability to feed and clothe our people. There is only so much we can do to provide for ourselves in such harsh terrain, and our stores run dangerously low. Bartering with the Storm Isles pirates isn't enough to fix that."

"You don't have to keep reminding us, we see it for ourselves," came the testy response. *"But she is not necessarily the answer, not how she has grown, a precocious bundle of anger and pride. We should have intervened sooner if we wanted to pin our hopes on her."*

"You know that was not possible." The second voice shivered with frustration, like this was something he'd said many times before. *"We are taking*

significant risks, I'm aware, but we have little choice. If we do nothing, Rithil, we face certain destruction."

"But taking the wrong course of action will only hasten that destruction."

A sigh. *"I know."*

Something about the tone of that sigh was sharp enough to draw Arya from sleep. She opened her eyes, blinking, into direct sunlight, only to glimpse a huddle of winged men nearby.

Winged men.

Shock flooded her and she sat upright, scrabbling for her sword. Sharply muttered words broke out at her movement, and wings rustled, air washed over her, and then a single Etherean stood above her, mostly hidden by the sunlight shining into her eyes. He didn't appear to be a threat, but even so, she lurched to her feet and drew her sword.

As she did so, another winged man dropped out of the sky to land a few paces behind his companion, holding a nocked bow pointed at her heart. The silver-white hair of both men gleamed too bright in the morning sun, and Arya had to blink a few times before she could look directly at their faces. They were lean, *too* lean to carry what had to be the heavy weight of the wings hanging from their backs. And unlike the Raiders and Shadeweavers, they didn't wear layers, only a simple tunic and breeches, with laced boots. They should be freezing.

Raven's balls, she'd fallen asleep on watch! And missed some kind of Etherean invasion? She rubbed at her eyes again. Nope, two winged men still stood in front of her.

"Put the bow down, Cerilla." The winged man closest to her spoke to his companion, then lifted his hands, palm open as he turned back to Arya. His wings were pale blue and he wore an aura of authority that the other man had lacked. There was something about him that nagged at her, though she couldn't quite place it. "I'm not here to hurt you, Raider Nameless. I would speak with you, if you will allow it?"

"Where did the others go? The ones you were talking to." She scanned the campsite frantically. But her Raiders slept on unharmed, Shadeweavers too, even Darmanin. The single Shadeweaver guard snored softly. She couldn't believe she'd fallen asleep on watch. She'd *never* done that. Arya's gaze narrowed in suspicion. "You put us to sleep with your healing magic?"

"We mean no harm," he repeated. "You are safe. In fact, I believe Cerilla brings good news."

"Elder." The second man took a step forward. "My warrior scouts have located and destroyed all remaining wraiths and shadowhounds."

Arya stared at him. "You did *what* now?"

The elder smiled. There was something naggingly familiar about him, but she couldn't quite place it. "We came to provide assistance in destroying the monsters that attacked your forts. Cerilla and his warriors have done an admirable job as you slept. Consider it a token of our good intentions."

Arya rubbed at her face. This was all feeling rather surreal, but she figured staring at the two Etherean like a goggling fool wasn't the best look for the leader of a shield. "How did you even know about that?"

"There is little that occurs in the Diamondfang that we are not aware of. You can be sure all wraiths and shadowhounds have been dealt with," Cerilla said. The politeness was overlaid with a tone of condescension, as if he assumed this would have been impossible without Etherean help.

Arya stared at him, torn between insult, confusion, and wonderment.

The elder seemed to recognise this. "Cerilla, leave us please. Raider Nameless will not hurt me."

Cerilla didn't look pleased about this instruction, but he didn't argue, simply lifted into the sky. His wings gleamed as they caught the sunlight. The remaining Etherean smiled at her. "Do I not look familiar to you, Raider Nameless?"

The moment he said that, it clicked into place, and her eyes widened. This was the man she'd seen in her dreams.

He was *real*?

"Who *are* you?" she asked.

"I am Salyarin, the elder of the Etherean. I am the equivalent of a High Warlord in your country." He gestured away from the camp. "Walk with me? My warriors watch over your camp, and no harm will come to you or yours while we are gone. It is best, however, that nobody hear what we speak of."

Arya baulked. "You let me wake a single Raider, one I trust, to keep watch. Or I don't go with you."

He let out a sigh. "Very well."

She crossed to where Laskin lay curled up and woke him with a touch. As succinctly as she could, she explained the situation, still not quite believing it herself. "Will you keep watch while I'm gone?"

He took this equably, although maybe that was just because he was still half asleep. Either way he sat up, pushed his blankets off, and made sure his sword was within reach. "Take too long and I'll rouse this whole camp to come after you."

"Thanks, Laskin." Arya returned to the elder, falling into step with him as he led her a short distance away to the banks of a frozen-over stream.

The Etherean paused here, his wings hanging loosely by his side. Arya found herself fascinated by the way his feathers ruffled in the icy breeze. His wings were so intricate—and they were powerful enough to carry him through the sky. Amazing. Abruptly, she had a flash of seeing those same wings in her dreams.

She slowly looked up to his face. "The dreams I've been having, they were real ... that was you? And in the last one, you saw me." But how... a shudder went through her. Magic.

"I've been trying to find you for a very long time," he said. "Too long."

She shivered as another icy gust of air swept through the trees. "Why?"

The elder held her gaze. "Because you are the true heir to the Andahari throne."

The moment froze as she waited for the joke to land, for a clarification, but ... nothing. He merely stared expectantly at her.

Arya coughed out a laugh. "That's ... Elder, I'm very sorry, but you're talking to the wrong person."

He gave her a knowing look. "I'm afraid I'm not. You *are* the true heir, and you are the only one that can destroy the Nightstalker and re-take the throne."

Arya lifted a hand to massage suddenly throbbing temples. The conversation was veering from surreal to fairy-tale territory. "And how is it that you know that, exactly?"

"That is a secret I cannot share. But I am certain, Arya Nameless. It is you." He gave her a sympathetic smile. "It's why I'm here so abruptly rather than taking time to properly introduce you to the idea. You were in immediate danger and needed our help."

She straightened. "You mean the wraiths and shadowhounds? We had that under control. And am I supposed to take you at your word that they've all been destroyed?"

"You don't understand." A grim look closed over his face. "Arya, those creatures were sent to find *you.* That's why we breached our exile and came—we had to make sure every single one of them was killed before any could either kill you or return to Andahar to report to their master that you'd been found."

She looked at him blankly. "Even if your frankly impossible claim was true, why would they be looking for me *now*?"

"We don't know for sure, but as the heir to Andahar you are a potential Sky Lord, Arya. We have little insight inside Andahar's borders, but given your age, it is possible that a wyvern has been born and that word of it reached the Nightstalker. He would know instantly what that meant."

Heir to Andahar *and* a Sky Lord. Arya shook her head, "Elder, it's just not possible. I'm not what you think I am. I have no magic, for a start."

His gaze searched her face. "Have you had dreams of a wyvern? Of anything unusual?"

She snorted. "My only unusual dreams are those I've had of you."

"Perhaps that is best for now," he said, almost to himself. "Without magic, you will be harder to track, and if there is no wyvern born ... but how then did he learn of you?"

"Or you've got the wrong person," she said again, more pointedly this time.

"I have not." There was so much certainty in his voice it gave her chills. "There are always five Sky Lords, Arya, which means there are four others.

You must find them before the Nightstalker finds and kills them too. Like he did to your grandfather, the last true king of Andahar, and *his* Sky Lords."

"Oh, I see. So I have to re-take a throne *and* find a bunch of special children?"

"I am not telling you this for your amusement!" Frustration marred his fey features. "It is imperative you hear what I say. You *must* find them."

"And how do I do that?"

"They will have a magical ability," the elder said, expelling a sigh. "I wish I could be more specific, but I believe you will know them when you meet them. It will be an instinct as strong as breathing."

Arya frowned as a thought occurred to her. "Being able to shapeshift into a shadowhound, is that the sort of thing you're talking about?"

The elder stilled, face turning grave. "That's exactly what I'm talking about. Do you know such a person?"

Arya said nothing, part of her unwilling to betray Darmanin's existence, even though she didn't understand the instinct to protect him.

"If you have, you *must* protect him, Arya." The elder's voice was thick with intensity. "I cannot stress the importance of it. He must be cared for. Do you understand?"

"I don't understand any of this!" she snapped.

"I appreciate that, but there was no other way," he said. "You are too close to the Diamondfang. I counsel you to leave, travel elsewhere in Dunidaen, as far south as you can go. The Nightstalker almost had you in his grasp, and he won't stop looking now he knows you exist. You threaten everything he's built."

She wanted to scoff again, but something in his face prevented that. "I know you warn me sincerely, but you're wrong. My place is here with the Raiders."

He gave a reluctant nod. "At least remember what I say, and be careful. That will have to do for now, Raider Nameless. Look for me in your dreams."

"What a delightful prospect," Arya muttered.

Her gaze trailed him as he winged into the sky, heading for one of the distant peaks. Once he was gone from sight, she shook her head and ran a hand over her eyes.

Born for a purpose. She snorted. What a ridiculous notion.

But ... the elder *had* given a reason for the monsters' presence that neatly fit their behaviour. Take out SheerRock so they could sneak through undetected to hunt her. Then once they'd picked up her trail—scent, magic, something else?—they'd tracked her to Icecliff Fort, looking to identify *which* Raider she was. It explained why they'd fled and dispersed after the attack from Icecliff without any apparent destination in mind.

Not all of them needed to find her. Just one hound or wraith. And then get back over the border to report to their master.

Arya sucked in a breath. That look of recognition in the shadowhound's eyes as it had crouched atop her. Could she *truly* have been what it was hunting for?

She laughed aloud at herself. She could be arrogant sometimes, but to think a hundreds-strong force of creatures had been sent over the border, had killed an entire fort of people, just to find her?

Ridiculous.

Arya turned and headed back to her shield. She arrived at the camp to find Raiders and Shadeweavers alike awake and staring warily up at the handful of Etherean hovering in the sky above. They were watching protectively as the elder had promised.

The moment they saw Arya appear, the Etherean warriors turned and winged higher into the sky, soon disappearing completely from sight.

"To be clear, they were Etherean, right?" Kait asked, wide-eyed.

"Indeed they were." Laskin nodded, one hand running over his stubble, a tell-tale sign he was mulling over something. A couple of the Raiders shot each other dark looks, no doubt remembering what Laskin had said the previous day about them having magic.

Wattin shook his head in wonder. "Never thought I'd see the day."

"Enough gawking." Arya clapped her hands. "Tack up and prepare for departure. Darmanin, the Etherean tell me they've tracked and destroyed the remaining creatures. Is that something you can confirm?"

"You can't trust their word on that." Darmanin stepped forward, arms crossed over his chest. His Shadeweavers hadn't moved to mount up either.

Arya snorted. "Like I can trust yours? At least no Etherean has ever murdered my shield-mates." She sighed. "Why do you think I'm asking you to confirm that they did what they said they did?"

"Why?"

"Why what?"

"The Etherean withdrew from formal relations with Dunidaen and Khadini at the same time as Andahar—" Darmanin began.

"I don't need a history lesson, Darmanin."

"—so have you asked yourself why they're breaching that agreement now to help a single shield of Raiders track down some wraiths and shadowhounds?"

She eyed him. No part of her wanted to pass on any of the elder's wild claims. She had no interest in being laughed off the plateau. "I imagine that, much like you Shadeweavers, the Etherean aren't too keen on having such a threat roaming through their home."

Darmanin's mouth tightened. Such a stubborn, angry boy. "Shadowhounds aren't getting anywhere near the peaks where the Etherean live, Raider Nameless. I doubt wraiths are either."

She wasn't arguing any further with him. "Are you willing to confirm the Etherean's claims or not?"

His mouth thinned, but he gave a terse nod.

"Thank you. We'll start making our way east to Icecliff, combing the mountains as we go. If you find any sign there are more creatures, come and let us know."

He stalked off without another word, and this time his Shadeweavers went with him. It was likely for the best. Instinct told her the Etherean were as good as their word—that and the fact that the elder had seemed so desperately worried about leaving any of them alive.

Raiders and Shadeweavers were enemies who had been forced by circumstance to fight together for a brief time. None were under any doubt that, now the threat seemed to be over, they would go back to killing each other.

It didn't exactly leave room for warm goodbyes.

Still, Arya's gaze lingered in the direction Darmanin went, the Etherean's words still echoing through her thoughts. He'd been so insistent, so urgent, that she protect Darmanin. Still, there was little she could do. He wouldn't come back to Icecliff with her, even if she thought that was a good idea.

She shook off her thoughts. Whatever the creatures' purpose in coming to Dunidaen, the threat they posed was neutralised. The Raiders at Icecliff had done their job. "Mount up," she called to her shield.

Charlin cleared his throat. None of the shield moved towards their horses. "Arya, what in raven's balls did an Etherean want to talk to you about?"

She shrugged. "To tell me his warriors had tracked down the remaining wraiths and shadowhounds. Come on now, let's get off this blasted cold rock. We'll sweep for creatures as we go, but unless we hear otherwise from our Shadeweaver tracker, we'll be sleeping in our warm beds tonight."

A ragged cheer followed her words. Everyone except Laskin headed for their horses. He gave her a look that suggested he knew very well there'd been more to her conversation with the elder. She lifted her eyebrow. He crossed his arms over his chest. She grinned and broke his gaze, striding over to her mare. He grumbled and followed.

A sense of warm contentment settled over Arya at the thought of returning to Icecliff. She wasn't sure why the Etherean had thought she could be the heir to Andahar. She was a Raider to the bone, a soldier comfortable with a sword in her grasp and a horse under her. And now that she'd earned the right to be promoted to shield captain, her days ahead were filled with new purpose. The urge to lead, to plan, to have a say and affect the outcome—it was as much a part of her as breathing. And now she'd finally get the chance to use it.

She ignored the little voice deep down that whispered that being queen of Andahar would give her even more power than she'd dreamed of.

It was only as the shield rode away, heading east towards Icecliff, that Arya realised something. When she'd raised someone with shapeshifting ability, the elder had immediately referred to them as a 'he.' Yet she hadn't *given* a gender. Had Salyarin already known whom she was referring to, and if so, why had he kept that from her?

Who was Darmanin?

Chapter 13

A Raider ran over as soon as Arya's shield rode through the gates of Icecliff and reined in. "Commander Lerin wants to see you at once, Arya."

"Of course he does," she muttered, then turned to the shield and lifted her voice. "See to your horses, then straight to the healers before anything else. Wattin, you make sure of that. Sleep in as long as you like tomorrow."

The familiar relief of being safe within high stone walls was palpable as it swept through the group, light chatter breaking out despite how tired they all were. Arya smiled at it, that shimmer of triumph sweeping through her again as she dismounted to head inside.

They'd done good.

Lerin sat at a large table in his quarters, concentrating on several pieces of parchment before him, a mug of something sweet-smelling steaming at his elbow. His hair was askew, his fleshy face grey with tiredness. Arya came to a stop and saluted sharply.

He glanced up. "Report, Raider Nameless."

Without fanfare, Arya gave a concise, detailed accounted of everything that had happened since they'd left the fort. She left out only the details of what the Etherean had told her in their private conversation. "We saw no sign of the creatures on our return, sir."

Lerin looked increasingly incredulous as she spoke of being helped by Etherean warrior scouts. "Etherean? Are you sure you weren't hallucinating from blood loss or exhaustion?"

"No, sir. The whole shield saw them, sir."

He shook his head. "Your report corroborates that of the patrols I've sent out, who identified no signs of shadowhounds or wraiths in the area. I think we can safely assume that they're gone. General Desomer has replacement shields en-route to SheerRock. Their first task will be to block up the underground road again and make sure it stays that way."

"That's excellent news." She hesitated. "Sir, may I ask about the status of my shield? I'd like to be considered as the replacement for—"

He cleared his throat, cutting her off. "Captain Robem has been assigned as your shield captain, and your shield will report to him in the drill yard day after tomorrow. More Raiders are being dispatched from elsewhere in Ravenstrike to bring you back up to your full complement of twenty. Dismissed."

Arya's jaw clenched, her heart sinking in her chest. "But sir—"

"You're not a shield captain, Nameless, and your shield needs one," Lerin said with an edge.

"Sir, in the past week I have ably demonstrated that I have what it takes to be a shield captain." She fought for a calm tone and barely managed it. She couldn't bear the thought of going back to following the orders of a captain again, not when she'd tasted the freedom of leading her shield. "You cannot argue with that."

"On the contrary, in the past week you have ably demonstrated your ability to ignore orders and undermine me in front of the other shield captains *and* our warlord. What did you think would be the consequences of defying me so openly in that meeting?" he bit out. "Not only that, but after you completed your mission, you went after the creatures without backup or the authority to do so, recklessly risking the safety of your undermanned shield. You further disobeyed direct orders by engaging Shadeweaver help. That is *not* the behaviour of someone ready to be a shield captain."

"I didn't engage Shadeweaver help!" she said, so stung by the accusation that she forgot to be deferential. "They helped of their own accord."

He lifted his eyebrows. "And you didn't arrest or kill them after the battle because...?"

"Sir, they–"

"They're criminals who hunt our kind, Raider Nameless!" he snarled at her. "Learn discipline and respect, and only then will I consider promoting you."

The contempt in his beady eyes undid her. She took a step towards him, fists clenching, refusing to bow to his command. She would never again submit to this cowardly fool.

Lerin rose slowly from his chair, his height and bulk looming over her. "You have something to say to me, Raider? You think you're better than me, that I should give you, a Nameless nobody, some respect?"

"I want nothing from you," she spat. "I'm done. You can find yourself another Raider. I'm out."

She didn't salute as she stormed from the room, slamming the door behind her.

Fury curdled as she stalked back to her barracks wing, and tears of frustration sprang to her eyes. All that she had done in the last few days, and *still* Lerin overlooked her. A lump rose in her throat, and her hands clenched into fists at her sides, nails digging painfully into her skin. She turned and kicked the stone wall of the corridor as hard as she could. Pain shot along her foot, only serving to make her angrier.

"Raven's balls!" she swore, hopping on one foot and cursing under her breath until the pain began to subside.

"Arya?" Wattin's voice sounded. He was coming along the corridor towards his room, a fresh bandage over a cut on his forehead, hair and beard damp from a wash.

Ignoring him, she stalked past and hauled open the door to her room to find it, fortunately, empty. Kait must still be with the healers. She sat on the edge of her bed and dropped her head into her hands.

Her resignation had been impulsive, but in that moment her pride couldn't have submitted to that man. And she didn't regret the words she'd thrown at him.

But come tomorrow, she would no longer be a Raider.

What had she done?

She glanced at the chest sitting at the end of her sleeping pallet. It was empty aside from her spare uniform and a small bag of coins that was her saved pay. She didn't even own any civilian clothing. She had no employable skills other than being a soldier. And although she could read and write, she hadn't had any education beyond that. The only real option she had was to find work as a labourer or a farmhand, or go to another State and hire on with their soldiers.

She would have to leave her shield-mates. Her fellow Raiders. The men and women who'd stood at her side for years. Never again would she patrol into the Diamondfang and experience that terrifying yet thrilling awareness of danger.

The magnitude of what she'd done hit Arya full force then. Being a Raider was all she'd known, all she loved. The thought of going back to Lerin to apologise flashed briefly, but she couldn't do it, couldn't go back to what she'd been. She yearned for too much more.

At least the Etherean elder was getting what he wanted, her leaving the Diamondfang. In her groggy exhaustion, a chuckle escaped her. That whole encounter had taken on a hazy quality, one already receding to the depths of her mind. She had far more immediate things to worry about. After sitting for a little longer, she rose, wearily made her way out of the door, and headed towards the healer's wing.

If she was leaving tomorrow, she'd best get her wounds seen to.

***

Sleep didn't claim Arya for long that night. Restless dreams had her tossing and turning, and she woke early. As soon as the blue light of daybreak filtered through her window, she shoved off the covers. Dread filled the pit of her stomach at the thought of leaving, but she recoiled with equal dread at the idea of going back to her shield, taking orders from someone else, someone new.

Her head dropped into her hands. She couldn't face the thought of telling Laskin any of this.

She would go and eat something. Food always helped her think better. Anyway, she'd have to get going early if she wanted any chance of making it down to the safety of Heathrock city before midnight.

The early dawn hallways were quiet, but outside the window, Warlord Ravenstrike's personal shield gathered in the entry yard. It looked like she was returning to Heathrock now that the crisis was over. No doubt she and the other warlords would be trying to figure out how to respond to recent events, to the possibility of Andahar stirring.

Another twinge of guilt and regret went through her. If invasion came, the Ravenstrike forts would take the brunt of it, and Arya wouldn't be here to help her shield-mates.

Maybe she should think about—

"Raider Nameless!"

She turned, startled. A man approached her with quick strides. He looked vaguely familiar: middle-aged, of average stature, with short-cropped red hair. Her still-tired mind took several moments to dig up why he was familiar—she'd seen him accompanying the warlord around the fort. "Yes?"

"I'm Magen, Warlord Ravenstrike's chief adviser. The warlord would like to speak with you before she departs."

She raised an eyebrow. "She wants to talk to *me*?"

"She does," he said with a slight smile. "And she doesn't like to be kept waiting."

Thiara Ravenstrike paced before a dying fire in her spacious but spare room. The warlord's blonde hair was tied back in a severe braid, and she wore plain but expensive riding clothes.

As on their previous encounters, she appeared confident and capable, despite being the first female warlord Dunidaen could remember—and not only that, but having the role thrust on her without any preparation. A flickering of respect shivered through Arya. It couldn't be easy. But there was envy edging the respect too.

The warlord spun to face her the moment the door opened. "I apologise, Raider Nameless," she said briskly, the words sincere but without warmth. "You must be sore and tired. I'll make this quick."

"Warlord." Arya stopped, saluted, then tucked her hands at the small of her back, legs slightly apart, back straight.

"General Desomer was my father's man, and he doesn't have many more years to serve before his retirement. He needs an apprentice. I want you to fill that post. If you accept, you'll be promoted to the rank of shield captain and return with me to Heathrock today."

Arya's mouth almost dropped open, only years of drill training preventing it, and a moment later she realised she was staring. "I apologise Warlord, I *am* tired, and I'm not sure I heard you correctly. You want to apprentice me to your general?"

Thiara's eyes raked over her, assessing and clearly finding her appearance wanting, then she spoke bluntly. "You're a stripling of a girl, barely more than a child, really. You are overconfident and reckless. Despite that, you were the clearest head in this fort this past week. More, you displayed a courage that is rare in anyone I've met, let alone in someone so young, and you inspired that same courage in your shield. You have a lot to learn, you do understand that, yes?"

"Yes, Warlord," Arya said, doing her best not to bristle.

"I have an instinct about you, Nameless, which I have decided to trust. Will you accept my offer? It will not be made again once I leave this room."

Arya blinked. The warlord of Ravenstrike couldn't *really* be offering to...

"I'm not promising you anything more than an apprenticeship," the warlord said, impatience beginning to edge her tone. "General Desomer has his faults, but he is a competent war leader. If he doesn't like you or believe you capable, you'll be done without a further word from me. However, apply yourself, and we'll see what happens in the future."

Cautious excitement spread through Arya, dispelling every trace of weariness she felt, even if only for a moment. She was being offered the opportunity of a lifetime—the ideal way out of her current dilemma. She would have to leave her shield-mates, but she'd still be a Raider ... and if Arya succeeded at an apprenticeship with the general of Ravenstrike State, who knew how far she could go, and in service to a warlord she might be able to genuinely respect and admire.

"I accept. Thank you, Warlord." She spoke fiercely.

"I require absolute loyalty," Thiara warned. "You will be in a position of rare trust in my household. If I found that you betrayed that in any way, my punishment would be swift and merciless."

"I would never—" Arya began protesting indignantly, but then she remembered who she was addressing. "I understand, Warlord."

Thiara Ravenstrike nodded. "We're riding out now. I want to be home before nightfall. Pack your things and meet us down in the yard."

"Warlord." Arya saluted and strode out.

The door closed behind her and she stopped, blinking. Had that just—?

A chuckle broke out from Magen, who stood outside. "Yes, that just happened. You'd better hurry. The shield is about ready for departure, and one of the first things you'll learn about the warlord is that she *hates* being kept waiting. I'll make sure Commander Lerin is informed that you're coming with us."

"I should—" She shook her head, trying to process how quickly this was all happening. "I should say goodbye."

"No time for that. She'll leave without you, don't doubt it."

Arya ran for her barracks. It took her a matter of minutes to find a pack and stuff it with her spare uniform and money, then she was leaving her room. She almost ran right into Laskin, who had clearly come looking for her.

"Oh, Laskin, thank goodness you're here!" She grabbed his arm. "I'm leaving, will you say goodbye to the shield for me?"

His eyebrows shot skywards. "Going where?"

"No time to explain, but the warlord has asked me to go with her." She hesitated, then threw her arms around him in a fierce hug before letting go. He rocked back, astonished. "Thank you for everything. I'm going to miss you all. Tell them that, will you?"

"I—" His face was still stunned when she pulled away.

"I'll miss you most of all," she admitted, swallowing down the emotion that wanted to rise. "Bye, Laskin." Arya sketched a wave and ran, exhaustion and soreness forgotten. The gates were being winched open as she emerged into the mounting yard.

Someone had brought her tired mare out of the stables, fully saddled. Arya attached her pack to the back of the saddle and then mounted up, barely even noticing the pain in her leg. The column of Raiders that made up the warlord's personal shield didn't seem surprised to see her join them. Though they didn't exactly welcome her, either.

And then the fort's bells rang out, and they were moving at a shout from the shield captain, the warlord's carriage lurching into movement. Arya glanced over her shoulder, and her heart clenched, wishing she'd had a chance to say a proper goodbye to her shield. At least she'd managed to see Laskin. He would tell them. Her mare clattered onto the main road as they increased speed.

Still, she kept glancing backwards, until the fort vanished from sight behind her, swallowed up by the Diamondfang.

Chapter 14

T hey hadn't long moved out of sight of Icecliff Fort when Arya was summoned to the warlord's carriage. Despite the bitterly cold day, the window where Thiara Ravenstrike sat was open to let in the watery sunlight. No other Raiders were within hearing distance, and Magen was sitting up with the driver, chatting away. Arya reined in by the window.

Thiara's glance raked her, always assessing. "I forced you into a quick decision. I don't apologise for it, but if we reach Heathrock castle and you've changed your mind, you'll be free to return to Icecliff. I won't write my instructions to Commander Lerin as regards your position until tomorrow morning, so you have some time to properly consider your situation."

"Thank you, Warlord, but I'm not going to change my mind," Arya said.

"You haven't slept or eaten properly in days, and you're no doubt in pain as well as exhausted. You are not in a fit state to make decisions that affect your entire future, Raider Nameless, and if you claim otherwise, you're a fool. I don't take on fools," the warlord said sharply.

Arya swallowed and nodded. The warlord knew nothing of her life, of what an opportunity this was for her, of how badly she wanted it. She would take this chance whether well-fed and rested or half dying on the slopes of the Diamondfang.

Thiara continued, "I will make you aware of everything that will be involved with your new position. You will sleep on it, consider carefully what I'm offering, and come to me with your decision in the morning."

It was an order, not a question, and Arya responded as such. "Yes, Warlord."

"The first thing you should know is that I intend to become High Warlord of Dunidaen," Thiara Ravenstrike said. "And when I do, that will have implications for whomever is general of Ravenstrike at that time."

Arya blinked in surprise. "You plan to stand for High Warlord at the State Council next year?"

Her education might have been lacking, but Arya at least knew that the State Councils—held every four years—were where the administration of Dunidaen as a whole was managed. Outside of that, States were essentially left to run themselves.

"No. Darien Eaglesoar is growing old, but he will remain High Warlord for at least another term. I will make my claim at the following Council," Thiara said.

"Five years is a long time from now," Arya said. Yet, given what Laskin had relayed about how reluctant the other warlords were to accept their first ever female warlord, was five years enough time to convince them that one could be High Warlord? "And yet not much time at all," she added without thinking.

Thiara glanced at her. "Why do you say that?"

Arya cleared her throat and tried to come up with something diplomatic. The silence lengthened.

"Spit it out, Raider. I won't bite at honest thoughts, but I will quickly become impatient with hesitation or prevarication."

"I heard that the other warlords were reluctant to accept a woman as a warlord," Arya said. "And so I wondered whether five years was long enough to convince them to consider one as a High Warlord."

A knowing look crossed Thiara's face, and she settled more comfortably in her carriage seat. "Well, you're no fool. That's a good sign. Ravenstrike is one of the strongest States in Dunidaen, but it has not exerted power or influence reflective of that status for many years. My father was a competent warlord, but too friendly with his peers to ever think of competing against them. My brother was of the same mould. I am not. I intend to restore the power and privilege of the House of Ravenstrike. You are right, however, in that achieving that will be a considerable challenge."

There was a note of ruthlessness in the warlord's voice that Arya found appealing. "You've been planning this for a long time," she hazarded a guess.

"I have *desired* it for a long time. But until circumstances made me a warlord, I never thought it could become a reality." Thiara Ravenstrike gave her a wolfish look. "And as to your point, the next five years are crucial. It is imperative that we use that time to demonstrate convincingly that a woman *can* be High Warlord."

The 'we' in that sentence filled Arya with a fierce pride, like she was being included in her warlord's plans. It prompted her to want to dive in immediately, learn more so that she could help her warlord achieve her goal. "What would you consider your biggest obstacle, Warlord? Will potential invasion from Andahar delay a High Warlord vote, for example?"

"Recent events could certainly be a threat to Dunidaen as a whole, and one we as warlords must respond to with speed and strength—but there will be opportunities for me to display Ravenstrike's strength and perhaps even to turn the situation to my advantage." Thiara gave her another approving look. "We have already done so, with how quickly and decisively my Raiders dealt with the creatures."

Her Raiders, as well as Shadeweavers and the Etherean. But Arya forbore to point that out. The carriage wheels creaked as they followed a bend in the road, a stiff breeze sweeping over them before gusting up into the mountains.

Thiara continued, "No, the single greatest threat to my ambitions is Mathas Crowtalon. He is a treacherous snake and wants the position as badly as I do. Crowtalon is a problem I must deal with decisively if I am to have any hope of succeeding."

Arya felt a start of surprise at the mention of Warlord Crowtalon—Darmanin's father. She dredged up everything she could recall of her conversations with Laskin about him, wishing now she'd paid better attention. Darmanin's face flashed into her mind, bringing with it the sharp memory of the elder's words, ringing through her mind ever since he'd spoken them.

Protect him. Could Warlord Ravenstrike be persuaded to offer the boy some kind of protection or help?

Hesitant, Arya ventured, "Are you aware that several years ago, Warlord Crowtalon expelled his second son from his household?"

"I had heard that, yes. There were some behavioural problems with the boy, if I remember correctly. And Mathas already has his heir in Andrian, his eldest son."

"I don't know if this could help you or not, but Darmanin Crowtalon is with the Shadeweavers. More, he was one of two Shadeweavers at Ranier's side when he spoke to my shield under truce. He seemed to hold some level of authority within the organisation."

Thiara raised an eyebrow, looking intrigued. "Describe him."

"He's young, but he's not really a child anymore." Arya tried to think of how best to explain it. "There's a sense of wildness about him and at the same time a core of steel, drive. I assume appearances are important when it comes to confirming warlords and High Warlords?"

"You assume correctly," the warlord said grimly, her gaze turning distant. "The vote can be won or lost on perceptions alone. People—and not just the warlords and vicelords— have a very specific view of what a warlord should be."

Arya snorted without thinking. "Starting with 'male'."

Thiara glanced at her, a quicksilver smile flashing over her face. "Did you learn anything about the behavioural problems that led to Darmanin being thrown out?"

"No." The answer came out of Arya without thought or hesitation. *Protect him.* Then she realised she'd lied to her warlord. Then she realised she was hesitating, and irritation was already forming on Thiara's expression, so she forged ahead, "But he's no well-bred warlord's son anymore. He's been with the Shadeweavers for years, and he's one of them now."

"Don't discount breeding so easily, Arya. Darmanin is the son of a strong warlord, and until the moment he was disowned, he would have had the full benefits of the education and training given to all noble children."

It was on the tip of Arya's tongue to point out that her warlord didn't know the Shadeweavers like she did, didn't know how hard, how ruthless and violent they needed to be to survive. But she held back—it wasn't really something that could be explained with words. Besides, she was desperately trying to figure out whether to walk back her lie. She wanted to.

But she couldn't. Something deep down wouldn't let her. *Protect him.*

"Did you know that the position of warlord isn't necessarily passed to the eldest born son?" Thiara asked. "Almost always the State Council will vote that way, but if the eldest son is simple, or sickly, or inappropriate in some way, the Council has voted in the past for a younger child."

Arya's eyes widened. "You think you could have *Darmanin* confirmed as Crowtalon heir instead of Andrian?"

"Andrian spent the last three years fostered at my house. He is a competent warrior, but I saw little sign of his father's drive or ambition. If Mathas becomes High Warlord, Andrian would automatically become warlord of Crowtalon if he is confirmed as heir, and from then on be no more than his father's puppet."

"Darmanin would be nobody's puppet," Arya said, again without thinking.

The warlord's gaze snapped to her. "*There's* the insight I was looking for. One assumes he doesn't have any love or loyalty to a father that threw him out of his home, either."

Now was the time to tell her. To warn Thiara Ravenstrike that her plan couldn't work, because Darmanin had magic, and once everyone found out, he would *never* be confirmed as heir. A woman was one thing—barely acceptable in the absence of any other options—but a magic-wielder? No, the hatred and fear of them ran too deep for that.

Instead she said, "Surely the Council would never vote in favour of a boy who spent so many years as a Shadeweaver?"

Thiara stared off into the distance, clearly thinking something through. "It will be a challenge, but no more so than the Council voting in a woman as High Warlord. The vote is still several years away. Many things could change between now and then."

The warlord fell silent, and Arya began to feel awkward, wondering if she had been dismissed in some way. But then her gaze returned to Arya's. "I will take Darmanin into my household, give him a home and continue his education." Thiara smiled slightly. "We'll rid him of that Shadeweaver wildness and turn him into a warlord's heir."

Arya was simultaneously impressed by the warlord's confidence and dubious about her ability to 'rid' Darmanin of anything. She had to tell her about his magical ability. Her plan was never going to work. Arya had set something in motion she desperately wished she hadn't. But Darmanin would be safe and protected in the Ravenstrike household, exactly what the elder had urged, exactly what Arya's instincts kept telling her. She wavered, torn.

"What is it?" Thiara demanded.

Arya cleared her throat, but she couldn't get the words out. "I just wondered ... why are you telling me all this? Especially since you said earlier that I'm free to change my mind and return to Icecliff."

Thiara Ravenstrike turned, her pale blue gaze holding Arya's with a fierce grip. "I'm telling you all this because I know full well you're *not* going to change your mind, Arya Nameless."

Chapter 15

Late afternoon, they rounded a bend to find Heathrock city laid out below them.

The dark-coloured stone buildings and winding cobblestoned streets clung to the easternmost face of the lower mountainside all the way down to the forested plains at the bottom. The exterior walls had stood, weathering time and mountain storms, for centuries. Snow covered the roofs and walls, a contrast in dark and light.

Arya thought it was glorious. Dark and forbidding and as resilient as the mountain it clung to.

The Raiders posted at the gates saluted sharply as their warlord's carriage trundled through. Their progress slowed as they wound their way down through the city's many levels. Arya stared around her, drinking in the hustle and bustle—the residents of Heathrock were a hardy lot, going about their lives weighed down by multiple layers of clothing merely to survive the cold of their home, and never letting it stop them. A little spark of excitement went through her at the thought she was going to be living close enough that she'd be able to explore the city in her time off.

Then they came to a temporary halt at a busy intersection, and all her excitement died when her gaze caught on a young man begging on the street corner. His layers were threadbare, ragged, and the rusted tin cup sitting in front of him looked empty. But it was the raw red brand scarred into the skin of his cheek that drew her attention.

A magic-wielder.

That circular brand was often used to mark those with magic. It made the threat they posed obvious to everyone and prevented them from getting work, or even somewhere to live. This young man was the example of what happened to magic-wielders when they were found out and *didn't* seek the protection of the Shadeweavers. Without shelter and the means to earn money for food and proper clothing, he was unlikely to survive the coming winter.

Her gaze shifted from the beggar to the warlord's carriage, the weight of the lie she'd told growing heavier. Darmanin was lucky his father hadn't branded him before throwing him out. Presumably it had only been to prevent anyone learning he'd fathered a magic-wielder.

No man or woman with magic in their bloodline would ever be allowed to rule Dunidaen. Arya wondered if Mathas was a secret magic-wielder himself, or whether Darmanin had received his ability from somewhere else in the Crowtalon line.

The column lurched back into movement, and the beggar vanished from sight behind them. Arya cleared her thoughts of him, but remained unsettled, despite her best efforts. Taze's words about magic-wielders had made her see things in a different light. What had that young man on the corner done to deserve his fate? Maybe he'd hurt someone with his magic ability, whatever it was, but Arya had heard stories of folk exposing magic-wielders as a way to inherit property or ruin a business competitor. Those people hadn't hurt anyone.

At the bottom level of the city, they turned on a wide road leading south out of the main gates—twice the size again of the top gates, and with more Raiders standing guard. Still, these gates stood open too, and lots of traffic moved in both directions. The entourage slowed once more as they approached a large intersection not far past the city—the road continuing south and branching off to the east, down into the lowlands of Ravenstrike.

They crossed the intersection and continued along the empty road heading south, where it ran along the edge of an escarpment before winding down through thick forest.

Heathrock castle, seat of the warlord of Ravenstrike, lay in a depression in the land at the foot of a frozen lake. Cradled by the lake to the east, and high mountains to its west and south, it painted an impressive sight, with its fortress-like structure built from the same dark stone as the city. Snow lay thick on roofs and walls but had been cleared from the road.

It was massive, easily as large as Icecliff Fort, and Arya's trained eye estimated there was room to barrack up to two battalions of Raiders inside its towering walls.

She wouldn't want to attack this place, even with a strong army.

The road flattened as it approached the gates, which were already being opened to admit them. The walls loomed high over Arya as she rode through into an enormous entrance courtyard, her neck craning as she stared upwards.

Grooms came running to gather the horses, and servants waited to attend the warlord and Magen as they disembarked. The yard—with stables abutting its eastern side—was large enough that at least five shields at a time could form up quickly in case of attack or need to deploy. Directly ahead, a set of stone steps led up to the main building of a sprawling castle, and to her right an inner wall looked down over proceedings.

"Raider Nameless?"

Startled, she tore her gaze from surveying the inner defences and found a servant hovering near her stirrups. "Yes?"

"The warlord would like you to accompany her inside," the young man said.

Not having forgotten the warlord's dislike for being kept waiting, she dismounted hurriedly and ran to catch up, falling in just behind where Thiara Ravenstrike and Magen walked, talking in quiet tones.

Arya followed them through a pair of heavy oak doors that stood open. A man waited inside. His easy smile widened as he approached Thiara, and they embraced briefly. "It's good to have you safely home," he said. "We've been so worried ever since General Desomer got your message about the attack."

Thiara returned what Arya assumed must be her husband's smile with genuine warmth. "It's good to be home, Matte. As you can see, we're all fine."

"And Icecliff?"

"The situation is resolved, for now at least." Her face was grim. "But I should be hearing back from the High Warlord any day. We'll have to do something about what happened, even if only to make certain invasion isn't looming."

"Let's hope it's not as bad as we fear." Matte glanced towards the chief adviser. "Magen, it's good to see you too."

"Lord Eaglesoar." Magen bowed his head. "If you don't mind, Warlord, I should get started on those tasks we discussed?"

"Please do. We'll talk later."

Thiara's husband turned his gaze to Arya before shifting it back to his wife, eyebrows raised. "You've brought a guest?"

"This is Raider Arya Nameless. I've asked her to apprentice to General Desomer. Arya, this is my husband, Lord Matte Eaglesoar."

"My Lord." Arya bowed her head, hiding her curiosity. With that name, Thiara's husband must be related to the High Warlord in some way.

If Lord Eaglesoar was surprised by his wife's rather unorthodox choice of apprentice to her general, he didn't show a hint of it. Instead, he gave Arya the same welcoming smile he had his wife. "I am glad to meet you, Raider Nameless. Welcome to Heathrock."

"Thank you, Lord Eaglesoar," she said, taken aback by his sincerity. It wasn't something she encountered very often from those so senior to her.

He turned to his wife. "If Arya is to join our household, she'll need to meet Rorin."

"I'll take her to him now." A light entered Thiara's eyes that Arya hadn't seen before, not even in greeting her husband. "How is he?"

"He was quiet while you were away, but I think that was just worry after we heard what was happening at Icecliff. He applies himself to his lessons and does what I ask of him." Eaglesoar hesitated. "I wish he had more children his own age for company. He must get so lonely."

Thiara touched his arm. "I might have an idea to help with that. Is he in his room?"

"Yes. I'll see you at dinner." He turned back to Arya. "If there is anything you need to help you settle in, please don't hesitate to let me know. I'm usually around—since my wife is busy running an entire State, it's down to me to make sure Heathrock doesn't fall into a ruin and that everyone who lives here gets fed and paid."

"I ... thank you," Arya replied. Husband and wife had shared a quick smile at his teasing words, but it left her uncomfortable. She wasn't sure how that meant *she* was supposed to behave around them.

"Come with me," Thiara told her and walked off, moving towards a wide, sweeping staircase.

The warlord didn't speak as she traversed a maze-like series of hallways and stairwells, and Arya became thoroughly lost in no time. Most of the corridors looked identical to her, the only difference being the tapestries hanging from the stone walls.

One thing she quickly assimilated was that while the forbidding exterior walls of the fortress bristled with Raiders, the interior of the castle had a complete absence of them. The warlord clearly trusted those inside her walls. Arya filed a note away to ensure that trust was well placed.

Thiara stopped abruptly before a large door at the end of a hallway. "I have a son, who will be my heir. His name is Rorin, and he's fourteen years old." She hesitated. "There is something you should know before meeting him. He's a mute."

Arya's eyes widened in surprise—she'd had no idea. Raider gossip obviously didn't extend to talking about the warlord's son, which very quickly told Arya how respected the family was.

Thiara Ravenstrike didn't give Arya any time to respond. She opened the door and strode in. Arya hesitated in the doorway for a moment, then followed the warlord inside. Her gaze went instantly to the boy sitting in the corner of the large, airy room, nose deep in a book. Thiara went to him and he leaped to his feet in excitement. They hugged warmly, the boy's thin arms tight around his mother's neck.

Arya stood awkwardly. She studied the room—windows on two walls gave the space plenty of light, and the ones to her right looked over the front walls and road to Heathrock city. Immediately across from her was an amazing view of the lower slopes of the Diamondfang.

Then mother and son moved, crossing to Arya. Rorin was small and thin for his age, with a shock of messy blonde hair like his father and faded blue eyes like his mother. Not knowing the correct protocol for dealing with a warlord's son, Arya dropped to a knee and held out her hand as if greeting a comrade. "Hello, Lord Rorin. I'm Raider Arya Nameless."

Rorin made a quick movement with his fingers, then reached out to take Arya's proffered hand. As they shook, the sweetest of smiles spread over his face. Inexplicably, it made her feel warm all over, and a matching smile spread across her own face. For a long moment, the two of them simply stared at each other. It was the warlord's voice that broke the spell a moment later.

"He returns your greeting," Thiara said. "Rorin has developed a sign language of sorts since he was rendered mute by an accident in his childhood. You'll learn it."

"I'd like that." Arya tore her gaze away from Rorin to nod at his mother, then looked back at her son. "I'm very pleased to meet you, Lord Rorin."

Rorin made another motion with both hands.

"He returns your sentiments," Thiara said, "and asks that you call him Rorin."

She frowned. "Is that all right?"

The warlord hesitated, looked at her son, and then back at Arya. Something was written in that gaze that Arya couldn't interpret. Sadness? Or maybe wistfulness. Whatever it was, it was unlike anything she'd ever seen in this proud woman's face before. She seemed to realise she hadn't responded yet and blinked, her imperious expression returning. "In private, yes, I'll allow it."

"Thank you, Rorin," she said. "And you may call me Arya. In private."

His mouth quirked, and he nodded vigorously.

The warlord cleared her throat. "Rorin, go and wash up for dinner, please."

The boy ran out, waving a farewell to Arya on the way. As he left, a servant appeared in the doorway. She was around Arya's age, with a kindly face and an air about her that Arya immediately warmed to. "Warlord, Lord Eaglesoar asked me to come and see that your guest is settled in."

"Thank you," Thiara said briskly. "Arya, this is Peemla, Heathrock's chamberlain. She'll show you to your room. Make sure you get some proper rest tonight. I'd like to see you in my office directly after breakfast tomorrow morning, and you can give me your official decision then."

Arya straightened, saluted. "Warlord. I'll be there."

Thiara hesitated briefly. "Rorin tends to make very quick judgements about people. It was clear that he liked you. It goes without saying that you are not to do anything to betray that."

"Never," Arya promised, the response instinctive and sure.

Thiara strode from the room without another word, and Peemla gestured for Arya to follow. After another long walk, she was shown to a room in another wing of the castle. It wasn't anywhere near as large, but it was private, with just one bed.

Peemla bustled about, opening the large, arched window to let in fresh air. "General Desomer's quarters are in this wing, as is my room, so you won't be all alone," she explained.

"What about the battalion commander and shield captains stationed here?"

"They have quarters in the barracks. You wouldn't have seen those when you came in, but they're in the south-western corner of the grounds. It's only a short walk there from the main castle where we are."

"Thank you," Arya said absently, staring around in wonder. "This is mine?"

Peemla smiled. "When you get hungry, you'll be able to find dinner down in the kitchens. All the household staff eat there. The family usually dines privately, although occasionally Chief Adviser Magen or General Desomer will join them."

"All right."

"I think that's about it. If you have any questions at all, just ask." Peemla paused at the door. "Welcome to Heathrock, Arya."

Arya waited until the door closed before wandering over to the arched window to the right of her bed. It looked out over a small garden. Farther back, she could see the trees of the forest beyond Heathrock's walls and the Diamondfang looming above.

She took a long breath, trying to expel the discomfort that had settled under her skin ever since she'd first stepped into the castle. Her new surroundings were so different to anything she'd ever experienced. Still, she was confident she'd made the right choice.

In time, she would adjust. This was her home now.

***

Unsurprisingly, a hot bath, full meal, and a long night's restful sleep didn't change Arya's mind about accepting the warlord's offer. It only made her even more eager to accept. Without the exhaustion dogging her steps, the discomfort she felt about her new surroundings faded and she felt like she could take on anything.

She *was* sore though, both stitched wounds in her arm and leg aching abominably. She let herself limp downstairs, managing to find her way back to the kitchens where she'd eaten the night before and hiding the limp the moment she spotted another person.

Peemla bustled in just as she was finishing a breakfast far more delicious than anything she'd ever had at Icecliff Fort. "The warlord is ready to see you, Arya. I can show you the way, if you like?"

"Yes, please," she said fervently. She had just been trying to work out how she was going to find the warlord's quarters. "You're a lifesaver."

"Did you sleep well?"

"I did, thank you. And your kitchen staff makes the best food I've ever tasted."

The young woman's cheeks pinked, and Arya was taken aback. "I mean it, Peemla. I can see why the warlord made you her chamberlain. Not only is the food good, but your staff operates like a perfectly drilled Raider shield."

"I don't know about that." Peemla turned pinker as they headed up a set of stone steps, climbing up three levels and turning onto the landing. "This is the office wing, where the warlord and the general work during the day. And here is the warlord's office."

"Thanks again for your help."

"I'll have some willow bark tea sent up. Don't think I didn't notice you pretending not to limp just now. You were hurt in the attack on Icecliff?"

"Nothing serious, but the tea would be wonderful," Arya admitted. "I'll see you later?"

"I … I look forward to that, Raider Nameless."

"Just Arya." She gave the chamberlain a parting nod, then straightened her uniform and knocked sharply.

The door opened and Thiara Ravenstrike stood there, barely reaching Arya's shoulder, eyebrows raised. "Well?"

Arya saluted as sharply as she ever had. "Offer accepted, Warlord."

"Good." Thiara came striding out into the hall, almost bowling Arya over in the process. "Follow me."

Arya hurriedly fell into step with the warlord as she continued speaking. "I've had word back from the High Warlord this morning. He has sent a missive to Andahar demanding an explanation for the border incursion." Thiara looked momentarily preoccupied. "We will see if the Nightstalker responds. I hope he does."

Arya blinked. Clearly there was going to be no settling into conversation. "Why?"

"If he ignores us … I suspect that will mean we have much to fear." She shook her head. "I've sent a message to Ranier. I'm hoping he'll be willing to release Darmanin to me, but I doubt he'll do it without naming a price."

"How are you able to contact the Shadeweaver leader?" Arya asked, astonished.

"I have my ways."

Arya was immediately intrigued. Nobody just *contacted* Ranier, the most dangerous man in Dunidaen. His location was as much of a mystery as his identity. Even his Shadeweavers had no idea where he was at any given time. "Warlord, if anyone knew you had direct contact with a Shadeweaver, especially their leader—"

"I'm aware of how it would look. That's my problem to manage, not yours, and I trust your discretion," she said with a pointed look.

"Nobody will hear of it from me," Arya promised.

"In the meantime, your first task will be to organise a bodyguard and weapons tutor for Rorin. He's old enough now that he needs both. Normally this would be General Desomer's job, but I want Rorin's guard to be chosen from among the Raiders at Icecliff Fort—those who have real combat experience. You know those men and women better than he does."

"I ... are you sure, Warlord?"

"I have given you my trust, Arya." A thread of irritation entered Thiara's voice. "You are not required to confirm every order I give you."

"Yes, Warlord," she said. "Are there any particular characteristics you wish me to consider when deciding whom to pick?"

"Only that you would trust them with both your life and Rorin's," she said, and they turned to head down the stairs Arya had just climbed with Peemla. Her leg instantly began complaining, but she forced the pain away as the warlord continued, "I'd like you back here tomorrow night if you can manage it. General Desomer will be returning from SheerRock and it's best you meet him as soon as possible."

Thiara stopped as they reached the bottom of the stairs, pulling a roll of sealed parchment from inside her tunic. "These are my orders for Commander Lerin as regards your new position, and the re-assignment of the two Raiders you select. Safe travels, *Captain* Arya Nameless."

Arya stared, blinking, as the warlord strode away. She was a shield captain.

The grin that spread across her face was blinding.

Chapter 16

Dusk was setting, bringing a sharp drop in temperature as Arya waited for the gates of Icecliff to be winched open. Once through, the screech of the winch still echoing through the yard, a quick word with one of the Raiders manning it revealed her old shield was off duty, and likely to be in the mess shortly for dinner.

A welcome sense of familiarity enveloped her as she stabled her horse and headed inside, exchanging greetings with those Raiders she passed. She would always feel at home, comfortable in her own skin, in this place.

Arya had known who she was going to pick for Rorin's bodyguard and weapons tutor the moment the warlord had given her the task, so she planned to speak with them both directly before taking the orders to Lerin. A gust of warm air redolent with the scent of bread and roasting meat washed over her when she stepped into the large space of the mess hall. It wasn't dinner time yet, so only a handful of Raiders were there; those having a warm drink before nightshift.

She'd just resigned herself to waiting for the dinner bell when she spotted Laskin sitting at the end of a long bench, reading a letter with a pint of ale at his elbow. Grinning, she made her way over, dropping to the bench opposite him. "Drinking away your sorrows at my departure already, I see."

He looked up, surprise flashing over his face. "Arya!"

"It's nice and warm in here," she said appreciatively, yanking off her gloves and unbuttoning her cowl before shrugging off her thick Raider cloak. "Looks like some snow is blowing in too—you must be glad you're not on wall duty tonight. Is that mead or cider you're drinking?"

He listened to this with a glower, waited for her to finish, then said, "You left without any explanation."

"I didn't have time, I'm sorry." She shrugged.

"Yeah, you look real torn up about it." His glower deepened. "What in the blazes did Warlord Ravenstrike want with you?"

"She offered me a position as apprentice to General Desomer."

Laskin's eyes widened to saucers. "She did *what* now?"

She grinned at his surprise. "I was as surprised as you are, Laskin, but there was no way I was turning it down."

"Uh huh." His tone spoke volumes.

"It's not a trick." She fished the parchment from her jerkin and waved it at him. "She's made me a shield captain. This is for Lerin, to make it official."

"Well, that's something," he grunted. "Why are you back here so soon then?"

"I'm here on her orders." She reached over the table to filch his mug and take a long swallow—cider, not mead. Ugh—before pushing it back to him, ignoring his scowl. "Fancy a new posting?"

"Posting to where?" he asked suspiciously.

"Heathrock castle. The warlord has instructed me to choose a weapons tutor for Rorin, her fourteen-year-old son, and she wants me to pick a Raider from Icecliff. You're my choice."

"Why?"

"Three reasons." Arya ticked them off one by one. "You're a good fighter, but more importantly you're steady and keep a calm head in a crisis. Rorin would be well-served to learn both those traits. And Laskin, you're a great teacher. You taught me everything that I know about being a Raider and I wasn't an easy student."

"I've never heard so many nice words about me come out of your mouth before," he grumbled. "What's the third reason?"

"I trust you to have my back in a fight, and that means I trust you to have Rorin's." She held his gaze. "I'm sure you can figure out all on your own what a heavy responsibility this posting would be. You screw up, and, well … bad things ensue, for both of us."

Laskin shrugged, scratched at the stubble on his jaw, then nodded. "I'm in."

It was her turn to look at him suspiciously. "That was too easy."

"These old bones wouldn't mind a break from the unrelenting cold and sleeping on hard ground of patrol," he admitted. "And you'll need someone to watch your back down there. Heathrock Raiders aren't going to be what you're used to."

"I can handle them." She swiped his cider again, swallowed a mouthful of its too-sweet contents, and gave it back, ignoring his filthy look. "The warlord also asked me to assign a personal bodyguard for Rorin. I'd like your opinion before I speak to him."

Laskin blinked in surprise when she disclosed her candidate. "Not the obvious choice," he said. "But I like the kid."

"Good." She rose to her feet, gathered cowl and cloak. "Then let's go talk to him."

"One day a shield captain and already issuing orders. I can't finish my drink first?"

"I think I might have finished it for you." She leaned over the mug, gave an apologetic shrug when she saw it was empty. "Come on, old man. I'll get you another one later. Something better than that sickly sweet swill."

A couple of her old shield members were drifting out of their dormitory rooms, heading down for dinner, when Arya and Laskin turned into the corridor.

"You're back." Charlin acknowledged her appearance without looking either surprised or curious about it. Or happy to see her.

She swallowed a smile. "Good to see you too, Charlin."

"Where have you been!" Kait demanded, planting hands on hips.

"I'll join you all for dinner in a bit and tell you the story," Arya promised. "I just need to take care of something first."

"You'd better." She scowled before trailing after Charlin down the hall.

Taze opened the door to the room he shared with Wattin and Etan when Arya knocked, brightening at the sight of her in his doorway. "You're back."

"Hello, Taze. Do you have a moment to talk before dinner? It won't take long."

***

Bad weather hit before midnight, filling the night with howling winds that didn't blow out for hours. Nobody got any sleep, and the pre-dawn found Arya, Laskin, and Taze in the stables saddling up their mounts in preparation for leaving at first light. Her youngest shield-mate had been even faster to accept her offer than Laskin, and she had to admit the idea that both men would be with her at Heathrock dispelled the edge of discomfort she felt about returning there.

A heavy layer of snow was already being swept to the edges of the mounting yard, while more continued to drift down from the sky. The horses did not look any more excited than the humans to be venturing outdoors, their heads hanging low and forlorn.

"Captain Nameless?"

Arya turned as a Raider jogged over to her, saluting. She'd enjoyed holding court in the mess the previous night, telling them all about her new circumstances, so most of the Raiders in the fort knew she was a captain now. A hot burst of pride filled her at the title, and she wondered when that feeling would fade. "What is it, Durin?"

"Commander Lerin wants to see you immediately."

"Why?" She'd already passed him the warlord's orders the night before. He'd read them, muttered something under his breath, then told her she was dismissed.

"He didn't say, Captain."

Arya thought about ignoring the summons, but Lerin remained a superior officer and she doubted Warlord Ravenstrike would take kindly to such insolence.

"I won't be long," she promised Taze and Laskin.

Lerin stood by the window of his office, face flushed with what looked like anger, a crumpled note clutched in his hand.

She saluted. "You wanted to see me, sir? If we could be quick, I'd like to get on the road before the weather closes in again. The warlord expects me back today."

"A patrol shield sent out two days ago failed to return as scheduled yesterday evening after being ambushed on their way back. Their surviving members managed to shelter out the snowstorm and rode in as soon as the weather calmed."

She stilled. "Surviving members?"

He rounded on her, spittle flying as he threw the words at her. "Four Raiders dead, killed in a Shadeweaver ambush, all so they could send us a *message.*"

Her glance dropped to the note in his hand, which she could now see was flecked with dried blood.

"Ranier wants to meet with you, *Captain* Nameless. Something about a request from our warlord." Disgust rippled over Lerin's face. "What is she doing communicating with that filth?"

Arya fought to keep any expression from her face, but her stomach dropped to her toes. Her warlord *didn't* understand the Shadeweavers well enough, and good Raider lives had suffered for it. Not only that, but Thiara Ravenstrike's ignorance may also have undermined her own position. Now Lerin knew the warlord was in contact with Shadeweavers, it would spread through every Raider at the fort within a day. They wouldn't take it well. "I'm just following orders, sir. You said he wants to meet *me?*"

"That's right. Time and place written down." He tossed the note at her. "You'll do as he wants before you go back to Heathrock, that's an order. I don't want any more of my Raiders killed because you didn't show up. And you might consider enlightening our new and *clearly* inexperienced warlord on the consequences of associating with murderous criminals."

"Yes, sir. I'll take a shield and—"

"I'm not risking more of my soldiers on this nonsense. You wanted Taze and Laskin so badly? You take them as your backup. Now get out of my sight."

Her mouth curled. "Sir, without backup—"

"You have your orders, *Captain*. Dismissed."

She wanted to leap across the room and break his nose with one well-landed punch. The urge beat at her with an insistence she found hard to fight down. Her body shifted forward, readying to move. He saw it on her face, and goaded, "Go on, do it. See where it gets you."

A single, indrawn breath, then another. It was what he wanted. To take her down because his warlord made him feel impotent.

She wouldn't give him the satisfaction.

Arya deliberately relaxed her muscles, steadied her breathing, fought down the anger until she could manage a controlled tone. Then she said, "One day I'm going to be your general, Commander. Think about that."

His contempt-filled laughter followed her out of the room.

The sound echoed in her ears as she walked, not able to distance herself from his quarters quickly enough. She was so heated that she barely felt the bite of bitter cold as she returned to the mounting yard. The sight of Laskin's familiar scowl took some of the edge away, though, and she calmed enough to explain Lerin's orders.

After she'd finished, both Taze and Laskin were silent for a long moment, as if they thought there had to be more and they were waiting for her to relay it. When it became clear there was no more, Laskin cleared his throat.

"So Ranier attacked a shield, killed four Raiders, and sent a message back with the survivors to request a meeting," he clarified, scratching at his beard.

"That about sums it up."

"And he's asked specifically to meet with you?"

"Correct again."

"And Commander Lerin refused to send a shield with you as backup."

"Delightful as ever, our favourite battalion commander."

"And you're going to do exactly as Ranier wants, and stroll off to this meeting in the middle of the mountains with no backup aside from Taze and me, just because you're pissed at Lerin?"

"You are *sharp* this morning, Laskin." Arya got her foot into the stirrup and swung into the saddle, fury still simmering. "What a good choice I made for Rorin's tutor."

Taze coughed to cover a chuckle. "We'd best get going if we're going to make it to this meeting point and back down to Heathrock before nightfall."

"You are not helping." Laskin scowled at him. "Want to try backing me up on protesting this insanity?"

Taze shrugged. "I do what my captain orders."

The older man grumbled as he climbed into the saddle. "Fine, don't listen to the most experienced Raider here. What would I know?"

"We're going to be fine, Laskin," Arya said bracingly as the bell rang and the front gates began to open. "What could go wrong?"

Chapter 17

"Are you going to tell us what this is all about at any point?" Laskin asked as they rode their horses along a barely-there trail leading to Ranier's nominated meeting point. "Unless you expect us to believe Ranier woke up yesterday morning and decided for no reason at all that he wanted to speak with a random Nameless Raider."

"I was ordered to be discreet."

"We're as discreet as can be," he replied glumly. "We're about to get murdered, after all."

She chuckled. "You don't think the three of us can take Ranier?"

Laskin snorted. "The three of us couldn't take Ranier even if he came alone and unarmed and with both hands tied behind his back. I'm not even sure a full shield could."

"What makes you so confident? Is he a magic-wielder?" she asked. Laskin wasn't prone to exaggeration, yet Ranier was a single man. And not so young anymore either. He'd first established the Shadeweavers somewhere around the time of the borders closing down—roughly forty years earlier.

"Nobody's ever known the answer to that. But you *do* know he's one of the two living men in Dunidaen who successfully ran the Dreadwater Gate into Khadini and returned to tell about it?"

Arya scoffed. "A ridiculous noble-born rite of passage I've never under-stood."

"Who is the other one?" Taze had so far been silent, riding in the lead, watchful.

"Mathas Crowtalon, right before he was confirmed as heir to Crowtalon State. It's how the heirs did it, back in the day. Proved their worth and made their confirmation a sure thing." Laskin huffed. "Until they stopped returning alive and States found themselves losing their heirs."

Arya's interest returned at that. Anything she could learn of Crowtalon might help her warlord. "How does successfully running the Dreadwater make them so invincible?"

"It takes a lot to survive the journey, an elite combination of general smarts, fighting skill, and survival knowledge. But it's not just that. There's something else about Ranier, he—"

"Almost there, Captain," Taze interrupted, hand on the hilt of his sword.

Arya and Laskin quieted, focus entirely on their surroundings. The rustle of icy air through the trees, the faint thump of snow falling from branches, the horses breathing. Everything seemed still, normal.

Arya found her gaze tugged upwards, towards the distant peaks, the memory of her conversation with the Etherean elder returning unexpectedly. It seemed increasingly unreal as time passed, yet it had only been three days earlier. He couldn't have been serious. Her, a Nameless Raider, an heir to magic and a throne? Inconceivable. Yet the niggle of unease remained. His claims fit the behaviour of wraiths and shadowhounds more neatly than any other she'd been able to come up with.

"What do we need to know before this chat?" Laskin asked in a low voice.

Arya let out a breath that frosted from her mouth, relieved to be distracted from her thoughts. "The warlord sent a message to Ranier requesting that he release Darmanin to come and live at Heathrock."

Laskin shot her an astonished look. "Does Commander Lerin know that?"

She gave a sharp nod. "Thanks to Ranier's little stunt."

"Captain." Taze's soft but urgent tone had them swinging their attention forward as their horses emerged from the trees into a small, snow-covered clearing. A Shadeweaver stood there, alone, hood thrown back.

Ranier. Even in the light of a sunny morning, his eyes were dark as coals, the jagged scar on his face making him seem not quite human. Arya dismissed the fancy, irritated at herself for letting Laskin's words get in her head. Ranier was as human as anyone else. As killable as anyone else. The sight of him brought her anger from earlier bubbling to the surface. More of her Raider comrades were dead at this man's hand.

His expression revealed nothing as he watched them approach. "Hello, Raiders. Not quite the force I was expecting. Is Ravenstrike running out of you?"

Arya lifted her hand in a gesture to Taze and Laskin to halt, then urged her mare forward a few more paces. Her hands were white-knuckled on the reins. "What do you want?"

"On the contrary. It was your warlord asking things of me." Ranier's voice was quiet but cutting, every word a weapon.

"And you decided an adequate response was to murder four Raiders and expose your warlord's private communications to the world?" Arya snapped.

He bared his teeth. "I have no warlord. And nobody has the right to approach me unless I ask for it. Four dead Raiders and your warlord's foolishness exposed was a cheap price to extract in order to remind her of that."

A snarl curled at her lip. Lerin she couldn't confront, but this man ... he was a wanted criminal. "You didn't really come alone, did you, Ranier? That seems foolish. I might decide there's a price to pay for my dead shield-mates."

"Empty threats only make you look like the child you are," he said. "You wouldn't dare touch me."

The Shadeweaver leader stood before her with no backup, trusting in his mystique to protect him, the second man today to treat her with contempt. Ironically, it was his words that turned her empty threat into action.

Because Arya *would* dare.

Arya kicked her feet out of the stirrups and lunged at him, sliding her dagger from its sheath as she did so. She was on him before he could react, and they crashed to the snow, her dagger stabbing for his kidney.

And in a blink she was on her back, Ranier above her, a knife at her throat. The metal had an odd blue sheen she'd never seen before, and the blade had to be ridiculously sharp—she could feel barely any pressure against her skin, yet a warm trickle of blood seeped down her neck. Metal rang as Laskin and Taze drew weapons, but Arya kept her gaze on Ranier, burning fury drowning out any fear or discomfort.

Contempt glittered in those dark eyes. "A child," he spat.

Snarling, she shoved upwards, ignoring his blade slicing deeper. She shoved his knife hand away and tried to bring a knee up into his chest. Then, somehow, she was face down in the snow, his knee pressing into the small of her back. She tasted blood in her mouth where she'd bitten her tongue. The weight above her shifted, and then his breath was warm against her cold ear. "It will be a long time before you can take me, Arya Nameless. This is your one pass. Try again and I will end you."

The weight on her back disappeared and she scrambled to her feet, spitting blood from her mouth. Both Taze and Laskin hovered, weapons out but clearly unwilling to attack while Ranier had held a knife to her throat. Blood continued to trickle down her neck.

Arya reached down to collect her dagger and sheath it, before lifting her hands to demonstrate they were empty. "What do you want from us?"

"Darmanin has consented to go to Heathrock, but he is mine, and therefore there is a price," Ranier continued, calm, as if nothing had happened, though his tunic was slightly askew, revealing an inky black tattoo climbing across his collarbone; it looked like part of a wing. His knife had vanished somewhere on his person.

"I don't have the authority to negotiate a price with you."

Ranier smiled. "I'm not here to negotiate. Your warlord will agree to take my daughter into her household—*and* under her protection—along with Darmanin. That is the price."

"If you think Warlord Ravenstrike will agree to take another Shadeweaver in and expose her household to that kind of danger, you're sadly mistaken," Arya said flatly.

"So much useless bluster." Ranier regarded her with pity. "As you said, Raider, you have no authority. Your warlord will decide how badly she wants Darmanin."

Arya's jaw clenched. Ranier held the upper hand. And all Arya could do was deliver the message. She *hated* being so powerless. "If Warlord Ravenstrike agrees?"

"She will signal her agreement by placing a black flag on her battlements within one day. Once I have that confirmation, I will send Darmanin and my daughter to Heathrock. If there is no signal, Darmanin stays with me and I will not enter into any further discussions." He paused. "You've already seen what will happen if your warlord tries to contact me again. The price *will* be higher next time."

Arya strode back to her mare and mounted. "I wouldn't hold my breath if I were you."

But Ranier was already gone, vanished into the forest.

"Let me see that cut," Laskin said, bringing his horse closer. "It looks deep."

"It's fine, leave it," she snapped, then spurred her mare on, leaving them both to follow.

She was too frustrated and angry to talk.

***

When Arya and her two Raiders rode through the gates of Heathrock in the late afternoon, they found the warlord herself emerging from the stables, Rorin in tow. Both were dressed as if they'd been out riding.

Arya swore under her breath. She'd expected to have a moment to prepare what she was going to say before the warlord would be available to speak with her. But the woman spotted Arya and came straight over as she, Taze, and Laskin dismounted.

"Captain." Thiara Ravenstrike glanced briefly at the two Raiders behind Arya, but then her expression changed as she caught sight of the wound on Arya's neck. "What happened?"

"Warlord." Arya saluted. "There's been a ... development as regards your request about Darmanin. It might be best if I brief you in private?"

"Understood." The warlord's gaze shifted back to the Raiders. "You've done as I asked?"

"Allow me to introduce Raider Laskin Carter as a weapons tutor for Lord Rorin, and Raider Taze Nameless as my choice for Lord Rorin's bodyguard."

Arya had expected Thiara Ravenstrike to baulk at Taze's obvious youth, but the warlord simply motioned Rorin forward. "Rorin, from now on, you will not leave the walls of this estate without Raider Nameless. When it comes to your safety, you will do as he says without hesitation. Am I clear?"

Rorin nodded, fingers flickering as he smiled a greeting at Taze.

"You will commence lessons with Raider Laskin immediately after breakfast tomorrow morning. As with Raider Nameless, you will obey him as you obey me."

Rorin signed again, eyes bright as he regarded the two Raiders saluting him. He clearly didn't think any of this was a hardship. Arya's heart went out to him—he seemed so happy just to have company.

"Lord Rorin," Laskin said. "I look forward to starting lessons with you. And I hope you will be willing to teach me also—your finger language is something I'd be very interested to learn."

"As would I, Lord Rorin," Taze said, brown eyes warm. "A secret language of sorts, no? It could come in very useful if you are ever in danger and we need to communicate silently."

Rorin's eyes shone brighter at these words. Arya held back a smile—she'd briefed both Taze and Laskin on Rorin's language, but they were exerting a clear effort to make the boy feel comfortable. She wondered if anyone other than his parents had done that before. It made her even more confident of her choices.

Warlord Ravenstrike seemed to feel the same way. Though she said nothing, her habitually cool expression softened as she addressed the two Raiders. "Raider Nameless, you'll sleep in a room adjacent to Rorin's. Peemla, our chamberlain, will see to anything that you need. Come inside and I'll introduce you to her. Captain, perhaps you could show Raider Laskin to his new quarters and then come directly to my office?"

"I'll be right there," Arya promised.

Taze gave Laskin and Arya a cheerful farewell wave and followed without hesitation as Thiara and Rorin headed for the main building. Grooms had already appeared to take their horses, so Arya turned to Laskin, who waited with saddlebags slung over both shoulders. "Come on, I'm *almost* sure I can find the way to the barracks from here."

When Arya returned to the main castle building, the entrance foyer was empty, and she paused there, orienting herself and trying to remember the way up to the offices Peemla had escorted her to the previous morning.

After two wrong turns, she found the right corridor and made her way along to the warlord's office at the end. The door stood ajar, the sound of voices drifting out. Arya was about to knock and enter when an unfamiliar woman's voice rang out, sounding utterly horrified. "You're not seriously planning to take a Shadeweaver under our roof? We'll all be murdered in our beds. Not to mention what the other States will think when they hear of it."

Thiara Ravenstrike responded, "Don't be ridiculous, Lanna. Darmanin is the son of a warlord. Besides, the warlords are a tad focused on potential war with Andahar right now. They're not really paying a lot of attention to whom I take into my household."

"A criminal outcast is what he is, no matter who fathered him. Have you even considered that there would have been good reason for Mathas throwing him out in the first place? Heirs don't grow on trees."

"I have exactly zero faith in Mathas' ability to judge character, and a great deal of faith in my household to straighten out whatever wildness there is in Darmanin," Thiara said dryly. "Besides, Rorin needs more children his own age around him. He's too isolated here."

"I can't believe what I'm hearing." Lanna's voice went up in pitch and volume. Arya winced at its shrill note. "You'd rather he spends his time with a grubby Shadeweaver child than my own two sons, his cousins?"

Arya let out a startled breath. This woman was the warlord's sister?

"Jenka and Warn spend more time tormenting Rorin than being his friend," Matte said, revealing his presence in the room.

A brief silence fell, and Arya hovered awkwardly, trying to decide whether to retreat down the hall and come back or announce herself and risk them guessing she'd overheard. But then Lanna spoke again, and Arya couldn't help the curiosity that kept her there.

"They're boys, Matte. They get rough sometimes, that's all."

"I'm not discussing this with you any further," Thiara said firmly. "It's my decision to make, and I've made it. Darmanin will join this household."

Lanna huffed a furious breath. "Putting that incredibly foolish decision aside, what possessed you to bring a stray Nameless here as apprentice to Desomer? She has no breeding, no experience, and probably no education. The Raiders will never accept her as their general."

"Have some compassion, Lanna, she's barely more than a child. Her lack of parentage isn't her fault," Eaglesoar protested.

"She's no child, Matte," Lanna snapped. "She was no doubt raised on the streets somewhere before joining the Raiders in order to get a roof over her head and food in her belly."

"You are right on that score, sister, she is no child." Thiara sounded impatient. "Arya is resourceful and tough. I have no doubt she has seen and done far more than any girl her age should. I have given her an opportunity, that is all. We will see what she makes of it."

"She's a mistake, and a bad one. I've no doubt the girl is a grasping opportunist," Lanna warned. "You are going to find it hard enough to hold onto your position as a woman, yet you insist on making things even more difficult for yourself with a series of bad decisions."

Arya's hands curled into fists.

A cold determination burned in her.

She would do whatever it took to succeed here. And one day, she would enjoy watching the smugness fall from Lanna's face as she became general of Ravenstrike. Lerin too.

"We'll see," Thiara repeated. "I've heard you out, and that is all the discussion I'm willing to entertain. Unless there's anything else, I'll see you at dinner."

Arya hurriedly knocked on the door to make her presence known, unsure if there would be time to scurry back down the hall and out of sight before someone left the office and spotted her.

Silence fell in the room, and then Lord Eaglesoar opened the door. Concern was etched all over his face, but he managed a smile of welcome for her. "Come in, Arya. I know you've got a report to make."

Arya's gaze went straight to the warlord's sister. Like Thiara, she was diminutive, and they shared similar features, though Lanna was rounder and had brown hair instead of blonde. Her blue eyes regarded Arya with barely concealed disgust, and she didn't bother acknowledging her as she swept out of the room behind Eaglesoar.

"My sister," Thiara said dryly as Arya closed the door behind them and saluted, forcing down her anger. "Beyond that, you should also know that she's married to Mathas Crowtalon's younger brother. Does that wound need stitches?"

Arya blinked at the sharp segue. "It's just a scratch, Warlord."

"At ease," Thiara said, then, "Who did that to you?"

As concisely as she could, Arya relayed the events of the day, starting with her meeting with Commander Lerin. The warlord listened without interrupting, though it was obvious from the slightly unfocused look in her eyes that she was thinking furiously about everything Arya was relaying. Eventually she finished with, "If you agree to his price, Ranier said you must reply by flying the black flag within one day."

"What possessed you to attack Ranier without provocation?"

"I..." Arya hadn't been prepared for that question, or the sharpness with which it had been asked. "He killed four of my Raiders just to make a point to you, and he dared me to—"

"Doing something on a dare is a childish reaction," the warlord snapped. "One you will have to grow out of, and quickly. I understand how it feels to be demeaned or considered incapable, Arya, but leaping at the culprit with a dagger is not the answer. All that demonstrates is immaturity and poor judgement."

"Warlord," Arya said stiffly.

"This is not a promising start for you," Thiara warned.

"Understood." She swallowed. "It won't happen again."

The warlord's index finger tapped idly on the edge of her desk, her gaze too knowing. "You're angry with me, for getting four Raiders killed."

"Shadeweavers are treacherous and violent, Warlord. Reaching out directly to—"

"I was not ignorant of the consequences, Arya," she said, quiet and sharp. "As warlord, I must weigh many factors when deciding on a course of action. There are sometimes no good choices. Nor do I have a responsibility to explain myself to a shield captain."

"Warlord." Arya bit her tongue, nodded.

Thiara held her gaze for a moment, seemed comfortable Arya had heard her, then changed the subject. "What do you know about this daughter of his?"

"I didn't even know he had one. Not even Raider gossip has mentioned her."

"What do you think I should do?"

"Refuse," Arya said. "Give up on Darmanin and cease all communication with the Shadeweavers. It puts you in a precarious position with your Raiders, and your plan with Darmanin already had extremely low odds of success. I don't judge those odds enough to risk losing the loyalty of your army."

The warlord smiled faintly. "A good response if protecting myself was my priority. But it's not. Being High Warlord is, and there's no way that's happening without weakening Crowtalon. Darmanin is my best bet to do that. I'll fly the flag first thing tomorrow morning."

"Warlord ... it will compromise the safety of this fortress to have two Shadeweavers living here." Not to mention how the Raiders here would react to it. "Have you discussed it with General Desomer?"

"I will as soon as he returns tonight." Thiara moved around to sit behind her desk. "And I will be relying on the both of you to ensure the safety of Heathrock is *not* compromised."

The door swung open then, and Magen strode in, parchment clutched in his hand, a harried air hovering around him.

The warlord rose from her chair. "Word from the High Warlord?"

Magen nodded. "He's ordering us to reinforce our northwest border with more Raider battalions from the south and has asked Crowtalon and Falconcrest to send shields of Lances and Aggressors to cover the resultant gap on our southern border."

Thiara frowned. "Has he received information that makes him think that's necessary?"

"No, warlord. At least, not that he says in his message. It's likely he's simply preparing for a worst-case scenario. You know how cautious he can be."

A little shiver went through Arya. He meant war with Andahar.

"I'll brief Desomer as soon as he rides in tonight." Thiara made a face. "The last thing I want is Crowtalon Lances inside my border."

"We might be grateful for them if it comes to the worst. And we don't really have any choice. His orders are clear—it's not a request."

Thiara's mouth thinned. "Noted. Now both of you leave me alone. I have much work to do. Arya, you'll report to General Desomer first thing tomorrow."

Arya saluted and followed Magen out. Out of sight of the warlord, his countenance changed—his brow was pinched, and he chewed on his lip.

"Are you truly worried about invasion?" she asked him.

Magen gave a dismissive wave. "It's not Andahar I'm worried about. I doubt very much the Nightstalker is looking to invade after all these years. It's Mathas Crowtalon. The warlord is right to worry about having his soldiers inside our borders."

Arya didn't understand—the Nightstalker seemed a far greater threat than a neighbouring warlord subject to the High Warlord's rule. But Magen was distracted, busy, and disappeared into his office before she could ask any more questions.

Maybe the general would have more answers when she saw him tomorrow. Anticipation filled her at the thought.

She couldn't wait to get started.

Chapter 18

Though much of the sprawling estate was still a confusion to Arya, she *had* managed to memorise the routes from her room to the kitchens, and from the kitchens to the third-floor offices, so she was on time when she presented herself at the general's door the next morning.

There was no answer to her knock, but just as she was beginning to wonder if she was too early, heavy footsteps sounded and a man appeared around the corner. He was no taller than she was, with weathered brown skin, greying hair, and an impressively bristling moustache. His broad shoulders looked capable of wielding a battle axe with ease, and he had a slight paunch that spoke of good eating or drinking. Or both. But her searching gaze stopped instantly on the gold trim of his bloodred Raider cloak.

"Sir." She saluted sharply.

General Desomer stopped, looked her up and down, and sniffed. "You must be my new apprentice."

"Yes, sir."

He stepped past her, opened the door, and walked inside, leaving her to follow. Beyond was a spacious corner room that looked out over the Raider barracks and drill yards. The space contained a desk in one corner near the lit hearth and an oval table along the windows with several chairs clustered haphazardly around it. Shelves full of books and parchment lined the walls.

Desomer went over to his desk, took off his heavy cloak and cowl with a grunt of relief, then opened a box of cigars on his desk and lit one up. After taking a long, blissful drag, he came back around the desk and perched on it, studying her. His presence loomed large, even without the bulky layers. "You're a scrawny waif of a girl, there's no doubt about that. Can you even lift a sword?"

"Yes, sir."

"I suppose we'll see about that. We serve at the warlord's pleasure, after all, even when she makes seemingly inane decisions."

"Sir." She bit her tongue on the protest that wanted to come out. If she failed with him, she was out. And she refused to lose this opportunity so quickly. So she kept a fierce stranglehold on her temper and promised herself to hold it no matter what.

"I am in command of ten thousand Raiders, Captain. That's fifty battalions. You think you can handle that one day?"

"Yes, sir, I do."

He barked a laugh. "She said you were arrogant. You have no idea what you're talking about, of course, but I'll soon see whether there's any substance under the bluster. And she did tell me I have full authority to cut you loose if I don't like you. I don't tolerate shirkers or those who can't follow orders. Clear?"

"Yes, sir."

"All right, well, stop being so bloody stiff and take a seat," he said in irritation. "I want to talk to you about what happened at Icecliff."

He went back around his desk to drop heavily into the chair. Arya perched on the edge of the chair before the desk, wary of saying or doing something wrong. The scent of his cigar was beginning to permeate the room, smoky and strong. "What would you like to know, sir?"

"Warlord Ravenstrike gave me her account last night, and I've received a detailed missive from Commander Lerin, too." Desomer snorted as he held up several pages filled with spidery handwriting. "He wasn't very complimentary of you."

"I'll bet," Arya muttered, before realising who she was talking to. "Sorry, sir."

Desomer's eyes gleamed in private amusement. "He's an ignorant fool who can barely tell one end of a sword from another. He got where he is because of family connections, not merit. If he doesn't like you, that probably means you're a half-decent Raider who has a mind of her own. Now, give me your account of what happened from beginning to end. Don't leave anything out."

Taking a breath, Arya ordered her thoughts and proceeded to report everything that had happened since her shield had left Icecliff Fort to deliver the new birds to SheerRock. He didn't interrupt, waiting to speak until she'd finished.

"There seems to be some confusion over the intent of this force of creatures." Desomer's eyes were on the papers before him. "What's your take on it?"

"The initial attack on my shield appeared strategic, sir. Our outriders were killed prior to the attack on the main column. At SheerRock, the creatures attacked at night and in the middle of bad weather, taking those in the fort by surprise. That's not generally how wild creatures behave, sir, magical or not. Not to mention, *someone* dug the tunnel through the rockfall in the underground road."

Desomer sat back in his chair, took another puff of his cigar. "What of Ranier's claims that the Nightstalker was testing our border defences?"

"I consider them credible, sir." She ignored her memory of the Etherean elder telling her that the wraiths and shadowhounds had come looking for *her*. The more time that passed since that conversation, the easier it was to ignore, to convince herself his claims were fanciful. "And it fits most of the facts."

"Most?"

"Their siege of Icecliff was broken easily and the creatures fled, dispersing into the mountains. It didn't seem to be a stern test of our defences, if that was the intention."

He didn't say anything further, so she tried, "Sir, if the Nightstalker *was* directing the creatures, he might try again, possibly with larger numbers. Without fully understanding their intent, we have to act as if it could occur again."

"Oh we *have* to, do we?" He lifted an eyebrow.

She cleared her throat. "I just meant—"

"No, you're right. Our warlord and chief adviser seem far more concerned about Mathas Crowtalon than anything else, but our job is to keep the borders safe and leave the political wrangling to them." He cleared his throat, sat forward. "About your apprenticeship. You'll drill with the shields here every morning. After that, you'll attend lessons with young Lord Rorin and these new fosterlings I'm advised we'll soon be getting. The afternoons and evenings you'll spend with me."

"Lessons?" Arya baulked. "Sir, I already—"

"You'll never be general of Ravenstrike without a thorough education," Desomer interrupted. "Don't insult my intelligence by telling me you received that while growing up on the streets of Aren."

Arya flushed. "Yes, sir."

"I expect you to work as hard in your lessons as you do in the drill yard and in your time with me. Clear?"

"Yes, sir."

"Besides, if our new warlord deems it necessary to put her young heir in a room with two Shadeweaver children on a daily basis, *someone* is going to need to make sure he doesn't get assassinated, and that someone will be you."

"Sir." She stifled an involuntary laugh.

He rose then, stubbing out his cigar. "You won't find things easy with the Raiders here. You've been plucked out of nowhere and given an opportunity many of them coveted. You'll have to prove yourself to them."

"Yes, sir." She winced inwardly. That was the sense she'd already gotten, but having him state it so plainly made it real.

"I'm not going to hold your hand. I'll teach you, but I won't cosset you."

She straightened her shoulders, offended by the very idea. "I don't need hand-holding or cosseting, sir."

"The arrogance on her," he muttered to himself, shaking his head. "Clear out and leave me to it. I've got a mountain of parchment to catch up on after redistributing shields all over the place to backfill SheerRock and make sure we're not left vulnerable anywhere else. Not to mention figure out where to put the reinforcements of Raiders I'll be summoning from the southern barracks on the High Warlord's orders. I'll give you today to yourself while I get on top of that. Your apprenticeship starts tomorrow at drill."

"Sir." Arya saluted and left.

As she closed the door behind her, a little smile crept over her face.

She *liked* General Desomer.

It was a shame he didn't seem to find her particularly likeable. Arya squared her shoulders. That was okay—she'd win him over.

Arya didn't plan on failing.

***

Darmanin Crowtalon arrived at Heathrock the following morning.

Returning from drill, Arya heard the shouts at the front gate that indicated someone was approaching and diverted by the kitchens, searching for Peemla.

Her first drill had been a miserable experience. Compared to the camaraderie of drilling with her shield at Icecliff, this morning had been a stiff hour where nobody spoke to her beyond issuing orders. Her drill partner had been uncommunicative, and she'd had to be at her sharpest to ensure the underhanded blows he tried to get in didn't land.

Thankfully, the chamberlain was there, overseeing breakfast being laid out on trays for the family. "Peemla? I think the warlord's two guests have arrived. Would you mind letting her and Chief Adviser Magen know? General Desomer too, if you can find him."

Peemla gave her a curious look, and Arya winced. Maybe she wasn't supposed to ask the chamberlain to do things. "Sorry, I'd do it myself, but I want to be in the yard when they come in, make sure everything is all right." She wasn't entirely sure what would happen once two Shadeweavers were allowed inside the gates and certainly hadn't ruled out some elaborate trap set by Ranier.

"Don't be silly," Peemla said as she headed for the door. "We've both got our jobs to do. Would you mind keeping them out front until the warlord is ready to receive them inside?"

"I can do that."

When Arya emerged into the frigid morning, the gates were swinging closed, and only one hooded Shadeweaver dismounted from his horse, wariness in every inch of his bearing.

"Hello, Darmanin," she called.

His head swung around, shoulders relaxing slightly. His cool grey eyes were watchful as she approached. "Raider Nameless."

"Captain, now." Arya's gaze roved over the purple bruising around his right eye and the swollen cut on his cheekbone. He'd dismounted stiffly, too, as if his chest or ribs pained him. "What happened to you?"

"Ranier doesn't much like it when his people disobey orders," he said, his tone inviting no further discussion on the topic.

So Darmanin had been punished for helping them against the wraiths and shadowhounds. A trickle of affront sparked in her chest on his behalf, even though he was a Shadeweaver and essentially a stranger to her. Maybe it *had* been the right thing to bring him here. She accepted his desire not to speak of it and looked over his shoulder. "Where's Ranier's daughter?"

"I've no idea," he said. "She lives in Heathrock city with a guardian. I've never even met her."

Arya frowned. "Ranier said he would send you both—"

More shouts sounded at the gate, and once again they winched open, allowing another rider through. In every way, the girl looked like a young noblewoman: clad in a lovely dress with a bright flower pattern, dark hair perfectly arranged in jaw-length curls, back impressively straight. Arya was surprised she wasn't riding side-saddle.

She wondered if this wasn't Ranier's daughter at all, and instead a guest of Thiara Ravenstrike's that Arya didn't know was coming. Would it be a faux pas for Arya to greet her if so? She looked at Darmanin, but he wasn't any help.

The girl dismounted, saw Darmanin and Arya standing by the steps, and came over. She was small, a good half a head shorter than Arya, but looked about the same age, or maybe a year younger. Arya's quick once-over to make sure the girl wasn't carrying a weapon revealed nothing unusual bar smudges of ink on the tips of her fingers.

"Hello." She seemed nervous, but friendly. "I'm Essa—my father told me I'm to live here from now on."

Arya cleared her throat. "Your father being Ranier, leader of the Shadeweavers?"

"That's right."

The girl had the same dark brown hair as Ranier, the same pointed nose, but they didn't share much else. "You're his daughter?"

"I am." She smiled, hands clasped neatly before her.

All Arya's doubts about this arrangement flooded to the surface. There was no way this girl was as innocent as she appeared. Not Ranier's daughter.

"You're suspicious of me," Essa said. There was a simple confidence about her that Arya instinctively respected. "That's fair, I'm aware of his reputation."

"Thanks for the permission," Arya said. "Why *are* you here?"

"To be honest, I've no idea why he sent me," she said, giving a little shrug. "But I have no immediate plans to start slitting throats or stealing things or otherwise making a nuisance of myself, if that helps."

"Oh," Arya managed. Darmanin made a sound that might have been a choked laugh.

"Are you Captain Nameless, then?" Essa studied her. "You're younger than I thought you would be."

"Am I?"

Essa cocked her head in Darmanin's direction. "Who are you?"

"Darmanin." He spoke tersely and didn't offer his last name.

An awkward silence fell. After a moment, Arya gave herself a little shake and decided to try discerning more of Darmanin's motives while they waited, since she'd failed so miserably with Essa.

"I thought Warlord Ravenstrike might have found it more difficult to roust you from your Shadeweaver home," she said lightly. "You being beholden to no man and all that."

His mouth curled slightly, as if he wanted to smile at her reference to their last conversation but held it back. "I have my reasons."

The conversation died again, and this time Arya was helpless to revive it. Essa seemed comfortable, though, her gaze taking in their surroundings with what seemed like genuine awe and interest.

"Captain?"

Arya swore in gratitude under her breath as Taze appeared from inside. "Warlord Ravenstrike and her family are ready to greet their guests."

Arya gave the two Shadeweavers one long, dubious, glance, then let out a sigh. "Darmanin, Essa, this is Raider Taze Nameless. He is the bodyguard to the warlord's son, Lord Rorin. You'll no doubt be seeing a lot of each other."

"I remember you," Darmanin said to Taze, giving him a slight nod.

"Hello!" Essa stuck out her hand. "So you'll be the one killing me ruthlessly but efficiently if I make any threatening moves towards Lord Rorin?"

Arya coughed, swallowing a laugh, while Taze's eyebrows shot skywards. But after a moment he shrugged and shook her hand. "That about sums it up."

Arya led the way up the stairs and into the entrance hall. Lord Eaglesoar and Rorin stood waiting to greet the newcomers while Peemla hovered discreetly in the background. The warlord strode in just as they did, Magen at her side. Arya's glance went straight to Rorin. He immediately offered her a cheerful wave. She smiled back.

Thiara Ravenstrike crossed to Darmanin. "Darmanin Crowtalon. Welcome to Heathrock. Do you agree to be a guest in my household?"

"Yes," he replied in that grave way of his. "On the condition that I am not ever to be handed over to my father."

"My word on it," Thiara Ravenstrike promised. "I am sure you have already guessed that there are several reasons I have offered you a place in my home. But among them is a desire for my son to have those of his own age around him. I ask for *your* word that while you are under my roof, you will do nothing to harm me or my house."

"My word on it, Warlord Ravenstrike." Darmanin bowed his head slightly.

Thiara shifted her attention to Essa. The warlord's face was impressively blank, but Arya wondered if she felt the same surprise Arya had on meeting her. "You are Ranier's daughter, Essa?"

"Yes, Warlord." She bowed her head too, tone polite and deferential. Arya eyed her like a hawk. If she made even the faintest of moves towards her warlord...

"Will you make the same oath that Darmanin has?"

"I give my word that as long as I am under the protection of this house, I will do nothing to harm it." Essa smiled easily as she spoke, no hesitation in her voice or bearing.

"If either of you do anything to hurt me or mine, you'll be dealt with quickly and permanently. Don't doubt me on this." Thiara Ravenstrike stepped back. "Rorin? Come and meet Darmanin and Essa."

He approached, face alight with curiosity, and stuck his hand out in Darmanin's direction. The unsmiling youth took it and said, "I'm pleased to meet you, Lord Rorin Ravenstrike."

"Same." Essa stuck her hand out too. "Am I supposed to address you formally? Or are things more relaxed here at home?"

There was something about her. A bubbly infectiousness that had Arya's entire bearing relaxing even though she was deliberately trying to maintain a watchful air around the girl.

Rorin seemed disarmed by it too, eyes bright as he signed with enthusiasm. Thiara watched, then hesitated before letting out a little sigh. "In private, you may address each other informally."

"Sister dear, what is all this?"

Arya turned as Lanna entered the room, instinctively on guard at the woman's tone. It was pleasant, but in an overly sweet sort of way. The mere sight of her had Arya bristling. She would never forget what she'd overheard.

"Lanna." Thiara's voice was flat. "I've already informed you about us taking on fosterlings."

"Oh yes, that." She gave a languid wave of her hand. "The latest in your series of foolish decisions. I'd best remember to turn the lock on my bedroom door tonight."

Rorin scowled, arms crossed defiantly, and Matte glanced at the woman with a look of fastidious distaste. Darmanin's expression closed over, and Essa shifted backwards, like she'd prefer to disappear into the tapestries and avoid the awkward family drama if that was at all possible.

Thiara's mouth thinned. "We won't be discussing this again, especially not in front of guests."

"I am your sister." An edge crept into that overly sweet voice.

"Yet *I* am warlord," Thiara said coldly.

The expression on Lanna's face turned calculating. "If the other warlords had known anything of the choices you would make, they would never have confirmed you."

"Then how greatly fortunate for me that they did not," Thiara said, then turned her back on her sister. "Peemla, show Essa and Darmanin to their rooms and give them a tour of the castle. Rorin, please return to your lessons."

Everyone dispersed, the warlord's tone ensuring they did it quickly and without fuss. Arya was left standing in the hall with Matte Eaglesoar, who looked troubled as he watched Lanna walk away.

"I'd best go with Peemla. Make sure she's okay," Arya managed, eyes trailing the chamberlain.

Matte's mouth twisted wryly. "I take it you don't trust our new guests any more than my dear sister-in-law does?"

"I'd just like to be sure." Arya ran after the departing figures.

The moment Darmanin saw Arya approach, he murmured something to Peemla, then stopped and waited for her while the other two continued on.

"Something wrong?" she asked him.

"No. I just needed to confirm something." He glanced around, lowered his voice further. "You haven't told Warlord Ravenstrike about my magic, have you? She would never have invited me here if she knew."

"What of it?"

"I'm no fool, Arya. I'm aware that Warlord Ravenstrike is taking me in for political reasons. I have no illusions that she cares about me at all beyond how she can use me," he said. "You lied to her." His gaze roved her face, as if searching for something he couldn't find.

Protect him. The urge rose in her again. There was something about this boy, this guarded, fierce, remote boy, that she wanted to shield from harm. She just wished she understood why.

Arya shifted uncomfortably. "I didn't lie exactly. I just didn't tell her everything."

"If she finds out, you'll be tossed out just as fast as me. Maybe worse."

As quick as a blink, the desire to protect faded, replaced by wariness. Arya took a step back. "Is that a threat?"

"I will hold to my oath to your warlord, Arya Nameless," he said formally. "You have nothing to fear from me while I enjoy the protection of his household."

A veiled threat then. If Thiara Ravenstrike threw him out because she discovered his magic, then he would have no reason to hold to his word.

"Understood."

"I hope you do." His gaze held hers.

"We'd best catch up with Peemla," Arya said. "If she gets too far ahead, I certainly won't be able to find her. This place is a maze."

As they walked, Arya tried to loosen the unease clenching tight in her shoulder blades. What had she set in motion by mentioning Darmanin to the warlord, then hiding a critical piece of information about him? Two Shadeweavers now living under this roof, both hiding secrets, both potential threats. And Arya couldn't watch them both constantly.

If anything happened to endanger the warlord or this household...

She would lose everything.

Chapter 19

Despite Arya's fears about Thiara Ravenstrike's decision to take two Shadeweavers under her roof, she hadn't expected for it to take less than a week for the situation to spin almost catastrophically out of control. In fact, initially, it went surprisingly well.

Rorin made no attempt to hide his delight at having companions his own age, and while Arya feared that he made himself too vulnerable in his naivety, both Darmanin and Essa had accepted his wholehearted welcome with nothing but reserved warmth. She saw no signs of the cruel superiority with which Lanna's older boys treated Rorin. In fact, Darmanin and Essa treated him no differently than they would any other boy roughly their own age—something that clearly made Rorin's eyes shine.

Then, on the fifth morning after their arrival, Arya ate a quick breakfast in the kitchens—seeking the comfort of Peemla's presence after another cold and uncomfortable drill with the Heathrock Raiders—before making her way to report to General Desomer. The rapping of her boots on the stone floor of the hallway leading to the office wing was the only sound in the deathly silent corridors, until the distant snatch of raised voices coming from outside.

Curious, she peered out the nearest window. Immediately below was an enclosed garden, beyond which stood the outer wall and the frozen-over lake.

"Raven's balls," she muttered.

Rorin was in the garden, backing away from two older boys—Jenka and Warn, Lanna Ravenstrike's two sons. The younger one, Warn, called out something that Arya couldn't make out, while Jenka—laughing—lunged forward and wrapped an arm around Rorin in a wrestling hold. Rorin strug-gled uselessly as Jenka brought him down to the ground, hard. Rorin clearly didn't have the strength or skill to free himself. Still, he fought against the bigger boy anyway, kicking and pummelling to no avail.

He couldn't scream, couldn't ask for help, couldn't make a sound.

Arya's temper flared white-hot and a snarl tore from her throat.

She banged her palm on the window, trying to get their attention, but the noise wasn't loud enough. She turned and sprinted back the way she'd come. Taking the stairs two at a time, she hit the ground floor running and accosted the first servant she saw, demanding, "Tell me the quickest way to the east garden."

His eyes went wide, presumably at the sight of her furious expression, and he stammered out, "Ah … straight down that hall and then … uh … second door to the right."

She left him gaping after her, sprinting hard, boots thudding on stone. When she reached the door he'd directed her to, she shouldered through it, one hand on the hilt of her sword—

But someone else had seen the altercation and gotten there faster.

Even as Arya spotted the tussling boys in the snow and started towards them, Darmanin, who had come running from the opposite direction, leaped onto Jenka's back, wrapping an arm around the older boy's throat and dragging him off Rorin with surprising strength given his slight frame.

Warn glanced between Rorin—lying on the snow, gasping for air, nose bloodied—and the bitterly fighting figures of Jenka and Darmanin, then made a move towards his brother, presumably intending to help him.

"HEY!" Arya used her best parade ground bellow, resting her hand on the hilt of her sword and standing tall and straight, knowing the layers of her uniform made her bigger and more imposing.

Warn immediately stopped in his tracks, boots sliding in the snow so that he almost fell. Jenka and Darmanin ignored her and continued wrestling, throwing wild punches that didn't hit anything. Then, even though he was smaller and younger, Darmanin got the upper hand. He scrambled above the taller boy and slammed a fist into his face. A blood-curdling snarl ripped out of him, and his body turned rigid. Jenka cried out in pain, nose smashed and bloody, curling around himself. Darmanin lifted his fist again.

"Shit, shit, shit," Arya swore, bursting into a run for the two boys and bellowing at Warn. "Get back. Rorin, stay down. Nobody move!"

She crashed into Darmanin, sending him to the ground, covering him with her body as he thrashed beneath her. His eyes had gone bright silver and long fangs slid down from his mouth. "Get control of yourself," she hissed in her ear. If he changed now, in front of Lanna's sons … "CONTROL!" she bellowed.

Another snarl tore out of him, and he continued thrashing, but she was bigger and stronger and more experienced. Eventually his struggles lessened, the light in his eyes fading, his features returning to normal. Once she was certain he was in control of his magic, she clambered to her feet, letting him do the same.

Jenka was rolling in the snow, moaning in pain, cradling his face. Clearly the kid had never taken a hit before. Arya took a few steps towards Rorin, wanting to make sure he was okay, but as soon as she did, Warn let out a yell of fury and leaped at his brother's attacker. Darmanin spun to face him. Metal flashed as he pulled a blade. He was hunched, eyes bright, nothing but feral violence written all over his face.

"Darmanin, no!"

She reached out, wrapped an arm around Darmanin's throat and hauled him away. Once again he fought her bitterly, gasping and kicking, the knife slashing through the air. She used her height and leverage to keep it away from her. Eventually she managed to wrestle him some distance away. "Enough!" she bellowed in his ear.

He stilled, and she let him go. Chest heaving, he lifted his hands in the air. "I'm done."

She held his gaze for a moment longer to be sure. "Don't you move an inch."

Arya turned back to the other three boys, adrenaline racing. Shit. Darmanin had just *pulled a knife* on a warlord's nephew. He would have used it, too, if she hadn't been there.

Rorin was on his feet, hand pressed to his nose. Unlike Jenka, there were no tears streaking his face. Warn helped his brother up.

"We were just horsing around, and you had no right to intervene, Nameless." Jenka looked furious now that the immediate flare of pain had faded. "Just because Rorin is such a pathetic heir that he can't even wrestle like…"

Jenka's words trailed off as he got a good look at Arya's face. Her fury must have looked truly terrible, because Jenka and Warn glanced at each other, then broke into a run for the garden exit, trying to slip past her.

Arya was quicker.

She swung around as Jenka shot past and grabbed him by the lapels of his shirt. Using the momentum of her swing, she slammed him up against the castle wall and placed her forearm at his throat. "Rorin, come here," she called.

Footsteps sounded and the bloodied boy appeared at her right. Arya looked into Jenka's face. "Apologise."

His lip curled and he remained stubbornly silent. Arya pressed harder on his throat until he was gasping for air. "Apologise!"

"I'm sorry, Rorin," Jenka gasped out.

"Me too," Warn muttered, eyes on his feet. To his credit, he hadn't abandoned his brother and continued running out of the garden.

She let go of Jenka and he dropped to the ground. "If I ever see either of you even *look* sideways at Rorin again, I won't go so easy on you. I don't care who your mother is. Are we clear?"

Jenka and Warn nodded.

"Get out!" she snapped "Now. Go!"

The two boys scattered, and Arya turned back to Rorin. "Will you go and wait over by the gate while I speak with Darmanin? He's really angry and I just need to make sure he calms down. Okay?"

Rorin shot a wary look between the two of them, then nodded and did as she asked. Arya faced Darmanin then. He hadn't moved, but his grey eyes remained bright with cold menace. He still clutched the knife in his hand, and a snarl ripped from his throat as she faced him. This was no child staring her down with a knife.

"If you'd tried using that on me, I'd have killed you," she told him flatly. "And if you use it on anyone in this household again, even bullies, I will do the same."

He said nothing, just continued to stare at her defiantly.

She lowered her voice but didn't lose the steel from it. "The same goes if you try turning into a shadowhound again. You do that and you're done. You are no longer a Shadeweaver. Is that clear?"

The moment held, but then the brightness in his eyes faded and he held out the knife, hilt facing her. "Understood."

She took it, tucked it into her weapons' belt. As she did, his usual expressionless mask settled over his features.

Arya waved Rorin over. "Let me take a look at that nose. Did he hurt you anywhere else?"

Rorin shook his head and she pulled out a kerchief from her pocket to gently wipe the blood away. The boy stoically endured her ministrations, then reached back and pulled a scrap of parchment and thin piece of charcoal from his vest pocket. He spent a second writing something, then held it up.

You helped me.

She nodded. "Those boys are bullies."

"I was trying to help also," Darmanin said stiffly. "They deserved my knife."

Arya gave him a look. He ignored it.

Tears welled in Rorin's eyes, and he scribbled something else. *Nobody has ever stood up for me before.*

"You're not alone anymore, Rorin," Arya said. "If this ever happens again, you come to me immediately. Understood?" He nodded, a tremulous smile breaking over his face.

"Good. Now both of you go and clean up and report to your lesson with Laskin."

"Captain." Darmanin hesitated before following Rorin, and the other boy paused at the gate, clearly curious, but leaving them their privacy.

"What?" she snapped.

"The shadowhound ... I didn't mean ..." He expelled a frustrated breath. "I can't control it yet. When I get angry..."

Her ire was still up and she wanted to yell at him again but stopped herself. Hard life aside, he was a fourteen-year-old boy. "You do understand how important it is that nobody here see you shapeshift, let alone attack someone? And not just because of the warlord's politics. You have a home here."

He nodded.

"You can learn to control it." At least, she hoped he could. She glanced at Rorin, let out a sigh at what she was about to suggest. "I'll figure out a reason for us to take rides outside the walls. We'll find a place in the forest where you can safely practice until it's second nature and fully under your control. Okay?"

He thought on that a moment, then nodded firmly. "Okay."

"Good. Now go."

***

After a brief search, Arya found Taze in the Raider barracks mess, eating with Laskin. It was still in the middle of post-drill breakfast time, so the space was close to full, though her two Raiders sat on their own. She ignored all the disgruntled looks cast her way as she crossed the room to them. "Taze!" she called out.

"Captain!" He shot up from his seat, saluted.

"Where is Lord Rorin right now?"

"I—"

"You're his bodyguard," she snapped when he hesitated. "That means you are supposed to know where he is at all times. Including when he's getting beaten up by a pair of bullies in the east garden."

Taze straightened. "How do I get to—?"

"It's taken care of."

"He's all right?"

"Apart from a bloody nose. But Darmanin got there before I could and now Jenka Crowtalon also has a bloody nose. That is going to be a problem."

Taze reddened. "I'm sorry, Captain."

"Sorry won't be good enough if Rorin gets hurt on your watch," she said, feeling better at being able to loose some of her frustration on him. "Now go, find him, and stay with him. That's an order!"

"Yes, Captain."

Laskin opened his mouth as Taze dashed off, but Arya cut him off. "Don't you start. You're due to give Rorin and Darmanin their lesson. Get to it—they'll probably need some patching up before you start."

He saluted. "Yes, Captain."

Once both Raiders were gone, Arya turned to see General Desomer watching from the doorway to the mess. The low-level chatter had fallen silent at his appearance, and she made her way over to him and saluted. "Sir."

He eyed her. "I'm glad to see you've already learned the skill of shouting at your command."

It was her turn to redden. "Sir."

"You have nothing to be embarrassed about," Desomer said. "Your Raider should have known where the young lord was. You were right to reprimand him."

"Yes, sir."

"Now, the story I just heard was that young Lord Jenka was set upon by a murderous Shadeweaver who broke his nose and threatened him with a knife, and that you then threw him against a wall and tried to choke him. What the hell happened?"

"I—"

"Save it for the warlord." His glower deepened. "She wants to see both of us, now."

He turned and strode away. Heart sinking, Arya followed. Despite knowing she shouldn't, she'd lost her temper at the sight of those boys hurting Rorin, but that didn't give her permission to touch a lord.

This wasn't going to be good.

Chapter 20

Arya stood beside General Desomer as they saluted before Thiara Ravenstrike's desk—the warlord stood behind it, looking furious. Magen was there too, leaning against the wall just off to the side.

"Is it true Darmanin pulled a knife?" the warlord demanded without preamble, looking straight at Arya.

"Yes, Warlord. But—"

"So if you hadn't been there, in all likelihood my sister's eldest son would be dead right now, murdered by *my* guest?"

Arya winced. "Darmanin was trying to protect Lord Rorin, Warlord."

"As much as I appreciate the sentiment, pulling a knife at a wrestling match is a little much," Thiara said witheringly. "Boys mess around all the time, it's normal."

"Warlord," Desomer said, "may I suggest that we accept bringing the Shadeweaver boy here was a mistake and send him away before something like this happens again?"

"I agree," Magen chimed in. "You can't afford to alienate your sister further. She has two sons who are legitimate heirs to Ravenstrike if she decided to put them forward."

Arya saw what looked like agreement forming on Thiara Ravenstrike's face, and blurted out, "Can I add something, Warlord?"

"What?"

She quailed at that face and tone but pushed ahead. "What I saw wasn't boys messing around. Lord Jenka had Lord Rorin in an unwilling headlock on the ground and he wasn't letting go. Darmanin pulled the knife because

Lord Warn went at him *after* I stopped the fight. I agree it was an overreaction, but it's not quite as much of one as you've been told."

Desomer shifted at Arya's side but said nothing. Magen lifted a hand to rub his jaw. She got the distinct sense both men wished she hadn't spoken. *Arya* wished she hadn't—what was she thinking? Darmanin leaving would be the safest thing for all of them, including her. If he wasn't here, nobody would find out she'd lied to her warlord.

Before Thiara could respond, the door slammed open and Lanna Ravenstrike walked in. "Why isn't the wretch gone yet?" she demanded, tone blisteringly hot. Then, her eyes landed on Arya and her face reddened with increased fury. "And why is *she* in here? She pushed my son against a wall and *choked* him. Jenka says he thought she was going to kill him."

"He's exaggerating!" Arya jumped in, indignant. "And I didn't choke him, I—"

"Arya, enough!" The warlord's voice ripped through the room, silencing everyone. Those pale blue eyes came to rest on her. "Did you shove Jenka against a wall?"

She gritted her teeth against all the excuses that wanted to come pouring out. "Yes, Warlord."

"She should be imprisoned for touching my son, as should the Shadeweaver brat," Lanna raged. "And you should be ashamed that you ever thought of bringing them into this household."

The words came almost distantly to Arya. She could see the resolve forming on her warlord's face and she felt suddenly sick. She was done. One flash of unchecked temper and she'd already ruined her chances here. Pushing Jenka against that wall hadn't been necessary.

Thiara Ravenstrike sounded almost regretful as she said, "Arya, I'm sorry, but you've crossed a line that I cannot—"

The door opened again for the second time, on this occasion revealing Rorin Ravenstrike. The boy, bruising already surrounding his swollen nose, faltered at the sight of so many angry adults, but then his gaze fell on Arya and he must have read the despair in her expression.

Rorin's face firmed and he came to stand beside Arya, fingers flicking as he signed a message towards his mother.

"Rorin, I appreciate what you're saying, but what happened was unacceptable." Thiara spoke to her son like an adult, but there was a gentleness there that didn't exist when she spoke to anyone else.

Rorin straightened his shoulders and kept signing, movements sharp with agitation. When he came to a halt he was staring at his mother with pure determination. It was the first time Arya saw that this boy had his mother's steel in him.

Thiara Ravenstrike held her son's gaze for a long moment, then gave a little nod. Her head lifted and she looked over at her sister, considering. "I have much to think on. Leave us."

Lanna's mouth thinned. "I'm not going anywhere until I see that dangerous trash removed from my son's home."

"You have my word here and now that neither Jenka nor Warn will come to any further harm under this roof," Thiara said, her voice granite. "Now, leave me."

Lanna's face flushed an even deeper red at the dismissal, and she looked around, as if seeking help from somewhere, but it wasn't forthcoming. Eventually, her mouth tightened in an echo of her sister's mannerism, and she swept from the room, slamming the door behind her.

Magen was the first to speak. "That was … dangerous … Warlord. If she were to go back to Crowtalon now, carrying tales of you communicating with Shadeweavers and taking two of them into your home? Not to mention the *first* thing she'll do is tell her brother-in-law that you've got his son."

"I cannot keep her prisoner here, Magen. Yet for many other reasons I think it would be best for us if she *did* decide to leave."

Magen clearly disagreed with this and sent a pointed look Desomer's way, as if asking for help.

"She won't stay here after that exchange," Desomer said abruptly. "She has no allies here and that woman needs someone to manipulate. She'll take her husband and run into Crowtalon's welcome embrace, I've no doubt about it."

"I agree. These events have placed us in a less than ideal position." Thiara rubbed worriedly at her forehead. "Yet we can do nothing now but make the best of it."

Magen cleared his throat, shot an apologetic glance Arya's way. "Warlord, if you removed Darmanin and Captain Nameless from your household, it would go a long way to alleviate any leverage Mathas Crowtalon could gain from what happened."

Arya's shoulders slumped of their own accord, body bracing to take the news she knew was coming. Bitterness filled her mouth, drying it out. She wanted to blame Lanna Crowtalon for everything, but deep down she knew this was her fault.

Thiara's gaze returned to her son, and she gave a little shake of her head. "Darmanin stays. And Arya, that was your one and only chance. Rorin can't save you again. Do you understand?"

Her head came up as astonishment thrilled through her. "I..." She swallowed. "Yes, Warlord. Thank you."

But despite the reprieve, Arya felt even worse. She'd put her warlord in an untenable position when she was supposed to be helping make her stronger.

"Out, all of you."

They left without another word, each preoccupied with their own thoughts as they filed into the hallway beyond.

Arya turned straight to Rorin. "What did you say to her?"

He tugged a fresh piece of parchment from his tunic and scribbled, before showing her. *You said I wasn't alone anymore, that I would always have you there to help me.*

"Right." She nodded, puzzled.

He turned over the page, kept writing, then showed her. *I told my mother that if I was her heir, then it was my right to give the same to you. That you are not alone and that I would always be there to help you.*

Arya couldn't swallow through the sudden lump in her throat, and she couldn't hide the sheen of tears in her eyes. Rorin grinned at that, then scribbled a little more. *Mama takes such oaths quite seriously, so I won't be able to use that tactic again. You better stay away from Jenka and Warn.*

She laughed, almost snorted. "Good advice."

"Arya!" Desomer's voice barked at her. He'd reached his office and was hovering in the open doorway. "Get in here."

"Yes, sir." Arya gave Rorin the warmest smile she could manage. "Thank you, Rorin."

Arya glanced over her shoulder as she entered Desomer's office. Rorin was still watching her and offered a little wave when their gazes caught.

She wasn't alone here. Rorin Ravenstrike would always be there. And not because he was a Raider who relied on her to watch his back in return for watching hers. Not because their survival depended on being there for each other. But simply because she was Arya. Even though she was a Nameless and he a warlord's heir.

She wouldn't ever forget it.

***

Arya took a seat before Desomer's desk, emotions still roiling. She braced herself, expecting to receive a solid chastening from the general too, but instead he said, "I've finished reviewing all accounts of the attacks on SheerRock and Icecliff Forts. You got very lucky with that strategy of yours, Captain."

"It was a good plan, sir," Arya said stiffly.

"It was a creative and daring plan, but a lot could have gone wrong. You got lucky," he repeated. "Still, you get credit for being the only one to come up with a halfway viable strategy. The way our warlord tells it, many others were keen on fleeing the fort and retreating to Heathrock."

"That's right, sir." She squirmed, trying to hold back what she really wanted to say.

"Spit it out."

She searched for the most diplomatic words she could muster, "Just now, Adviser Magen seemed concerned that the warlord's position might be compromised by her sister, and it made me think..." She trailed off as her attempts to find diplomatic wording failed.

Desomer gave an impatient grunt. "If you're trying to tell me something, then stop dancing around it like a fool and say it."

"Commander Lerin does not respect the warlord. He was ... reluctant ... to do as she ordered during the attack. And now he's learned of the warlord contacting Ranier. I worry about his loyalty, sir."

He took a puff of his cigar, eyed her. "Your observations are noted, Captain."

"Yes, sir." She waited a beat, but clearly he wasn't going to engage any further on the topic of Lerin. She then ventured, "Can I ask, what was so bad about my plan?"

He grimaced, sat back in his chair, laced his hands over his stomach. "What would you have done if the Shadeweavers hadn't come to your aid?"

"I—"

"What if a larger force than you expected had surrounded you when you rode out of the fort?"

Arya didn't look away. "That was always a risk, sir. Commander Lerin wouldn't send out scouts, so we had no sense of numbers. The priority was that we drew enough of them in to allow the second force of Raiders to break the blockade, or at the very least understand better what was facing us."

Desomer nodded slowly, holding her gaze for a moment as he tapped ash from the end of his cigar. She couldn't for the life of her tell what he was thinking. "You said the other day that if the Nightstalker *was* testing our border defences, he might try again, and in greater numbers next time. We'll have new shields arriving from the south to bolster our numbers within the week. What do you think we should do?"

Arya didn't hesitate. "I'd increase the number of shields in all three forts and develop a more effective warning system between them—something faster and less vulnerable than birds. None of the three fort commanders should wait more than a day for word from the others. If a message doesn't arrive on schedule, then the fort goes into defensive mode and riders are immediately sent here, and to the other forts, to raise the alarm."

"If we increase the number of shields in those forts," Desomer said, "it will be standing room only in there. Our soldiers will barely have any room to move, let alone any personal space. Morale will drop quicker than the temperature on a winter's night, not to mention the difficulties it will cause for sanitation, illness, supplies. And what, exactly, would be a faster system of communication than birds?"

"I ..." she started, then stopped.

"You answered my question just now without even taking a breath to think about it. That's a poor way to come up with a plan, Captain."

Her face burned at his scathing tone. "Yes, sir."

"Birds we'll have to rely on, but we *can* improve the warning system. I'm implementing a daily check-in for each fort. Windfall to SheerRock to Icecliff, and Icecliff to Windfall." He tapped the desk with an index finger, thinking. "If a check-in is missed, a bird will be sent here to notify us immediately. All forts will go into defensive lockdown, and we'll deploy a force of three shields from Heathrock to the fort that missed check-in. Thoughts?"

"There will be occasions when a bird doesn't arrive for non-nefarious reasons; weather or predators," she said slowly. "But given what's happened, I think the risk worth it. And false alarms could serve as good practice drills for a time when the threat is real."

He nodded. "You'll be writing the orders on the new procedure to all three commanders today." A brief smile flickered at his mouth. "Commander Lerin will enjoy that, I think."

Arya tried not to smile, and instead paid close attention as the general kept speaking.

"We can't just focus on the Shadeweavers anymore; we need to maintain a closer watch on the pass over the Diamondfang, as well as the underground road—at least until the High Warlord hears back from Andahar. We'll run more frequent patrols from Icecliff and SheerRock to ensure the integrity of the roadblocks, at least once a month." He took a puff of his cigar. "You look about to burst, Captain. Go on, give me your thoughts."

"Sir, the Raiders based here at Heathrock don't have any experience riding patrols through the Wraith Forest or the Diamondfang, let alone battling Shadeweavers or wraiths and shadowhounds. I imagine that is the same for those posted elsewhere across Ravenstrike who are coming here to reinforce our numbers." It was rare that a Raider volunteered for posts at any of the three forts—they were far too isolated and cold. It was usually the newest, youngest, poorest recruits who were sent up there, and they rarely left unless they were promoted high enough up the chain. "I don't mean to sound cocky, sir, but basic Raider training doesn't prepare you for riding patrols up there."

"If you have a point, feel free to get to it," he barked.

Arya shifted. "The three patrol shields you talked about deploying in the event a fort missed check-in? I recommend recalling some of the Raiders from Icecliff and mixing them with the Raiders here to form those shields. Then if the alarm *is* raised, you'd at least be sending experienced Raiders to help."

Desomer considered her words for a moment, then leaned forward, stubbed out his cigar, and began gathering the parchment on his desk into a single untidy pile. "By tomorrow afternoon, you'll have a list for me of the Raiders you'd like to recall from Icecliff to join the new shields. You'll head one of them, and the training of all three will be your responsibility."

"Yes, sir," Arya said eagerly.

"Your point about inexperience is a good one," he said, almost to himself, then looked up and straightened, returning to his papers. "Right, well, you have some orders to write, Captain. Make sure they're sent out before dinner."

***

That night, Arya woke from a restless sleep filled with dreams she couldn't quite catch hold of. After fruitlessly trying to get back to sleep, she tossed off her covers and promptly swore as the frigid night air wrapped around her. She yanked on pants and shirt in a hurry before lacing up her boots and shrugging on her thick Raider cloak.

Slipping out of her room, she kept her stride brisk in a futile attempt to warm up. As she walked, she wrapped her cowl around her neck and buttoned that up too. The halls were dark and empty; the kitchen staff wouldn't be up for at least another couple of hours.

Cold, ice-filled air gusted around her as she pushed open the external kitchen door and stepped into the garden beyond. Following the stone pathway through to the outer walls, she climbed the steps up to the top of the battlements surrounding the castle, the exertion slowly beginning to warm her.

One of the Raiders on guard duty looked up as Arya reached the top of the steps. When he recognised her, a scowl flashed over his face and he turned away. Sighing inwardly, she nonetheless gave him a quiet greeting as she passed.

The Heathrock Raiders were just as much of a close-knit group as those at Icecliff Fort, and while an outsider would eventually be accepted with the passage of time and shared danger, she doubted it was going to be as easy for her. They hated that she'd been handpicked by a warlord they were still uncertain about to apprentice to their beloved general.

And after today, she was going to have to lead and train three shields of these soldiers.

This time she let the sigh out. She'd reached a more isolated section of the wall where she could stare out into the night. Immediately below, the frozen surface of the lake glinted in the moonlight.

Movement in her peripheral vision had her turning as a shadowy figure approached, resolving into Taze's familiar lanky stride. He came to stand beside her, a rueful smile on his face. "Can't sleep, Captain?"

"No. You as well?"

"Yep."

They stood in comfortable silence for a long time, both relishing the cold air and company of the other.

After a while, Taze spoke. "It's so different here, from Icecliff or Aren."

Arya looked at him in surprise. Neither of them had ever mentioned the bond they shared, surviving as cold, hungry Nameless on the streets of Aren.

They'd recognised each other the moment Taze had arrived at Icecliff Fort with the latest crop of recruits almost a year earlier, but neither had ever directly spoken of it. When he'd been assigned to her shield the next day, however, something wound tight in Arya had eased.

"Having our own rooms is the worst part," she said, huffing a breath of scorn at herself. "I've never slept alone before. It's so damned quiet."

"There were always at least, what, six of us sleeping in those abandoned warehouses in Aren?" he agreed. "And with the Raiders you're always barracked with others."

"We'll adjust," she said confidently. "It will just take some time."

He nodded. "How are things going with General Desomer?"

Arya shrugged. "He's grumpy and blunt, but I like him."

"The Raiders here speak very highly of him. Apparently, he's regarded across Dunidaen as among the best of the State's generals but very set in his ways. Not one for creative thought."

"Well, he hasn't thrown me out yet, which I'm treating as a ringing endorsement of my apprenticeship, even though I don't think he's convinced about me yet," she said. "Not that I can say the same of the Raiders here. You'd think I'd bathed in a vat of bear piss before attending morning drill the way they all steer clear of me."

Taze hesitated. "I won't lie, there is a lot of muttering and discontent in the barracks. There's this one Raider, his name is Arken ... have you met him?"

"He's in the warlord's personal shield, isn't he?" Arya confirmed. "He was insufferably civil the first morning I attended drill but has gone out of his way to avoid talking to me since."

"Laskin told me he's the younger son of one of the State's vicelords. It was generally expected he would be chosen as General Desomer's apprentice. He's also very well-liked around here, so..."

"The Raiders all think I stole his rightful position." Arya groaned. "Wonderful."

"I'd be careful of him. He holds a lot of influence."

"Noted," she said. "What about you? How are you and Laskin settling in?"

"They're wary of us, but you know how Laskin is, he can get along with an angry ice bear. I think we'll be fine with a bit of time." He hesitated a moment. "About this morning, Captain, with Lord Rorin. It won't happen again, I promise. I take my role very seriously."

She reached out, squeezed his shoulder in acknowledgment of that.

"It's strange, I've never really looked into the future before," he mused. "Life has always been about surviving the moment."

"Until now," Arya murmured.

"Until now," he agreed before offering her a small smile. "There is plenty of floor space in my room and a nice soft rug at the end of the bed. You're welcome to bunk in with me tonight. My snoring should help you sleep."

She smiled. "I'd like that."

They headed back inside together, Taze tossing her one of his blankets and a pillow before rolling into his bed. Arya curled up on the rug at the end of his bed, muscles relaxing at the sound of his soft breathing nearby.

She felt warm. Content. This must be what home felt like. Family. Different to the rough camaraderie of her shield-mates. Deeper, steadier, a feeling of security she'd never had.

And as that realisation came to her, a cold slide of dread followed it.

All of a sudden she had a lot to lose, and her position felt incredibly precarious—there were so many things that could result in it all being taken away from her. If the warlord found out she'd lied about Darmanin. If Essa or Darmanin did something on Ranier's behalf that hurt the warlord or Rorin. If Arya failed to succeed in Desomer's tasks.

And as much as she'd buried her conversation with the Etherean elder away … she couldn't stop the occasional memory of his assertion that the Nightstalker had been looking for her. Maybe Darmanin too. In the wildest, most farfetched possibility that what the elder had said was even remotely true, what he wanted from Arya would tear her away from all this.

She shivered, and burrowed deeper into the blanket, even though she wasn't cold. The warlords would deal with the Nightstalker and all would be well.

She closed her eyes tight and repeated it to herself over and over until she slept.

Chapter 21

Arya's arrow struck the middle of the target with a satisfying thud. Pleased, she loosed another three in quick succession, gaze narrowed against the dim light. Heavy clouds obscured the dawn, and a light snowfall drifted over the drill ground. She'd been up since pre-dawn to get some practice in and work off the unease that continued to plague her.

A glance towards the hulking barracks showed the first of the warlord's personal shield members trickling outside. She took a steadying breath, bracing herself for another morning drill with the Raiders of Heathrock.

None of them acknowledged her as they filed past on the way to the weapons' rack. Arya greeted them anyway. "Morning, Cusper, Joffer," she said agreeably. "You too, Riter."

Riter gave her a nod but didn't look at her, and the other two pretended not to have heard her. In the week since her late-night conversation with Taze, she'd taken to eating most of her meals in the barracks mess rather than in the castle kitchens, hoping it would help the Raiders see her as one of them.

So far it had made no difference. As far as they were concerned, she was a Nameless orphan who hadn't earned anything as a Raider yet, especially not a prized apprenticeship with the Raider general. Still, the time she spent in the mess had taught her some useful things. For a start, they weren't a unified bunch.

The warlord had three personal shields, a primary and two backups, while the remaining shields barracked at Heathrock were responsible for protection of the castle and nearby city. Laskin had told her that most of those in the warlord's personal shields were sons and daughters of Ravenstrike vicelords. It was clear to Arya that they thought they were better than the rest. The other Raiders sensed this and resented it accordingly.

Not that such division would help her. It gave her *two* factions to win over, and in the time she'd been here, she'd made no progress with either. It was a problem. A critical one. If she didn't earn their regard, she'd never be able to hold her position. And it wasn't just about determination to succeed in her ambitions anymore.

Now it was about the life she wanted to build for herself as part of the Ravenstrike household.

Arya turned back to the target and continued loosing arrows, using the focus archery required to temporarily free her mind from its worries. Moments later—four more arrows bristling in the target—she sensed someone approaching. She drew the bow again, loosed, smothered the little smile that wanted to break out when it hit the centre.

"Being a good archer isn't going to make you a general," a voice drawled. "You'd be better off accepting your limitations and stepping aside for someone better qualified."

Ah. She knew this voice.

"Arken." Arya turned to face the tall Raider, keeping her posture deliberately relaxed. He was older than her, probably in his mid-twenties. She'd paid more attention to him after Taze's advice, noting for herself how well-liked he was. He had a natural charm and affability, which meant even those not in the warlord's shields liked and respected him. On that fact alone he would have been a good choice as Desomer's apprentice. "What limitations might those be?"

His eyes gave her a slow, insulting once-over. "The list is so long, and I wouldn't want us to be late for drill."

He hadn't yet addressed her by rank, or saluted, which was a break in protocol and an insult to boot, but she kept firm hold of her temper. "So you're just over here wasting my time then?"

He smirked, glancing around. Most of the shields were out of the barracks by now, standing around in small groups, chatting—some surreptitiously watching her and Arken. Barring the shields on guard duty on the walls, or on scheduled days off, that made for almost a hundred Raiders.

Instinct rippled through her, warning her to be very careful, but she kept her focus on Arken, eyebrow raised, waiting for a response.

"You're the one who's wasting everyone's time." He crossed his arms over his chest. "The warlord made a mistake in bringing you here. A Nameless has no right to be anything more than a soldier on the border."

Her anger flared, seeping through her control like water running through holes in a dam.

"Arya." Laskin's warning tone sounded behind her.

She glanced back, surprised to see him there. She could tell from the look on his face he thought it was a bad idea for her to push Arken, but her temper and pride were telling her otherwise.

Arken was the source of most of the negative feelings about her. She'd ignored the muttering so far, had swallowed her pride and put her head down, hoping to prove her worth by training hard and not shirking. It wasn't working.

Her gaze narrowed as she assessed the situation. Arken had thought to put her in an impossible situation by needling her in front of an audience of Raiders; either he'd provoke her into doing something that would get her thrown out, or she'd concede in front of everyone and undermine her credibility even further.

Arya grinned inwardly, suddenly confident. Energy sparked through her. Little did Arken know how badly Arya responded to being put in impossible situations.

She gave him the same insulting once-over that he'd just given her. "And why should any of us listen to you? All I see standing in front of me is a pretty boy who hasn't lifted a sword in a real fight in his life."

His mouth curled. "I could take you any day."

She leaned forward, holding his gaze. "Prove it."

"Now?" Arken snorted, like he thought she was joking.

"Any time that suits you." She cocked her head, lifting her voice. "If you'd like to go and polish your boots and brush your hair beforehand, I'm happy to wait."

Her words carried, exactly as she'd hoped. Those who hadn't already stopped their chatter to watch them now did so, and a loose circle of sorts formed around Arken and Arya. A few glanced towards the entrance gate, probably hoping Randin, the battalion commander of the shields based at Heathrock, didn't show up to stop this.

"You're a fool to challenge me here," Arken said, huffing a laugh.

"Are you willing to prove your words or not?" she snapped.

He shrugged, shifted into fighting stance, and lifted his training sword. "Bring it on, Nameless."

She glanced over her shoulder at Laskin, ready to catch the training sword he tossed her way. He looked all kinds of annoyed with her, so she winked at him. His scowl deepened.

Arya closed her gloved fingers around the wooden hilt of the sword and tested its weight, using a moment to study her opponent. Arken was a good head taller than her, broader, and much stronger. She'd seen him at practice every morning and judged him among the best fighters of those stationed at Heathrock—quick on his feet and sound in fundamentals, with what appeared to be a solid ability to read his opponent.

She would have to end this fast if she wanted to win. The longer the fight lasted, the more of an advantage he would have with his superior size and strength.

A snowflake landed on Arya's eyelid as she swung the blade then shifted into fighting stance. She brushed at it irritably, not taking her eyes off Arken, and said, for his ears alone, "Give me your best shot, pretty boy."

He came at her without hesitation, sword whipping through the air as he cut at her head. Arya stepped aside, lifting her sword in counter. Their blades cracked loudly through the morning air.

Arken disengaged and they circled each other. With each of his next three blows, Arya took his measure, testing his speed and reflexes, settling into the fight. The first thing Laskin had ever taught her was that winning wasn't about who was the strongest or fastest, or even the most skilled; it was about who was the smartest. If you could outsmart your opponent, you could win.

And Laskin was a good teacher.

They circled a few more times; blow, parry, blow, counter. Snow continued to fall. Everything was silent apart from the loud cracking of their blades. She could feel the intensity of the Raiders' interest prickling along her shoulder blades.

In one lightning-fast move, Arken got inside Arya's guard and slammed his blade into her shoulder. The pain made her swear loudly—the hit would leave a nasty bruise later—but she was impressed by the move.

Arken had clearly expected his blow would force her to drop her sword, but Arya had taken far worse hits than that, and she didn't slow at all. Instead, she merely stepped back, swinging the sword to demonstrate she was undeterred. The pain-fuelled anger warmed her, gave her strength and confidence, and she used it to launch her first attack.

She'd seen enough now to win this, and it was time to end it before the advantage swung to him.

Arken countered skilfully, swiping aside both blows before counterattacking. She dodged aside, her blade a blur as she defended herself, moving instinctively as she waited for that one particular…

There it was.

Arken finished off a sweeping cut by reversing his blade up over his head, preparing it to slash down too fast for her to avoid. He'd done it twice now, almost scoring blows both times, and so she was ready, waiting for the right moment as his blade came slicing…

Arya brought her sword up, meeting Arken's as it came down with all his strength. For a brief millisecond, she pushed back, allowing him to think she was bracing against his blow. Then, just as his muscles bunched to press more effort into the stroke, trying to smash through her guard with sheer strength, she dropped her blade and stepped to the side.

Arken stumbled forward, abruptly off balance as the counterforce of Arya's blade vanished. Quick as a blink, she shifted closer, bringing the hilt of her sword down hard into the middle of his back. He grunted and stumbled to his knees. She stepped again without hesitation, curled her free hand around the back of his neck, and slammed her knee up into his face. Cartilage crunched under her blow and blood spurted into white snow.

To his credit, Arken gave only another grunt of pain before staggering back to his feet, reaching for his fallen sword. Blood streamed down his face and dripped into the snow. Arya kicked the sword out of his reach then slammed her boot, hard, right into his midsection. The breath whooshed from his lungs and he fell back to the ground, gasping for air.

She dropped her sword and crouched over him, pressing one knee into his chest before reaching out to close a gloved fist around his throat. She rested her other hand palm down in the snow beside his head.

"Are we done?" she asked. His breath wheezed as he stared up at her, and she loosened her hold enough that he could talk. "Are we done?"

He swallowed, coughed. "Yes."

"Yes, who?"

His jaw tensed. "Yes, *Captain.*"

"Don't ever challenge me again, Arken."

She tightened her fist on his throat, waited until his face turned red from lack of oxygen, before she let go and stood up. She fetched her sword and tossed it back to Laskin in one movement. The yard full of Raiders had gone utterly silent, onlookers stunned by how quickly and ruthlessly she'd taken Arken apart.

Arya barked into the silence, "Drill should have started ten minutes ago. Stop shirking and get to it before the commander appears and puts us all on privy duty."

They got to it.

Laskin approached. "Captain—"

"Don't start, Laskin. That had to be done."

He rubbed at his nose, clearly trying to hide amusement. "I just wanted to tell you that General Desomer is here."

"Shit." She turned and winced at the sight of Ravenstrike's general standing at the edge of the drill yard with Rorin, Taze hovering in the background.

"Good luck," he said bracingly.

She crossed the ground in quick strides, stopped, and saluted before the general. A stab of pain went through her shoulder at the movement and she had to bite down a wince. Arken had gotten her good.

Rorin stood at Desomer's side, his fingers flickering briefly in a greeting to Arya. She ignored him, all her attention on her general.

"I knew that was coming," he barked, "but I couldn't help you. You understand?"

"Yes, sir." She hesitated, relaxing as it seemed she wasn't to be chastened. It made her bold. "Sir, I want Arken gone. I don't want him here at Heathrock stirring discontent among the Raiders and turning them against me."

"What did I tell you about thinking through your plans before talking to me about them?" he said sharply.

"Sir," she said stiffly.

"Your Raiders from Icecliff are arriving this morning. When we meet later, I want to go over the formation of the new shields. After *thinking* about it for more than a minute, you tell me then what you want to do about Arken, and I'll see that it's done."

"Yes, sir."

"Here's my second piece of advice to you. Sending your problems away is never the best way to deal with them." Desomer's gaze moved past her as Arken came limping past, supported by Cusper. "Go and get your shoulder looked at. It was a nasty blow and there could be worse than bruising." He paused, then muttered, "You fight like someone with a brain and you can take a hit. Not bad, Captain."

Arya beamed from ear to ear. "Thank you, sir."

He scowled and stalked off.

Chapter 22

Rorin followed Arya to the healer's wing in the barracks and watched as the healer brusquely poked and prodded at her arm and shoulder before rotating it in every direction he could think of. Taze remained on guard outside the door.

Arya endured these ministrations as best she could before snapping out, "Well, is it going to fall off or not?"

The man sniffed and finally stepped away. "There's no joint damage far as I can tell, though it's going to swell up some. Don't use that arm for the next week in drill, but make sure you keep it moving—the last thing you need is for the joint to stiffen up." He pressed a hessian bag filled with snow against her shoulder. "That stays on for at least twenty minutes before you leave here. Do the same at least once a day until the swelling goes down."

Rorin sat himself on a chair beside her once the healer had gone, fingers flickering. *"It must hurt."*

It took Arya a moment to work out what Rorin had said. Although she'd been spending at least an hour every night after dinner learning his sign language, it was going to take time to become fluent. "I've had worse. What were you doing down in the drill yard so early this morning anyway?"

For this, he pulled out his parchment and charcoal. *General Desomer wanted me to watch drill before my lesson with Raider Carter. I think he wants to make sure I understand the Raiders and how they work.*

Arya studied the boy's face, sensing there was something else he wanted to say. "What is it? You can ask me anything."

"I just think..." Rorin signed, then his face cleared and he started scribbling on the parchment. *It was harsh, what you just did. Arken was beaten. You didn't have to kick him.*

Arya thought carefully about how to respond to that. She didn't want to give him a flippant answer. "Sometimes it's necessary to make a display of strength. Arken challenged my position in front of almost a hundred Raiders. If I'd backed down, or failed to put him down properly, he would have continued undermining me. It will be hard for him to do that now I've bested him so decisively."

"Will I have to do that?" He didn't seem pleased at the idea.

"Not in the same way." She reached out and squeezed his shoulder. "You're the son of a warlord. You will have people like me to do the brutal and messy work for you."

He frowned, wrote again. *But being a warlord ... by your logic, I'll have to make displays of strength too. To solidify my position. Especially because I'm a mute.*

Arya was impressed by the boy's perceptiveness. "That's true. But as far as I know, warlords don't solve their disputes by fighting it out in the drill yard. You'll have to find other ways to display your strength."

"Better ways," he signed determinedly. Or, at least that's what she *thought* he'd signed.

A cleared throat at the door had them both turning. Arya was surprised to see Essa standing there. As usual, she wore a lovely floral-patterned dress that fell almost to her ankles, although Arya couldn't see much of it through the fur-lined cloak she wore. Her dark hair was hidden under a woollen hat pulled down low over her ears.

Arya had seen little of the Shadeweaver leader's daughter outside of their formal lessons each morning—between keeping a close eye on Darmanin, figuring out how to win over the Raiders, and completing all of Desomer's tasking, Arya hadn't had time for figuring out how much of a threat the girl might pose. Still, it remained one of the many worries simmering in the back of her mind. "What brings you here?" she asked.

"I came to let you know Rawson is looking for you, Rorin." Essa brightened while both Arya and Rorin made a face. Essa was the only one who seemed to enjoy the hours they spent with Rorin's tutor every morning.

Rorin passed his parchment of writing to Essa, asking for her thoughts on their conversation—and no doubt wanting to delay having to attend their lessons.

Essa read his words and thought for a few moments before replying in a considered way. "The difference, Rorin, is that you were born into your position, so your people, and the other warlords, will be predisposed to accept you, even as a mute. Arya was born with nothing, so she has to prove to everyone that she can lead. You have room to make mistakes. She doesn't."

"*That doesn't seem fair.*" Rorin frowned.

"Fair or not, Essa is right." Arya hopped off the healing table and gingerly shrugged her cloak back on, hiding her interest at how perceptive Essa had just proved herself to be. "Come on, let's go."

The three of them, and Taze falling in behind, trailed out of the barracks and along the path to the main castle. Arya was no more excited to get to lessons than Rorin and gladly followed his slow pace.

"It doesn't help," Essa spoke suddenly at her side, voice pitched low. "You being so obviously dismissive of our lessons. Rorin clearly idolises you, and he takes your lead."

Arya shrugged, shifting the bag of snow against her shoulder. "I don't know why the general insists I attend. I'm a soldier, not a scholar."

Essa gave her a look. "He's doing right by you. You *will* fail if you don't have an education. And Rorin needs one even more if he's going to succeed."

The girl's voice held no sharpness or censure, and Arya took no offence—she was right. The opportunity Warlord Ravenstrike had given her was beyond anything she could have asked for, even the parts of it she didn't like. "I'm curious as to why you care so much about either of us succeeding."

"I have been given an opportunity too." Essa paused. "It's not what I expected, being here. It's ... whatever his mother's political motives, Rorin has welcomed us into his home and made it ours too. I don't want to put that at risk."

Those words were so similar to Arya's feelings about being at Heathrock that she shivered. She didn't really want to have anything in common with Ranier's daughter.

Ahead of them, Rorin hauled open the outer door and waved them inside before bounding ahead again. Taze walked at his side, a little smile on his face as Rorin's fingers flickered busily. He was picking up the finger language far quicker than the others.

Arya turned her gaze back to Essa, deciding to probe a little. "Is there something or someone you think *will* put it at risk?"

Essa shrugged.

Right. So the lack of trust went both ways. Arya tried another tack. "Did Rorin tell you about what happened in the garden last week?"

Essa cut a sharp glance her way, considering. "He did, and I can understand why Darmanin did what he did. I imagine that where he comes from, it doesn't pay to mince about when there's a threat. What surprises me is that Warlord Ravenstrike let him stay after pulling a knife on her nephew. Or that she let *you* stay after you put hands on him."

It was an impressively nuanced understanding of the event, and Arya's gaze narrowed. "Something tells me that if you'd been in Darmanin's position, you would have realised the context and not drawn that knife."

"My, is that a compliment?" A quick smile flashed over the girl's face.

Arya scowled.

"You do realise the position you put the warlord in?" Essa said. "Lanna Crowtalon will almost be back to Crowtalon by now. There are any number of things Warlord Crowtalon could do with what she'll tell him, starting with demanding formal retribution for an attack on his nephews."

Arya winced. Lanna had left the day after the altercation, as Desomer had predicted. "I don't need telling more than once, Essa."

Essa's gaze studied her thoughtfully, but she said nothing further.

Ahead of them, Rorin reached their classroom and heaved a sigh before opening the door and waving them inside. As she took her usual seat at the back of the room, Arya was mindful of Essa's words and tried to keep the reluctance from her face. Darmanin was already there, and Rorin sat beside him.

Surprisingly, Essa took the seat beside Arya, and leaned over to murmur, "I spent my whole life in Heathrock city, in a very nice house with three meals a day and enough hearths to keep me warm on the coldest winter days. I lived with my guardian, who mostly kept to herself. My only other company was the occasional visits from my father and the tutor who taught me to read, write, and dress and behave like a young noblewoman. Being here has been ... wonderful in many ways, but I'm also too accustomed to being on my own. So it's also been an adjustment that I don't always enjoy."

Arya eyed her. "Why are you telling me this?"

"Because you want to know." Essa settled back in her seat.

At the top of the room, Rawson cleared his throat. "Enough chatter, please. Pay attention."

Arya straightened. She paid attention as best she could—or at least made it *look* like she was paying attention. Truth was, she'd understood very little of what was going on since starting these classes. She certainly wasn't going to admit that to anyone, so today she kept a focused look on her face while allowing her thoughts free rein, primarily considering Desomer's instructions to her. What to do with Arken?

Her train of thought drifted again after a while—the ceaseless throbbing from her shoulder and drips of melting snow from the bag pressed against it forming a pool of water on the desk—wasn't helping her ability to concentrate. She found herself glancing sideways. Essa focused on the lesson with a fascinating single-mindedness, gaze not shifting from the top of the room, but even though she was clearly listening to everything Rawson said, her right hand moved busily the entire time, doodling on her parchment.

By the end of the lesson, the parchment was framed with a beautiful border of complex ivy spotted here and there with blossoming roses. It looked so real Arya was surprised when it didn't keep growing off the edges of the page.

That explained the ink or paint the girl constantly had spotting her fingertips and clothes. She was an artist. A good one.

Why did Ranier want her here at Heathrock? He clearly had the resources to provide his daughter a comfortable upbringing without needing Thiara Ravenstrike's help. Or risk having the warlord of Ravenstrike holding a piece of leverage over him.

The Shadeweaver leader didn't do anything without good reason. He'd placed his daughter here for a reason, and Arya doubted it was a good one. The question was whether Essa knew of his purpose, and if so, would she go along with it.

The sooner Arya figured that out, the better.

Peemla came bustling down the corridor just as they were finally freed from Rawson's endless droning, bringing the news that the Raiders from Icecliff had arrived.

"Thanks, Peemla." Arya caught Rorin's eye. "You all go ahead to lunch, I'll need to go and meet them."

His shoulders slumped, but he signed anyway, *"See you later, Arya."*

Arya diverted from Peemla in the entrance hall, with the chamberlain promising to let General Desomer know the Raiders had arrived. The small group was dismounting as Arya came down the front steps, looking around them with expressions ranging from interest to awe to the same discomfort Arya had first felt on arriving.

"Well, well, well." She lifted her voice to draw their attention. "I've never seen such a raggedy lot in my life."

They turned almost as one, straightening and saluting her, clearly relieved to see someone familiar. A swell of gladness swamped her at the sight of them, and a smile tugged at her mouth. "Etan, you've recovered well," she greeted the rangy man.

"Yes, Captain!" he said. "I'm ready for action."

"Glad to hear it. Wattin, are you ever going to trim that beard to regulation length?"

"Never," he assured her.

She chuckled. "Charlin, you brought that big battle axe along with your scowl, I see. And Allicen, you'd better get that shirt tucked in quick smart or I'll throw you on privy duty for a week."

"Captain." She saluted sharply before quickly fixing her shirt.

"Kait." Arya greeted the remaining Raider, and she grinned. "How much did Commander Lerin tell you all about your re-assignment?"

"He said he'd received orders that we were being deployed to Heathrock castle and that we were to leave immediately," Charlin said sourly. "No 'thanks for saving our asses recently' or anything. Just 'get out of my face.' Real heart-warming stuff."

"He said some choice things about you too," Kait added. "Didn't realise he had such a mouth on him."

"He used some words *I'd* never heard before, and that's saying something," Etan huffed.

Arya smirked. "I'm sorry for the abrupt manner of your re-assignment, but it came at my request. You're here to join three new shields we'll be training to deploy in the event there is a problem at one of the forts again. Or to be the first line of defence if it comes to the worst with Andahar."

"You mean we'll get sent into the fight if those creatures attack again?" Wattin asked.

"Or if anything or anyone else does, yes." Arya stepped forward, lowered her voice. "Don't tell them this, but you're here to teach these soft Heathrock Raiders what real combat is and how to survive it."

"I'm glad something is being done about reacting better if the same thing happens again," Charlin grumbled.

Arya nodded. "You'll find Laskin in the barracks. He'll get you settled in." She gave quick directions on getting there. "I want you reporting to drill first thing tomorrow. Welcome to Heathrock."

Grinning and joking among themselves, they shuffled off. Arya watched them go with a smile that stayed on her face as she returned inside to report to the general for the afternoon. She came to a halt in surprise at seeing him standing at the top of the steps, straightened, and saluted. "Sir, I was just heading up to your office."

"You have good instincts, Captain," he said.

She was thrown by this unsolicited compliment. "How's that, sir?"

"At ease, that shoulder must be killing you," he said, then gestured for her to fall in with him. "I read the reports on the Raiders you requested be assigned here from Icecliff. They're all from the shield *you* led during the attack. Watching you greet them just now confirmed my suspicions."

"Suspicions about what, sir?" she asked.

"They're your people. Bringing them here was a deliberate move to try and bolster your support among the Raiders at Heathrock."

Arya winced. Had it been that obvious?

They reached his office, both shedding cloaks and cowls before sitting in their now-customary positions on opposite sides of his desk. Their days always started off this way, Desomer asking questions, teaching something, or giving her orders. Then they'd usually separate to carry out their tasks. It was quickly becoming a routine she enjoyed.

Once settled, Desomer continued, "I hope you've chosen well—the *wrong* people and they'll only sow more division, and we'll end up with three factions inside this compound. Your supporters, the nobleborns, and everyone else." He eyed her. "If that happens, it's on you to fix it."

"That's not what I'm aiming to do, sir. Yes, I did want some familiar faces, but these Raiders are steady and experienced. They're the example I want *all* Raiders here at Heathrock to meet."

"Barely two weeks here and already you're fashioning *my* army in your own style," he growled. "I'll be the one deciding what the example is for Warlord Ravenstrike's army if that's all right with you, Captain Nameless."

She flushed. "Yes, sir."

A knock came at Desomer's door, and the general barked out an invitation to enter. Arya was taken aback to see Arken enter the room, though the sight of his swollen nose and black eye filled her with satisfaction and she had to fight back a smirk. The Raider limped over to Desomer's desk and kept his gaze resolutely away from Arya the whole time.

"You look a little worse for wear, Raider Rosenthal," Desomer remarked.

Arken stood straight, despite how painful that must have been, and saluted. "I'm fine, sir. I'll be back at drill tomorrow."

"You don't look fine," the general barked, then widened his gaze to include both Arya and Arken. "I don't tolerate infighting among my Raiders. What happened on the drill yard this morning will end there and never happen again. Am I clear?"

"Yes, sir," both Arya and Arken muttered.

"Arken, she put you down fair and square. Not to mention you called out a soldier of higher rank in front of a hundred Raiders," Desomer continued. "That means I'm not going to help you. Captain Nameless has earned the right to decide what will be done with you."

"Yes, sir." Arken's gaze flickered briefly to Arya, anger and resentment smouldering in them. "I suppose I'm to be sent to Icecliff or SheerRock. Or are the eastern mines the nastiest place you can think to send me?"

The look in his eyes and the contempt in his voice had Arya's temper flaring again, quick as a flash. It was on the tip of her tongue to send him to privy-guarding duty at Icecliff for the rest of his Raider career.

But a glance at Desomer checked her. She'd come here to learn from him, an experienced general, and that meant listening to his advice. He'd also made some good points just now about her Icecliff Raiders. She truly didn't want further division.

She turned back to the general. "Sir, my recommendation is that Arken is re-assigned out of the warlord's personal shield and placed in charge of one of the three new shields you're creating."

Desomer's eyebrows shot upwards. "You want me to *promote* him?"

"Yes, sir."

He stared at her a moment longer before shrugging. "I said the decision was yours, so consider it done. Captain Rosenthal, report to the yard first thing tomorrow to meet your new shield. Dismissed."

Arken was so surprised he almost took a step back. "Sir, I—"

"Not a word," Desomer warned. "Go on, get out of here before you say something you regret."

Arken saluted, his shocked glance lingering between Desomer and Arya for a handful of heartbeats before he turned and strode from the room.

"What the hell was that all about?" Desomer demanded as soon as the door closed behind him.

"Arken is a good Raider, sir," she admitted reluctantly. "He's probably the best fighter at Heathrock, and he's well-liked and respected. He is due for promotion, and he probably would have received one if I hadn't come along. He *was* going to be your recommendation to the warlord to be your apprentice, was he not?"

Desomer glowered. "I hadn't firmly decided yet, but ... yes."

"And that tells me your opinion of the man and his leadership potential." Arya paused. "You told me to deal with my problems instead of sending them away, sir."

"This won't make him your friend," Desomer warned. "He'll chafe at anything you give him."

"I understand that, sir, but it *will* show the rest of the Raiders here that I'm willing to give them what they've earned, and that I won't be petty."

His gaze narrowed. "I suppose you want me to put one of your people in charge of the third shield?"

"No, sir." Arya shook her head. "Captain Derrin would be my recommendation. I've seen the way he treats his shield during morning drill. From what I can tell, he's the most-liked captain here at Heathrock, but it's not because he's easy on his shield."

"Are you sure?"

"I can't go putting my own people in charge, sir. That would only increase resentment. But I do need to ensure the soldiers that lead the other two shields are competent. Arken and Derrin are capable, and their appointments will be popular. My people will have no issue taking orders from either man."

Desomer sat down. For a moment, he eyed her, considering. Then he reached forward, picked up one of his cigars, lit it, and took a long drag. "There's a fair to middling chance Warlord Ravenstrike might have been right about you, Captain. If you can learn to get past your temper and pride on a consistent basis, you have the instincts to be a real leader one day."

A grin spread across her face. "Yes, sir."

He harrumphed. "Focus on the first part of that sentence, not the last. Challenging Arken this morning was a risky gamble that could have ended very badly for you. Time, hard work, and patience would have achieved the same outcome, yet you couldn't hold your temper or your patience longer than a fortnight." He waited a beat to make sure that sank in, then continued, "Now, let's talk about the distribution of Raiders in these shields." He gathered the papers, shoved them at her. "Start writing."

***

Arya wasn't surprised when Arken approached her in the barracks mess that night after she'd read out the new assignments—there had been cheers at the news of Arken's promotion. Laskin joined her to eat, but while the rest of her ex-shield-mates had all come over to say hello, they sat down with their new shields. Quiet pride filled her at this.

"Captain," Arken said stiffly.

She looked up at him. "Captain. Can I help you?"

"I'm not sure what you hoped to achieve earlier, but everyone here knows I'm the better candidate to be General Desomer's apprentice."

"I know that's what *you* think," she said. "But I know different. You'll figure that out eventually."

Arken's mouth tightened. "Your briefing on the new shields' responsibilities ... Captain Derrin was a good choice."

"Yes, that's why I made it."

The Raider hesitated. "What happened in the yard this morning won't happen again. I recognise that you beat me, and I accept that we must now work together. That doesn't mean I am conceding that one day you will be general instead of me."

"Understood."

"Good night, Captain. I'll see you at drill tomorrow."

"Hopefully a more productive one than this morning?" she asked with a smile.

"I will make sure it is so." He nodded, grim-faced, and strode away.

Arya returned to her bowl of stew, only looking up after a few moments of silence to find Laskin watching her, a look of amusement on his face.

"What?" she snapped.

Laskin's smile widened as he rose with his empty bowl. "Oh, nothing. You enjoy your dinner; I promised to join some of Robem's shield in a card game and they'll be waiting for me."

"I hope you lose everything," she called after him.

He laughed and waved farewell before disappearing through the door. She chuckled to herself as she went back to finishing her dinner. Once done, she rose from her spot at the end of one of the benches and dropped her tray off. Her shoulder ached abominably, so her immediate plans were a long soak in a hot bath before finishing off the work Desomer had set her earlier.

"Evening, Captain."

Arya started as the greeting sounded right beside her. It was from another Raider—she'd stepped back to let a small group of them come through the door before heading out. He was past before she realised he was addressing her, but then the soldiers filing in behind him offered a nod or hello as well.

She stared after them, suppressing a grin.

Some of the weight on her shoulders lessened slightly. She *could* do this.

Chapter 23

In just over a month, winter had officially arrived, not that it hadn't felt like winter for weeks already in the north. The Raider reinforcements from the south arrived as well. Arya joined General Desomer one afternoon to find him fuming over a report he'd received of a fight breaking out between Raiders and Falconcrest Aggressors at a barracks on their southern border.

"Damned Nightstalker better respond to the High Warlord soon so we can send those Aggressors and Lances home, or we're going to have a mini civil war inside our borders," he grumbled at her.

"You look worried about more than a brawl between Raiders and Aggressors, sir."

He sat down with a huff. "We're not prepared for war, Captain."

That was all he'd say on the matter, changing the subject immediately after, but those words stayed with her.

Arya began the painstaking work of training the three new shields, trying to find the balance between letting them know they had a lot to learn without making them think she felt she was superior to them.

It often didn't go well.

"They can see every time you get frustrated at them," Laskin pointed out one day. "Be more patient."

"They have no idea what it's like going on patrol when a Shadeweaver ambush could hit you at any moment, let alone a snow leopard or a life-threatening blizzard," she grumbled.

"Which is why you're teaching them."

"I can't teach them when they don't accept they need to learn."

Essa was another problem she struggled with. She worried that the girl was so close to Rorin all the time, and though Arya tried to be around as much as possible, she was often drawn away by her duties as apprentice to Desomer.

"What's on your mind? I can hear you thinking from here." Taze's voice was teasing, but Arya let out a sigh. She'd just settled at the foot of his bed, wrapped in blankets, but knew she probably wasn't falling asleep anytime soon.

"I—"

Both sat up in surprise when a knock came at the door. It was Rorin, thick cloak over his nightclothes, a mischievous smile on his face and a note clutched in his hand. On it was scribbled, *Will you both come to my room?*

"Are you all right?" she asked in concern. His nose had healed up weeks earlier, and he certainly didn't look sick.

"*I'm fine. Please come,*" he signed.

Arya shared a look with Taze but shrugged and fetched her own cloak from the door. They nodded to the Raider on guard at the end of the hall and filed into the young lord's room.

"Did you have a bad dream or something?" Taze asked.

Rorin shook his head vigorously, pointed at them both, and then in the direction of Taze's room, then signed simply, "*Are* you *both okay?*"

Arya took a moment to figure out why he was asking that, then smiled in understanding. "We're used to sleeping in a room full of people, so it's been hard for us to sleep alone. Don't worry, we'll get used to it."

"We will," Taze agreed. "But it's kind of you to ask the question, Lord Rorin."

Rorin made a face at the title, then turned and made a gesture for them to follow him over to his closet. Opening the door, he stepped inside, and Taze and Arya watched, bemused, as he shoved hanging clothes to each side to reveal the back wall. There, he fumbled with something, and the back of the closet slid sideways.

Rorin glanced back, gave them that mischievous grin, and beckoned. Arya went first, finding herself in a dark, narrow corridor behind the wall of his room. Her chest closed over immediately, her breathing descending to panicked gasps, until she realised she could stand up straight and move her arms. It was dark but not too confined. She swallowed, calming, and was glad of the darkness that neither Taze or Rorin had seen her reaction.

"Hidden corridors?" Taze asked in surprise.

"You'll have to make sure these are guarded," Arya said to Taze immediately. "It's a vulnerability."

Rorin tugged on her sleeve and the three of them returned to his well-lit room. There, he picked up a nearby piece of parchment and charcoal and started writing. The fading fire in his hearth cracked and popped as they waited patiently for him to finish. *Nobody knows about the hidden passageways but me, and I think they're only internal. I can show you where they all go. I thought, if you're lonely at night, you could use them to visit each other, or me. I don't mind keeping you company. I get lonely too sometimes.*

Unexpectedly, tears prickled at Arya's eyes as she read this message. Taze's gaze had gone suspiciously dark too.

"Thank you for sharing your secret with us, Rorin, it's an honour," Arya told him. "Still, Taze is going to have to search all of the passageways, make sure there isn't an entry point that could be a security risk."

"*I understand.*" Rorin signed, shoulders slumping a little.

"You are a good man, to risk your secret to try and help us," Arya said quietly. "As long as Taze can make them safe, we won't tell anyone."

A little smile flickered over the boy's face. "*Do you both want to sleep in here tonight?*"

"I don't know about Taze, but it's much warmer in here." Arya grinned.

"I'll go fetch our blankets." Taze headed for the door.

While he was gone, Rorin wrote something and showed it to Arya. *I'd like to show Darmanin and Essa. They might get lonely too.*

Arya hesitated. "The passageways are your secret, so it's your choice. But when you make that decision, keep in mind that if their existence is ever compromised, they'll have to be blocked up. Remember where Darmanin and Essa came from."

Rorin nodded gravely. *We shouldn't make judgements on them just because of where they come from.*

"No," Arya agreed. "But when you have something to protect, it's not always wise to make too-quick judgements on trusting people, either."

I don't think Darmanin or Essa will hurt me.

Taze returned carting a pile of blankets, and Rorin busied himself helping them create two warm nests to sleep on, even sharing the quilt from his bed. A couch sat at the end of his bed, which Arya took, and it was far more comfortable than the floor in Taze's room.

She stayed awake, thinking, worrying, as she often had since arriving at Heathrock. Tonight, though, her thoughts worried away at a different topic than usual. She feared how trusting Rorin was, how his need for friends and company might obscure his good sense. Might lead to him getting hurt.

Arya had a true home for the first time in her life. A family. Rorin Raven-strike had given her that. So had Desomer in his gruff way, and Peemla with her unhesitating acceptance of Arya into the household. Even Darmanin and their strange shared kinship.

She had to make sure they were safe. At all costs.

***

Several days later, Arya skipped breakfast after drill. A quick peek into the castle kitchens confirmed that Rorin, Darmanin, and Essa were all there enjoying breakfast before lessons started.

Confident she had enough time for what she needed, Arya went upstairs into the guest wing. The door to Essa's room was unlocked, and Arya slipped inside before closing it quietly behind her.

The bed was unmade, clothes strewn in a pile over one chair, though the floor was clear. A faint scent of lavender infused the room. The table under the window was covered with pieces of parchment, a myriad of beautiful drawings. After she flicked through them—finding nothing alarming—her gaze lifted, looking out the window. It faced the east garden.

Arya stepped away and looked around the room. She didn't have much time. After a quick rifle through the desk drawers, Arya methodically searched the rest of the room. Dresses hung in the closet, along with thick scarves and furs. Boots were haphazardly scattered on the floor, undergarments tucked in a pile on the closet's single shelf.

She spent a few moments running her fingers along the back wall of the closet and finding the catch that sprung it open. It was hard to move, getting stuck halfway, but eventually she got it open. There was a passageway behind it, just as Rorin had said.

Arya made a note to remind Taze to ensure the passageways didn't have any external entrances. But even if they didn't, it made her uncomfortable knowing Essa could get to Rorin's room undetected if she wanted to.

A shiver ran through her at another thought: did the passageways have an entrance into Warlord Ravenstrike's room? She made another note to have Taze check that as a priority.

After closing the door and stepping out of the closet, Arya surveyed the room once more. It was a large space—Thiara Ravenstrike had been generous in the quarters she'd assigned Ranier's daughter—but there weren't many obvious hiding places.

There was *something*, though. Arya was certain of it. Essa was not as uncomplicated as she seemed.

Frustrated, she turned to leave, but her eye caught on the thick tapestry hanging on the wall above the girl's bed. She crossed to it, then sat on the edge of the bed to unlace her boots—scuffed boot prints on the sheets would make it obvious someone had been in here. Once she'd tugged them off, Arya clambered onto the bed and lifted the surprisingly heavy cloth.

"Well, well, well." A smile curled at her mouth. "Not so uncomplicated after all."

A square piece of padded hessian had been fixed to the wall behind the tapestry, charcoal lines marking out a target. The fabric at the centre of the target was torn from multiple hits, and when Arya looked closer, it was clear they'd hadn't been made by arrowheads. Besides, the room was large, but not large enough to fire a bow.

Knife points. Essa was using the target to practice her knife throwing. Which meant...

Energised, Arya let the tapestry fall back and dropped off the bed to hurriedly lace up her boots. Then she lifted the girl's mattress and let out a quiet whistle at the rolled-up piece of leather sitting under there. Arya lifted it out, unrolled it on the bed. Three throwing knives sat inside it—but there were straps for two more, and from the wear in them, they'd been used.

Essa was walking around Heathrock armed. A shiver went through Arya at the thought.

What was Ranier's daughter hiding?

***

Peemla was supervising when Arya arrived in the kitchens for a late breakfast. She was relieved to find Essa, Rorin, and Darmanin had already finished and left. Without a word, the chamberlain fetched a plate, filled it with Arya's favourite—fluffy scrambled eggs, crispy bacon, warm bread, and thick butter—and placed it before her.

"You don't have to serve me, Peemla."

"I'm aware of that, Captain. But a nice home-cooked breakfast always makes one feel better. You look a little glum this morning."

The young woman didn't say any more than that, just squeezed Arya's shoulder and returned to her work. After some internal debate while she ate, Arya decided not to confront Essa about her knives. If she did, the girl would just find another way to hide things, not to mention being on guard that Arya was watching her so closely. This way, Arya at least knew what she was hiding.

Laskin's appearance broke her from her thoughts—he usually met Rorin and Darmanin here for their lessons after they'd washed up from breakfast. He sat opposite Arya and snagged a piece of her bread. "Mmm, Peemla makes the best bread."

"Go get your own," she said sourly.

"Not all of us can be the chamberlain's favourites," he said with a mourn-ful sigh.

She made a face at him.

"Some of the Raiders are going to the city tonight for a drink at The *Arms*." Laskin stole another bite of bread, chewed, swallowed, ignored her scowl. "I was told to invite you."

That almost brought a smile to her face. She had yet to be directly invited to join the Raiders on their social time, but occasionally now they'd make it known to Laskin or Taze or one of her ex shield-mates that she'd be welcome to join them. "Thanks, Laskin."

Fortunately, Rorin and Darmanin—Taze in tow—appeared before Laskin could eat any more of her breakfast, and they set off for their weapons' lesson.

"Taze, do you have a moment?" Arya called him back.

"What's on your mind, Captain?" he asked, sitting down and making no attempt to steal parts of her breakfast. "You look worried."

She filled him in on what she'd found in Essa's room, keeping her voice low so only he could hear.

"I'll keep an extra close eye on her when she's with Rorin," he promised immediately. "But..."

"What is it?"

"I'm starting to think she's okay, Captain. I genuinely sense no threat from her."

She scowled at him. "Except for the fact she's carrying around two hid-den weapons at all times."

"We both carry a sword around in this castle without nefarious intent," Taze pointed out. "And given who Essa is, I'd be more surprised if her father *hadn't* taught her to defend herself. Don't forget she's all alone inside the castle of a warlord who hunts her father and his people."

"I could accept all of that, except..."

"Except?"

"I can't figure out why *Ranier* wanted her here. He certainly didn't do it for no reason."

"Good point. Should we—"

Taze's question was interrupted by the sudden ringing of bells through the castle. Arya straightened as she recognised the new alert pattern Desomer had set up.

A check-in with one of the forts had failed.

"I have to go." Arya leaped to her feet. "I could be gone a few weeks. Make sure you keep a close eye on—"

"Essa and her secret knives. Got it, Captain. Stay safe and good luck."

As Arya sprinted for the mounting yards, all thoughts of Essa and Shadeweavers fell from her mind. It was time to put her new shields to the test.

Arya was among the first to arrive in the mounting yard. Arken and Derrin were almost as fast, which she was pleased to see. The Raiders of the three shields also responded with decent speed given they'd never done this before, appearing in the yard armed and dressed.

It went quickly downhill from there.

"Arya!"

She swore under her breath at the sound of the general's voice a short time later. It took her a few moments to figure out in all the chaos where he was, then run to meet him at the top of the steps leading into the castle.

"What's all this?" he barked at her.

She surveyed the yard—a chaotic scramble of sixty Raiders trying to organise themselves and their horses into individual shields and failing miserably—and searched for the right words. Arken and Derrin were trying to sort things out, but they'd never worked together before, and their attempts to help were making things worse.

The sight of Charlin standing off to the side with his horse, watching proceedings with evident amusement, made her want to be swallowed up by a hole in the ground.

She couldn't imagine anything like this ever happening at Icecliff.

"At this rate, you won't be out of the yard before midday," Desomer continued. "SheerRock could be taken out three times over by the time you get there."

"Yes, sir."

"What are you going to do about it? Wraiths could be eating their way through a hundred more Raiders as we speak!"

"I—"

Desomer gave her a glower, then turned away and bellowed at the top of his lungs, "Everyone stop!"

It took a long few moments for the Raiders to cease their frantic preparations and face the general, embarrassing her even further.

"You'll be pleased to know that there is no failed check-in," Desomer told them all in scathing tones. "Which is good news, noting none of you were able to organise yourselves to respond with anything approaching discipline or speed."

Arya felt her face flush red. "You were testing us."

"Good thing I did," he harrumphed, then lifted his voice again. "Make sure you do better next time. A good first step might be trying it again, right now."

The Raiders all saluted, and Arya muttered, "We will, sir."

"Leading a single shield well-practiced in working together is a different thing than leading multiple shields," Desomer told her. "You've never done it before. You'll have to learn."

"I will," she promised.

Once the general had gone, Arya headed back down the steps to meet Derrin and Arken, who looked as shamefaced as she felt.

"We should have thought of this," Derrin said glumly.

"No shit," Arya snapped. "Come on, let's try it again."

Arken cleared his throat. "Perhaps a plan before we try it again? Otherwise we'll just have the same chaos."

She bit down hard on the dismissive reply she wanted to make, because he was right. "What do you suggest?"

***

After a long and trying day working with the three shields, Arya took up Laskin's invitation of a drink in town. As dusk fell, she saddled up her horse and rode out.

The temperature dropped with the fading of the day and Arya pulled her cowl up over her head as her mare entered the city gates, forced to slow to a walk given how busy the main streets were. She rode up through two levels of winding city streets before reining in outside The Ruined Arms.

It was warm inside, and cheerful music filtered through the hum of conversation. Arya spotted Laskin sitting with a couple of shield captains and went to get a drink from the bar—making sure to get a round for each of them—before going to sit down, taking her cowl and cloak off with a sigh of relief and throwing them on the pile with the others.

"Captain." Derrin acknowledged her with a smile and thanks for his drink. At least after the day they'd had he was still talking to her.

Laskin tipped his head at her. The others at the table acknowledged her too, even if they weren't jumping for joy at her presence. It was progress, and she was determined to keep making more of it.

Time passed in pleasant conversation. Arya was halfway through her third mug of ale when a new musician took over. This man's music was particularly good, a far sight better than anything else she'd heard here before. She twisted in her seat to look towards the corner of the room where he played. He sat cradling a lute, fiery copper curls tied loosely at his nape, eyes half closed as he sank into his music. He was barely older than her, maybe eighteen or so—young to have such skill.

"His name is Chiarn," Derrin said over the noise of the inn when he caught her looking. "Notice how it's more full than usual in here tonight? People heard he would be playing. He's been gaining popularity with every town in the north he's travelled to."

"I'm sure he's popular with the ladies, as well," Arya said, watching him open those sleepy eyes to wink at a pretty woman clapping in appreciation.

Torren chuckled. "I heard he got run out of Saunders last month for sleeping with the mayor's only daughter."

Saunders was Ravenstrike's largest mining town, where there was a Raider barracks—Arya presumed Torren had heard this through the Raider gossip network. She laughed and turned back to the table, dismissing the singer from her mind. He was handsome enough to consider taking to bed—she enjoyed either women or men as bedding partners—but she was already sorted in that department.

"Who's up for a game of cards?" Laskin asked, pulling a well-worn pack from his pocket.

Arya snorted. "The last time we played, I beat you soundly. You still owe me five silver pieces."

"And now's my chance to win them back," he said.

"I'll play," Derrin said.

Arya drained her glass, about to agree when she caught sight of the inn owner's daughter, Tiya, entering through the swinging door from the kitchens, carrying a tray of cleaned mugs that she passed to the bartender. When her bright blue eyes fell on Arya, she smiled and lifted an eyebrow in question.

Arya hesitated briefly, but not long. Tension still lined her shoulders and neck from her massive failure earlier that morning, and there was one sure-fire way of soothing it outside a hot bath. "I've got a better offer, boys." She rose from the table. "Don't let Laskin fleece you again, Derrin."

Laskin snorted as he caught sight of Tiya. "A better offer indeed."

Arya crossed the inn, following Tiya as she pushed through the swinging doors into the corridor leading to the kitchens.

"Hello you." Tiya reached out to her waist, tugging her in for a kiss. Her unusual silver-white curls brushed against Arya's cheek, light as a feather. Arya sank into the kiss, eyes closing in the simple pleasure of the contact. They'd met on one of Arya's first visits to the inn, on a night when she'd been feeling particularly despondent over her reception among the Raiders and before she'd started sleeping in the same room as Taze or Rorin. She'd sat alone at the bar, and Tiya had made a point of talking to her, sensing her loneliness. She was funny and relaxed and exactly what Arya had needed to take her mind off everything.

"Hello yourself." Arya frowned as her hands settled on Tiya's hips. The girl was waiflike, all skin and bone. "Does your father not earn enough to feed you?"

"Step-father. And you'd be surprised at how much I eat." Tiya tossed her head and smiled archly. "I'll be finished up here shortly. Wait in my room?"

Arya leaned down for another kiss. "Don't be too long."

"Oh, I won't." Tiya winked, slipped her room key into Arya's palm, then ducked back into the inn, calling over her shoulder, "And I'll bring some honey wine."

Arya was about to make her way upstairs when Laskin pushed through the doors from the inn. "Urgent message from the general. He says the warlord wants you both right away."

Any disappointment Arya might have felt about missing a night with Tiya was overshadowed by equal parts curiosity and concern. She passed the key back to Tiya with a quick apology and headed straight out into the icy night to mount up her mare.

Desomer was waiting for her in his office, and the moment she knocked at his door, he rose from his desk and waved her after him down the hall to the warlord's office.

The door was open, and Thiara Ravenstrike looked up as they entered. Magen was there, as was Matte Eaglesoar. Both Desomer and Arya saluted then stood at attention.

"Thank you for coming so quickly," Warlord Ravenstrike said briskly. "It's late, so I won't bandy about. I received a missive from High Warlord Eaglesoar only an hour ago. The Nightstalker has proposed a summit between our two countries so that"—her eyes dropped to a piece of parchment—"'*we may discuss in person the offensive claims made in your recent missive after decades of peace and silence between our two kingdoms.*'"

For the first time since Arya had met him, Desomer looked startled. "Where?"

Thiara Ravenstrike gave them a grim look. "The Nightstalker and his wyvern are coming here."

Chapter 24

'Here' turned out to be Ravenstrike State—specifically, Windfall Fort, the third of Ravenstrike's border forts and the one that perched above the massive port city of Aren.

All six Dunidae warlords, in addition to the High Warlord, were travelling to the summit, which was set for exactly one month from when the Nightstalker had sent his missive.

"Real flexible in setting deadlines for us to show up," Desomer grumbled ceaselessly. "It's no diplomatic summit. It's a meeting organised and chaired by a foreign king. High Warlord Eaglesoar should have pushed back on the date, at the very least, if not outright refused."

"There is good for us in this," Magen pointed out each time Desomer complained. "Holding the summit in Ravenstrike and having all the warlords travel here reflects well on our importance as a State."

The general came straight back with, "Maybe if the High Warlord had chosen the location. But he didn't; the Nightstalker did. He's turned us into naughty children being summoned to the tutor's office."

"It's not quite as dramatic as all that," Thiara Ravenstrike said. "The southern warlords will be able to travel faster to Aren via ship, and the fort is a defensible location if the Nightstalker tries anything. Which seems unlikely, given he says he's travelling alone on Xaphistryl."

"A great bloody big wyvern," Desomer pointed out, then lifted his hands in surrender when the warlord levelled a look on him.

Arya had mixed feelings. She'd been desperately hoping the whole Nightstalker situation would fade away into memory, but now he was coming to Dunidaen, bringing all the dangers to her position rising to the surface again.

At the same time, being part of something like this, negotiations on a grand scale, was everything she'd ever wanted, and Desomer would be taking her with him to Aren. She ignored the little voice in her head that whispered that Salyarin would be horrified at the idea of her being in such close proximity to the Nightstalker.

The elder clearly believed Arya was Andahar's lost heir, but that didn't mean it was true. She had no magic, she reasoned, no wyvern. Besides, she was far too low in rank to come anywhere near direct contact with a foreign king.

No, she would go to Aren and soak in the experience. And hopefully the summit would resolve any lingering frictions between the two kingdoms and Arya could come home and focus on learning to be the future general of Ravenstrike.

She was soon too busy to worry about any of it anyway.

Desomer was responsible for the security of their trip to Windfall Fort, and Arya was occupied for every spare moment leading up to their departure; writing orders, checking supplies, ensuring Raiders' weapons were ready, horses were shod, and making sure anything else Desomer tasked her with was carried out in quick and efficient fashion.

It meant even less time with Rorin, Darmanin, and Essa, which bothered her given what she'd learned about Essa's knives, but Taze assured her he was keeping a close eye. She managed a couple of trips outside the walls with Darmanin, where they found an isolated spot in the foothills for him to practice. As uncomfortable as it was for her to see him use his magic so openly, he did seem to be improving his control over it.

"Stop looking so worried," Darmanin said as they rode back to the castle one morning. "I'll be fine while you're gone."

"What makes you think it's you I'm worried about?" she grumbled. "You're actually lower on my list right now."

He gave her a look. "Not everything is your responsibility, Arya Nameless."

She hesitated, then, "You'll keep an eye on Essa while we're away?" Essa and Darmanin weren't coming to the summit, Thiara Ravenstrike having no desire to advertise the fact she'd taken two Shadeweavers into her household.

"Are you asking me to make sure she's safe, or make sure everyone else here is safe from her?"

Arya looked away, toying with her reins. "Both, Darmanin."

He lifted an eyebrow. "Have you asked Essa to do the same as regards me?"

She huffed an exasperated breath. No, she hadn't. "Believe it or not, I trust that you'll hold to your word to Warlord Ravenstrike. I don't trust Essa because I don't understand her father's motivations in placing her here."

"I'll look out for her," he said quietly.

***

Thiara Ravenstrike arrived at Aren the day before the summit, accompanied by her husband, Magen, Desomer, Arya, and the warlord's personal shield of Raiders. Rorin rode with his parents in their carriage—the warlord had been insistent on him accompanying them, noting the opportunity for her future heir to learn.

They made their way up a long, paved road that connected the port city to the imposing fort that stood in the lower reaches of the Diamondfang, looming high above. The High Warlord's flag—the Eaglesoar emblem of a golden eagle on blue background—flew on the battlements.

And then they were riding through the gates into a busy entry yard. The warlord's shield was well practiced at dispersing to manage their horses at visiting stables, so Desomer and Arya were free to follow the warlord, her husband and son, and Magen, straight into the fort.

Delight shimmered through Arya. *This.* This was what she'd wanted so badly. To accompany those who mattered, to be involved in the decision making rather than being left outside to stable her horse and find something to eat in the mess.

"Warlord Ravenstrike. Welcome."

Arya stilled instantly at the sound of that voice, a hand falling to the hilt of her sword. Her body unconsciously shifted into a fighting stance and her practiced gaze swept the dim interior, searching for what every instinct in her identified as a threat.

The man who'd spoken stepped out of the gloom. He was tall, broad-shouldered, with light-brown hair and a neatly trimmed beard, and he was richly dressed, with hints of violet and black throughout his clothing. Arya blinked at the dissonance. This man appeared to be a lord, not an assassin or Shadeweaver. Desomer levelled a scowl at her and she relaxed her stance, dropped her hand away from her sword.

"Warlord Crowtalon." Thiara's voice was terse. "As this is my fort, I'll welcome you here, and not the other way around."

Arya whipped her head between them. *This* was Darmanin's father? The warlord who stood between Thiara Ravenstrike and her ambition to be High Warlord? From the corner of her eye, she saw both Matte Eaglesoar and Rorin shift closer to Thiara.

Crowtalon bowed his head. "I was merely being polite. And since I arrived before you, I have organised a dinner for this evening, once all warlords have arrived. It will give us an opportunity to ensure that we are all ... unified ... before tomorrow. I have some ideas about how we should present ourselves. Your fort mess has been advised to prepare the appropriate food."

The words were polite, reasonable, and yet ... the way he spoke them, the look he levelled on Thiara Ravenstrike. It was challenge and contempt all wrapped together. Rorin bristled at her side, echoing Arya's feelings. How dare he give orders to a Raider mess?

"I'll be there," Arya's warlord responded simply. She didn't seem inclined to engage in a battle of wills in her entry foyer. But she did turn and walk off, ceasing the conversation before Crowtalon could.

"Thiara," he called after her as they reached a set of steps. "How is my son?"

She turned, held his gaze. "I assume you know far better than I do how Andrian is. I'm surprised you didn't bring him."

His mouth tightened, slightly. "You know what I'm asking."

"My understanding is that you only acknowledge having one son, Mathas?" Thiara lifted a single eyebrow.

Crowtalon took a step forward. Arya wasn't sure what he planned to do or say, only that there was menace oozing from every line of his body. Again she reached for her sword. But then a group of men clattered through the doors from outside, most wearing a green and brown uniform. A big, gruff-looking man strode at their head, his eyes taking in the tableau before him.

"Warlord Ravenstrike." His voice boomed loudly enough to carry to the stables outside. "Damned annoying that you beat me here, but there it goes. Pleasure to see you."

"Warlord Hawkesdale. Welcome to Ravenstrike." What Arya thought was a genuine smile crossed Thiara Ravenstrike's face.

"Thank you." Hawkesdale's gaze shifted to Mathas Crowtalon. "Hello, Crowtalon."

"Hawkesdale." Crowtalon bowed his head, then turned and strode away.

Thiara's shoulders relaxed slightly. "Please make yourself comfortable, Gelfrey. There's a dinner planned this evening if you can make it. Crowtalon wants to make sure we all show a unified front tomorrow."

"Oh he does, does he?" Hawkesdale grunted. "The man hasn't realised he's not High Warlord yet, I take it? All right, I'll be there. Interesting times we find ourselves in, Thiara."

"Interesting indeed. There's another matter I'd like to speak with you about while you're here, if you can find time for it?"

"How intriguing." He bowed his head. "And of course I will make time. See you at dinner."

***

To Arya's disappointment, she wasn't invited to the dinner, and so she spent the evening with Rorin, doing some of the work their tutor had set for them to complete while away.

She was up at dawn the following morning for drill, even though she was distracted enough to take a few good hits—a mixture of anticipation, excitement, and little bit of fear of what the day might bring making it hard to focus.

The missive from the Nightstalker had been low on detail, and nobody knew exactly when he planned to arrive. Given none wished to miss it, they started gathering out in the entrance yard not long after the watery winter sun had fully risen over the horizon.

"Look at them all waiting around on a foreign king, like he's worth wasting their time," Desomer grumbled.

Personal servants hurried about, bringing their masters hot cups of tea and platters of food. Each warlord had also brought their chief adviser and general, or the captain of their personal guard, so it made for a busy yard. She recognised Crowtalon and Hawkesdale—one remote and watchful, the other loudly proclaiming his enjoyment of the crisp morning and buttery roll he was eating. High Warlord Darien Eaglesoar leaned on another man's arm, his stooped shoulders and shock of white hair proclaiming his increasing age. Arya picked out the Eaglesoar, SparrowWing, and Falconcrest warlords by their rich dress and colours.

Desomer continued, "Warlord, I recommend we all go inside. When he shows, then we can make a song and dance about his arrival. The power imbalance here is already lopsided enough."

"I'm in agreement with you, General," she remarked. "But to hear the warlords talk at dinner last night, they're as afraid of what it means that the Nightstalker is coming here as they are excited to see this mythic figure in the flesh. If I go inside, they won't follow, and then I'll be the only warlord to miss his arrival."

That conversation was Arya's first direct taste of the limitations of Thiara Ravenstrike's influence. Or that of any individual warlord. It now seemed clearer why she so strongly wanted to be High Warlord.

"Dismissed, Arya," Desomer told her then. "I expect you to attend once the Nightstalker arrives and the summit starts, but only for learning purposes, understood? You stay at the back of the room with Lord Rorin, and you do nothing to draw attention to yourself."

"Understood, sir."

Thiara turned to her. "You are to impress those same instructions on my son, also."

Arya saluted again and then weaved her way through the crowded yard to the steps leading up to the front entry, her intention to find Rorin and give him a sparring lesson while they waited.

But just as her boots hit the top step, a scream tore through the morning. The sound froze Arya in her tracks at the same time as it sent a thundering compulsion to hide flooding through her body. She sucked in a shocked breath, then gritted her teeth and fought the feeling, one hand reaching for her sword as she turned back.

A shadow washed over the sunny courtyard and another scream tore through the air, this one challenging, both deep and high-pitched all at once.

The cry of a wyvern.

The compulsion to flee and hide deepened to an almost unbearable urge. Arya swallowed, shook her head. She'd heard the fantastic rumours that a wyvern's call could freeze a man in his tracks, send entire armies fleeing in terror, but she'd never credited them. When, through sheer will, she was able to master her reaction enough to take in the scene below, she found those in the entry yard experiencing a similar reaction. Some—including Warlord Falconcrest and Darien Eaglesoar—were even backing uncon-sciously towards the steps. Only two figures remained standing straight, apparently unshaken, gazes fixed on the sky.

Thiara Ravenstrike and Mathas Crowtalon.

She had a moment to be impressed by the sheer strength of will they displayed before another shadow swept over the courtyard. This time the scream was unbearably loud and directly overhead. An enormous, winged shape dropped out of the sky, sending the Raiders on guard scattering as it landed on the battlements beside the gates.

The Nightstalker's wyvern was enormous—the man on her back tiny in comparison. Xaphistryl lifted her serpentine head to roar another challenge, her outspread wings stretched almost the entire length of the southern wall. Her fangs had to be as long as Arya's arm, and she rose at least two stories high, ink-black scales rippling in the sunlight. The shadow of her presence cast the courtyard and everyone in it into darkness.

As the echoes of her deafening roar forced those gathered to press hands to their ears, her sweeping tail knocked into a parapet, sending thick stone crumbling to the ground as if it were chalk. Something inside her told Arya this was deliberate, a show of strength and invincibility.

An instinct for self-preservation had Arya backing slowly away, inside the fort. She was too exposed as the lone person at the top of the fort steps, and even though she believed the Etherean elder was wrong about her, she still didn't want the Nightstalker's attention to fall on her.

Because now she knew.

She hadn't even seen a hint of his magic, yet she already knew. Why Dunidaen had been so frightened of the Nightstalker that they'd shunned and feared all magic-wielders since, for fear they might join his ranks.

This Sky Lord was an existential threat.

Chapter 25

Heart still racing and palms slick with sweat, Arya went straight to fetch Rorin and Taze. The young heir was waiting with poorly concealed impatience in his room.

"*Was that screaming his wyvern? Is he here?*" Rorin signed the moment she walked in. "*That cry … it made me want to crawl under my bed and never come out.*"

"He's here." She held up a hand to stop him as he went to rush past her. Suddenly, she was unsure whether Rorin being in the same room as the man who rode that wyvern was a good idea. "Remember, we stay at the back and out of sight. We're here to observe and learn only."

"*Yes, yes, I know already, Arya.*"

She still held him back. "The Nightstalker … he's dangerous, Rorin. You stay out of his notice."

He clearly read something on her face because he nodded more seriously this time. "*I trust your judgement and will do as you say. Can we go now?*"

"Taze, keep a close watch," she ordered as they left the room, even though she didn't need to. He was as watchful as she'd ever seen him. Clearly that wyvern's cry had affected him, too, even inside the walls.

By the time Arya and Rorin entered the elegantly converted mess hall—Taze remaining outside with the guards posted there—it was full to bursting. Apart from the Raiders of Thiara Ravenstrike's personal shield lining the walls, rows of benches facing a dais at one end of the hall were filled with chief advisers, personal shield captains, a general or two, family members, and scribes.

When Rorin moved forward, aiming for a lone remaining space at the end of one of the benches, Arya tugged him back. Ignoring his protesting expression, she drew him along the back wall among the gathered Raiders and staff who didn't warrant a chair. Once they were situated, and she was confident they didn't stand out, she finally turned her attention to the dais.

The Nightstalker instantly drew her attention. He wore his black hair swept back from his face, highlighting fey, ascetic features and pale skin. He was tall, too, lean and sinewy, his dark clothes perfectly tailored to show his frame to best effect. But none of that was what drew the eye.

It was his magic.

Or at least, she assumed that's what shimmered in the air around him with every gesture, every movement. Not visible, but just *there* somehow. Not only that, but for a man who had to be at least sixty, he didn't look a day over thirty years old.

Arya swallowed, looked away as a sense of vertigo swept through her. Her heartrate had sped up and her palms were sweating again. By the time she'd taken a few deep breaths and settled, the warlords had seated themselves and the High Warlord began speaking.

"Welcome to Dunidaen, King Lucius." Darien Eaglesoar spoke with a courtier's grace. "We thank you for travelling all this way to discuss the recent misunderstanding on our shared border."

There were a few rustles and murmurs throughout the room at that phrasing, but nobody spoke out.

"We have been at peace so long, High Warlord." The Nightstalker sat relaxed in his chair, one booted foot stretched out, both arms laid casually on the armrests. "It would be a shame to ruin that because of baseless accusations, would it not?"

Darien opened his mouth, no doubt planning a polite reply, but Mathas Crowtalon beat him to it. "The High Warlord's missive merely sought understanding of why you dug through the underground road and sent wraiths and shadowhounds into our country, Your Grace."

"The wording was polite enough, but it clearly accused me of planning invasion," the Nightstalker responded. "Which is offensive and untrue."

"You killed hundreds of Dunidae soldiers without provocation." This from Thiara Ravenstrike, quiet but firm. "And now you claim to be *offended* that we demanded to know why? You would be wise not to treat us as fools, King Lucius."

The Nightstalker went still, head cocked—like a hawk surveying its prey, Arya thought—as he turned to the Ravenstrike warlord. A ripple went through the air around him, but it was gone as quickly as it had come. "Those deaths were ... unfortunate, Warlord, and not my intention."

She was fearless, quick as a striking snake. "So you didn't *intend* to take out the fort guarding the underground road in the hopes of getting more of your wraiths and shadowhounds into Dunidaen without detection? That happened by accident, did it? How convenient."

Darien Eaglesoar cleared his throat. "What Warlord Ravenstrike means, Your Grace—"

"Perhaps now isn't the time to fling accusations at each other," Mathas Crowtalon cut in. "If you are so offended by our suspicions of invasion, King Lucius, would you enlighten us as to the reason for your incursion into our borders?"

Arya began to see why Crowtalon was such a threat to her warlord. He'd initially taken over the conversation from the High Warlord with ease, and the old man seemed happy to let him do it. Then he'd sidelined her warlord when she'd attempted to wrest control back, while simultaneously managing to rebuke her for being rude. He looked strong up on that dais, too, calm, and clearly unbothered by the sheer danger the Nightstalker exuded.

"A fair question." The Nightstalker pressed his hands together, offering a grave nod to Crowtalon. Arya wondered if anyone else was buying the false politeness. "It came to my attention that there were ... malcontents in our shared border region that present a threat to my rule and the stability of Andahar. I sent my wraiths and shadowhounds to find them."

"One might wonder why you didn't simply ask for our assistance in hunting these malcontents rather than invading without permission," Thiara said coolly.

The Nightstalker's mouth tightened, only slightly, but almost every warlord at that table cowered. "Every single one of my wraiths and shadowhounds was killed. *I* might wonder whether you did that to prevent them from either killing or delivering to me those I hunted."

Arya was hard pressed to hide a gasp. The Etherean elder had been right. Assuming the Nightstalker was telling the truth, he *had* sent those creatures to find someone. She swallowed. It couldn't be her, of course. But still, the elder had been right in part.

The Nightstalker looked up suddenly, his gaze roving the room. Arya felt a sharp tug in her chest, a closing grip that demanded submission. Cold sweat broke out over her skin at the sensation of that touch, like the burn of cold iron pressed against bare skin on a bitterly cold winter's day.

Someone tugged on her sleeve. Rorin. She swallowed again, tried to look at him, but the *thing* pulling at her was forcing her to turn towards the Nightstalker, to break free of the crowd along the wall and walk towards him. To reveal herself.

Her breath grew short in her chest the longer she fought the compulsion, and her fists were clenched so hard at her sides that her nails, dug into her palms, drew blood. Fear curled in her stomach. She couldn't fight it. She ... her breath quickened to near-panic levels.

What was he doing?

Warm fingers closed over hers, squeezed. She let the hand pull her, instinctively knowing it was safe. But as she let herself be pulled away, the fierce grip in her chest grew stronger, more demanding. Her ribs felt as if they were being pulled through her skin. Arya tried to focus, but everything was a blur, her breathing too loud in her ears, her head ringing.

Dimly, she heard a door click shut. The warm hand in hers kept tugging, gentle but insistent, and it took everything she had to let it, but she did.

And then her boot tripped, and she sprawled forward, crashing hard to the ground. The pain of slamming her left shin into stone was sharp and intense and snapped her out of whatever fog it was that had gripped her.

She looked around, blinking, trying to understand where she was. She'd tripped on the first step of a narrow stairwell. Rorin crouched on the step above her, worry written all over his face as he signed at her, over and over again. *"You okay? You okay? You okay?"*

She swallowed. "It was you that dragged me out of there?"

He nodded. *"What's wrong?"*

"I think ... I don't know." She looked around. "Where's Taze?"

"Still around guarding the front. I brought you out a side door."

She was sweating, shaky, vaguely nauseous. She needed a moment of space, a chance to breathe. "Can you help me upstairs. Your room?"

He reached out a hand, helping her to her feet. The compulsion had lessened now, the pain seeming to break some of its hold, but it was still there, and she needed Rorin's help to force her reluctant legs further away from the mess hall.

At some point on the journey, the compulsion faded completely. As soon as they were through the door into his room, Rorin started signing. *"It was him, wasn't it? The Nightstalker did something to you?"*

"I don't know what he did ... but yes, it was him." She sank down on Rorin's bed, head between her knees, trying to regain her equilibrium. When her heartbeat finally steadied, she looked up to meet his concerned blue gaze. "I think you might have saved my life just now."

His impish grin flashed out. *"Well now we're even, then."*

Dread crept over her. "Who saw what happened?"

"I took us out quietly. Side exit. Everyone was watching the front. I made myself look really bored, so if anyone did see they'd think that's why I was sneaking out." Rorin paused. *"I waited until the Nightstalker was looking away before moving. He was talking to the warlords, but looking around the room at the same time. It looked like he was searching for something. I thought it best he didn't see us leave."*

Gratitude filled her. In the most vulnerable moment of her life, she'd been able to rely so completely on a fourteen-year-old boy, and he'd come through for her.

"Your instincts are good. Thank you."

"Why do you think he affected you like that? Was he using his magic on you?"

She rubbed at her still sore chest. "Did anyone else look like they were affected like me? Did anyone stand up or walk out into the open?"

"I was mostly focused on you, but no, I don't think so. You should stay here till he leaves," Rorin said. *"But if you're okay, I'd best go back so mother doesn't notice me gone too long."*

"Stay at the back," she warned him. "Don't come to his attention. And when you leave, make sure you take Taze with you."

"I will," he promised. *"And I'll let mother and General Desomer know that you ate some bad fish at breakfast so had to leave early and I helped you get back here."*

She managed a smile for him. "Now it is me who is in your debt, Rorin Ravenstrike."

Once the door closed behind Rorin, Arya sagged onto the bed, closing her eyes. She felt like she'd gone on a three-day patrol in a blizzard and fought her way through multiple ambushes.

Then, fear still lurking, she forced herself to recall what had happened. The Nightstalker had told the warlords he'd been looking for rebels, and then he'd suddenly looked up, as if something in the room had caught his attention.

After that it was blurry, but something inside her had responded to the Nightstalker, had wanted to do as he demanded.

Reveal herself.

She relaxed slightly at that thought. Someone in the room had caught his attention, but he hadn't known who. He'd used his magic to try and force her into the open, to learn her identity. But Rorin had gotten her out before that had happened.

Arya didn't even try to lie to herself. Nobody else in the room had responded the way she had, or it would have been obvious—she'd only gotten away with it because she was right at the back of the room and Rorin had made such an effort to be discreet.

The Nightstalker had sensed her there, and he'd wanted her. If she put that together with what Salyarin had claimed...

His wraiths and shadowhounds *had* come to Dunidaen searching for her.

Arya let out a long, shaky breath, and curled up, closing her eyes tightly.

She couldn't be what Salyarin said. She didn't want to be.

But she was. She was the lost heir to Andahar.

Chapter 26

When the door opened later that afternoon to admit Rorin and Taze, the sight of them was a welcome relief after so much time alone dwelling on what had happened. Her head throbbed dully.

"How are you feeling, Captain?" Taze asked.

"Better." She waved off the question. "How did the rest of the summit go?"

"*I'm not entirely sure.*" Rorin signed. "*I couldn't hear all of it, but the Nightstalker made some demands, and it caused a lot of consternation between the warlords. General Desomer looked even grumpier than usual.*"

"The Nightstalker left right after," Taze added. "I got a look at his wyvern—she's magnificent. And terrifying."

Arya straightened her uniform. "I'd best go find the general."

"*You should stay here.*" Rorin's look was pointed. "*And rest until your stomach settles properly.*"

"I'll be fine, Rorin." She gave him a reassuring smile as she shrugged on her cloak and left.

The Raider on guard outside the warlord's quarters let Arya through without question, or even a glare, which she didn't fail to notice. Inside, though, any pleasure she might have felt at that vanished abruptly. Desomer was just settling into a chair near the hearth, as was Magen. Matte Eaglesoar sat between them, and Thiara Ravenstrike paced in front of the fire. The mood was so grim it was palpable.

"What happened?" Arya asked without thinking, before wincing and saluting sharply when all eyes turned to her.

Thiara's gaze raked her. "Rorin said you were sick."

"Bad stomach," Arya managed. "I still feel a little queasy, but it seems to have settled."

"You vomit in front of me and we're done, Nameless," Desomer barked from his chair.

"Understood, sir," she said.

"All right, gentlemen." Thiara addressed the room. "Thoughts?"

Relief cascaded through Arya. The warlord was going to let her stay. She told herself to remain quiet and not do or say anything that might get her dismissed.

Desomer started. "Warlord, that wasn't a summit. That was the Nightstalker taking the opportunity to waltz in here, threaten us to our faces, and demand we do as he wants or else."

"I'm not an idiot, General," Thiara snapped. "I do realise that."

"Had to be said," he grumbled.

"It may not be as bad as all that," Magen counselled. "After all, General, you have increased our watch on the pass and the underground road and put an effective warning system in place. If the Nightstalker does move again, we'll know about it faster and be better prepared."

"You heard the High Warlord after the Nightstalker left. He's going to withdraw the Aggressors and Lances he sent here to bolster our Raiders—and he expects me to take full responsibility for securing the border." Thiara's mouth thinned. "I fear he does not fully appreciate what happened here today."

Arya swore inwardly. It sounded like she'd missed a meeting of the warlords after the summit.

"No doubt he was distracted by all the little power battles between you and Crowtalon," Desomer said, mostly under his breath.

When Thiara rounded on him, fury on her face, Desomer sank further into his chair, but Magen cleared his throat and waded in. "If you manage the High Warlord's expectations successfully, your case to be his successor becomes immeasurably stronger. What other warlord can claim to have single-handedly kept our country safe from a threat as powerful as the Nightstalker?"

Thiara's gaze narrowed, and she stopped pacing for a moment as she considered that.

Desomer cleared his throat. "I'm sorry, Warlord, but the Nightstalker just told us that if we don't assist him in hunting down and handing over the 'malcontents' threatening his throne, he will do what is necessary to quell the threat himself. We know what that means."

Arya went cold. She suddenly felt incredibly exposed, like somehow they would all magically know she was the one the Nightstalker was looking for. The fire in the hearth suddenly popped, and she literally jumped.

Thiara gave her an unamused glance, then waved a hand at Desomer. "The High Warlord seemed to think we could make a show of doing that well enough to satisfy him."

"He's wrong," Desomer said. "We don't know who these malcontents are, nor could the Nightstalker provide any descriptive details except that they are magic-wielders and have taken refuge in the northwest of Raven-strike."

"What of Crowtalon's suggestion?" Magen asked, so quiet in comparison to Desomer it was almost comical. "It has merit, Warlord."

"I'm no more a fan of magic-wielders than anyone, Magen, but agreeing to hand over any magic-wielder we capture in Dunidaen to the Nightstalker is a dangerous precedent to set," she said. "They are Dunidae citizens. Agreeing to such a thing is an affront to our sovereignty."

"Yet it is a painless way of giving the Nightstalker what he wants. And by doing it, we wouldn't only be securing our country but ridding ourselves of its most dangerous elements."

A cold sweat prickled on Arya's skin, and it was a fight not to let herself shift anxiously from foot to foot. She could see the sense of what Magen was saying, but what would it mean for her ... for Darmanin too. But also for Shadeweavers who'd attacked and killed her friends and comrades, she reminded herself.

And what about the branded man she'd seen begging on the streets of Heathrock? What had he done that he deserved to be handed over to a foreign king, presumably to be slaughtered?

Desomer snorted. "Let's not beat around the bush. The Nightstalker is setting up invasion quite nicely. The minute we don't do what he wants, or he decides we're not doing enough to find and hand over these rebels, he has the excuse to invade us on the grounds of securing his country."

"I respect your strategic judgement, General, and I do not necessarily disagree," Magen said. "But the point remains that there was a good reason the Nightstalker didn't invade Dunidaen after he stole the Andahari throne—and hasn't in the years since. We have a strong army—"

Another snort. "You saw that bloody wyvern. She could eat a shield of Raiders in the blink of an eye."

"—that he must think carefully about before challenging," Magen finished. "Not to mention the cazaix weapons that the Khadini can wield against him. If we can calm any fears he has about Dunidaen harbouring threats to him, there is a good chance he'll be content within his own borders."

"The Khadini have those weapons, not us," Desomer argued. "Nobody has gone through the Dreadwater Gate and run the rapids since Crowtalon, so it's not even like we have a bunch of warlords and their heirs running about with stolen cazaix blades that could threaten a wyvern."

Arya frowned. Why did cazaix blades matter?

"That sounds good to me," Thiara remarked dryly. "We send Crowtalon and his cazaix sword off to face the Nightstalker and his wyvern."

Matte shifted then, rising to go to his wife and lay a gentle hand on her shoulder. At that touch, she finally ceased her constant pacing, and offered him a little smile. Magen and Desomer shared a look.

A silence fell, and Arya couldn't help herself. She had to know. "Warlord, General. Can I ask … how were things left with the Nightstalker?"

Desomer let out a heavy sigh. "He 'apologised' for sending wraiths and shadowhounds across our border without notice and killing Raiders, promised to be a good neighbour from now on, but made it clear in no uncertain terms he wants these rebels hunted down and handed over."

Thiara looked up, as if she were watching the day's earlier events play out on the ceiling. "The High Warlord accepted his apology and assured him that the full Council of Dunidae warlords and vicelords would discuss the best way to provide the assistance he requests. The Nightstalker agreed to wait for word after the State Council, implied unpalatable consequences if the proposal wasn't to his satisfaction, then left."

Arya swallowed around a dry throat. Suddenly the cosy room felt stiflingly hot and she wished she could take her cloak off. "How does the Nightstalker even know about these malcontents, or where they are?" The elder had said something about a wyvern being born that might have tipped off the Nightstalker to her existence, but that wouldn't tell him *where* she was in Ravenstrike. Or even that she was in Dunidaen at all. Not to mention there was no wyvern.

Thiara sighed heavily. "When the coup in Andahar happened, some of those who fought against the Nightstalker fled over the Diamondfang. He chased them down and killed them—it's what brought us so close to war back then—but there is a chance some slipped his hunter's net. His magic would likely warn him of their existence."

Arya's gaze flickered to her in curiosity—there'd been something in Thiara's voice then ... some odd emotion she couldn't quite pin down.

"Our spies and scouts haven't reported anything about Andahari rebels causing trouble in our State," Desomer pointed out. "Or even existing. And anyone that fled Andahar after the coup would be pretty old by now."

"Let's say out loud what the Nightstalker heavily implied and what we all know must be true," Thiara Ravenstrike said flatly. "He believes more Sky Lord potentials have been born. That is the only threat he'd take seriously enough to consider war with us."

"And they're running around the Diamondfang?" Magen asked sceptically.

Thiara looked suddenly weary. "If the Nightstalker truly intends invasion, we cannot stop him; we can only prepare. I will raise the possibility at the next State Council and push for a Dunidaen-wide response. In the meantime, we continue our close watch on the border. That is the best we can do."

The conversation moved on then, Magen and Desomer offering their thoughts on the various warlords' responses to the Nightstalker summit, Thiara contributing now and then, Matte rarely. Desomer lit a cigar, and the strong scent of it drifted through the room on smoky tendrils.

Arya tried to pay attention, but her mind kept drifting. The sweat was clammy on her skin, and fear lodged like a boulder in her stomach. If those gathered in this room knew that she was the one the Nightstalker wanted, and possibly Darmanin too, would they hand them both over to safeguard their country?

Of course they would. A Nameless and a Shadeweaver youth was a small price to pay for preventing a war that would cost innumerable lives, damage the country, and still not be guaranteed to win.

She tried to steady her breathing and calm the fear. She was no threat to the Nightstalker. She had no intention of trying to steal his throne, no matter who she supposedly was, an intention even more certain after seeing him today.

She had her life here, in Dunidaen, as future general of Ravenstrike. If she did nothing, made no moves, surely the Nightstalker would stop worrying about her existence. She repeated that to herself over and over.

She just wished she could believe it.

***

The following morning, the fort descended into chaos as warlords and their retinues began departing for their home States. Desomer was cranky, and the warlord's shield could tend to itself, so after drill, Arya checked in on Rorin—being roused from bed by his father—then headed downstairs, her intention to go to the stables and make sure her mare was tacked up and ready whenever Desomer gave the order.

She'd barely slept the night before, and even drill hadn't worked out her anxiety about the events of the past few days. Distracted, she rounded a bend to the top of the stairs leading down to the entry foyer.

And came to a halt at the sight of Mathas Crowtalon standing at the bottom of the steps with Thiara Ravenstrike. Her mouth was already opening to apologise and back away when she realised neither of them had seen her. She went still.

"Brave of you, to challenge me so openly," her warlord was saying. "I am a warlord, just like you, Crowtalon."

"You're a disgrace to the title of warlord." He hissed the words, his voice worlds away from the charming, controlled man he'd presented so far. "Your sister has told me all about what you're doing up there at Heathrock."

"If that's truly how you think, then I look forward with great anticipation to how uncomfortable you're going to be when I'm High Warlord." A little smile played at Thiara's mouth. Arya was impressed and astonished by her temerity.

"That will never happen," Mathas said quietly. "I will make sure of it."

"Careful, Mathas, that sounded like a threat. What would the other warlords think?"

He took a step towards her. "If you use that boy against me, Thiara Ravenstrike, I will destroy everything and everyone you hold dear. Be certain of that."

Before she knew what she was doing, Arya was stepping loudly down the stairs, half-drawing her sword from her sheath so that its crisp ring sent both warlords' gazes swinging her way. "Warlord Crowtalon. Please step back from my warlord."

"You're the apprentice Lanna told me about." Mathas' expression turned calculating. "How dare you address me so?"

She held his gaze. "I am a Raider sworn to my warlord's service. You can understand my desire to ensure she is safe, I am sure?"

"Arya, enough!" Thiara snapped out. "Mathas, leave, before I make a formal complaint to the High Warlord that you openly threatened me in my own home."

Crowtalon's gaze swung back to her, almost amused. "Until next time, Ravenstrike."

Arya clattered the rest of the way down the steps as the man strode away. "Warlord, I apologise, but I will never stand by while you are being threatened—"

Thiara waved a weary hand. "He was just posturing. There was no need to rise to the bait."

But he hadn't been, and they both knew it. Guilt abruptly swamped Arya. Her warlord, Rorin, they were all in danger. If Arya handed herself over to the Nightstalker, there would be no need for him to invade, and Thiara could focus all her energy on Mathas Crowtalon.

"No, Arya." The warlord's voice was quiet, but sharp enough to bring Arya's attention snapping to her.

"Warlord?" She frowned.

"You might be thinking it would be better for all concerned if you handed yourself over." Those ice-blue eyes met and held hers. "It would not. Further, I give you a direct order here and now that you will do no such thing."

Arya reeled. Was the warlord ... did she know?

"We never speak of it, not ever again," the warlord finished quietly, steel in her voice. "But make sure you heed my will in this."

She turned and strode off, leaving Arya gaping after her.

"There you are!" Desomer's voice bellowed from the top of the steps. "You're to ride back to Heathrock now, pick up your shield and Arken's, and head out on patrol. You'll split up—one to check the underground road, one the mountain pass."

"Yes, sir."

"Now, Captain, not tomorrow," he barked when she didn't move.

Arya blinked, saluted, and turned for the stables, trying to get her roiling thoughts in order.

How long had her warlord known who she really was?

Chapter 27

The long line of forty Raiders trotted along the road approaching Heathrock castle in perfect formation. Arya rode at their head, cowl pulled down against the icy wind that tugged at her clothes and weapons.

The sight of the imposing walls of Heathrock was a welcome one after ten nights spent sleeping out in the unforgiving weather of the mountains. Not that she would have slept well in a warm, soft bed. Not after the events of the summit. Her head still hurt when she allowed herself to think about it.

Arken rode over once they were through the gates. "Any orders before I dismiss my shield, Captain?"

"It's been a long patrol. Let them get inside," she told him. "A day off tomorrow, too, before returning to duty."

He acknowledged that and wheeled his horse away to pass on her orders. A series of weary whoops followed his announcement of a day off. They made for a jostling, cheerful group that loudly agreed on hot cider and a card game as they headed towards the barracks.

Arya tried not to let the sight get her down. Arken's shield was slowly becoming as confident and skilled as hers or Derrin's in patrolling the forest and mountains. But he continued to rebuff every attempt she made to get them on friendlier terms. *That* she could live with. More problematic, however, was the fact that his shield adored him.

What truly bothered her was that, deep down, she wasn't convinced they'd listen if she ever had to overrule his orders one day. And failing here—losing her future as general of Ravenstrike—was now even less of an option than it had been. She had to make it work. Not just because she loved this life, but because it was her shield against all the implications of being the person the Nightstalker hunted.

She dismissed those anxieties with a huff. More immediate problems loomed on the horizon. She couldn't help a sweeping glance of the walls, making sure the right number of Raiders were up there and everything was calm.

"Captain?" Charlin called out. "Do we get a day off too?"

She chuckled, forced away the shadows. Everything would be fine. She just had to keep her head down and work hard. "Same orders for you lot. Now get away with you all. I'm sick of the sight of you."

"We'll have a mug of mead waiting for you tonight," Etan promised.

And they would. While not as ebullient as Arken's shield, Arya's shield was quickly becoming exactly what she wanted—as competent and resilient as her shield from Icecliff. And she could feel their respect for her.

Inside the castle, the cavernous entrance foyer was empty, but the sounds of quiet chaos drifted from the great hall directly across from the main doors. Her boots echoed on stone as she crossed to it and paused at the threshold, an unbidden smile stretching across her face. All her worries fell away, and she revelled in the simple joy of having a home to come back to.

And a family.

The hall was abuzz with servants preparing for the warlord's formal Winterfest eve dinner—a way for the warlord to thank her vicelords for their work in support of Ravenstrike. This year, it would be the vehicle by which she prepared them for the upcoming State Council and deliberating on the Nightstalker's demands.

The usually drab hall had been transformed for the occasion. Sprigs of holly and fir hung from all the doors and above the arched windows lining its western side. Sparkling green and red ribbons hung between them, interspersed with tiny golden bells that rang gently in the always-present draft. Frost collecting on the windowpanes added to the cheer, as did the roaring fires in the hearths. Tables, perfectly set, sat ready to be adorned by festive, ostentatious spreads of food and drink.

Arya's smile widened as she recalled the conversation she'd had with Desomer about Winterfest prior to the summit. "A bunch of lords and ladies dressed like peacocks and clamouring for the warlord's attention like spoiled children," he'd muttered when she'd asked about it. "A ridiculous indulgence of finery and wealth if you ask me."

"I'm guessing a mere shield captain such as myself doesn't rate an invite, sir?" she'd asked, trying desperately to keep a straight face.

His scowl could have killed. "You'll be part of planning the security for it. I want this castle secure while we're hosting a group of feckless and indulgent Very Important People."

Arya pushed off the wall reluctantly—she'd best get to Desomer's office to report in—just as Peemla walked into sight.

"Arya, welcome home!" Peemla's eyes lit up at the sight of her. "We missed you. It must have been a strenuous patrol. You look so tired."

"It's good to be back," Arya said, heartfelt, then pointed into the hall. "I can't believe what you've done with the space. It looks stunning."

Peemla looked surprised at the praise. A stab of annoyance reverberated through Arya, not for the first time. Did nobody around Heathrock ever appreciate the woman's efforts? Peemla might be household staff, but there was nothing lesser about the work she did, day in and day out, without ever asking for recognition.

"This is the biggest event of the year, and those attending need to be suitably impressed," Peemla said. "I can show you what I was thinking, if you like?"

Arya hesitated—she really should report in—but Peemla looked so enthusiastic, and honestly, she could use a little bit of time in the woman's company. "Go on, then."

The chamberlain immediately started talking, leading Arya down into the hall and explaining her ideas on the decorating and how she planned to seat the vicelords so that there wouldn't be any friction.

"Warlord Ravenstrike is lucky to have you," Arya said once the chamberlain finished. The woman had the mind of a master tactician, the way she juggled multiple threads and brought them together seamlessly, all the while making it look easy. "How *did* you come to Heathrock, Peemla?"

"My father was the stablemaster here before he died," she replied, grief flashing briefly over her face. "The old warlord took me into his household staff after it happened, and when Warlord Ravenstrike was confirmed, she made me her chamberlain, even though most people here thought me far too young."

"Let me guess." A smile tugged at Arya's mouth. Peemla seemed roughly Arya's age. "She had an instinct about you."

"She honoured me."

"She chose well," Arya said. "Now, if you need any help, I'd be glad to lend an extra hand."

"I wouldn't dream of bothering you, you're so busy already. I'd best get to the kitchens and make sure dinner preparations are happening smoothly. We still need to feed the castle, especially now you and your hungry Raiders are home." Peemla's eyes twinkled.

"We are most obliged." Arya gave her a sweeping bow, making the woman flush red and then chuckle before hurrying away, muttering a list of tasks to herself.

Before Arya could head back out and up to the general's office, she spotted Essa passing Peemla in the doorway leading to the kitchens. A look of relief crossed the girl's face at the sight of Arya.

Arya lifted an eyebrow as she came over. "What is going on?"

"You're back, thank goodness." Essa smiled, and as usual it filled her face with warmth and character. Each time she saw that smile, Arya's suspicions about the girl faded another inch, even though she told herself that was unwise. "Rorin is currently in the kitchens spiking the festive mead."

Arya rolled her eyes, trying not to be amused. "And Taze is letting him do that? He'll be skinned alive."

"You know Taze can't gainsay anything Rorin wants to do." Essa let out a sigh. "Maybe he'll listen to you."

Arya was torn. More than half of her thought the prank was a wonderful idea and immediately wanted to join in. The rest of her understood how important it was that this dinner go off smoothly. "All right, where are they?"

"Did something happen on patrol?" Essa asked as they walked. "You seem tired, more so than usual."

Arya was saved from replying as Rorin barrelled into the hall, Taze following at a more sedate pace. Rorin's face lit up at the sight of Arya, and his fingers launched into a flurry of movement. Taze remained a step behind, at attention.

"*Arya, you're back!*" he signed, then paused. "*Are you okay? You look—*"

"Friendly warning. If one more person tells me I look tired, I am going to strangle them. Warlord's sons are not exempt," she said, keeping her voice firm, arms crossed over her chest. "I hear you've been spiking the mead?"

Rorin's grin widened, and he nodded unrepentantly. "*Just a little extra rum.*"

"Rorin, I understand the impulse, but it's important that this dinner goes well. Your mother needs to make sure her vicelords are ready to vote the way she needs them to when the Council discusses the Nightstalker issue. You do understand that, yes?"

"*It will help,*" he signed with a perfectly innocent expression. "*Relaxed vicelords make for vicelords less likely to plan to undermine my mother.*"

Her mouth twitched. It was hard to argue with that. "Did you get the whole bottle in?"

Rorin grinned, signing with his hands that every single drop had been poured in.

"What about—" Essa started, then stopped as two servants walked past carrying a keg of ale. Moments later, Darmanin appeared from around the corner, gaze searching them out before coming over.

"Good, you're done. Peemla is back in the kitchens," he said, then nodded at Arya. "Welcome home, Arya."

"You were a *lookout* for Rorin?" Arya asked in surprise.

He shrugged.

"Who's up for escaping these walls for a bit?" Essa suggested. She often felt chafed inside the fortress. "I'd love to do another drawing of the lake."

"We could go ice-skating while you draw," Darmanin suggested; he too preferred to be outside.

Rorin signed enthusiastically, indicating his agreement.

"You'll go with them," Arya said pointedly to Taze, and he nodded.

"*Will you come too, Arya?*" Rorin implored her.

"I've just spent days outside in the freezing cold. I think I'll let my bones warm up a little before I venture out again." The shadows from her patrol returned with a whisper. "Besides, I need to report to General Desomer."

Rorin signed. "*Then come after. Please, Arya?*"

She sighed, then conceded. "I'll do my best."

"We'd love to see you if you can make it," Essa said, then linked her arm with Rorin's. "Lead the way, Dar."

Darmanin hesitated slightly at the nickname. Arya shared a look with Taze before turning to head in the opposite direction. The shortening of Darmanin's name was something Taze had been the first to do, without thinking, but soon they'd all picked it up. Each time they used it, Darmanin had an odd little reaction. It wasn't displeasure, she thought, because he'd never asked them to stop, but she wasn't sure what it was. Maybe one day she'd ask him.

As she walked, reluctantly, away from them, she couldn't help but think of her new knowledge. The reason she'd been so unsettled and restless since the summit. What had her real family been like? She had to assume her parents were dead, or she wouldn't be the direct heir to Andahar, but did she have younger siblings over the border? Cousins? Aunts or uncles?

But even as she wondered that, she heard Essa and Taze's laughter drift across the hall. It prompted Arya to turn and see Rorin signing vigorously, eyes alight, clearly the source of the amusement. Even Darmanin was smiling. She let out a breath.

It didn't matter who else might be in Andahar.

Her real family was here.

Nobody answered her knock at the general's door, and she was debating where to start looking for him first, when the door to the warlord's office at the other end of the hall opened and he appeared.

"We've just started," he said brusquely. "I was about to send a servant to fetch you. What took you so long?"

"Sorry, sir." Arya made quick work of striding down the hall. Seeing who was inside, she realised it was the warlord's regular meeting with Magen and Desomer where they managed the affairs of the State.

The warlord sat at the head of the table by the windows, Magen at her left, and Desomer's cigar smoked in a tray beside his seat. Arya saluted sharply, then took an empty seat on Desomer's right.

"Welcome home, Arya," Thiara Ravenstrike said, and Magen gave her a friendly smile.

Arya accepted that with a nod, still unsure what to think about the last interaction she'd had with her warlord back at Windfall Fort. But the woman was as brusque and cool as always and showed no sign the conversation had ever happened.

"Report," Desomer demanded of Arya without any niceties.

"Both patrols performed well, sir," she said. "Captain Rosenthal's shield checked on the underground road, and mine went up to the Diamondfang pass. No signs of disturbance at either location. But..." She hesitated. She'd been hoping to discuss this privately with the general before it was presented to the warlord, but she didn't want to delay informing him.

His gaze sharpened. "What?"

Arya had learned by now that hesitation or prevarication only made the general yell, so she gave the facts. "We stayed overnight at Icecliff Fort on our way up and back from the pass, and I spoke with some old shield-mates. Sir, Commander Lerin hasn't sent a single patrol up to the pass since you issued the order over two months ago. He has grown slack on the daily check-ins and has convinced the other two fort commanders to do the same."

"Is this Raider gossip or information you trust?"

"The latter, sir."

"And your shield-mates' views on why this is the case?"

"Commander Lerin does not believe that the wraiths or shadowhounds will return, or that they'd pose a threat to us if they did. He instead focuses Raider patrols closer to the fort, where he seeks out and provokes Shadeweaver encampments into attacks. He thinks this will impress the warlords and get him a promotion as your replacement."

Desomer harrumphed. "Your shield-mates are interestingly well-informed on the inner workings of their commander's mind."

Arya fought not to squirm. Shield Captain Sapontis had heard Lerin say exactly what she'd just relayed in a meeting, but she didn't want to betray the woman. "Yes, sir."

Desomer abruptly turned to face Thiara Ravenstrike. "He needs to go, Warlord. I told you this after the recent attacks. I cannot guarantee you a secure border while that man sits in charge of Icecliff Fort, and we can ill afford a rogue commander up there while the Nightstalker pays such close attention to the region."

"He can't be fired," Magen said immediately. "For the same reasons he couldn't when you first raised it. Warlord, he is the brother of your most important vicelord. Lord Lerin controls Ravenstrike's share of the mines on the eastern border, and we are already faced with addressing his skimming off the top of those profits without losing his support. If we remove his brother from a position of power—"

"You don't need to tell me the consequences of losing Lord Lerin's loyalty, Magen," Thiara said, irritated. "But I must balance the security of my position with the safety of this State. If Dunidaen is invaded because I failed in my duty of protecting our border, I am guaranteed to achieve the inglorious pleasure of being the first ever warlord voted out of her position."

Arya had to bite her tongue to stop herself from jumping into the debate. While Magen's arguments were sensible, she was firmly with Desomer. Lerin had to go ... the border would be unsafe as long as he ran Icecliff Fort. Nor could Lerin's blatant disregard of his general's orders be ignored. She inwardly urged Desomer to argue his case more strongly.

"Captain Nameless said herself there is no sign of threat on the border," Magen said patiently. "Warlord, you cannot remove Commander Lerin. Not now, at least."

Thiara looked at Desomer. "Is there another position you could give him? One which is of equal symbolic importance but not as much of a risk to our security?"

"No," Desomer barked.

"Think about it." The warlord held his gaze until he gave a sharp nod. "And while you're at it, tell him to stop provoking Shadeweavers. I don't want us distracted by tussling with Shadeweavers with the threat of Andahar hanging over us."

"Warlord—" Magen began.

"I get the reports of dead Raiders just like you both do." Her voice held a note of warning in it. "We need as many Raiders as we can get right now, Magen. I suspect if we limited ourselves to only intervening when their criminal activities stretched beyond the mountains or threatened our citizens, those reports would grow a lot less frequent."

"The last thing you can afford is to be seen as soft on Shadeweavers, particularly once word gets out of you fostering two of them here," Magen protested. "In fact, going hard on them is an easy win for bolstering your strength, and killing or arresting their magic-wielders might solve the Nightstalker threat at the same time."

"I concede your point," she said, after a moment of tapping her fingers on the tabletop. "As for the other thing, I will speak with Vicelord Lerin at Winterfest, sound him out about the mines and his brother, and judge for myself how much his support wavers."

Arya tried not to let her disappointment show. She shifted in her chair and Desomer gave her a quelling glance, as if sensing her discontent. She stilled.

Magen cleared his throat. "The State Council isn't far off. All it will take is a handful of your vicelords expressing a vote of no confidence—"

"Enough, Magen!" Thiara snapped.

"You told me Crowtalon openly threatened your position at Windfall Fort. If you ride into this year's State Council emphasising your recent victory on the border, in addition to a new policy of hunting down and rooting out all the Shadeweavers in your State—*and* supporting his move to hand over the magic-wielders to Andahar—it will undermine any attacks Crowtalon makes on your strength or ability to rule," Magen said patiently. "It's a good way to start preparing your bid for High Warlord at the following State Council, too."

Arya shifted again, unable to help herself. She couldn't parse *how* she felt about the strategy Crowtalon had suggested or whether she wanted Thiara Ravenstrike to support it. On one hand, she saw clearly how well it would play politically for her warlord. But on the other ... how could she stand by while Dunidae magic-wielders were handed over, probably to be killed, when she was the one the Nightstalker wanted? A dull ache started up in her temples.

The warlord's gaze switched to her, and she gave a very slight head shake. Arya swallowed and stayed silent. Her warlord's direct order bound her, no matter how guilty she might feel.

"Politics is all well and good, but nobody is going to give two figs for who is High Warlord of Dunidaen if we're overrun by Andahar." Desomer glowered at Magen. "Warlord, if you want me to run your army and secure your State, I need the latitude to remove the weak links."

"Exaggeration will only serve to test my patience," Thiara said crisply. "General, I'm asking you to be creative. Re-position the weak link rather than remove it."

"A good army isn't creative. It's disciplined and structured," he insisted.

"I'm not debating this any further." The warlord rose from her chair. "I have things to see to for tomorrow night. We'll pick this up after Winterfest."

She strode from the room without another word. Magen gave Desomer an apologetic look as he followed her out. Desomer gave an annoyed grunt and rose from his chair. "Wait here," he barked at Arya. "I need a word with Magen."

The door slammed behind him, and Arya wandered over to the windows, processing everything she'd just heard and prioritising what she wanted to ask. It was never her place to speak in those meetings unless asked directly—she was allowed to attend them only because she was the general's apprentice—but once Desomer returned, she could ask questions as long as his patience lasted, which was rarely very long.

The warlord's office had a clear view over the frozen lake to the east of the castle walls. Taze, Essa, Darmanin, and Rorin were out there skating. As she watched, Taze tripped and went sprawling onto the ice. Even from a distance, she could imagine the laughing grin Rorin wore as he watched the Raider try to scrabble back to his feet. It made her smile and eased the tension in her shoulders.

The door clicked open and Desomer stomped back in. He took one look at her face and grunted. "Go on, then."

"Sir, if Vicelord Lerin is *anything* like his brother..." Arya took a breath. "Then he's already planning a vote of no confidence in the warlord. I wouldn't be surprised if Commander Lerin is going after the Shadeweavers in support of his *brother's* bid for the warlord's position."

Desomer gave a sharp nod. "Maybe, but it'll do him no good if Vicelord Lerin can't get anyone else to support him. Magen seems convinced nobody will yet, and he's usually right on these things."

"Yes, sir. What should we do about the lapsed border checks?" she asked.

"I'd pay a visit to all three forts myself to emphasise my orders, but we're leaving for the State Council within a fortnight, so there's no time, and we'll be gone for months." He stubbed out his cigar in a huff.

Arya hesitated, then, "Sir, wasn't it Arken's uncle that you promoted to command SheerRock Fort after it was attacked? Perhaps if you gave Arken some time off over Winterfest to visit his uncle, he could have a quiet word, make a request for his uncle to be more vigilant no matter what Lerin tells him."

"Now *you're* playing politics too?" he grumbled, but it was half-hearted. "It's worth a chat to Magen—we'd want to make sure we weren't making things worse. I don't know where Arken's family sits politically. Vicelords Lerin and Rosenthal could be bosom buddies for all I know."

"Yes, sir," she said. "My shield—and Derrin and Arken's—we could cover the border while you're gone. We can do regular checks of the pass and underground road. That should suffice until a decision is made at State Council about how to respond to the Nightstalker's demands."

"You'll have to, and to be honest, I'd trust the three of you doing those patrols over anyone Lerin sends." He waved her off. "You're dismissed. Back on duty after Winterfest."

"Sir." She saluted and headed for the door, stopping when he called her name.

"Almost forgot. Warlord says you're to join us for the family lunch at Winterfest. Don't know what's possessed her, but there you go."

She stifled a smile. "Thank you, sir. I'll see you there."

Warmth filled her as she closed the door and headed in the direction of her rooms. Warlord Ravenstrike wanted her at the family meal. *Her,* a Nameless.

But that warmth faded quickly, the shadows of the summit and her recent patrol returning to settle uneasily in her bones. It tugged at her peace of mind, knowing those roads had been unguarded. Anything could come across—again—and they wouldn't have warning in time.

And if it did, it would be her fault. Because the Nightstalker wanted her.

Arya's stride quickened as she headed to her quarters. She'd intended on joining Rorin skating, but instead she took off her boots, cloak, and cowl and sat down before her fire, parchment and quill in hand.

She'd draw up a patrol schedule for the time until the general returned from the State Council, make sure the roadblocks were checked regularly. It would make for a long and tiring few months for her three shields, but it would be good for their training.

It was only as she started working that the tension in her shoulders began to unwind. Even so, it didn't fade entirely.

After all, two months had passed between anyone checking the roadblocks. Anything could have come through in that time. Anything smart enough to have learned from the last time and removed any traces of its passing.

She told herself she was being silly. After all, if anything *had* come through, it would have made itself known by now. And the Nightstalker had promised to wait until Dunidaen came up with a proposal at the State Council.

"They're looking for you, Arya." Unbidden, the elder's words came back to her. Her quill paused over the parchment, ink dripping as her attention drifted. How long would the Nightstalker keep searching for her? Surely he'd give up when she made no threatening moves towards him.

Arya gave herself a shake and refocused back on her planning.

She would make sure the border stayed safe, single-handedly if she had to. It was her responsibility now.

Chapter 28

Arya felt someone shaking her shoulder. "What?" she mumbled, reluctantly opening her eyes. Rorin hovered at her bedside. He signed something, but it was too dark to make out his flickering fingers. "I can't see what you're saying."

Rorin heaved a frustrated sigh and pointed to her closet, where the passageway entrance was open. The message was clear: he wanted to her to follow him.

Arya eyed him. "Where's Taze?"

Rorin rolled his eyes. Pointed.

"All right, I'm coming." Arya jumped out of bed. It was freezing, so she put on warm socks and boots and carried her quilt with her. The two of them entered the passageway behind her room. Taze was waiting just inside and gave her a nod of greeting.

Since learning about the passageways behind the walls, she and Taze, and then Darmanin and Essa, had explored them all. They'd worked out the quickest route that connected all their rooms—iron rungs hammered into stone served as ladders between levels—and had used it so often they could now move through them in the dark without the need for a light.

When they reached his room, Rorin pulled out a key and unlocked the door that slid sideways into the back of his closet. The locks and keys had been something Arya had insisted on to ensure the passageways remained secure. The five of them were the only ones with keys.

The darkness of the closet greeted her as they slid it closed behind them before pushing through the hanging clothes and emerging into Rorin's bedroom. A fire crackled in the hearth, but the room was empty. He waved her over to the balcony door, which he'd left ajar.

"What are we doing?"

Rorin merely pointed, but Taze caught the edge in her tone and replied promptly. "Rorin wanted to have his own private Winterfest party."

By the time Arya stepped outside, Rorin was already on the balcony railing, scrambling up onto the roof above. Heaving a sigh, she climbed up, then—stretching up and gripping the ledge tightly—she swung herself onto the sloping castle roof.

Darmanin was already there, and Essa too, though every part of her was hidden beneath multiple layers of fur, so it could have been anyone, really.

Three stories high, the residential wing rose to the same height as the exterior walls but not as high as the centre of the castle, which housed the great hall. It meant they couldn't see the eastern walls from where they sat—instead, they could only peer down into a narrow courtyard that separated the residential wing from the great hall. Tonight, light spilled out into the courtyard below from the windows lining the great hall. The warlord's Winterfest eve dinner was in full swing.

"*Now we're all here!*" Rorin signed with a pleased smile, then tossed Arya a flagon. The sky above was clear, the moon bright enough she could read his signing clearly enough.

She caught the flagon and sat beside Essa, taking a healthy swig and enjoying its spiced taste. "Is this the mead you spiked?"

Rorin nodded proudly.

A gust of icy wind swept over the castle and both Rorin and Taze shivered. Arya gave the young lord a look. "Couldn't we have your personal Winterfest party inside where it's not dangerously cold?"

Essa's voice drifted out from somewhere inside the pile of clothing beside Arya. "That's what I said."

He shook his head vigorously, then swept his arm out as if to say, "*Look at the view we have from here.*"

Arya shrugged and tossed the flagon to Darmanin; she figured if all of them shared it equally, there wasn't enough liquor in there to make being on the roof too dangerous. He caught it and took a tiny sip before passing it to Taze. Taze sensibly put it down beside him. With a mischievous grin, Rorin swept it up and chugged a few mouthfuls.

"Careful, Rorin. I don't want you falling off this roof on my watch. Your mother would have me skinned alive," Taze said.

"And me." Arya reached over to take it from him.

"*We have to celebrate properly tonight*," Rorin signed in protest. "*We won't be together next Winterfest.*"

The mood immediately sobered. Approaching fifteen years old, Rorin had reached the age for fostering, an ironclad tradition among the warlords of Dunidaen. When Thiara Ravenstrike left for the State Council in Gateport in two weeks, both Rorin and Darmanin would travel with her. The two boys would spend the next three years with Warlord Gelfrey Hawkesdale and his household in their seat of Darulan.

She'd liked what she'd seen of Hawkesdale at the summit, though she did wonder how Thiara had managed to get him to agree to take Darmanin as well, given Darmanin's father had not been consulted. Her warlord was one impressive woman.

Her heart ached at the thought of Rorin's imminent departure, though she'd been careful to hide it. It had been there since their first meeting, then solidified when he'd stood up for her with his mother, and again during the summit, but Rorin Ravenstrike cut through all Arya's instinctive defences. It was him she first looked for when coming back from patrols, *his* safety she most thought about when reviewing the security of the fortress, and his company she never grew tired of, despite their difference in age and life experience.

Yet, she was forced to admit to herself that it wasn't just him she would miss.

Her suspicions of Essa and Darmanin had relaxed, if only because neither had said or done anything to keep them alive. Darmanin retained a wildness about him that Arya sensed didn't come entirely from having spent years with the Shadeweavers. But he'd never again drawn his knife on anyone in Heathrock, and in every sense, he'd honoured the promise he'd made to Warlord Ravenstrike on his arrival.

Essa kept her distance—the only one of them not to frequently seek out company in each other's rooms at night—but she never failed to bring a warmth to their group with her musical laughter or a beautiful drawing. Arya felt calm in her presence in a way she never had before, not even with Laskin or Rorin.

If she and Ranier were planning something, it was a long game. Arya told herself she couldn't discount that, but it seemed less and less plausible when laughing at a joke Essa had made or feeling gratitude well up when the girl helped her in lessons, brushing away thanks every time Arya tried to give it.

Another gust swept over the roof. Even Arya shivered, and she pulled her quilt higher up her shoulders. Through the large, arched windows of the great hall below, Thiara Ravenstrike came into view, nursing a glass of wine. Her husband appeared at her side a few moments later. Matte said something that made Thiara chuckle. He then took her arm and led her out of sight, presumably to go and speak with more vicelords. Arya wondered if they'd spoken with Vicelord Lerin yet.

Arya glanced at Rorin, caught the look of sadness on his face as he, too, watched his parents. "What is it?" she asked him.

He shook his head, looked away.

She would have pushed harder, but movement in the courtyard below caught Arya's attention—always wary of Rorin's safety. Her fingers tightened into fists when Lanna Ravenstrike strolled into sight with her husband, Mathas Crowtalon's brother, Daskinal. What was *she* doing here?

"Here comes the shrew," Essa warned in a loud whisper.

"Shush, she'll hear us," Darmanin said.

Essa snorted. "I don't care."

"I'm surprised your mother invited her back here," Arya said, turning back to Rorin.

"She didn't. Lanna arrived last week, claiming regret over their disagreement and wanting to mend fences. She left her boys in Crowtalon, though. I doubt it's a

coincidence that the timing of her arrival coincided with the exact amount of time it would have taken for Warlord Crowtalon to return home after the summit and send her back here as his spy." Rorin picked up the almost-empty flagon and hefted it as if he were going to throw it at his aunt.

Darmanin reached out to lay a hand on the boy's arm. "You can't afford to make an enemy of her any more than your mother can," he told Rorin gravely. "You know she wants to see Jenka as warlord of Ravenstrike one day."

Rorin's face clouded, and he signed vigorously. "*She thinks I cannot be warlord because I am mute.*"

"Your friends know different, Rorin," Arya told him. "What she thinks won't matter."

Both Essa and Darmanin gave Arya a surreptitious look, as if that were wishful thinking, but said nothing. Rorin hesitated, but then he put down the flagon. Seconds later, Taze began humming a ditty under his breath, and Arya and Essa joined in. Rorin started clapping in time with their singing, but they were all horribly out of tune.

Arya caught sight of Darmanin's amused smile, and it stilled her laughter. She couldn't remember ever seeing him smile openly before. It looked strange, to see his grave face so transformed. He caught her looking, and the smile faded a little. "Don't stop," she murmured. "You should smile more."

"You say that like it's easy," he said just as quietly.

"All right." Essa rose abruptly. "That's enough sitting on a freezing roof. I'm going inside—Rorin, if you come with me, I'll do a drawing of us all that you can take with you when you leave."

That got the young lord up, and he scrambled recklessly off the roof, almost giving Taze and Arya heart attacks in the process. Arya went last, making sure they all got down safely.

When she dropped back down to the balcony, she found Darmanin still there, staring out into the night. His thin frame shivered as he leaned on the stone ledge. Arya lifted her quilt and spread it across his shoulders, enclosing them both in its warmth. "I haven't had a chance to ask how you're feeling." She dropped her voice to a murmur. "About the summit. Your father's proposal about magic-wielders."

She hadn't told him about the Etherean elder's warnings. He'd be safer not knowing, nor did she want to put the guilt she felt on his shoulders.

"My life was already forfeit if the wrong people learned of my ability." His voice was flat, almost uncaring. "Dunidaen handing me over to the Nightstalker is no different from being branded and refused shelter, employment, or food here."

She opened her mouth, closed it. It was clear he didn't want to talk about it, but her question only reminded her how confused *she* felt about the proposal. She'd already lied to her warlord to protect Darmanin, and the stakes of that lie had increased dramatically after the summit. "If you want to be alone, that's okay," she said finally. "But you could probably do it somewhere where you won't freeze to death."

He didn't look at her. "I like the cold."

Arya glanced yearningly towards the door inside. Then she sighed. "You don't have to talk." She rubbed her hands together for warmth. "But it's nicer not to be alone on Winterfest eve. Unless you'd prefer me to go inside with the others?"

Darmanin was silent for a long time, but he didn't ask her to go, and slowly the warmth of the quilt soaked through them both. Eventually, he turned towards her. "Haven't you always been alone on Winterfest?"

Arya shrugged. "Well, at first I had my foster father in Aren. He was an ex-Raider, retired due to injury, so Winterfest was usually just the two of us sitting and sharing whatever he could afford to buy from the markets. After he died, Winterfest was no different than any other day. And then once I joined the Raiders, I was always around people, but they weren't family. I've never known any different."

"So not alone, but lonely."

She shook her head. "No, I've never been lonely. The rough companionship of the Raiders was enough for me." Or, it had been. What she was finding here at Heathrock ... with Rorin and Desomer and Peemla, and Darmanin and Essa too. It scared her. Her unexpected and unlooked for bond with them had the potential to hurt more than any physical pain she'd ever suffered. Because she knew all too well that anything gained could be just as easily lost.

"I knew different once," Darmanin said eventually. "Then my mother died on Winterfest eve."

Arya sucked in a breath. "Oh, Dar. I'm so sorry. I didn't realise."

"She and my father had a terrible fight that night, and she left and went walking in the forest near our home. She must have gotten lost or walked too far … nobody noticed she was gone until the next morning and my brother Andrian and I raised the alarm. They found her frozen body later that morning." Darmanin paused, then spoke with ferocious bitterness. "They shared a room. My father should have known she hadn't come back. He did know. And he did *nothing*."

Arya reached out to take his hand. His skin was cold, and she clasped his hand between both of hers, not knowing what else to do or say. After a moment, he kept talking.

"I was eleven. I used to love Winterfest before that. My mother would make funny little hats for everyone to wear at the family meal—she used to pick fresh snowdrops to put in each one—and she had my father's chamberlain fill the table with candles that smelled like cinnamon and vanilla." He paused. "When she died … my father sent Andrian off to fostering then threw me out. It made me realise that she had been the only thing that had been stopping him from doing it."

Silence fell as Arya searched for what to say. "I met your father at the summit. You're nothing like him, Dar. Not in any conceivable way."

He turned to her, grey eyes luminous, fingers squeezing hers hard. "You mean that?"

"I mean that," she said firmly. "Now, I can't pretend to know what it's like to lose a beloved mother, but in coming here … for the first time in my life, I feel like I belong somewhere. It's strange, and surprising. Dar, maybe you could see it the same way I do?"

He tensed slightly. "We both know why Thiara Ravenstrike took me into her household, Arya. Her interest in me is purely political."

"Rorin's isn't," Arya said firmly. "He treats you like a brother. And mine isn't either."

I lied to my warlord for you. The words lay unsaid between them.

"Don't get me wrong. Because of Warlord Ravenstrike, I will have an opportunity to strike back at my father one day." Darmanin paused, mouth tightening. "I'm going to kill him, just like he killed my mother."

He spoke so fiercely that Arya didn't want to treat his words lightly. "I don't blame you," she said, giving his hand a squeeze. "We haven't gone on one of our rides in a while. How about we head out early tomorrow morning, before the family lunch?"

He nodded and stood, shrugging off the quilt. "I think I'll go back to bed now."

Arya followed him inside, watching as he murmured goodnight to Rorin and Essa and left through the closet. Chairs had been set up in front of the hearth for Essa to draw them, but Arya noticed that none of them were sitting on the chairs—in fact they were all standing much closer to the balcony door.

"How much of that did you hear?" she asked dryly.

Rorin's expression was angry and defiant. "*If he needs help killing Mathas Crowtalon, I'll be the first to put up my hand.*"

"Be careful what you say, Rorin," she warned, not unkindly.

Rorin shook his head vigorously and began signing. "*I never had a brother until he came. I want to help.*"

"Sometimes there's not much you *can* do," she said, feeling the truth of those words at the same time felt how hard it was to accept. "Come on, it's time to get back to bed. We can find a time for Essa to draw us when Dar is feeling better."

He nodded sadly, shoulders slumping.

Essa waved goodnight and ducked into the closet, Arya following, feeling equally sad. A tug on her shoulder had her turning, watching as Rorin stood there, hands flickering. "*I never had a sister, either, until you came.*"

Arya swallowed, stunned. "Rorin, I..."

"*Good night, Arya.*" He smiled, waved.

Still stunned, Arya slid closed the closet door and locked it.

"He loves you very much." Essa's voice came out of the darkness.

Arya started. She'd forgotten the girl was there. "You sound like that troubles you."

"It's going to get tangled, especially now the boys are off to be fostered. By the time they come back, things will be different." Essa paused. "The heir to Ravenstrike cannot treat one of his army's shield captains as a sister. The warlord is treading dangerous enough ground giving Darmanin the status of a warlord's son by fostering him."

"Because he was a Shadeweaver."

"I am rather uniquely placed to understand how deep the hatred and fear of the Shadeweavers runs," Essa said quietly.

"You're very perceptive," Arya told her. "I hope you can also perceive that you're as important to Rorin as Darmanin or I are. That you're as important to all of us."

"Is there a warning in those words, Arya Nameless?"

"I still don't know why you're here, Essa, and the closer you get to Rorin, the more you're in a position to hurt him. I'll kill you before I allow that."

"I mean them no harm. Arya, I swear it." Essa reached out unexpectedly, squeezing her hand. "Maybe one day you'll believe that. It's the Nightstalker we must fear—at least, it is what the warlords will do to assuage his demands and protect themselves that we must fear. If protecting Rorin is really your priority, perhaps you should focus on that."

Before Arya could think of how to respond, Essa was gone, taking a turning in the passages that led to her room.

Chapter 29

The following morning, Arya stood huddled in her cloak and cowl, watching as Darmanin practiced shifting from his human form to his shadowhound one. It was a clear day, fresh snow covering the ground and a winter sunlight setting the peaks alight around them. They were a good hour's ride from Heathrock, in an isolated clearing. Their horses grazed nearby, noses digging through the snow.

"It looks like it's getting easier," she offered as he returned to his human form, trying to stop her teeth from chattering as she spoke. The first few times they'd done this, she'd stared, mouth agape, as Darmanin employed his shapeshifting magic, but now she was accustomed to it.

"It is," he acknowledged. "While you were gone on patrol … when Lanna and my uncle arrived … I got angry, seeing them. Really angry. But holding back the shift didn't take as much effort as it used to, not like when I fought Jenka and Warn."

"Good." Her breath frosted as she expelled a relieved breath. "That's really good, Dar."

"Thank you for your help, Arya." He offered that with his usual grave solemnity.

She snorted. "I've literally done nothing aside from stand in the snow and freeze my ass off while watching you use your magic."

He held her gaze. "I don't think you understand how impossible it usually is for a magic-wielder to be given a safe space to practice."

She waved a hand. "Okay, one more time and then we'll head back. I'm supposed to meet with the general before Winterfest lunch and you've got weapons practice with Rorin and Laskin."

Darmanin took a deep breath, settled, then Arya watched as his limbs began changing. It did seem more fluid than the first time she'd seen it, and faster too. Soon a black shadowhound stood in the snow, large enough that his head stood as tall as her ribs. He shook himself, then padded out of the clearing, taking the time to stretch out his limbs, practice running on four legs rather than two.

She stood, shivering, until he came back. But when he did, there was an odd tenseness about him, and he was frowning when he shifted back into his human form.

"What?" She asked. "Shadeweavers or predators nearby?"

It was always a risk when they were alone like this, but Darmanin had assured her that his shadowhound's nose would pick up their scent well before any danger could stumble across them.

He hesitated. "I scented Essa."

Arya stared at him for a moment, then turned and strode for her mare. "Show me."

"Arya—"

"Show me, Darmanin."

Darmanin shifted back into shadowhound form and loped off. Arya set her mare after him, bringing Darmanin's horse behind her. He headed in the direction of Heathrock, presumably following the scent he'd picked up. Eventually she followed him into another clearing ... this one marked by footprints.

"Essa's prints?" she asked Darmanin once he was back in human form.

"Judging from the scent, yes." He studied them with human eyes. "They're small like her feet too."

Arya stared around them from the saddle. "What was she doing out here?"

"I don't know."

A grimness fell between them. She could think of only one reason the Shadeweaver's daughter would hike out into the Wraith Forest on her own.

A meeting with one of them.

"She might have been painting out here, or drawing," Darmanin said. "Or just taking a walk. You know she loves hiking."

"She also hates it when it's this cold. Let's follow the tracks back, make sure they lead to the castle," she said.

Darmanin nodded and mounted, and the two set off. The tracks led in a wandering line back to the walls of Heathrock castle, as if Essa had been searching for something, rather than knowing exactly where she was going.

"Let me handle this," she told Darmanin as they unsaddled their horses in the stables. "Say nothing to anyone."

"All right, Arya." He hesitated. "There were no other tracks in the snow, no indication anyone else was there."

"I've encountered at least one Shadeweaver who didn't leave tracks. One we both know. Are you telling me he isn't capable of hiding his scent from you? Or that there aren't other Shadeweavers who could do the same."

Leanir. The name hovered between them, and Darmanin looked away, clearly troubled.

She smiled, touched his arm. "See you at lunch, Dar."

***

"One of the unsung but critical responsibilities of being a general is managing the logistics of such a large force," Desomer said, then, "Arya!"

Arya jerked her attention away from the window. In the drill yard below, Darmanin and Rorin were at weapons practice with Laskin. As usual, Rorin was swinging his wooden sword around with more enthusiasm than skill. Darmanin was slight, but he was quick and focused and had excellent footwork. He never attacked until he had an opening, and sometimes he would wait a long time before getting it. His patience bordered on eerie.

The sight of the boys had her dwelling on what she and Darmanin had seen in the forest. Thinking of it left a sick lurch in the pit of her stomach.

Desomer's voice intruded again. "What has you as distracted as a bumblebee in a field of flowers?"

"Sorry, sir." She gave him her full attention. "What do you make of Essa, sir?"

"The Shadeweaver's daughter?" He seemed startled by the question. "She's pleasant to everyone and dresses and carries herself like she's a warlord's daughter. It's a well-practiced façade."

"You don't think it's real?"

Desomer snorted. "She's Ranier's daughter. Our warlord was mad to take her in and you'll never convince me otherwise. Can we get back to work now?"

The general sat at the long table near the windows, multiple pages of documents laid out in front of him. Arya joined him, gaze narrowing. His usual punishment when she'd done something wrong was drowning her in paperwork. "Am I in trouble?"

He snorted. "No. You're doing well enough. And you've not made any major missteps. *Yet.*"

"Most of the Raiders here still don't think I should be your apprentice," she muttered.

"Then you'd better figure that out."

"I will, sir. And I won't make any major mistakes," she assured him.

He gave an exasperated sigh. "Of course you will. Every leader does. The key is to learn from them and not make the same mistake twice."

She nodded, because that's what he expected, but inwardly she promised herself she wouldn't mess up. She wanted his position one day more than she'd ever wanted anything. And if she succeeded here, ignored the Etherean elder's claims, the Nightstalker would face no threat from her. Then maybe Dunidaen would be safe.

The look Desomer gave her indicated he knew very well she was humouring him, but he didn't push it. "Right. We need to discuss the State Council."

She brightened. "Will I be going with you, sir?"

"Not this time." He looked up, catching her face falling. "These things happen every four years, and sometimes in between if there's a need, so you'll get plenty of opportunities in the future." He scowled. "And trust me, it's not all that interesting. It will be two weeks of politics and posturing about the Nightstalker. Your patience wouldn't last a half hour."

Arya simply nodded. He'd brought this up for a reason, so she'd let him get to it in his own time. Desomer put down his quill and looked at her. He seemed uneasy, which was uncharacteristic for him. She could count on one hand how many times she'd seen him uncertain.

"I understand that being brought into Warlord Ravenstrike's confidence about her plans must be gratifying for you," he said. "I also understand how it must feel to be a Nameless welcomed into a household as you have been. But don't forget that when it comes down to it, you and I, and everyone else that works for Warlord Ravenstrike, are tools that she will use in furtherance of her goals. You are not family, and she is as ruthless as any male warlord I've met."

"I'll keep that in mind," she said. Her heart, her instinct, told her he was wrong. But her brain, the one he and Rorin's tutor were teaching her to use ... suspected he had a point.

"Good." His voice turned brisk, and he sat forward. "You've been learning all the administrative and logistical details of running a Raider army, and with passable patience too." He gifted her a single look of acknowledgment. "You'll still be doing all that, but you also need to start learning to *think* like a general."

Desomer rifled through the piles of parchment on the table until he dug out a map, which he then unrolled. The detail showed southern Ravenstrike, with the States of Falconcrest to the east and SparrowWing and Hawkesdale to the south. The northern tip of Crowtalon was visible too, right at the bottom. While Arya watched curiously, Desomer collected a jar of small, coloured stones from a nearby shelf.

He placed a grouping of red stones over Heathrock castle on the map and more on the three forts in the Diamondfang, as well as the other towns in Ravenstrike that held a Raider barracks. He then placed a large cluster of purple stones on the Ravenstrike-SparrowWing border and used pieces of string to lead from the purple stones south to three different SparrowWing cities, with Seelan, a massive trading centre, the farthest away to the south.

"These represent Raiders?" Arya pointed to the red stones.

"Yes. The purple stones are an invading force of Crowtalon Lances. Each stone represents five hundred Lances. The pieces of string are supply lines. You're at Heathrock, and you've just received word from your scouts about this invasion. What do you do?"

"Why are we talking about invasion from within Dunidaen when the Nightstalker…" Arya's words died at the look on his face, and she cast her gaze back to the map. "Sorry, sir. Well, the first thing I'd do is fire my scouts," she said dryly. "How did five thousand Lances cross the entire State of SparrowWing and camp on our southern border without me knowing about it?"

Desomer sat back in his chair, arms crossed. She sighed, turning her attention back to the map. Five thousand Lances was about half of Crowtalon's standing army. Heathrock and its surrounding areas garrisoned roughly the same number of Raiders, and she'd put her money on Raiders over Lances in an even fight any day.

Leaning forward, she picked up most of the red stones over Heathrock, and the ones from the nearest garrisons, and moved them directly south until they were planted in front of the invading force. She then sat back. "That's what I'd do."

Desomer raised an eyebrow. "You don't want to think about that, for maybe … I don't know … another thirty seconds?"

"No, sir."

"In that case, just to clarify." He uncrossed his arms and sat forward to knock ash from his cigar. "Your plan is to march half our entire army directly south to meet the invading force?"

"Yes, sir," she said. "It's a strong force of Lances. I think it best to counter it with an equally strong force. Raiders are more mobile and have an advantage over Lances because of their ability to shoot from horseback at distance. An equal number of Raiders should be able to deal with that invasion force well enough."

He dropped the cigar and put his face in his hands. "It's worse than I thought," he muttered, mostly to himself.

Arya stiffened. "Sir?"

"Let me demonstrate the outcome of your well-thought-out and highly detailed strategy." Desomer sat forward and moved all the stones back to their original positions. "Now, when you first receive word of the invasion, provided that you can get all twenty-five shields moving out of Heathrock and nearby garrisons instantly, which would be impossible, how long do you think it would take them to ride south?"

Arya shrugged, glanced at the map. "A week, pushing the pace?"

"Closer to two. In the meantime, the Lances will be moving north at a slower pace to protect their supply lines." He moved the purple stones a third of the way into Ravenstrike. "They would get about this far in two weeks."

Arya frowned; she hadn't considered the forward movement that Crowtalon would make.

"Your army has managed to race south in two weeks, instantly after you received the report." Desomer moved the red stones. "The horses are exhausted from the pace you set, and Raiders are surviving on dwindling rations because you haven't left time to set up supply lines. When the two armies eventually meet, the well-fed, well-rested, and heavily armoured Lances will be facing a weary group of Raiders on similarly exhausted horses.

"If their general is smart, he'll run straight through you and march north for Heathrock, which is now open and vulnerable because you've only left a single shield behind to defend it. Once he holds that, he is at leisure to pick off the rest of your army from his new stronghold in the north, including any force of Raiders that tries to attack the walls of Heathrock from the forts. Windfall Fort might succeed in blockading Aren and preventing him from shipping in supplies or troops, but that's the best we could hope for."

"Oh," Arya bit her lip.

Desomer removed the stones before rolling up the map. "While I'm in Gateport, you will drill all the shields here at Heathrock in preparing for an instant march south. You will work out the time it takes to marshal five thousand Raiders from here and the surrounding garrisons, establish supply lines, and get them moving. Then you'll figure out how to do it faster. You'll need to inventory our supplies and make proposals on what we'd need to acquire to be better prepared. I'll expect a full report on my return. Commander Randin will be made aware of your tasking and that he is expected to cooperate. Any questions?"

"No, sir," she mumbled, face hot.

He gave her a hard look. "What do I keep saying about thinking things through?"

She opened her mouth—she *had* been getting better at that—but closed it. He was right. "Yes, sir. I'll do better."

"There is a *massive* difference between leading a shield of twenty Raiders and an entire army. You're not even close, Arya Nameless, so get that into that overconfident and cocky brain of yours."

She stilled the flare of temper at his brusque words. "Sir. I get it."

"Good. Now, you weren't wrong about the Raiders being more mobile than the Lances, and having an advantage in being able to fire from a distance," he said. "What you didn't consider is that the Lances are less mobile *because* they're heavily armoured. You could fire away all day at those shields they carry and not injure a single Lance if they're riding in proper formation. And our mobility, while an advantage, can also make us more vulnerable in the wrong situation. We wear no armour, and while the thick layers we wear *might* turn away an arrow shot from distance, it won't do anything to stop a broadsword or a lance from running right through us."

He'd switched from censorious to brusque teaching in a blink and Arya found her temper dying as quickly as it had come. Desomer didn't hold grudges and he wasn't cruel. He'd given her the message he felt she needed to hear and now he was helping her to get better.

She responded in kind. "In that case sir, why don't we wear armour and use longbows with greater punch?"

He gave her an uncharacteristic smile. "Because we're more mobile and have a distance advantage over most foes *without* those things."

"But you just said—"

"Dunidaen is a unified country. The States were set up to co-exist mostly autonomously, but peacefully. That's why each State has its own style of fighting force, so that if Dunidaen were ever threatened, we could put together a complete army with the capability of fighting in several different ways."

Arya straightened. "So we have heavy and light cavalry in Crowtalon and Ravenstrike respectively, longbows in Hawkesdale, armoured infantry in Eaglesoar, and light infantry in Falconcrest. I assume SparrowWing is different because of the terrible fires they get during the summer?"

Desomer nodded. "SparrowWing was initially a force of scouts and trackers, but yes, their State is made up almost entirely of open, grassy spaces, so those scouts and trackers became Firefighters. If it ever came to war, though, they'd do a good enough job at their original purpose."

She started to see the reason for this lesson now. Desomer *was* thinking about invasion from Andahar. But there was one thing that didn't add up. "That all makes sense sir, but doesn't that mean no provision was ever made for civil war in Dunidaen?"

"Correct. If that ever happened, well, every State would have strong advantages *and* key vulnerabilities against any other State. That's when a good commander becomes critical—their ability to understand their force's weaknesses and its strengths, and then exploit those to his or her advantage," Desomer said. "Not that it will ever happen, of course."

"Sir, when you return, could we do this exercise again? I'd like to come up with a better response, and then I want to understand how you would do it so I can learn from that."

He stifled a smile. "You'll have months to come up with a different response—it better be a good one."

"Yes, sir."

"You won't have as much time as you think," he said then. "While I'm gone, you'll have responsibility for maintaining a watch over the border entrances—you have the autonomy to organise that how you see fit. Battalion Commander Randin will be in charge of Heathrock in my absence, but

I've let him know you have full control of the three alert shields and their activities."

Pleasure warmed Arya. "I won't let you down," she promised.

"See that you don't," he grumbled. "I'd much prefer it if your first major misstep wasn't allowing an invasion of our borders while I'm away."

Arya swallowed, excitement dying abruptly at that thought. "Yes, sir."

Desomer stood abruptly, sending half the pieces of parchment nearest him flying across the table. "Come on then, it's nearly time for Winterfest lunch. Don't want to miss that, do we? Not when Peemla is organising it."

The leap of anticipation that went through her at the thought quickly died. Essa would be at lunch. What was she going to do about that situation, especially with the warlord and Desomer about to leave Heathrock? She'd have to tell the warlord, even though everything inside her protested doing that, knowing it would likely mean Essa being expelled from the household.

What had she been doing in that damned forest?

That question went round and round in Arya's mind as she and Desomer made their way down to the castle's formal dining room, the general complaining the whole way about his old knees on the stairs. Magen was already there when they arrived, as were Peemla and Commander Randin.

Arya didn't get a good look at the table until she sat down, and when she did, unexpected tears pricked her eyes and she couldn't stop the delighted smile that spread over her face.

But who had…? Arya looked over at Peemla, who gave a secret smile. "It wasn't me, Captain."

Essa's laughter heralded the arrival of the boys. She was the first to appear, Rorin and Darmanin trailing behind. Both stopped in their tracks as they got a good look at the table.

Small candles lined the centre of the tabletop, filling the room with the scent of cinnamon and vanilla. Perched in front of each table setting were silly-looking hats, each one different and clearly having been put together with an artistic hand.

And every hat had a bright snowdrop pinned to it—freshly picked that morning.

Rorin looked straight at Essa, who was staring hopefully at Darmanin, then a beaming smile lit up his face and he reached out to wrap an arm around Darmanin's shoulders. The young shapeshifter merely stared at the table, grey eyes sheened with tears.

Essa had done this?

Arya put on her hat, then picked up Desomer's and held it out to him, making sure to wipe the grin from her face. The general glowered but reluctantly took the thing and put it on his head. With a wry smile, Magen followed suit. Peemla was already wearing hers. Rorin darted forward, dropping into his seat so enthusiastically it rocked and almost sent him flying backwards, then put his hat on too.

Darmanin crossed to the table and sat down at his place opposite Arya, saying nothing. After a moment, he reached out, gently running his fingers over the hat sitting in front of him. Then, he picked it up and placed it over his dark hair. When he lifted his head, he was smiling.

"Are they okay?" Essa asked quietly. "I wasn't sure if—"

"They're perfect," Darmanin said simply. "Thank you."

Essa relaxed, then gave a dramatic shiver. "It was *freezing* out in the forest this morning, so I'm glad my near-hypothermia was worth it."

Arya bit her lip, a surge of guilt flooding her at having doubted Essa once again. She'd been out in the cold looking for snowdrops to make Winterfest a happier time for Darmanin, not sneaking off to meet with Shadeweavers.

Her gaze met Darmanin's and she saw the same guilt reflected there.

Thiara Ravenstrike and her husband entered, and everyone stood, attention going to the front of the room. The warlord's gaze narrowed slightly at the sight of the hats and candles, but she didn't say anything as she sat down.

"*Mother, Papa, please put your hats on,*" Rorin signed, then looked at Darmanin as he continued. "*It's a new family tradition we'd like to start. For all of us.*"

The warlord reached for her hat and put it on, Matte Eaglesoar following suit. Then she raised her glass. "Happy Winterfest, everyone."

"Happy Winterfest," came the resounding response.

The warlord actually smiled. "Let's enjoy lunch."

"You were right, Arya," Darmanin said as she spooned creamy mashed potatoes onto her plate before passing the bowl along. "About us being family."

Their gazes met and held, that wonderful smile returning to Darmanin's face.

"Arya, do you want these blasted beans or not?" Desomer barked in her ear.

"Yes, sir." She looked away to take the tray from Desomer. After spooning beans onto her plate and then passing it to Peemla, she glanced back at Darmanin. He was leaning across to say something to Rorin. Rorin grinned in response and nodded vigorously.

Towards the end of the lunch, when everybody was stuffed full of food and drink, Matte Eaglesoar stood to toast the household. "As you all know by now, this celebration is a sadder one than usual. It's the last Winterfest that Rorin will be sharing with us for a while." Matte ruffled his son's sandy mop of hair. "Thiara and I will be diverting to Hawkesdale on our way to the State Council, where Rorin and Darmanin will be fostered for the next three years."

Arya joined in the clapping and clinking of glasses, but only half-heartedly. She glanced across the table, caught the flash of tears in Essa's eyes before she blinked them away, the way Darmanin and Rorin shifted closer to each other almost unconsciously, and the look of concern on Magen's face as he watched Darmanin.

She had many things to protect now. Not just her own life and future, but that of her family too. Her State. She had to do more than just wait for the State Council to decide about the Nightstalker.

It was time to talk to Salyarin again.

Chapter 30

The day after Warlord Ravenstrike left for the State Council, taking Rorin, Taze, and Darmanin with her, Arya took her shield out on a patrol—filled out now with Laskin, who hadn't travelled with Rorin. Gelfrey Hawkesdale would provide his own weapons tutor. They passed Icecliff without stopping and continued along the road to the pass.

She took the opportunity to question Laskin about something that had been nagging at her; it was the first opportunity she'd had since the summit. "I thought the run through the Dreadwater Gate to steal cazaix weapons from the Khadini was just a foolish noble's game. But after the summit, Desomer and Magen talked about cazaix as something that keeps the Nightstalker at bay. Why?"

"Well." Laskin scratched at his beard. "It *is* a foolish rich person's game. There are ways to get cazaix without running the dangerous Dreadwater rapids into Khadini and risking your life sneaking past their border guards. But the way I understand it, cazaix metal inhibits Sky Lord magic. It is also the only weapon that can inflict damage on a wyvern."

"I see." That *was* interesting. And made it clearer why the Nightstalker had hesitated about invading all those years ago. There was something that could counter his magic.

There was a moment's silence, then Laskin asked in a low voice, "He's looking for Sky Lord potentials, isn't he?"

Arya started. "What?"

None of Laskin's usual teasing or dry amusement was on his face. "The Nightstalker told the warlords that he's looking for rebels, but a handful of cold and half-starved rebels managing to survive in the Diamondfang are no threat to the Nightstalker's rule. What he really meant is that he's looking for Sky Lord potentials."

"Our warlord thinks as much," Arya conceded. "You told me he killed all the Sky Lords, though."

"Yes. But there were always five, Arya. The king or queen of Andahar and their Sky Lord council. When one died, a new Sky Lord would be born into one of the Sky Lord Houses who would grow to make five again. That was part of the magic of Andahar."

She scowled at him. "Why do you know so much about everything?"

"Mainly so I can annoy you." He chuckled. "My father was a storyteller, and he loved tales of magic and Sky Lords and heroes. My sisters and I reaped the benefits of that in his bedtime stories." There was a note of wistfulness in Laskin's voice.

"He sounds like a good father," she said softly, then, "What *is* the Nightstalker's magic exactly?"

"Nobody really knows. The way I heard it from Da, each Sky Lord possessed a particular kind of magic, an ability unique to the House they were born into. That's how they got their names. Windspinner and Flamewielder were two of the Sky Lord Houses I recall him telling stories about. Inkweaver too, and their mysterious archive. But the Nightstalker was always shrouded in mystery. My father thought he'd somehow managed to get more magic, unnaturally, and that's how he was able to kill the others and bring down their Houses."

A thought came to Arya unbidden—which House had *she* been born into? Which magic was she meant to have? But she dismissed the fancy from her thoughts. She clearly had no magic. *Yet.* The single word shivered through her. She hoped it stayed that way. If she never evinced any magic, she'd never be a threat to the Nightstalker's incredible power.

As if reading her mind, Laskin cleared his throat, lifted an eyebrow. "You're suddenly quite curious about the Sky Lords. What did the Etherean want to talk to you about—that morning you woke me to watch the camp? You never told me."

A call came down from the front of the column before Arya could figure out how to respond. Glad of the reprieve, she spurred her mare down the line.

They'd reached the pass.

It looked as untouched as the last time Arya had ridden up months earlier. Even so, she had them all out of the saddle, crawling over its surface to ensure they missed nothing.

Once they'd confirmed it was intact, Arya left the shield in Laskin's hands, claiming she wanted to scout the area to make sure all was well. They seemed happy enough to put this down to her being extra careful in Desomer's absence, though Laskin gave her a suspicious look as they rode off. She hoped he'd forget about his question before she saw him again.

As soon as the shield was out of sight, Arya turned her mare off the road and into the trees. Keeping careful watch for predators and Shadeweavers, she made her way to the snow-covered plateau where the Etherean elder had first come to speak with her.

There, she dismounted and set about making camp. Shelter if bad weather blew in and enough wood to keep a fire alive all night. She gathered water, then settled before the warmth of the crackling flames. She made sure she was out in the open, so any Etherean scout flying high above would see her.

And then she waited.

***

Salyarin came at dawn the following morning. After a restless night's sleep on cold, hard ground, Arya was already awake, huddled close to her fire.

"Arya." He looked relieved to see her, pale blue wings rustling as he dropped to the ground. He didn't appear the slightest bit cold, even though he wore only a simple jerkin and breeches. It made her shiver just to look at him. "I am glad to see you well, especially after the Nightstalker crossed the Diamondfang recently."

"Elder." She bowed her head in acknowledgment of his rank, then relayed the details of the summit. He looked increasingly dismayed, turning white when she spoke about being in the same room as the Nightstalker, though she left out what had happened when he'd used his magic on her. She had no desire for anyone to know about that weakness. "He was … I can understand why everyone is so afraid of him, now that I've seen him and Xaphistryl together."

"Is that why you've come?" His face brightened. "To take up your heritage?"

"No." Arya took a breath. "I've come to make a bargain with you, Elder."

His relieved expression turned wary. "What kind of bargain?"

"I accept that the Nightstalker is looking for me, but you are wrong that I am a threat to him. I have no magic and no intention of trying to take his throne."

"Arya, you must! You—"

"What is it exactly you want me to do?" she challenged. "Hike over the Diamondfang to Andahar, announce to everyone I see that I am the lost heir and a potential Sky Lord, somehow build an army without the Nightstalker knowing about it, then use that army to defeat the most powerful man alive and his equally powerful wyvern?"

"It is not as simplistic as you make it sound," the elder said stiffly. "You *do* have magic, magic that will take its own time to reveal, but it is there. You will have a wyvern too. And other Sky Lords to help you."

"Even if that were true, he killed the last Sky Lords when they were fully trained and grown," Arya pressed. "I have no army, no proof that I am anybody's heir, and no knowledge of Andahar. I have no means of unseating the Nightstalker, and no desire to. My home is here, Elder. My family is here. My future is here."

He opened his mouth, as if to argue further, but abruptly shut it. "Then what bargain do you wish to strike with me?"

"My general believes the Nightstalker is laying the ground for invasion under the pretext that Dunidaen is sheltering threats to Andahar. I think he could be right. Either way, we must keep a closer eye on this border than ever before. I need to make sure he does not and cannot cross it with an army."

"You mean you seek to relieve your guilt over being responsible for the Nightstalker's renewed interest in Dunidaen," the elder said reprovingly.

Her shoulders tensed, stung by his accusation, how it landed too close to home. "I am not responsible for his actions or his choices. I want your help, Elder. I want your Etherean scouts to help us watch the border."

Once the words were out, she almost wanted to take them back. If her warlord knew she was treating with the Etherean, if *any* of the warlords learned of it...

"And why would I agree to that? Your Dunidae warlords wouldn't want our help if they knew you were asking for it, and I have no desire to draw the Nightstalker's attention to my people."

"Our mutual interest lies in me not being discovered," Arya pointed out. "We both benefit from the Nightstalker giving up on the fact that I am to be found here or that I pose any threat to him. By helping me watch the border, you prevent more wraiths and shadowhounds coming through that could find me or attack your home. We will keep our contact discreet, and neither Andahar nor Dunidaen need ever learn of it."

The elder regarded her for a long moment, a calculating expression on his face. "I would require something from you if I were to agree to this."

"What?"

"I told you there would be four others, Sky Lord potentials. You intimated you already knew one. If you promise me to protect them to the best of your ability, I will help keep watch on your border, Arya Nameless."

She baulked. "I don't know who they are."

"You will, in time. Promise me, and we have a deal."

Arya didn't have to think about it for longer than a moment. She stepped forward, offered the winged man her outstretched hand. "My word on it, Elder Salyarin."

"And my word on it, Captain Nameless."

Once the winged man had gone, vanishing into the low, grey cloud presaging a snow fall, Arya stood there for a long time, staring out over the mountains.

She'd done what she could. Now she would go back home, pull out Desomer's maps and coloured stones, and work on a strategy that would impress him. Continue training her shields to be even better. Figure out how to improve the Raiders' opinion of her. Write letters to Rorin in Hawkesdale.

Arya saddled up her mare and set her in the direction of Icecliff. She'd re-join her shield, take them back to Heathrock city where they could enjoy a drink at The Ruined Arms and she could see Tiya.

A smile spread over her face at the thought of all those things. She had a family now, a home and a purpose, and she wasn't going to let anything interfere with that.

PART 2

Chapter 31

Nearly three years later

Arya splashed cold water from the stream onto her face before standing and stretching. More alert now, she pulled her jerkin back on and then buckled her sword belt around her waist. A small smile crossed her face as it settled comfortably on her hip; the weapon no longer dwarfed her like it had the waiflike, under-fed fifteen-year-old girl who'd enlisted with the Raiders. Now, at twenty years, she easily carried its weight.

Not far off, Laskin tossed a bucket of water over the dying fire, making it hiss, and she could hear the casual chatter of the shield as they prepared to leave. She should join them, but instead found her gaze tugged inexorably upwards, towards the highest peaks of the Diamondfang. Over the past three years, she'd regularly slipped away from her patrol to meet with one of the Etherean warrior scouts—confirming all was well. This time, it hadn't been a simple warrior there to meet her; it had been the elder himself.

She'd eyed Salyarin suspiciously when he'd landed in the clearing and offered that faintly condescending smile that seemed unique to the Etherean. "Arya, it's good to see you."

"Is something wrong?" Her stomach dropped at the thought. For three years, there had been no sign of danger from Andahar. It had been long enough that she'd convinced herself the danger was over. That she'd dealt with the problem and could forget about it. That the Nightstalker had seen no threat emerging and left it alone.

"We have seen no sign of wraiths, shadowhounds, or any other creature from Andahar moving through the mountains," he assured her. "As always, we fly as close as we dare to their north-eastern border and see no signs of a troop build-up or anything else that might indicate an intent to invade."

"But…"

"Our agreement has held for almost three years, Arya Nameless, and I thought it time to review the terms." That air of authority he carried edged his voice, reminding Arya that she was effectively negotiating with a man that held the status of a king or High Warlord. The Dunidae warlords would have a fit if they found out. "The Sky Lord potential you once spoke of—are they safe? Have you found any of the others?"

"Yes, and no," she said flatly. Darmanin was safe, as far as she knew, and due to return from Hawkesdale with Rorin any day now. Even though she had her suspicions Salyarin already knew it, she'd never revealed Darmanin's identity to the Etherean. Nor did she intend to.

"There are still three—"

"I cannot go actively searching for magic-wielders, Elder, not without putting myself at risk. You know that already." She eyed him. "But that's not why you came today."

He let out a sigh. "You know that our magic is in healing?"

"Yes." It was the reason the Etherean had chosen self-exile when the borders closed. Arya thought the Dunidae warlords foolish for ignoring an aerial kingdom that could bring such useful magic to an alliance, but in the time since the Nightstalker's coup and aversion of war, the Dunidae fear of magic had turned into hatred. Arya put a lid on that thinking before her own confusion and guilt on the issue of magic-wielders rose up to distract her.

"Recently, our strongest healers have felt … it's hard to explain, but something like a blight, when they're using their magic." Unadorned fear closed over his face. "Arya, I came today because I fear the nazal are stirring again."

She eyed him, reading his fear as genuine. "Connect those two things for me."

"Our healers have felt this before, decades ago when the nazal were active and hunting Sky Lords. The nazal are the greatest threat you face beyond the Nightstalker himself … if he has sent them to hunt you, then you are in extreme danger. You have no hope of surviving a nazal. They are your bane, Arya."

"What *are* they?"

"Creatures of the Nightstalker's creation. They aren't human but can appear so—they can wear many disguises and have potent abilities at their disposal, including powerful sensing magic. They are a threat not just to you, but any other potential Sky Lords."

"We've successfully faced down wraiths and shadowhounds, Elder, surely we can—"

"The nazal are like nothing you've faced," he said, louder now. "Even as a fully-fledged Sky Lord at the height of your powers you would find them a test."

She didn't want to believe him, because if she did, it would mean the Nightstalker hadn't given up. Worse, it meant he was escalating his search for her. And what would that mean for Dunidaen? For her Raider comrades and her family? But Salyarin wasn't making this up. He believed it.

She let out a sigh. "How do I protect myself from them?"

"The only way is to stay hidden. We cannot overstate how vulnerable you are to a nazal."

"I appreciate the warning, but the Nightstalker is quiet. I pose no threat to him. Perhaps these monsters are stirring for another reason, or maybe your healers are wrong."

"I know you want that to be true, but—"

"It *is* true. It has been for three years now." She recognised the edge in her voice and wondered if the old Etherean could see that she was trying to convince herself as much as him.

Irritation had flashed over the elder's face, but he didn't argue any further. "Do not use your magic, under any circumstances. Do not draw attention to yourselves. If a nazal is near, you probably won't even know it."

"I can do that," she said. "And thank you, for the warning. I know it is sincerely meant."

He spread his wings, then paused. "You still have the candle we gave you? My dream-walking ability is incredibly draining, but I can reach you in your sleep if there is a need. If my healers are right, you might need to reach us urgently."

"I have," she assured him.

"Then light it if you need to speak with me, and I will come to your dreams. Be careful, Arya Nameless. More careful than you've ever been before."

Those had been his parting words, before he'd taken flight and she'd watched in fascination as his massive wings carried him away from her.

Now, Arya shook away the memory of that conversation and the disturbing news she'd learned at Icecliff during the patrol, allowing her good mood borne of a sunny morning and the companionship of her shield-mates to return. As she walked through the trees towards the horses, she called the order for the shield to mount up. A series of cheerful acknowledgments came back.

On reaching the horses, she reached out to stroke the silky nose of her stallion, a cheeky chestnut named Zeke. He snorted at her touch and butted Arya's hand, searching for food.

Laskin gave her one of his looks as he joined her. "That horse was a rich gift for the warlord to give you for your coming of age."

"Raven's balls, Laskin, you never stop harping like an old woman. That was over a year ago now. Don't tell me you still have doubts about my apprenticeship to General Desomer?"

"I never had doubts about your ability to succeed him one day," Laskin said. "That doesn't mean I'll ever understand why Warlord Ravenstrike chose a stripling Nameless girl to apprentice to her general. Or why you're still his apprentice even as his retirement age grows closer."

"I'm no stripling Nameless girl anymore," she said sharply. Arya had grown tall in the years since her first arrival at Heathrock, and repeated drill and conditioning exercises had built muscle and strength into her lean frame. She was fiercely proud of this fact.

He snorted. "No, but you're hardly old and grey, either."

"Like you?" she asked innocently.

Laskin glowered at her. "You're in a good mood today."

She sobered. Laskin never riled her just for the sake of it. He watched her back, always. "Do you really think the warlord will change her mind about me succeeding General Desomer?"

"The woman wants to be High Warlord. Every single one of her senior advisers needs to be influential and powerful for the other warlords to even entertain voting for her. Desomer is one of Dunidaen's most respected generals and Magen is the son of a powerful vicelord. Having a Nameless as Ravenstrike general … I just don't see her letting it happen. When it comes down to it, she'll pick Lerin or Arken, whichever of them gives her the most political clout."

Her heart sank, some of her good mood evaporating. She already knew this, deep down, but Laskin's words made if feel more real.

"Then why would she have apprenticed me in the first place?" It was an argument she threw out to hold him off, but one she didn't have a good answer to. Although … she'd wondered often over the years about that moment in Windfall Fort, when it had seemed Thiara Ravenstrike knew exactly who Arya was and given her a direct order not to hand herself over to the Nightstalker. Could that knowledge have had something to do with why the warlord chose her to be Desomer's apprentice?

"I don't know, but something else you should be thinking about?" He leaned closer. "Arken still doesn't like you, and we all know how Lerin feels about you. If one of them becomes general…"

Laskin didn't need to spell that one out for her. Her Raider career would be done.

Further conversation was forestalled as Arya swung into the saddle and picked up the reins. The rest of their shield adjusted girth straps and stirrups before mounting. She lifted her voice, sending it ringing through the trees. "Shield, let's ride."

She rode at the head of the column, where she could be alone with her thoughts. It was late summer in Dunidaen, barely a week from the arrival of autumn, which meant dappled sunlight shone through the leaves of the forest as they rode, dispelling its usually gloomy air. Her shield had spent the past three weeks patrolling between Icecliff, SheerRock, and Windfall

Forts, and now they were returning home after a final trip up to the Diamondfang pass.

They weren't riding long before they emerged from the Wraith Forest and onto the main road between Heathrock city and Icecliff, and by midday they were entering the city gates.

The streets were busy, the sun hot on their backs as Arya led them down the winding cobblestone streets to the entry gates at the bottom level. She couldn't help but notice—as she always did now—how many more beggars with branded cheeks lurked on the street corners.

At the State Council three years earlier, Thiara Ravenstrike's powerful arguments about Dunidae sovereignty had succeeded in modifying Crowtalon's original proposal that all magic-wielders captured in Dunidaen should be handed over to Andahar. A full convocation of the Council had agreed on sending captured Shadeweavers only—as criminals, they were a burden on Dunidae society, and the warlords had no compunction about handing them over.

The Nightstalker had proclaimed himself satisfied with that arrangement—after all, most Shadeweaver magic-wielders lived in the Diamondfang where he'd claimed the malcontents were—and there had been no rumblings from across the border since. It had also meant that magic-wielders no longer joined the Shadeweavers for safety in the same numbers they once had, instead taking their chances in not being found out or surviving on the streets of bigger cities if they were.

Yet some warlords and vicelords—Falconcrest and Crowtalon leading the charge—continued to push for all magic-wielders to be given to Andahar.

Arya hated all of it. She understood well the threat that magic could pose, but every time she saw one of those beggars, she simply could not summon an acceptance of the way they were treated. And every time she thought of Darmanin, she struggled to even be okay with the idea of sending magic-wielding Shadeweavers to Andahar.

They were Dunidae citizens, and criminals or not, they should be dealt with by Dunidaen, not shipped off to a foreign king. Arya had always assumed the Nightstalker killed the magic-wielders sent to him, but sometimes she wondered. Would the Nightstalker—

"What do you think he does with them?" Laskin spoke suddenly from where he rode beside her, accurately interpreting her thoughts as he often did.

"I only know what you do, Laskin. That after their arrest, the Shadeweaver magic-wielders are held in Aren until one of Andahar's navy ships comes along every six months to pick them up."

"Do you think…" He hesitated. "If he's looking for Sky Lord potentials, what happens if all these magic-wielders we're sending over are no more than that; Dunidae citizens with a bit of magical ability."

"Then I assume he gives up on his paranoid notion that there are Sky Lords wandering around the Diamondfang looking to unseat him from his throne," she snapped, irritation boiling over.

Laskin seemed to sense her irritation wasn't directed at him, because he gave her a look. "You're antsy today."

She snorted. By now they'd left the city and were on the road out to Heathrock castle. Despite her unease, anticipation began to thrum through her. "I'm always antsy when we can't go faster than a walk."

"You don't fool me." Laskin snorted. "You're impatient to get home because Lord Rorin and Darmanin are due to return from Hawkesdale any day now."

She shrugged nonchalantly. "It will be good to see them."

"You've written letters to Rorin at least once a month since he left, sometimes more," Laskin said. "I'd bet a pile of gold coins you'd never written a letter in your life before that."

"He was homesick at the beginning. I was just helping him settle in."

"And after that?"

She turned and glowered at him. "Ravens' balls, Laskin, leave it alone will you!"

"Yes, Captain," he said with a mostly straight face, probably the only person in Heathrock that could get away with teasing the apprentice to the general of Ravenstrike. "It will be good to see them. They're good boys."

"They were good boys nearly three years ago. They could be horrible youths by now," she pointed out. "You know what Warn was like."

Lanna Crowtalon's second son had fostered at Ravenstrike—a gesture of civility Thiara had made in an effort to keep relations with Crowtalon on an even keel—and had only returned home a month earlier. A wastrel who preferred lazing about to doing anything productive, not a single person at Heathrock had enjoyed Warn Crowtalon's stay, and in the end, Desomer had banished him to Icecliff for far longer than he had Andrian Crowtalon when he'd fostered with Ravenstrike years earlier.

Laskin grimaced. "Excellent point."

Soon, they rounded a corner and the seat of Ravenstrike was laid out before them. The lake, unfrozen in summer, gleamed green in the sunlight, and the surrounding mountains of the Diamondfang were snow-free apart from their very peaks. But Arya ignored all that. Her gaze scanned the battlements, looking for ... there. She let out a loud whoop.

"What is it?" Laskin looked as if she'd gone mad.

She pointed. "Rorin's home! Look, the flags are flying. Take charge of the shield, Laskin."

Arya urged Zeke into a gallop down the road and the stallion's hooves clattered through the open gates into the castle. Raiders that had been part of Rorin's escort home, as well as the grooms taking care of their horses, scattered frantically as Arya came in at full speed, then reined Zeke into a stop just before the main castle building.

A groom came to take Zeke and Arya ran up the steps, sword tapping against her leg. At the threshold she paused, gaze scanning the gaggle of people gathered in the entrance foyer greeting each other with varying levels of enthusiasm.

She searched the group, not resting until ... her eyes widened as she finally spotted what she was looking for.

Rorin, the future heir to Ravenstrike, had returned home.

Chapter 32

Gone was the skinny boy Arya had met when first arriving at Heathrock. A tall, gangly, seventeen-year-old now stood in the entrance foyer, signing an enthusiastic greeting to his parents. But while his messy blonde curls were now tamed by the traditional short braid that marked him as the son of a noble house, the same merry sparkle still lit up Rorin's blue eyes.

He seemed to sense as soon as Arya appeared because his gaze shifted, going straight to her. A delighted grin spread over his face. He broke into a run, and she moved with quick strides to meet him halfway. He was as tall as her now, and he threw his arms around her and lifted her off her feet in an energetic hug. Laughing, she hugged him back, pleased beyond measure to see him. Eventually, he let her go and began signing. "*It's so good to see you, Arya. We missed you!*"

Nearly three years. It had been too long, and letters weren't enough. Even so, Arya didn't realise just how deeply she'd missed Rorin until this moment. She found grounded again, seeing him, having him near. "Welcome home, Rorin," she murmured.

His blue eyes brightened, and he drew her into another hug.

When they parted, Darmanin appeared at Rorin's shoulder, grave as ever. "Hello, Arya."

Her eyes widened in surprise as she let go of Rorin. Darmanin too, had grown. He stood a good head taller than her and, dressed in black fighting leathers, looked far less the gangly youth than Rorin. He wore his black hair in the same short braid, and his features had hardened. Darmanin would never be handsome, but his high cheekbones and light grey eyes made him striking.

Unexpected delight swept through her at the sight of him, and she instinctively reached up to press her palm lightly against his chest. "Hello, Dar."

That little smile of his crept over his face, and he bowed his head, one hand reaching up to touch hers. Something inside her tightened. Or pulled. Or settled into place. She wasn't sure which it was.

Taze appeared then at Rorin's side, saluting sharply. "We missed you, Captain."

Arya blinked, tearing her attention from Darmanin to stare at Taze. "I thought you were done growing." The whip-cord thin young Raider had filled out with muscle and length, but his warm hazel eyes remained unchanged. "It's good to see you, Taze."

"*We have so much to tell you!*" Rorin signed. "*Come and eat lunch with us?*"

"You can make your patrol report after lunch, Captain," Thiara Ravenstrike said when Arya looked her way. "I'd actually like to see both you and Raider Nameless then."

"Warlord." Arya saluted. "We'll be there."

Thiara turned to her son. "Rorin, I look forward to seeing you at dinner tonight."

"*I'll be there. I love you.*"

Thiara smiled and reached out to touch Rorin's arm before she and Matte departed. Still grinning, Rorin linked arms with Arya and began dragging her away. "*You look different.*" He signed. "*You still have that fierce glare I remember, but look at you, you're stunning.*"

Arya snorted. Fortunately, she was saved from having to reply when Rorin, Taze, and Darmanin's attention all shifted suddenly elsewhere. Rorin even stopped his incessant signing mid-gesture.

Essa had arrived, probably alerted to Rorin's arrival by the shouting and laughter. While Arya was every inch a warrior, and dressed and behaved like one, Essa had grown into a self-assured young woman who carried herself like the daughter of a warlord. "You're back!" she said, clapping her hands with delight, green eyes shining.

"It's good to see you again, Essa." Darmanin bowed slightly, making her snort.

"*We missed you!*" Rorin signed so vigorously his fingers were a blur. "*We have so much to tell you both.*"

"Yes. Poor Warlord Hawkesdale." Taze's mouth quirked. "I think he was glad to see the back of us."

"*That's because he was terrified you were trying to corrupt his daughter.*" Rorin grinned at his bodyguard.

"You didn't?" Arya rounded on Taze.

"I did nothing of the sort, Captain," Taze said firmly. "I cannot say the same for Rorin."

"*I did not!*" Rorin said, his signing so indignant it barely made sense.

"I want to hear all about this." Arya laughed. "Come on, Peemla's cooked up a massive spread to welcome you home, I'm sure."

***

Immediately after lunch, Arya and Taze reported to the warlord's office. General Desomer was there too, standing straight-backed to one side of the warlord's desk. Arya was still glowing from seeing Rorin but did her best to school her features into a sober expression.

"Any issues during your patrol?" the warlord asked.

"None, Warlord. The roadblocks remained undisturbed, and while we saw signs of Shadeweaver activity in several locations, we weren't attacked." She mentioned nothing about her conversation with the elder, of course, and tried to make it sound like she wasn't leaving anything out—something she'd become well-practiced at.

"Good. You'll pass on details of those locations to SheerRock and Icecliff to follow up on," Thiara ordered.

"Yes, Warlord." Arya managed to reply *just* quickly enough so that her hesitation wasn't obvious.

Warlord Ravenstrike's harsher policies on cleaning up Shadeweaver activities had gone down well at the last State Council, so much so that she'd kept them up, allowing Commander Lerin free rein to track down and destroy any encampment his patrols found. It meant they found and captured more magic-wielders that sought refuge with the Shadeweavers, too, which kept Andahar happy. The one time Arya had tried raising with the warlord how Ranier might respond to her approach—particularly given she was fostering his daughter in her household—Thiara had dismissed her concerns and made clear she did not consider it important enough to discuss further. In her view, Essa was now a member of the Ravenstrike household and all remnants of her Shadeweaver origins had been polished away.

It was one of the very few times Arya had ever felt genuine anger towards her warlord. For an incredibly smart woman whose strategic mind was ahead of even Desomer's, she could be stunningly ignorant of some things.

Desomer didn't seem overly bothered by the warlord's policy either. Arya had tried to reconcile herself to it, but largely failed. Shadeweavers had murdered her shield-mates, people she liked and respected. They could be violent in conducting their criminal activities and plagued trade throughout Dunidaen. Yet ... when Arya went on patrol, she made no particular effort to find Shadeweaver encampments and didn't question herself too closely as to why.

"Raider Nameless." Thiara addressed Taze next, drawing Arya from her thoughts. "My intention in assigning you as my son's bodyguard was that you would be able to win his trust and confidence. You know Rorin well by now, and you know the way his mind works." Thiara pierced Taze with those penetrating, faded blue eyes. "I am promoting you to shield captain and placing you in command of a new shield that will be Rorin's personal guard, just as I have my own personal shield. If anything happens to him, I will hold you responsible."

Surprise flashed over Taze's face, but he rallied quickly. "Thank you, Warlord. Can I ask ... do you believe there are any specific threats to Lord Rorin's life?"

The warlord sighed. "It would take a lot for any of the warlords to consider raising a hand against a potential heir … too much, even, for Mathas Crowtalon. Still, Rorin is my only child and there are other dangers closer to home than rival warlords, as we all discovered some years ago." "No harm will come to your son, Warlord. I'll make sure of it," Taze said.

"It would be too provocative for me to assign Darmanin his own personal shield for protection," Thiara said. "And if it came down to a choice between protecting Rorin or Darmanin, you will choose Rorin. But in all other instances, I expect you to protect Darmanin too."

"Yes, Warlord."

"Good," Thiara said crisply, including Arya in her gaze now too. "Warlord Crowtalon's chief adviser, Nain, will be arriving here in a week. Darmanin is to be kept out of sight at all times while he's here. Mathas no doubt knows Darmanin is at Heathrock, but I'd rather not make it obvious. I met Nain at the last State Council—Crowtalon had just appointed him. He's a slimy but observant man, and no doubt he'll be looking for anything he can take back to Mathas to use against us."

"Yes, Warlord." Taze and Arya agreed simultaneously.

Magen knocked and entered, and Thiara Ravenstrike glanced at Taze. "Dismissed."

Taze saluted and left, and Magen closed the door behind him. "You're discussing Nain's visit?"

Thiara nodded. "Your expression tells me you're bringing me more headaches."

Magen gave her a pained smile. "A message arrived this morning from High Warlord Eaglesoar. He's had a formal missive from Andahar."

The attention in the room sharpened. A cold fist closed abruptly around Arya's chest.

"King Lucius notes the number of magic-wielders we've been sending him is growing smaller, and further claims that none of those we've sent so far are who he's looking for." Magen glanced at the curling parchment in his hand. "Eaglesoar says the Nightstalker pointed out how patient he's been, then politely implied we are deliberately sheltering these threats to his throne. Crowtalon presumably got the same news from Eaglesoar a few days ago because he's also sent a message that says he wants us to discuss the situation with Nain while he's here. He's proposing a quick and decisive response to the Nightstalker."

"Oh he is, is he?" Thiara said dryly.

Arya fought the urge to close her eyes, to make herself as small and as close to invisible as possible. She'd done her best to brush aside Salyarin's recent warning, but for the Nightstalker to reach out now … the timing couldn't be coincidental.

"Warlord, we'll need to be careful," Magen said. "Khadini was furious when they learned we'd treated with the Nightstalker three years ago without advising or including them. Even the Icefolk were unhappy. We—"

"Yes, yes, I know. If we respond without discussing it with them this time, they'll be even angrier, and it's incredibly important we maintain good relations with Khadini and their cazaix if the Nightstalker gets restive again." She waved a dismissive hand. "Except that Mathas Crowtalon disagrees and thinks consulting them shows weakness on Dunidaen's part. No doubt Nain will be parroting that when he arrives."

"I wish you luck with him," Desomer grunted. "I assume you won't need me for any of your discussions, Warlord?"

"No. Foreign relations aside, he's here to complain about the trade deficit between Crowtalon and Ravenstrike. Again." The warlord smiled coolly. "Not that he's going to get anywhere with those complaints."

Desomer nodded. "Understood. Warlord, noting the missive from the Nightstalker, I recommend an increase in patrols of the underground road and Diamondfang pass."

"Do it," she said. "Dismissed, General. Captain."

Back in Desomer's office, they moved over to the table by his windows. As she took a chair, Arya's usual anticipation was dimmed by a heavy layer of dread weighing on her chest. These sessions with Desomer had become her favourite of everything they did together, but today the news from Magen had unsettled her too badly to feel excitement.

He spread a map of Ravenstrike and surrounds on the table's flat surface, then placed stones on the map; red in Heathrock and purple crossing the border through SparrowWing. Then he used string to lay out three supply lines for the invading forces.

Once he was finished, he lit a cigar, sat back in his chair, and asked the ritual question. "What would you do?"

Arya took a deep, steadying breath, and dispelled her troubled thoughts, allowing her mind to become completely focused on the problem. She spent some time surveying the map and the Crowtalon numbers. When she began moving stones, she did it carefully, thinking her way through each move and its potential consequences before making it. A couple of times she moved stones back and started again. At some point, Desomer finished his cigar and returned to his desk to start working through the untidy pile of parchment that always sat there.

Over an hour had passed before Arya sat back. "That's what I'd do, sir."

Desomer grunted, signed something, then came to take a look. After a moment, a reluctant smile crossed his face. "Not bad, Captain."

She'd marched four thousand Raiders south, slowly enough to establish supply lines along the way. The two forces met in the middle of Ravenstrike in a cluster of red and purple stones. Meanwhile, two red stones had galloped south from small garrisons in the east and west of the State they'd established in the past three years. While her main force marched south, these two flanking units attacked and destroyed the Crowtalon supply lines, then turned north to hit the Lances from behind. The purple stones found themselves surrounded by red, stranded in the middle of Ravenstrike.

Desomer's smile faded as quickly as it had come, and he leaned forward to put all the stones back where they'd started. He then opened a draw and pulled out some blue stones, placing them along the Crowtalon supply lines. "Falconcrest have allied with Crowtalon and are using their Aggressors to protect the Lances' supply lines," he said. "Think on that overnight and report your counter to me when we meet tomorrow."

"Yes, sir." She bit her lip, mind racing, already thinking about what she would do.

"Tomorrow, Captain." Desomer hefted himself out of his chair. "Right now, we have to review shield placements. We've got a higher than usual number of requests for re-assignment this month and three shield captain vacancies to address. We'll also need to move rosters around to increase patrols to the pass and underground road."

Arya stifled her sigh and followed him to the desk. Paperwork was her least favourite part of this job. Still, she had some thoughts she'd been wanting to raise. "Sir, if I may?"

"Go on."

"I recommend you promote Laskin to lead my alert shield. I think he's wasted outside a leadership role."

Desomer eyed her. "And what will you be doing instead?"

"Well." She cleared her throat, as always doing her best not to wilt under his withering stare. "You know over the past few months I've been taking a few of the different shields here out on patrol?"

"If you've a point, hurry up and get to it."

"Yes, sir. I'd like to keep doing that. It's a good way for me to get to know the individual Raiders better, their strengths and weaknesses, and let them see more of me too."

Initially she'd begun this to try and win the loyalty of the Heathrock Raiders—as outwardly confident as she was about succeeding Desomer one day, the doubts were never far from the surface. But the more she'd ridden with different shields, the more it had made her see things she hadn't before.

"And?" Desomer knew there was more coming.

"Well, sir, it seems to me that some men and women are under-utilised, while others have been given duties their talents don't suit. I think we should mix up the shields so that we can make each individual shield a more well-rounded and effective unit." She also saw this as a way to start breaking down the divide between the 'noble' Raiders from important families and the others at Heathrock. It would be hard for a vicelord's daughter to maintain disdain for the blacksmith's son who'd just saved her life in a Shadeweaver ambush.

"That's not how it's done," he barked. "Those men and women have been together for years. They know each other's tendencies."

"Familiarity also breeds complacency, sir."

"Not if they've got effective captains and a strong battalion commander."

"Sir—"

"Enough. The shields stay as they are."

She stifled a flash of irritation. He was wrong on this; she knew it in her bones. And if the Nightstalker was stirring again, they needed the strongest army possible. "Yes, sir."

"The rest of your recommendations are solid. I'll promote Laskin and you can keep taking the other shields out on a rotating basis."

That seemed counter-productive, falling short of proper change, but Arya tried not to let her impatience show. She'd put her idea aside for now but not give up on it. One day, she would have free rein to make these types of decisions.

If Warlord Ravenstrike made her general on Desomer's retirement.

Suddenly, in the space of a day, a secure border … her future … it all seemed incredibly precarious. Her shoulders firmed, refuting that thought.

She'd figured it out three years ago, and she'd do it again. And again. However many times she needed to secure her future and the safety of her home.

Chapter 33

A few days before Nain's arrival, Rorin decided he wanted to ride into the city for the afternoon and insisted on Darmanin and Essa going with him—it would be Darmanin's last opportunity to move around freely until Crowtalon's chief adviser left Heathrock. It was one of Arya's rare days off, so she joined them. Taze and his new shield deployed around them.

It was a relief to escape the walls for an afternoon. Arya loved her home at Heathrock, but the imminent presence of Warlord Crowtalon's chief adviser meant all formalities—including perfectly attired uniforms, polite language, and a grumpy Desomer—had to be adhered to for the duration of his stay. Not to mention the constant, underlying dread that had been with her since hearing the message from High Warlord Eaglesoar.

The season was shifting from late summer into early autumn, and while the day was sunny and clear, there was already a bite to the air that presaged the cooler weather. It wouldn't be long before snow covered this road again. Summer was only a brief respite from snow in the north, unlike in the States to the south like SparrowWing. Laskin had only been telling her that morning about the fires in SparrowWing—apparently, they were having the worst fire season they'd had in decades.

"It's a nice day," Rorin signed. Arya still had not ceased being impressed by how he'd learned to ride without needing reins to guide the horse so that he could communicate while in the saddle. *"Cuttlefish Inn?"*

Taze sent a questioning glance in Arya's direction.

"Taze doesn't get to decide where we go," Rorin signed in annoyance. *"Nor do you, Arya, as much as I love you."*

"So you'll decide everything we do, then?" Essa asked mildly. "Being you're the heir to Ravenstrike, I suppose."

Rorin flushed hotly. *"That wasn't what I meant."*

Taze and Arya shared a look. Rorin had immediately chafed at his parents' increased protectiveness since his return from Hawkesdale—initially set off by the creation of Taze's shield, then worsened by extra requirements from his mother that restricted what he could do without her permission. Arya understood his frustration. He was no longer a boy, after all. But she also knew how critical he was to Thiara Ravenstrike from both a personal and strategic perspective.

"Peemla mentioned at breakfast that Chiarn is in town, which means he'll be playing at The Ruined Arms," Darmanin said, breaking the awkward silence. "I'd like to hear him play."

"That's a good idea, Dar," Rorin said. *"I don't think I've ever heard better music than when we heard him play in Darulan."*

Taze wisely kept his mouth shut but gave Arya a surreptitious nod; he had no concerns with that location.

"I'd love to hear him play too," Essa said.

"The Arms it is." Arya's enthusiasm for that idea filled her voice, and Essa gave her a sidelong look of amusement, knowing full well Tiya was the reason for Arya's excitement. The innkeeper's daughter had become increasingly busy over the years as she took on more and more of the running of the place, and it meant Arya saw less of her these days. Still, she thoroughly enjoyed the nights they did get to spend together, valuing both Tiya's ability to make her laugh and relax, and the fact she'd never asked for anything permanent or serious.

The afternoon sun failed to lighten the gloomy city of Heathrock in any significant way, as if the city was determined to remain dark and brooding no matter the season. Arya liked that about it.

The Ruined Arms was a lot more than just an inn popular with Raiders these days. In fact, most Raiders now frequented other places as The Arms had become increasingly expensive in line with its growth in popularity. In a canny move, Tiya had struck a deal with Chiarn that meant he played in The Arms exclusively whenever he came to Heathrock city.

The talented musician was in a particularly good mood as the afternoon faded to dusk, enthusiastically playing a series of upbeat, rollicking tunes to the enjoyment of the packed and rowdy inn.

Buoyed by the energy in the room, Arya relaxed as they sat around a table talking. Rorin's good humour returned soon after sitting down and taking his first sip of ale, and the three young men relayed tales of their time in Hawkesdale, with Arya and Essa filling in some of the gaps of what they'd missed while they'd been away from Heathrock.

Taze's Raider shield was dispersed around the edges of the room and at each of its entrances. They were a discreet presence and didn't try to hold back those who recognised Rorin and offered a greeting as they passed his table. Rorin responded to each with a friendly smile of acknowledgment. He seemed at ease, shaking their hands or speaking with them for a few moments, even though such close contact had both Arya and Taze on edge.

"Be careful, Lord Rorin," Taze murmured after the third shaken hand.

"*I might be a warlord's son, but it is these people I will rule over. An accident of birth does not make me any better than they are,*" he responded.

"My lord." Taze accepted this.

"A warlord's son faces different dangers than a tailor frequenting an inn," Arya pointed out. "Your attitude is admirable, but don't let naivety blind you from the realities of your position."

"I think a little more naivety would serve our ruling class well," Essa said.

"*Essa is right.*" Rorin signed before Arya could say anything. "*And you won't change my mind.*"

Arya lifted her hands in submission and changed the subject. "Tell me more about Hawkesdale's Longbows. I've heard their skill in archery is almost magical."

Rorin launched into an accounting of one archer he swore he'd seen fire blindfolded and still hit the shot. At one point, Essa pulled out a piece of parchment and her ever-present charcoal stick and began sketching Chiarn as he played. Arya nudged her with an elbow. "Makes for a good subject, doesn't he?"

"He has such an interesting face, don't you think?"

"A handsome one at least." Arya chuckled. "I could introduce you, if you wanted?"

Essa made a face. "I don't want to bed him, Arya. He's just a good subject to draw. See how he sinks into his music, the expression on his face when he plays?"

"If you say so." Arya shrugged and sat back.

Later in the evening, Arya left the hot, crowded space to go outside and use the privy. Chiarn had finished playing earlier, and now one of the local bards had taken over. Part of her was hoping to catch sight of Tiya.

It had been months since they'd spent a night together, which Arya was content with, but tonight, with Rorin being home, she felt good and wanted to share that mood. It was still warm outside, but a cool breeze had sprung up, shivering across her hot skin. Music and laughter spilled out from the inn. There was no sign of Tiya anywhere though.

Coming out of the privy, she heard something spark, then saw a brief flash of flame as someone near the doorway lit a cigar. At the same moment, she felt a prickling along her skin; it wasn't a painful sensation but distinctive, nonetheless. The figure detached from the shadows by the doorway, a lit cigar dangling from his fingers, revealing a familiar face.

"Hello, Chiarn," Arya greeted him. "Good set, as always."

He gave her a sweeping, exaggerated bow. "Thank you, Captain Arya Nameless. I was hoping to see you here, even though most of your Raiders have abandoned this place for cheaper drinking holes."

"Where's your flint?" she asked, ignoring his flirtatious remark.

He frowned, puzzled.

She pointed to his cigar. "Where's the flint?"

"Oh." He shrugged. "It was old. I tossed it." He stepped closer, a little smile on his face. "Don't go inside yet. It's a beautiful evening out here."

Arya chuckled. She'd never bedded Chiarn, although it probably wasn't much of an exaggeration to say that half the patrons of the inn had, at one point or another. But that didn't stop him from trying every time he visited. She'd been tempted in the past, particularly when Tiya had been absent for a while, but despite his flirtation, it had never really gone anywhere. Something held her back. "Maybe another time."

"I'll look forward to it." He went back to leaning against the inn wall, puffing on his cigar, giving her a wink as she passed him to go back inside.

When they emerged from the inn roughly an hour later, the city streets were still busy. Taze was hurrying them up—Rorin had a strict curfew and was required to be back within castle grounds by midnight.

"*Stop nagging, Taze. We're moving,*" Rorin signed good-naturedly.

Taze frowned, gaze scanning the surrounding street. His shield deployed around them, not as quickly as Arya would have liked, but they were still new and hadn't adjusted to working together yet.

"Rorin, you—" Darmanin's words were drowned out by the loud whinnying of a panicked horse, followed by multiple shouts of alarm. Seconds later, there were several crashing thumps and then a girl's scream, high and loud, abruptly cut off. Then, after a moment's frozen silence, a series of raised voices.

Rorin broke into a run in the direction of the sounds, Darmanin reacting quickly enough to be close behind him as Rorin ducked down a narrow alleyway. Arya and Taze cursed and sprinted after them. The alley emerged into a main street linking two levels of the city. Rorin and Darmanin had gone left along the street.

Where the street ended, at a large market square—a rare section of flat land—a small crowd gathered near where a cart had overturned. The horse hitched to it stood lathered in sweat, snorting, his ears pinned back. The crates that had presumably been inside the cart now lay scattered and broken over the ground.

"What happened?" Essa caught up, panting, and asked the nearest bystander.

"Horse panicked, bolted across the square," a man tossed over his shoulder. "One of the wheels caught in a rut and flipped. I think it hit someone."

Rorin darted forward, pushing through the crowd. Arya swore, following, then stopped dead when they broke through. A man crouched amidst the fallen crates, shoulders shaking, heart-rending sobs coming from his hunched figure.

Darmanin and Essa stopped beside her. A stifled gasp came from Essa but Darmanin's silence was as grim as Arya's.

A girl lay near him, maybe ten years old. One of the crates had fallen on her legs and midsection, pinning her to the ground. She was unconscious, her skin deathly pale. Even in the dim light cast by the lanterns lining the edges of the square, it was clear she was in a bad state.

"Give us some room!" Arya shouted to those clustered around. "Move back, please. And someone make sure that horse doesn't bolt again."

Taze pushed through, hand on his sword, snapping an order to his shield. The Raiders formed a circle around the site and kept the crowd behind it.

"*We need to move the crate off her.*" Rorin's fingers flickered.

"No, that could do even more damage." Arya shook her head. "Taze—find out if someone's called a healer. We need one here fast."

"Arya—" Essa started, but was cut off as Darmanin knelt beside the girl, turning his gaze to the man.

"Sir, are you her father?"

He sucked in a breath, rocking. "I don't know what to do. I don't know what to do."

"What's her name?" Darmanin's voice was cool and steady.

"Mira." Saying her name launched him into more broken-hearted sobs.

"What's in the crates?" Darmanin asked him.

Tears streaked his face. "I don't know, I don't know. What do I do? My baby girl."

Taze moved, one eye on Rorin, one peering inside the nearest broken crate. When he looked up again, his expression was grim. "Linen cloth, bolts of it, and packed full. It would take a few of us to lift it."

Rorin signed. "*What if we shift the crate very slowly? It could be doing worse damage the longer we leave it there.*"

Arya didn't know how to answer that. She was no healer.

"Her heartbeat is weakening." Darmanin had two fingers pressed against the girl's neck. "But I'm not confident we could coordinate multiple people to lift it slowly and gently enough to prevent more damage—it could hasten her death rather than save her."

"Arya, can you move the crowd farther back?" Essa asked quietly.

"Why?"

Darmanin turned and caught Arya's eye. "Do as she asks."

She hesitated, confused. Essa was scrabbling in the pocket of her dress, searching for something. A moment later she pulled out the parchment she'd been sketching Chiarn's image on earlier and flipped it over to the blank side. Then, determined expression in place, she shifted to kneel beside the girl. Darmanin moved closer to her, angling his body so that her actions were hidden.

Arya hesitated briefly then searched out Taze. "Move the crowd farther back."

"Stop!"

As quick as a blink, a wiry figure wriggled between the circle of Raiders holding everyone back and slid down beside Essa, a hand clamping over her wrist where she'd begun sketching something.

A very familiar figure.

"Tiya?" Arya hissed. "What are you—"

"Wait for my word before doing anything. Clear?" The innkeeper's daughter ignored Arya, gaze steady on Essa's.

Essa nodded. "I understand."

Arya glanced between them, uneasiness pooling in the pit of her stomach. She turned to Taze. "Get everyone back farther. Now, Taze!"

He snapped out a series of orders. Arya looked around—it was dark, and they weren't near the edges of the square that were well-lit by lanterns, but there was enough light that *she* could see the fallen girl and her immediate surrounds. She'd just have to hope the crowd was far enough back that anything going on was too indistinct to see.

But what *was* going on?

A prickling sensation crawled under her skin. Her unease deepened. A faint blue glow appeared in the palm of Tiya's right hand as she slowly moved it over the girl's chest.

Magic.

"Raven's balls," Arya swore under her breath. "Taze, get the father out of there. Now."

He moved without hesitation, but the girl's father grabbed Arya's arm when Taze tried to move him away. "What are they doing to my daughter?"

"She's hurt and my Raiders have some basic healing skills, that's all. I want to give them room to work," Arya said as gently as she could. "We need a proper healer, though. Can you make sure someone has gone to fetch one?"

He swallowed, nodded, looking dazed as he allowed Taze to escort him away. Anxiety climbed through Arya's chest and took a stranglehold over her breathing. If *anyone* noticed Tiya using magic, with Arya and a shield of Raiders standing by and letting it happen instead of arresting her...

She snapped out of her panicked spiral when Tiya spoke to Essa, so soft she could barely hear the words. "You can start now, but you have to go incredibly slowly, so I can work as you go, understand me? If you're not confident you can do that—"

"I can." Essa began sketching, steady lines on the parchment. It was too dim for Arya to make out what she was drawing, but the prickling sensation under her skin grew almost uncomfortable in its intensity. Darmanin shifted again, doing his best to keep the actions of both women hidden.

The panic rose again. What should she do? Expose Tiya and arrest her? It was the only way to guarantee they'd all come out of this with their futures assured. The thought took hold, but then ... that would mean exposing whatever Essa was doing too. Not to mention, the girl was mortally hurt. If Arya stopped them now, she'd die.

Where was that damned healer?

Something creaked, shifted, then thudded. The crate. Somehow it wasn't *on* the girl anymore. Rorin tugged on Arya's sleeve, the question clear in his expression.

"I have no idea," she muttered. "But don't look surprised. Keep your expression calm, like all this is normal. Can you do that?"

He nodded, his face smoothing over, shoulders relaxing.

"Good, Rorin," she murmured.

Panic clawed at her, barely suppressed. Sweat trickled down Arya's back and beaded on her forehead. All it would take would be for one person to see the light, to notice the crate shifting...

Her nerves were already shot, so the sound of a scuffle had her spinning, hand on her sword. Someone else had pushed through the crowd and stood at the cordon of Raiders, staring in the direction of the fallen girl, confusion etched all over his face.

Chiarn.

As she watched, he rubbed idly at his bare forearm, as if it prickled, just like her skin was ... her chest tightened further. "Cusper!" she snapped at the nearest Raider. "Move him off."

Cusper responded immediately, pushing Chiarn back behind the first row of the crowd. Thank everything Taze's shield were facing outwards, concentrating on keeping people back, and not on what was happening by the fallen girl. If this crowd knew a magic-wielder was right there, this scene could turn into a riot, and there was no guarantee her Raiders would try to stop it.

"Healer's here!" a voice shouted.

The crowd rippled as a tall woman appeared, a bag slung over her shoulder. Her voice rang out, firm and authoritative. "Let me through please."

"Essa, Tiya, stop!" Arya hissed, deliberately not looking in their direction.

"It's all right, we're done." Essa's voice was laced with exhaustion. Tiya looked up, met Arya's gaze, then rose to her feet and slipped away as quickly as she'd come, vanishing into the crowd beyond the cordon before Arya could do anything to stop her. Darmanin wrapped a steadying arm around Essa's waist and discreetly helped her to stand.

That was all they had time for before the healer reached them. Arya shifted aside to give the healer room to kneel beside the girl. Darmanin and

Essa moved back too, and Arya stared in astonishment now that her view was clear.

The crate was no longer on the girl; instead, it sat on the ground right beside her, almost leaning on her. Her complexion had colour back in it and her chest rose and fell in a steady rhythm. The healer kneeled, examined the girl in a sweeping glance. "What happened here?"

Darmanin spoke first. "It looked at first like the crate hit the girl directly, but I think more of its weight hit the ground than her, fortunately. I suspect it gave her a glancing blow, and she fell and hit her head on the ground, which knocked her out." He lied coolly and with confidence. "We just checked to make sure she wasn't bleeding anywhere then waited for you."

"I hope you didn't move her at all," the woman said in disapproval, then began thoroughly examining the girl. A moment later Mira blinked her eyes open, dazed.

Arya was still staring at Mira, stunned, when a sudden sense of danger stabbed through her. She sucked a breath in and stiffened, forgetting all about Mira as she scanned the crowd, her gaze catching on a hooded figure standing among the onlookers.

Early autumn in northern Ravenstrike wasn't hot, but it was still far too warm for hoods or cowls. At least for anyone native to the State. Whoever it was, their build and stance told her it was a man. And the moment she looked at him, the sharp pulse of danger she'd felt reverberated through her again.

Wrong. Wrong. Wrong.

She was careful not to allow her gaze to stick on the hooded man, continuing her slow scan of the whole crowd. She didn't want whomever it was to realise she'd marked him. Turning aside, she murmured to Taze, "We need to get out of here. Now. But all casual like, you hear me?"

The young Raider nodded and touched Rorin's arm. "Let's let the healer do her work so the girl can go home, Lord Rorin. It's time for us to leave."

Darmanin opened his mouth to protest, but Arya levelled a look on him that made him close it instantly. Essa simply nodded; she still seemed dazed. At an order from Taze, the Raiders dissolved the cordon and surrounded Rorin and his group in a protective formation.

At a quick but not too hurried pace they left the square and headed back to their horses. As they walked, the pulse of danger faded, though echoes of it remained, like an oily residue on her skin. When they reached their tethered horses, Arya closed on Essa before she could mount and snatched the parchment still crumpled in her hand.

Essa froze but said nothing, instead watching Arya with wide eyes.

Angling her body away from the others, Arya uncurled the parchment. On it was a perfect rendering of the fallen girl, only the drawing depicted the fallen crate *next* to the girl's body, rather than on it.

Mouth thinning, she crumpled it back up and handed it back to Essa. "You burn this the second we get back. Is that clear?"

"I already planned to," she said quietly.

"Good." Arya lifted her voice. "Hurry it up. Let's go."

They mounted without incident and headed straight down to the city gates on the bottom level. The sense of danger faded completely once they were on the now-empty road back to Heathrock fortress, but Arya couldn't help glancing over her shoulder every few seconds.

She only stopped when Rorin caught her doing it and asked what was wrong.

"Nothing." She smiled. "Just monitoring Taze's shield and their formation. It's not bad, given the shield is newly formed."

"Thanks, Captain," Taze said proudly, understanding exactly what she was doing. "Hear that, lads and ladies? We're doing good. A shot of rum for everyone at dinner in the mess tomorrow."

A series of whistles and quiet cheers came in response to that, draining any tension that remained with the group. Only Taze and Arya remained surreptitiously watchful.

Arya couldn't help thinking of Essa's drawing. How Mira had been dying—Arya was certain of that—but then suddenly was alive and well. What had Tiya and Essa done?

They'd come so close to disaster.

Even now, she couldn't believe nobody had noticed what was happening. A chill wrapped around her heart. Maybe someone *had* noticed.

Who was that man in the crowd watching them?

Chapter 34

Yawns were breaking out as they dismounted in the entry yard, Rorin and Essa the main culprits.

"Taze, will you have someone from your shield escort Essa and Darmanin to their rooms?" Arya asked. "Rorin, I need a word."

Darmanin went without protest, but Essa kept shooting little glances over her shoulder at Arya and Rorin as she was led away.

"*What is it?*" Rorin asked once they were alone, Taze hovering a short distance off.

Arya searched his gaze. "I assume you understand the implications if anyone in that crowd, or one of the Raiders, saw what happened earlier?"

"*You mean that Tiya and Essa probably used magic to help that girl and we let them do it?*" Weariness etched its way into Rorin's features, and she suspected it wasn't just physical tiredness.

"Yes."

"*I would never be confirmed heir. You'd be expelled from the Raiders. My mother would have trouble keeping her position, let alone competing for High Warlord. But even worse than that, Tiya and Essa would be thrown out of their homes and left to starve, unless they joined the Shadeweavers and risked being arrested and shipped to Andahar, where they'd probably be killed by the Nightstalker.*"

Seeing it laid out so bluntly made her stomach lurch with nausea. Her shoulders tensed. "So what do you plan to do about it?"

"*Nothing.*" Rorin seemed confused she would ask that question. "*Nobody did see, and they saved that girl's life. You're going to do nothing too, right?*"

Arya hesitated.

"*This is Essa we're talking about.*" Rorin frowned. "*She's our friend. I would never expose her. Even if she has magic, I know she'd never use it to hurt anyone.*"

She expelled a long breath, surprised he was so calm about this. "But the implications, Rorin..."

"*It will be fine. Nobody saw anything.*"

His confidence was misplaced, but it was late and she wanted him to be right. "All right. Go on and get some sleep. We'll talk tomorrow."

"*Good night, Arya.*"

"Rorin?"

He turned, and she stepped up to him, voice low. "We don't discuss this at all, even in private, while Crowtalon's chief adviser is here. If you have questions, or want to talk, wait until he's gone."

"*Understood.*"

Once Arya had seen Taze escort Rorin safely inside the castle, she climbed the steps onto the battlements. From there, she walked the entire length of the walls, gaze scanning the dark forest that surrounded them to the south and west, noting the calm surface of the lake to the east, and finally returning to study the dark, empty road approaching the castle.

Nothing moved. Nothing seemed out of place.

Even so, disquiet itched at the back of her mind, and she was relieved to see Laskin approaching. Presumably the Raiders on watch had noticed her unusual night patrol and sent their shield captain to find out what was wrong. She was glad it was him on duty.

"You were back dangerously close to curfew," he commented. "Enjoy testing Warlord Ravenstrike's temper, do you?"

She leaned against the stone beside him, ignoring the jest. "I want you to be extra vigilant tonight."

He studied her, the teasing humour fading from his face. A moment later, he called out to the nearest Raider. "Kait?"

"Captain!" she saluted sharply.

"Wake up Captain Rarik and tell him his shield will start their shift early. Captain Nameless wants a double guard on the walls tonight. The duty rosters can be re-organised in the morning."

"Yes, sir." Kait darted off, full of energy as always despite the late hour.

Arya made a face. "General Desomer will make *me* re-do the duty rosters, you know. And Rarik will be pissed at me for dragging him out of bed at this hour." Even so, she relaxed slightly. With a double guard on the walls, nothing would get close without being spotted.

"What's going on?" Laskin asked quietly.

She hesitated, but Laskin waited her out. He had always been a good sounding board, one she could trust implicitly, and there was no reason to doubt that now. "There was an incident in the city after we left The Ruined Arms."

He rewarded her faith in him immediately by ignoring the revelations about potential magic use by Essa and Tiya and instead narrowing in on what mattered. "You think the man in the crowd was a threat?"

"There was something about him, more than just the fact he was wearing a hood and cloak in this weather. It was a sensation I didn't like."

"And you think the danger is connected to whatever Essa and your tavern girl were doing?"

"Unclear, but..." Instinct thrummed deep and true. "Maybe."

He kept his voice low. "Has Essa displayed any kind of magic before?"

"No." Arya's jaw clenched in anger. "But clearly both she and Darmanin have hidden it from me. I *knew* she was hiding something, dammit! This whole time, I knew. I should have trusted my instincts."

He gave her one of his looks. "Are you angry that she has magic and hid it—which, for a magic-wielder in Dunidaen, is a very sensible thing to do—or that by having it, she puts your entire existence here under threat."

Arya tensed. "It's more than just *my* existence."

Laskin let out a long breath, lifting a hand to run over the short stubble on his head. "Right. Tiya grew up in that city; she'll be fine. But if someone noticed Essa using magic ... that could be very bad. If it got out that Warlord Ravenstrike was sheltering *two* magic users in her household, both linked to the Shadeweavers..."

Arya took a steadying breath. "I could be exaggerating the danger. It was dark, and it would have been almost impossible to see what Essa and Tiya were doing, especially with Dar covering them. I couldn't even see clearly, and I was standing right there."

"Then why was he watching you?"

Arya shifted, feeling suddenly tired. "Lots of people were watching. Rorin *is* the heir to Ravenstrike. The warlords are relatively settled right now, but the next State Council is only a little over a year away, and there's already gossip about whether Rorin will be confirmed because he's a mute."

He caught her weariness. "We'll keep a tight watch, Arya. Go and get some rest. Nothing is getting over these walls tonight. I promise you that."

Exhausted, Arya nonetheless set a candle burning—it gave off an unusual green-tinged light—in her window before falling asleep. One of Salyarin's scouts had passed it to her in one of their earliest meetings, and a shiver went through her at the memory of her recent meeting with Salyarin and his now-prescient words about her needing to contact him.

She knew it would take a certain amount of luck for one of his patrolling warriors to be traversing the skies over Heathrock on this particular night, so she was surprised to find her eyes blinking open in the same moonlit hallway that had haunted the dreams of her younger years, only this time she could clearly see the Etherean elder standing before her.

"*Arya. What is wrong?*" he asked immediately.

She gave him a suspicious look. "How frequently do you send patrols over Heathrock?"

"*Is that what you summoned me to ask? I warn you that I cannot hold this dreamscape for long, especially when communicating with one not of my kind.*"

She told him about the message from the High Warlord. "And," she added, "something happened tonight."

He frowned. "*There was a clear image in your mind as you spoke just now, sharper than anything else. A young woman. She's small, dark hair. Dressed well. Who is she?*"

"Her name is Essa. Why, what's wrong?"

"*I've warned you about this. The Nightstalker has not stopped searching for you. And clearly, he is growing impatient. Your friend's use of magic, unshielded as it was, may draw him or his hunters to you.*"

"We destroyed every wraith and shadowhound that crossed the border, and nothing has crossed since. We've made sure of it. The border blockages are intact," she argued, rubbing at her temples, even though that made no difference in a dream. "Nothing is going to find me!"

"*And what makes you think it was only wraiths and shadowhounds that came through four years ago?*" he asked quietly.

She stilled. The silence hung heavy between them as his point sank home. The dream landscape seemed to be flickering at the edges, the drapes and the walls becoming slightly less distinct. Was he losing the connection?

"*What we want, and what is true, are often two very different things,*" the elder said, almost gently. "*We made a deal, you and I. You promised to keep the others safe.*"

Arya sucked in a breath. "Wait … did you see Essa so clearly in my dream because she is another Sky Lord potential?"

"*I cannot be certain.*" He hesitated. "*But from what I saw … no … sensed is a better word … when you spoke of her, then yes, I think so. You will have a powerful connection with these four people, even if you don't feel or acknowledge it.*"

"Raven's balls, could you be any more vague?" she snapped. "What danger should I be looking out for, exactly?"He waved a hand as she opened her mouth to ask more questions. The hallway was becoming increasingly transparent, its edges fading to nothing. "*We don't have time; you are a long distance away and dream-walking is powerful magic that drains quickly. I will have my warriors patrol the Diamondfang even more closely. At the same time, you must stop using your magic. They will use it to track you.*"

"I don't have magic," Arya said flatly.

The elder shrugged. "*You haven't grown into yours yet. But the others too. They must keep it hidden.*"

"Wait, why don't—"

But the elder was gone, his dream construction vanished as abruptly as it had come. Arya's eyes snapped open into the darkness of her bedroom at Heathrock. The headache still throbbed at her temples, a single reminder of the dream that was now fading into unreality. She turned over under the covers, wide awake now, staring into the darkness and wondering if any of it had been real.

All her hopes that the Nightstalker would go away, that the elder had been wrong. They were crumbling to dust inside her. Frustration welled, and she wanted to scream it into the night.

She'd promised the elder she'd keep Darmanin safe, and now Essa too. She would do that, she had to, because she needed Etherean help in watching the border. But she also allowed herself to accept that she'd do it anyway. She could never stand by while either was arrested and sent to their deaths.

She had to figure out something. Some way to make the Nightstalker believe she was no threat to him. That none of them were.

It was the only way out.

Chapter 35

Arya cornered Essa and Darmanin as they left breakfast the next morning and dragged them upstairs to her room. After closing the door, making sure the closet was empty and the window firmly closed, she rounded on them both. "Explain what happened last night. Now."

"You saw," Darmanin said. "The girl's injuries looked worse than they were."

"Don't take me for a fool, Dar," she snarled, temper rising. "You either, Essa. You and Tiya did something—I *felt* it. You were using magic, weren't you?"

Essa seemed startled. "You felt it?"

"Start talking, or I'm going straight to Warlord Ravenstrike!" It was a bluff ... well, mostly it was a bluff, but it worked well enough.

Essa glanced around, lowered her voice. "My drawings. Sometimes they ... sometimes I can make what I draw real."

"Sometimes?" Arya demanded.

"Only when I intend for it to," she admitted.

Arya rounded on Darmanin. "And you knew about this?"

"I overheard Ranier talking about his daughter one night, about something she'd done as a small girl." Darmanin glanced Essa's way. "So when she was sent to live here along with me, I paid close attention. I noticed how good her drawings were and I figured out the rest."

"Why didn't either of you tell me?"

"Now you're taking *us* for fools," Darmanin said coldly. "You're the one who helps Warlord Ravenstrike hunt down and arrest Shadeweaver magic-wielders so they can be handed over to Andahar to be killed."

She reeled at that, then snarled, temper spilling over. "Do you see me doing anything but reacting with anger at your dishonesty?"

His eyes flashed silver, the beginnings of a matching snarl escaping from his throat. She didn't shy from it, merely held that furious gaze. "Have I *ever* treated you any differently from anyone else?"

"No." The word grated out of him.

She stepped back, included Essa in her gaze. "Is there anything else the both of you haven't told me?"

Darmanin said nothing, but his left hand fidgeted at his side, toying with the piece of flint he always carried on him.

Essa sighed. "No."

"You put Rorin in danger last night, not to mention this household," Arya said. "I won't have that. If either of you use your abilities again without my consent—I don't care what it's for—I won't expose your magic, but I'll tell Warlord Ravenstrike whatever I need to make sure she throws you out on your ears. Am I clear?"

"Very," Essa said evenly.

"What do you mean, we put Rorin in danger last night?" Darmanin demanded. "You made it sound like there was a specific threat."

Arya hesitated.

"If you demand our trust then you have to give it," he said.

She sighed. "There was someone in the crowd, watching Essa and Tiya, I think. It didn't feel right."

His eyes bored into hers. "Are you sure?" Arya glared.

"I am sorry," he said gracefully, all his rigidness fading. "It was wrong of us to keep this hidden from you."

She waved an irritated hand, turning to Essa. "Tiya. How long have you known her?"

"I don't." Essa looked surprised. "I've seen her at The Arms of course, but we've never actually spoken before. But the crate *did* land on that little girl. All I did was draw it moving off her slowly enough that Tiya could heal the damage as it shifted."

"From now on, you don't draw in sight of anyone but me or Dar. And you keep away from Tiya. I don't want anyone seeing the two of you together ever again."

Essa's face fell. Arya felt bad but instantly pushed the feeling aside. There was no room for softness here.

Darmanin crossed his arms. "We shouldn't discuss this out loud again unless it's critically necessary."

Arya waved them to the door. "I've told Rorin the same thing. I'll tell him I've spoken with you both, but it will be safer if you don't raise it with him."

"Rorin..." Darmanin hesitated. "He...?"

"He loves you both and would never do or say anything to harm you. He needed no convincing to agree to keep Essa's secret."

"He doesn't hate me then?" Essa asked, her voice small.

"Not even a little bit." Arya let out a sigh. "Now go on and get out of here before I lose my temper again."

Darmanin left without another word, but Essa paused on the threshold, looking thoughtful.

"That's why the knives?" Arya asked her, finally understanding.

Essa shrugged, seeming unsurprised that Arya knew of them. "My father knew the consequences if anyone learned of what I can do and insisted that I be able to defend myself. I learned and became good at it because he was right. And I brought them here with me, and wear one always, because I'm in the home of a warlord who would kill or imprison me if she knew. But I'll never use them unless I'm forced to."

"All right," Arya said simply.

"You're risking a lot for both of us." The thoughtful look returned to Essa's expression. "I wish I knew why."

Arya huffed a breath. "So do I."

***

Arya woke with a start, heart pounding, chest tight. She lay still in the dark, the sense of dread pervading her so strong that she fully expected some enemy to leap out at her from the darkness around the bed.

But nothing did.

The shadows of her room were still, the rays of moonlight shining through the cracks in her curtains unbroken. She sat up carefully. Her heart raced, and despite the appearance of everything being fine, the fear of something bad about to happen was like a blanket smothering her.

Something was wrong.

She was certain of it like she'd never been certain of anything in her life.

"Move, Arya," she told herself, quiet but fierce.

In the next heartbeat, she threw back the covers and dashed across the floor to the closet. Yanking out shirt and breeches, she dragged them on. Next, she tugged on her boots, not bothering with the laces, and buckled on her sword belt. She moved frantically, as if something were chasing her, even though her room was clearly empty.

Once dressed, she paused. What to do next? She considered lighting a torch, but instinct warned her not to. Something was out there, and she didn't want it to know she knew.

Darmanin.

When she concentrated, she felt his presence in her chest, like a string gently being pulled taut. It might even have been what had woken her. The knowledge that Rorin and Darmanin often slept in the other's room for companionship sent renewed fear flooding through her veins, cold and insidious. She wished she hadn't decided to sleep in her own room this night.

Which room to go to first: Rorin's or Darmanin's? One was her heart and the other instinct.

Rorin.

Decision made, urgency flooded her. The urge to sprint with every drop of speed she had to the residential wing, yelling for Raider backup the whole way, was almost overwhelming.

She fought the urge back. The danger felt too imminent, and whatever the threat was, she didn't want it warned that she was coming, that she was alert to it. Besides, there was a more direct way to Rorin's room than running through the castle hallways.

She didn't linger any longer.

Arya pushed through the clothes in her closet and plunged straight into the secret passageways inside the walls.

The darkness was complete, and she was alert for any sound, any indication that someone was in there with her. As she moved, swift and sure despite the dark, anger uncurled. The thought that someone might be intent on doing harm in *her* home sparked her always-simmering temper. It was that, more than anything, that cleared the fog of dread from her mind.

Quietly, she unlocked the wooden door that was the entry into Rorin's closet and stepped inside. After carefully sliding through the clothes hanging there, she curled her fingers around the handle of the right-side closet door.

Before doing anything, she closed her eyes and listened, straining to hear anything beyond the doors.

Nothing. Complete silence.

Taking a deep breath, she turned the handle and cracked the closet door open *just* enough that she could get a view of the room. After the complete dark of the passageway, the faint moonlight coming through Rorin's curtains seemed as bright as a midsummer day.

Her shoulders relaxed minutely at the sight of Rorin, asleep on the bed between the closet and the window. The floor around his bed was equally empty, dark, but ...

Arya froze.

A plush couch ran along the foot of Rorin's bed—the place Darmanin, or Arya, usually slept when they wanted company overnight. From her vantage point, she couldn't tell whether Darmanin *was* sleeping there, but a hooded figure was balanced over it.

Metal flashed in the moonlight, a blade being lifted.

Arya burst from the closet, bellowing an alarm at the top of her lungs to the Raiders posted outside the door and leaping up onto Rorin's bed so she could throw herself across the space and into the assassin.

She collided with him an instant before the blade would have sliced into Darmanin's neck—he *was* sleeping there—and they crashed hard to the stone floor at the base of the couch. Her left kneecap slammed into the ground, sending fiery pain stabbing up her leg. Grunting, Arya fought to keep the assassin underneath her while trying to draw her dagger. In the moonlight, she caught a flash of brown eyes, a stubbled jaw. Otherwise the assassin was utterly silent as he struggled beneath her with an intimidating strength and agility. After a few moments he managed to get an arm free and drove a brutal elbow into her midsection, sending the breath whooshing from her lungs.

Gasping, she fell back, mouth moving as she fought desperately to suck in air. She scrabbled at the floor, trying to get enough purchase to rise, but she couldn't breathe. Her vision spotted.

Loud thumping came from the door, the yells of Raiders outside reverberating through the room, but it wouldn't open. The assassin rose to his feet and spun, gaze searching ... then he straightened and went straight towards Rorin's bed, where Darmanin was backing away. Arya clawed at her throat, desperately trying to suck air back into her starved lungs. A prickling sensation broke out all over her body.

She managed to roll and stick out her leg to trip the assassin up before he could reach the bed. Pain spiked in her knee at the collision, but she gritted her teeth and forced down the agony before dizziness overtook her.

Rorin, dishevelled from sleep, scrambled out from under the covers. He jumped in front of Darmanin without hesitation. Enough air trickled back into Arya's lungs that she could rasp out, "Rorin, get clear. Try and figure out what's jamming the door!"

But it was too late. The assassin recovered his balance and went at Rorin as he tried to dash for the doorway.

A low growl reverberated through the room. Silver eyes flashed, bone cracked and twisted, and then a black shadowhound stood where Darmanin had been. The second growl was louder, deeper, sending the hairs on the back of Arya's neck standing straight. The shadowhound leaped at the assassin, forcing him to dive away mid-lunge at Rorin.

Rorin kept going, sprinting for the door. Arya staggered to her feet, blinking away spotty vision, breath finally beginning to fill her lungs. She put herself between the assassin and Rorin, making sure he and the door were behind her. The shadowhound leaped again at the assassin, fangs bared. But the man shifted out of the way with unnatural speed, and Darmanin, unable to anticipate the dodge and check his momentum, crashed into a wooden chest before hitting the floor awkwardly, claws scrabbling on stone.

The shouting and thumping from the door increased in volume—it was a matter of time until they broke through.

She only had to keep the boys safe until then.

Arya swore as Rorin ignored her orders and abandoned the door to place himself between the assassin and Darmanin. The assassin advanced on Rorin just as deliberately as he had Darmanin, knife glinting as he struck fast and low.

Darmanin growled low and deep, shoving Rorin aside with his bulk and moving into the path of the knife. Arya covered the distance just in time, leaping onto the assassin's back, wrapping an arm around his neck, and hauling him backwards before the knife could land.

"Get the door open!" she screamed at Rorin, desperately trying to get him away from Darmanin. If the boys separated, the assassin couldn't get them both at once. Anything to make it harder, to stall for time.

An elbow slammed into her ribs, dislodging her hold long enough for the assassin to lunge at Rorin again. He was ridiculously fast on his feet. Darmanin leaped, snapping for his throat, but again, the assassin sidestepped. Still, it brought him into Arya's path, and she grabbed his cloak from behind, yanking hard enough to get him off balance. Using that momentum, she swung him around and sent them both slamming hard into the far wall.

Before he could recover, Arya yanked her dagger from her belt and stabbed for his throat. Unbelievably quick, he twisted in her hold, and the dagger went into his shoulder instead. As they struggled, the hood fell off, and Arya's eyes narrowed in recognition. "Leanir!"

She yanked the dagger out, aiming to stab again, but with a powerful heave, he threw her off him, his fist sinking into her ribs as soon as he had room for the wind-up. He aimed a kick that she barely avoided, and then he was on his feet and running for the window she only now noticed was open.

In one graceful swing, he was out the window and gone.

Chapter 36

Arya dropped her bloodied dagger and slapped a palm against the wall, trying to keep herself upright. That last punch had fire spreading through her ribs. Her vision swam. A moment later, a wiry arm slid around her waist and helped her stand. It was Darmanin, having changed back into his human form.

Rorin hovered in front of them, signing frantically. *"Are you okay? Arya, you're bleeding, ARE YOU OKAY?"*

Arya shook her head, wheezing. "Not my blood. You both need to ... the door. Go!"

But as the words left her mouth, wood splintered and an axe-head appeared, causing a wide crack down the middle of the door.

Rorin ignored it, his attention firmly on Arya. *"Are you okay?"*

She had the presence of mind to say, quiet and firm, "You can't say anything about what you saw."

He glanced between her and Darmanin. *"You'll explain later?"*

"We will," Darmanin promised.

Two more hits and the door was down, Raiders pouring in, Taze in the lead. At that exact same moment, alarm bells began pealing throughout the castle.

"Captain!" Taze's jaw was set, fingers white-knuckled on his sword hilt. "What happened? Are you all right?"

Arya took a pained breath but stood straight. "I'm fine, just a bit banged up. Rorin and Dar are fine too. The attacker went out the window."

Darmanin added, "It was an assassination attempt on Rorin. Just one man, but a skilled professional."

Taze looked around the room to make sure the threat was gone, then back to his shield. "Filen, get Lord Rorin and Darmanin out of here and down to the main hall. You and the rest of the shield stick close to them and don't let them out of your sight. I'll go and inform the warlord."

Rorin found himself being bundled away by Taze's shield. Darmanin hesitated but, at a look from Arya, allowed himself to be taken away too.

Taze turned back to her as soon as they were gone. "I'm sorry, Captain. We should have—"

"It was Leanir," she cut him off. Explanations could come later. "Go, inform the warlord and General Desomer and then stick close to Rorin and Dar. I'll meet you in the main hall as soon as I can."

"Where are you going?" he called after her as she limped for the door.

"He could still be on the grounds. I need to make sure we're all safe." Outside the door, she paused at the sight of Charlin, leaning on his axe, rumpled, as if he'd been woken suddenly from sleep. "That was you who got through?"

He nodded. "That's thick oak, that door. Taze sent Filen running to get me when they realised the lock was jammed."

"Good work, Charlin." And good thinking by Taze. She clapped him on the arm and went to walk away when realisation slammed into her, and she stopped abruptly.

"Something wrong, Captain?" he asked.

"I want you to go to Essa's room, right now. Make sure she's okay, and then escort her to the great hall with Lord Rorin and the others. Quickly, now!"

Charlin saluted and ran off, axe hefted and ready.

Turning in the opposite direction, Arya forced herself into a run, steps almost perfectly in time with the still-ringing bells. Her knee throbbed, and her chest was on fire, but urgency gripped her. As she emerged from the castle into the cool night air, Raiders were gathering in the drill yard, dressed and armed. It looked like almost all of them were there; impressively efficient. As soon as they spotted her, conversation died.

"Arken, Derrin, Laskin!" she bellowed.

The three men appeared quickly from within the throng, coming to stand at attention before her. She cradled her ribs with one hand, trying to make it easier to speak.

"There was an assassination attempt on Lord Rorin." She made a quick decision to go with Darmanin's version of events. It was the easiest story to tell, and for all she knew it could be the right one. "Arken, Derrin, get your shields mounted and searching the forest around the castle walls for any sign of the assassin coming and going. Laskin, take your shield and search every building and every bit of space inside the grounds to make sure he's not still here. He went out Lord Rorin's bedroom window. This man in dangerous, so stay in pairs at all times."

"And if we catch him?" Arken asked.

"You bring him in alive so we can question him."

Derrin hesitated, gaze flicking up and down her rumpled attire. "You all right, Arya?"

"A little banged up but nothing serious. Go, get out of here!"

They turned as one, diving back into the yard to pick out their shields and lead them at a run for the stables. By then, all Raiders not on duty had turned out of the barracks and were lined up in neat rows in their shields.

Neither General Desomer nor Commander Randin were there, so Arya stepped up in front of them, and they fell silent, their attention unwavering. It surprised her a little, their willingness to turn to her, but she filed it away to consider later. "There was an assassination attempt on Lord Rorin just now. He's fine. It was one assassin, a Shadeweaver. Captain Rarik, your shield will bolster the Raiders already on the walls tonight to double the watch. The rest of you go back to bed and get some rest—we'll need to be prepared for whatever response Warlord Ravenstrike and General Desomer decide to make to the attack." She clapped her hands. "There will be an extra shot of rum at dinner once this is all over for such an efficient turnout in the middle of the night. Go to it."

Their unanimous and hearty salute drowned out all the pain in her body, even if only for a moment.

By the time Arya made it back to the main hall, General Desomer was there with the resident healer as well as Warlord Ravenstrike, Magen, and Lord Eaglesoar. Taze's shield was spread protectively throughout the space, focused on the huddle of Rorin, Darmanin, and Essa.

Essa spotted her first. She leaped up and ran over, concern written all over her face. "Arya, are you okay?"

"Are *you* okay?" Arya searched her face. "Nothing came after you?"

"No, I was sleeping when the alarm bells woke me. Before I could decide what to do, your Raider showed up at my door."

"Good, that's good." Arya's eyes closed in relief. It was then, when she could be sure everyone was okay, that pain engulfed her like a wave. She fought not to sway on her feet.

"You look hurt." Essa reached out, then seemed to think better of it.

"I'm fine." Arya forced herself to straighten up and walk over to the group.

The warlord wore an expression of controlled fury that cowed every person present. The healer was checking Darmanin over carefully—he seemed to have already ensured Rorin was fine—while Thiara Ravenstrike demanded details about what had happened.

Desomer turned away from the warlord to bark at Arya. "What orders did you give?"

She saluted and relayed them. "Is there anything else you want the Raiders doing right now, sir?"

"No, those were good orders." He scowled. "At ease, Captain. Sit down before you fall down."

Arya slumped into the nearest chair. Her knee throbbed mercilessly and her ribs stabbed in pain every time she spoke or inhaled too deeply.

"Should I ask the healer to look at you next?" Essa asked quietly, touching Arya's shoulder while she watched Rorin signing.

She shook her head. "I'm fine."

"*An assassin got into my room and tried to kill me and Darmanin,*" Rorin explained with remarkable aplomb, even though his expression indicated it wasn't the first time he'd relayed this. *"Arya foiled the attack and managed to drive the assassin away before he could harm us."*

"Two shields of Raiders are searching the immediate area around the castle, and another is combing through the grounds inside the walls," Desomer relayed the orders Arya had given when the warlord turned to him with a questioning eyebrow. "If he's still nearby, we'll find him, but I suspect he's long gone."

"How did he get inside the damned walls in the first place?" the warlord demanded furiously.

Arya shifted, wilting under that gaze, even though it wasn't directed at her.

"It's unclear, Warlord."

Thiara turned to Arya. "Did the assassin say anything to you?"

"No." Arya sat up straighter. "He was silent the whole time."

"How did you learn about the attack in time to foil it, and why didn't you raise the alarm?"

"I didn't know an attack was taking place, Warlord," she said honestly. "I woke up earlier, and I ... it felt like something was terribly wrong. My first thought was to check on Rorin. I'm glad I did."

"How did you get into his room?" she asked. "I thought the lock on the door had been jammed."

"Melted wax in the lock." Rorin signed at Arya in explanation. *"Taze found it."*

"I..." Arya hesitated again, glancing at Rorin, whose shoulders were already slumping. But she couldn't lie directly to her warlord. "I used the passageways behind the walls to get in."

Thiara's mouth thinned. "I see. And how long have you all been using those without my knowledge?"

They all stared at the floor. The warlord didn't have to say anything further for her displeasure to weigh on them.

"We are fortunate for your instincts, Arya." Matte wrapped an arm around his son's shoulders. "I cannot tell you how grateful I am for your actions tonight."

"I owe her my life," Rorin signed simply. *"Dar and I both do."*

Thiara's mouth was a thin line. She did not seem mollified.

"Warlord," Magen ventured for the first time. "We should consider the implications of an attack on Lord Rorin. Especially given Crowtalon's chief adviser is scheduled to arrive tomorrow."

Thiara Ravenstrike let loose an expletive that would have impressed Arya's saltiest Raider. "First, we ensure the safety of my son and this castle. We can worry about the political implications once the assassin is caught. Questioning him might illuminate the matter further."

"You ordered a double guard on the walls two nights ago, Captain," Desomer said to Arya. "Why?"

Arya looked up, taking strength and reassurance from Essa's light touch on her arm. "There was a man in the city when we went there for a drink. He's not the same man who attacked Rorin tonight, but I felt like he was paying undue attention to us, so I bolstered the watch just in case. I had no evidence that he was a threat, so I didn't come to you with it. I'm sorry, sir."

Desomer shared a glance with the warlord. "More instinct, hmm?"

"Are you sure the man you saw in Heathrock city was not the same man who attacked you tonight?" Thira asked.

"Yes, Warlord. I recognised tonight's attacker. His name is Leanir; he's a Shadeweaver. He murdered one of my shield members back when I was at Icecliff." She didn't add that Leanir had been one of the Shadeweavers that had helped Icecliff Fort fight off the wraiths and shadowhounds.

"A Shadeweaver?" Thiara's eyes widened in surprise. "Darmanin, do you know this man?"

"Yes," Darmanin replied quietly. "He's their best contract assassin. Tonight may have been the first time ever he hasn't completed a kill."

"Which means he'll be coming back." Essa had murmured the words so quietly only Arya heard them, and she gave her a startled look.

Essa was right.

Desomer stroked his beard. "A contract killing, then. But no matter how good he is, he wouldn't have gotten inside these walls and into the castle unnoticed without help—it's possible the person you saw in the city the other night, and maybe others, were doing reconnaissance. We know Ranier has a network of supporters that carry out such activities for him.”

“Tell us more about this man you saw,” the warlord demanded.

“Warlord, to be clear, he struck my attention because he was wearing a hood and cloak on a warm night. But he made no threatening moves and did nothing else to rouse suspicion. I just got an odd sense about him.” Arya didn’t want a search for the assassin skewed in the wrong direction just because she’d had a bad feeling, even if she’d been certain at the time that the hooded man boded ill.

Quick bootsteps sounded outside, and they all turned as Arken strode in, slowing his pace to a brisk walk before stopping and saluting. His cheeks were flushed, green eyes bright. He’d found something. “Warlord. General.”

“Report,” Desomer said.

“No tracks in the ground surrounding the walls, but my shield found signs of travel along the road towards Heathrock city,” Arken said, crisp and fast. “They looked fresh enough to have been created sometime within the last few hours.”

“Nobody rode in or out of the castle tonight, did they, General?” Thiara asked.

“No, Warlord.”

“We shut Heathrock city down, right now,” the warlord ordered. “It stays closed until we find the man Arya saw and anyone else that helped this assassin.”

“Warlord.” Desomer hesitated. “Closing down the city will stop all trade in and out, and finding one man in a city of thousands will be a challenging task. It will take time.”

Arya jumped in without thinking. “It’s odd that Leanir left a visible trail.” She ignored Arken’s dark look and the warlord’s withering stare. “And why would he flee into the city rather than escape into the Diamondfang or the Wraith Forest, where the territory is familiar to him and he can hide more easily?”

“I don’t much care to consider an assassin’s logic at this point, Captain. If there’s any chance he’s gone to ground inside Heathrock city, I want him caught—him *and* his helpers," Thiara said. "Take as long as you need, General. Nobody attacks my son without consequences."

The tone of the warlord's voice sent chills down Arya's spine, and nobody dared to dispute her course of action any further. Desomer nodded briskly. "Arya, Arken, with me."

"I wasn't trying to undermine you," Arya muttered to Arken as they trailed Desomer out. "But don't you think it's strange that an assassin who got in and out of these walls without leaving a trace couldn't manage to make his way to the city without leaving signs of his passing?"

Arken's jaw was tight, but he gave her a sharp nod. "You could have raised it after, rather than right in front of the warlord, though."

"I could have," she conceded. "And I will, next time."

Desomer came to a halt in the entrance foyer outside the great hall. "Arken, you and your shield will deploy straight to Heathrock and cover the lower city gates. Find Derrin on your way out—his shield is to go with you and cover the top city entrance. I'll send more shields after you to cover the smaller exits and close down the intersection before the early morning traders start moving."

"Sir." Arken saluted and strode out.

"Let's you and I figure out who to send after them while keeping enough security here at the castle in case the Shadeweaver comes back to try again," Desomer told Arya before turning for the stairs.

She took a breath, tried not to wince at the stabbing pain in her ribs, and started up after him.

It was going to be a long night.

Chapter 37

By dawn, General Desomer had sent out messenger birds carrying orders for shields from outlying barracks to ride for Heathrock castle immediately. When they arrived, they would supplement those he'd used to close the city.

Arya worked tirelessly at his side. When he caught her swaying on her feet not long before dawn, he intervened. "You're hurt and exhausted, Captain. Clean yourself up and get a few hours' rest, then report to me in the city at midday."

When she climbed the stairs to the residential wing of the castle—unable to resist the urge to check on Rorin before allowing herself to rest—it was to find both he and Darmanin in Rorin's room with a guard of six Raiders manning the door.

"Captain Nameless is inside with them," Cusper assured her when she asked.

Confident they were safe, Arya limped to her room, ribs protesting with every movement. After closing the door behind her, she leaned back against it, unsure she could make the trip to her washstand, let alone get out of her uniform and climb into bed.

She allowed herself to rest there for a moment, before heaving herself off the door and slowly taking off layers, wincing with every move. The cold water of a wash helped her feel a little better, and she finally dropped face-first onto her bed with a groan, knee and ribs both aching abominably.

Then her closet door opened.

Rorin and Darmanin filed out, followed by Taze and Essa. Arya cracked an eye open. "What are you doing here?"

"I wanted to make sure you were okay," Rorin signed, determined. *"Taze's shield is already outside your door. One shout and they'll pour in here."*

Essa carried a tray with a steaming pot and cup as well as a bowl of something that smelled delicious. "Peemla told me General Desomer had dismissed you and she gave me this tray to bring you. She looked very worried."

"I'm fine," Arya grumbled, heart softening at the chamberlain's kind gesture.

"Oh yes, you look the very picture of good health," Essa said tartly. "Food or tea first?"

Arya scowled at her, but Essa merely waited her out, and she sighed. "Is that Peemla's beef stew?"

"It most certainly is." Essa waited while Arya dragged herself up to a sitting position, resting her back against the headboard, and passed Arya the bowl. Then, Essa took a seat on the bed, making sure not to jostle her.

Taze took up a guard position at her door, while Rorin sat on the opposite side of the bed and Darmanin pulled up a chair. They all remained quiet while Arya ate hungrily until the combination of pain and exhaustion reclaimed her and she put the bowl down, feeling vaguely ill.

Essa promptly poured a cup of the tea. "Peemla put willow bark in it, so it should help with the pain."

"Thanks." Arya took the mug and sipped, closing her eyes as the warmth spread through her. Her thoughts were groggy with exhaustion, but she didn't make any effort to get them to leave. The sooner they made sure their stories were straight, the better.

Darmanin shot a look at Rorin. "She's needs rest. We should leave her alone."

Essa moved to shift off the bed, but Arya shook her head.

"No, we need to talk. Taze, come over here. You should probably hear this too, and I don't want to shout it across the room and risk anyone overhearing."

Rorin caught her gaze. *"Will you tell me what I need to know?"*

"You drink your tea, Arya. I can start the story," Darmanin said. He kept glancing at her in concern, which caused her irritation to spike. At least if he was talking he'd stop looking at her like that, so she nodded.

In short, clear terms, Darmanin explained about his magical ability, and Essa's, as well as what Essa and Tiya had done with the injured girl in the street two nights earlier. Throughout, Rorin shifted on the bed like he was sitting on a nest of fire ants, but he allowed Darmanin to finish without interrupting.

"The assassin was after *you*, Dar, not Rorin?" Taze jumped in before Rorin could ask anything, brows furrowing.

"It's unclear," Arya said. "When I came into Rorin's room, Leanir was hovering over Darmanin with his knife."

"*But he went for me when I tried to protect Dar,*" Rorin continued. "*It's equally possible he was after me but wanted to take out Darmanin first, in case he woke and interrupted.*"

"I worry about the timing of this given what happened two nights ago," Taze said. "What if the attack was connected to that?"

Darmanin shook his head. "Tiya and Essa were the ones who helped the girl, not me or Rorin."

Essa straightened abruptly. "What if whoever Arya saw *thought* Darmanin was the healer? You were shielding what Tiya and I were doing, weren't you, Dar? From a distance, it could have looked like *you* were the one using magic."

Arya shook her head. "Leanir and the Shadeweavers have known about Dar's magic for years. They took him in *because* of it. If Leanir was after Dar last night, it wasn't about magic. And I think it's doubtful that someone who hates magic enough to contract an assassin to kill a magic-wielder would employ another magic-wielder to do it."

"You're right—we should focus on the fact Leanir is a contract killer," Darmanin said. "The simplest explanation is that someone contracted the Shadeweavers to kill Rorin or me, or both of us. The fact he went to Rorin's room, not mine, indicates Rorin was the target."

Arya turned that over in her mind. It made a lot of sense. And if Leanir was as good as Darmanin claimed, it made even more sense that when he'd found Darmanin sleeping in Rorin's room, he'd tried to take that potential threat out first, before going on to complete his kill.

"Why Rorin and not Warlord Ravenstrike?" Essa asked, frowning. "Kill her and the State falls into disarray, because Rorin hasn't been confirmed as heir and hasn't come of age yet. Killing Rorin doesn't achieve anything like that."

Rorin looked sceptical too. "*Dunidaen is at peace, despite the political wrangling between the warlords. None of them would dare to hire a Shadeweaver assassin to act against another warlord.*"

"My father is capable of anything," Darmanin snapped.

Rorin's signing became incredulous. "*You're suggesting that Warlord Crowtalon hired a Shadeweaver assassin to kill the future Ravenstrike heir?*"

"He threatened your mother three years ago, didn't he?" Darmanin said.

A tense silence fell. Darmanin's mouth was set in a familiar stubborn line, and Rorin was flushed with frustration. Arya drained the remnants of her tea. The willow bark had soothed the edges of her pain, so she took a breath, breaking the silence.

"There is something else I should tell you." She hesitated. Whatever its purpose, last night's attack had driven home to her the dangers that Essa and Darmanin faced—and, by association, Rorin. She'd pretended to herself for too long that she could protect them all by simply keeping her head down and watching the border. No longer. Without the knowledge she had, they couldn't protect themselves, and last night had proven that she might not always be there to protect them. They deserved to know.

"Arya?" Essa asked in puzzlement when the silence drew out.

She took a breath, surprised at the depth of her reluctance to say it out loud, as if, by doing that, she would make it real. "It's something I have kept to myself for many years, but I think it's time that you know."

She sensed Darmanin's gaze fall on her, wariness written in the depths of his grey eyes. Guiltily, she looked away from him and faced Rorin. She always felt safe talking to him.

"Many years ago, during the attack on Icecliff … you remember that the Etherean helped us?"

They all nodded.

Arya shifted uncomfortably. "At the time, their ruler, a man they call their elder, spoke with me privately."

Darmanin's mouth tightened. "What did he say?"

Taking a breath, Arya focused on the mug in her hands and related to them everything Salyarin had told her that day and since. A confused silence met her words.

"*You made a bargain with him? Without any kind of authority?*" Rorin signed incredulously.

"I—"

"You're saying that you, Darmanin, and I are Andahari? Not only that, but we're potential Sky Lords?" Essa looked blank, like she didn't understand.

"The elder thinks we are, yes."

"Impossible," Darmanin said flatly. "My father is Mathas Crowtalon, you all know that."

"And your mother?" Arya asked. "You and Andrian are only half-brothers, aren't you?"

His face darkened. "Yes, but my mother was from Falconcrest, a cousin of Warlord Falconcrest's."

"Are you sure?"

"Of course I'm sure," he snapped. "What the elder told you is wrong."

"I never knew who my mother was," Essa said quietly. "My father always refused to tell me. He said she'd died soon after I was born."

Rorin frowned. "*What about your parents, Arya?*"

She shrugged. "I'm a Nameless, Rorin. I know nothing about them. They could be from Khadini for all I know."

His smile quirked. "*Not with that fair skin of yours. Icefolk, maybe, but definitely not Khadini.*"

"So *we're* the reason for the Nightstalker's sudden interest in Dunidaen?" Essa said quietly. "We're the reason Shadeweaver magic-wielders are being rounded up and sent off to have who knows what done to them in Anda-har?"

Arya didn't like the look on Essa's face. "We've done nothing wrong, Essa."

"We're lying to Warlord Ravenstrike and placing her son in danger for a start," Essa said heatedly. "You yelled at Dar and me about trust, but you've been hiding this from us the whole time."

"I was trying to protect—"

"You don't get to make unilateral decisions about my life," she said, eyes flashing.

"She's right." Darmanin crossed his arms over his chest.

"*We should tell my mother*," Rorin signed, trying to break the tension. "*She could help keep you safe if she were better informed.*"

Arya hesitated, wondering whether to tell them of her suspicions that the warlord already knew who Arya was, but Darmanin spoke before she could decide.

"Telling the warlord would only make things worse."

Essa's mouth thinned. "You don't want her to kick you out, you mean, because you want to be named Crowtalon heir. And that's more important to you than Rorin's life."

Arya sucked in a breath. Essa's cleverness could sometimes be cutting, and in this instance, it was sharp and cold.

Darmanin turned white. "She'll kick you out too, Essa. Is that what you want? We're both Shadeweavers, in case you'd forgotten. If we're exposed as magic-wielders, we'll be sent to the Nightstalker—which is apparently *exactly* what he wants."

"Enough!" Arya raised a hand, recognising a brewing fight. Essa and Darmanin could be equally stubborn when they got their minds stuck on something. "For now, we say nothing to the warlord. Rorin, we'd be placing your mother in an impossible position politically if she knew she had two magic-wielders under her roof. Her position is safer if she doesn't know. If *nobody* knows."

"Exactly," Darmanin said in satisfaction.

Essa didn't respond, but she'd sunk into a mutinous silence. Rorin merely seemed worried.

Taze spoke into the tense silence. "What do we do about all this? If Rorin is marked by a Shadeweaver assassination contract, they only end when the execution is carried out. And if the Nightstalker isn't giving up on hunting Arya and Essa and Dar, then—"

"*Perhaps we should all get away from Heathrock for a time?*" Rorin suggested.

"How are we going to do that?" Arya asked. "I doubt you or Dar are going to be allowed to step one foot outside these walls for a long time. Not to mention Dar is confined to his room until Nain leaves."

"*We'll come up with something,*" Rorin signed optimistically. "*In the meantime, I will have my parents ensure Dar is guarded as closely as I am.*"

"Not necessary," Darmanin said. "I can protect myself."

"That shadowhound was much bigger than the last time I saw it." Arya smiled at him, trying to lighten the mood. "Almost full grown."

"*I wish I could shapeshift like that,*" Rorin signed.

"No you don't," Darmanin said shortly, then rose to his feet. "It's time to go. Arya needs sleep."

"You should never have hidden that information from us." Essa was still angry, her words clipped. "We had a right to know."

Arya opened her mouth to make some kind of excuse, point out she'd only learned Essa was one of the potential Sky Lords a handful of days ago, but the young woman was already gone.

"*I love you, but they're right,*" Rorin said. She accepted it stiffly, annoyed at their anger with her.

As soon as the door closed behind Rorin and Taze, Arya gingerly lowered herself back to the bed and drew the covers up over her head, wanting to block out the world and everything in it. Guilt niggled at her. She'd honestly thought she'd been doing the right thing in keeping what Salyarin had told her hidden. But she'd been wrong. She *had* been making decisions about their lives, and if they'd done that to her, she'd be beyond livid.

She'd just have to hope they forgave her.

Despite her exhaustion, sleep was difficult to come by.

Chapter 38

Arya woke with frustration simmering alongside her still-there guilt. Essa and Darmanin had reacted understandably, and it wasn't them she was truly angry at. She hadn't asked for any of what the elder had told her, didn't want it. Why couldn't the Nightstalker just leave them all alone? She pushed off the covers, huffing a breath at her childish petulance.

Her knee ached as she stood—it had swollen and stiffened up while she slept. Her ribs hurt too, and while the healer had confirmed they weren't broken, just bruised, it certainly *felt* like they'd cracked into a few different pieces. Wincing, she bandaged her midsection tightly on the healer's instructions, then limped down to eat a quick meal in the kitchens.

Her thoughts were busy, distracted by the previous night's attack and the subsequent conversation with Rorin and the others, as she headed for the entry hall on her way out to the stables. She was several paces inside before she realised it was busy with people.

Nain and his party had arrived.

Magen was there, Peemla too—the chamberlain organising servants to carry the Crowtalon chief adviser's luggage and that of the clerks he'd brought with him. It was a blustery day outside, and the travelling party were in the midst of pushing back the hoods of their cloaks while Magen greeted them officially, his words carrying as he promised that Warlord Ravenstrike was on her way down.

Arya, doing her best to discreetly slip around the edge of the hall, found her gaze snagging on the man she'd already deduced was Nain, simply from the deferential way those around him behaved. He wore a light travelling cloak, and as he lifted a hand to push his hood back, revealing short-cropped blonde hair and a narrow face, she froze. It had only been a blink that she'd seen him standing there with his hood on, but...

In that moment she'd seen the man from the market square who'd been watching them that night.

Nain's build and stance was similar, but it wasn't just that. She felt the same sense of unease now, looking at the chief adviser, that she had that night with the man watching them.

She blinked, rubbed her eyes. Nain couldn't have been in Heathrock city when he would have been on the road, travelling from Anduil in Crowtalon. Weariness must be affecting her judgement.

She'd hesitated too long, staring, and Nain's gaze shifted. Arya instantly turned away and kept walking, keeping a fixed soldier's look on her face as she strode around the edges of the hall and out the door. Her heart raced the whole way until she was out of his sight.

She calmed as she performed the familiar routine of saddling and bridling Zeke and mounting up. Even with the tight bandaging, she couldn't help wincing as the stallion's gait jolted her sore ribs.

The entire ride out to Heathrock city, she kept coming back to that single glance she'd gotten of Nain in his hood and cloak. She *was* tired, and it had been dark that night. But something inside her refused to accept she'd imagined it.

The intersection where the main road branched off into the lowlands was in a state of noisy chaos as Arya came upon it, drawing her sharply from her tangled thoughts. A line at least a mile long clogged the road leading up to it, where Raiders were turning people around. Dust filled the air as carts and horses jostled to move. Arya rode past, glad she wasn't on that duty.

Raiders from Arken's shield stood guard outside the closed and locked city gates, their horses grazing nearby. The nearest, Allicen, saluted at Arya's approach and opened a side gate for her to ride through.

"General Desomer has set up in the Trading Hall. He asked us to tell you to meet him there," Allicen told her.

She nodded her thanks. "How are things going out here?"

"Bored as crap, Captain," Etan called over. "But at least the weather's mild. Beats standing out here in the wind."

She smiled. "Stay alert. It might seem quiet, but that Shadeweaver snuck up on us good last night."

The streets of the city were eerily empty as Arya rode upwards, heading for the Trading Hall on the fourth level of the city, roughly halfway between the top and bottom entry gates. Raiders stood or sat horses on every main intersection, and many residents seemed to be staying inside. Those out to fetch food or try and keep their businesses open looked at her in open curiosity as she rode by.

A gaggle of people were gathered in the square outside the Trading Hall, muttering to each other, dissatisfaction hanging over them like a cloud. On seeing Arya arrive, they began drifting in her direction, so she hurriedly dismounted and tethered Zeke before ducking up the steps. Dealing with a group of disgruntled traders was not on the list of things she wanted to do today.

Once inside, Arya stopped, wincing as she took her weight off her injured knee. She hadn't wanted to limp up the stairs in full view of the those outside, but it had hurt to move normally. Not to mention the constant throbbing of her chest. She took a deep breath, but slowly, and stood still until the pain subsided.

An enormous space opened up before her. It was usually full to bursting with trestle tables laden with goods of all kinds displayed for barter or sale, but the hall was now empty, most of the trestles packed up and pushed to the sides of the room. Dust and straw drifted in the air and scattered over the floor empty. Her nose tickled.

General Desomer stood where two trestles had been dragged together in the middle of the empty space, in conference with Laskin and Derrin.

"General." Arya saluted as she joined them. "Do you have a moment?"

He nodded and stepped aside, but before she could say anything, he peered at her. "How are you feeling?"

"I'm fine, sir."

"Knee giving you any trouble?"

"No, sir."

"What about those ribs?"

"I can barely feel them, sir." She continued before he could press her more, "Sir, Chief Adviser Nain was arriving when I left to come here."

"And?" he snapped impatiently when she hesitated.

"He looked ... that is..." She winced. In her mind, she'd been certain, but saying it aloud it now seemed ridiculous. "He looked just like the man watching us in the city the other night, sir."

Desomer scowled. "I thought you said you didn't see his face?"

"That's right. He was cloaked and hooded. So was the chief adviser when he rode in earlier. His build, the way he moved, it was the same, sir."

"You think Crowtalon's chief adviser was skulking around the city watching you three nights ago. For what possible purpose—"

"Watching Darmanin, sir," she said quietly.

Desomer grunted. "Even if your farfetched, and frankly unbelievable, theory was true, we're already making sure Darmanin doesn't go anywhere near Nain while he's at Heathrock. You said yourself the man you saw didn't do anything suspicious or threatening. We've got more important things to worry about right now."

"Yes, sir, but—"

"Enough."

He turned back to the table, but as he did, Derrin addressed him, having just received a report from one of his shield. "Sir, are you aware of the people gathering outside? Annoyed merchants, by the look."

"Merchants do tend to get annoyed when you close down an entire city for an indefinite period of time to look for a needle in a haystack." Desomer glowered. "Any other obvious pieces of information you'd like to point out to me, Captain?"

Derrin wilted. "No, sir."

Desomer harrumphed and swept his arm in an arc, addressing Arya. "There are antechambers that we're using for interviews with any business owner, resident, or guest within two blocks of every possible exit and entrance from the city—let's hope someone saw these Shadeweavers entering or leaving. We're doing the same for all homes and business fronting the market square where you saw the suspicious man. It's going to take days to get through them all."

"How are you making sure you get everyone?" she asked.

"We're starting with those we know and asking everyone we speak with to give us a list of people they know who live or work near them. Derrin's shield is out fetching people and bringing them in." Desomer jabbed a finger at the pieces of parchment on the trestles. They contained lists of names, with some crossed out. "Arken is already interviewing, and the three of us were about to start a new round. Take one of the Raiders as support and join in. You can use the last room on the right."

"Yes, sir. Have you gotten anything useful yet?"

He sighed. "Just a lot of gossip and rumour so far. Once we get a credible lead, we can concentrate our efforts better, but until then we're going to have to wade through a lot of crap."

Arya moved off, then paused. "Laskin, do you have a moment?" He nodded and joined her as she left the hall. "Has anyone checked on The Ruined Arms?"

He glanced up in surprise. "Why?"

"Can you send someone? Make sure Tiya and her father are safe and sound."

Laskin wasn't a stupid man. "You think Leanir's attack might have had something to do with whatever Tiya and Essa did to help that girl?"

"No—it all points to a contract killing. But given the timing, I'd just like to be sure. And while you're at it, is the singer Chiarn still in the city?"

"No," Laskin replied. "I was in The Arms yesterday evening. We went there to hear him play, but he'd already left the city that morning. Why?"

She hesitated.

"You think *he* was involved?" Laskin's eyebrows shot up.

"No." She hesitated again; Chiarn's reaction to Essa and Tiya had niggled at her, but she might have been imagining it. She'd been panicking that night, worried that anyone might see what was happening. "The timing of his departure is curious, though."

"Next time he's in town, we'll have a chat to him," Laskin promised. "Not much we can do until then. I'll send someone to check on Tiya and her father."

"Thanks. I'd best get to it."

"I'd move quickly if I were you," he advised. "The city isn't going to stay quiet and well-behaved for long, especially if this carries on longer than a day or so."

"Our warlord wants the assassin found, Laskin."

He lifted an eyebrow. "You think this is the best way to do it?"

"I do. People need to understand what the consequences are of going at Ravenstrike House. *Or* sheltering those that do." Arya meant every word.

"Right you are, Captain," he muttered.

Arya found Wattin on guard outside the room Desomer had sent her to, his inscrutable expression not shifting when he saw her. "Captain." He saluted.

She returned the smile. As much as her standing had gradually improved among the Raiders at Heathrock in the past four years, she always appreciated having a familiar face from her old Icecliff shield at her back. And Wattin's laconic air belied how sharp he was. "Who's in there?"

"His name is Indal. He owns the Golden Duck inn on Fisher Street."

Arya paused in the midst of pushing open the door, glancing back with interest. "That inn faces the square where the girl was hurt the other night, doesn't it?"

"That's right, Captain."

"Watch him carefully while I ask the questions." She walked into a small room, where sun shining through a window high in the wall illuminated specks of dust floating in the air. Sitting on a chair on one side of a table, facing her, was a short, balding man with plump jowls and a harried demeanour.

"Your name is Indal?" she asked briskly, sitting opposite him. Wattin took up position against the wall behind her.

"Yes." He nodded, glance shifting between the two of them, the hand on his thigh tapping out an impatient rhythm.

"I am Shield Captain Arya Nameless. I need to ask you some questions, and then you're free to go."

"I know who you are." The tapping increased in pace. "Everyone in town knows who General Desomer's apprentice is. Why do you need to ask me questions? I don't know anything about the assassination attempt on Lord Rorin."

"I presume you've had the usual number of guests staying at your inn over the past month?" she asked.

"Yes. I own one of the most popular inns in the city, and summer has only just ended, so it's our busiest time of year. My rooms have been booked out all month." His mouth thinned. "Until now, that is. None of my booked guests can enter the city, and my current guests can't leave. I am losing money every day this goes on, Captain."

She ignored his irritated tone. "Has anything strange happened during the last month?"

"Strange like what?"

Arya lifted an eyebrow, holding his gaze and keeping a tight rein on her temper. "Anything out of the ordinary? Odd? Unusual? Something that caught your attention?"

"No, nothing like that."

He'd answered far too quickly to have thought about it properly. In addition to the tapping fingers, he'd started shifting in his chair. He wanted out of this room.

"What about your guests?" She forced her voice to remain calm, pleasant. "Were there any that looked dangerous, or stood out from the others? Perhaps someone that kept to themselves and didn't socialise with the other guests?"

"I don't think so." He sighed noisily. "What's all this about, anyway? You think the man that attacked the warlord's son was staying at my inn? Captain, there are upwards of thirty inns in this city."

"Even so. Please take a moment to think about it."

He didn't. "My inn is a very busy place. I don't have time to notice much about the characteristics of my guests."

Shouts in the street outside caught Arya's attention. She motioned for Wattin to go and find out what was happening. Indal glanced curiously over his shoulder towards the window as the door closed behind her Raider. When he looked back, open irritation had settled in his features, his veneer of tolerant politeness beginning to fade.

Hesitating, Arya gambled. "Did you have a guest staying the last few nights? Tall, blonde hair, very thin-looking?"

He looked at her in disbelief. "Blonde and tall? Multiple guests fit that appearance, Captain."

"Do you keep records of your guests?" she asked.

"Why would I?"

Arya bit down on her temper once again, though it took an effort. She wasn't going to get anything more out of him.

A knock came at the door. "Wait here please, sir."

She was up and out the door quickly. Wattin hovered there. "There was a bit of a scuffle with some of the traders, Captain. They're angry at losing a day's trading and didn't take it well when Captain Derrin told them we could be here for days. General Desomer has gone out to talk to them."

"How many are out there?"

"At least fifteen or so, but more were trickling in." Wattin hesitated.

"What is it?"

"Didn't like the vibe, Captain."

Arya sighed. If Wattin didn't like it, she'd best go and see if Desomer needed any help. She opened the door to the room and told Indal he was free to leave, then gestured for Wattin to follow her as she headed down the long corridor.

"Captain, do you really think we're going to find the assassin here in the city?" Wattin asked.

"The warlord's orders are clear. We have to try." She glanced at him. "But I don't think a Shadeweaver assassin leaves tracks accidentally. I doubt very much the trail that Captain Rosenthal's shield found was left by Leanir."

"Unless he did it deliberately."

Arya stopped mid-stride, her mind suddenly clearing like sun shining through a cloudy sky. "You mean, if he *wanted* us to know he'd gone to ground in Heathrock city?"

"Sure. Or wanted us to think he had."

"Why would he want us to follow him into the city?" she murmured, mostly to herself, as they resumed walking. "The only reason he'd do something like that would be to…"

She quickened her pace into a run. She should have thought of this already. Would have if she hadn't been distracted by arguments with Essa and Darmanin and fanciful notions about Crowtalon's chief adviser. Shit.

"Captain?" Wattin ran after her, startled.

Ignoring the pain stabbing through her knee, she ran down the hall and burst out into the afternoon sunlight at the top of the steps, pausing only long enough to take in the scene. The group of traders had doubled in size since her earlier arrival, but they weren't doing anything more than gesturing unhappily, some with raised voices.

General Desomer was out there, astride his horse, dealing with them while a handful of Raiders sat their horses in a loose circle nearby to make sure the situation was contained.

"What is it?" Wattin stopped beside her, hand on the hilt of his sword.

"What if Lord Rorin wasn't his target last night? Or at least, not his only target?" She kept scanning the wide street outside the Trading Hall, but aside from Raiders positioned in the main corners there was nothing obviously wrong. "What if, by leaving those tracks, Leanir was trying to draw us out?"

Wattin saw what she meant immediately. "Outside the protective walls of the castle."

The square was open. *Too* open.

Arya broke into movement again, running down the steps and across to where the general sat his horse. Her movement drew their attention, and Desomer turned in the saddle, a frown settling over his grumpy features.

It happened so fast she didn't quite catch it.

A faint hiss, a whisper of air over her shoulder, and then Desomer was toppling off his horse, almost in slow motion, crashing facedown to the cobblestones. His horse reared, letting out a shrill whinny. Everyone froze in a tableau of shock.

Some instinct—like a string inside her that connected her to something else, something she hadn't been aware of before—thrummed and Arya dived to the left just as another arrow ploughed into the cobblestone where she'd been a second earlier.

"Archer!" she screamed, even as she was rolling, coming to her feet, eyes scanning the rooftops to identify where those arrows had come from. "ARCHER!"

There. Above the Trading Hall. A figure rose to its feet, gave her a mocking salute, then turned and vanished from sight.

Leanir.

"The general's down!" Wattin roared into the silence that followed. "General Desomer is down!"

Arya spun, heedless of the fact there might be more than one archer, and ran to the general's fallen figure. One of the traders had grabbed the reins of the spooked horse, but they were all moving off the street in a panicked huddle. "Get under cover!" she yelled at them. "Faster, go!"

She turned back to Desomer. He was unconscious, sprawled on the cobblestones, blood from the arrow embedded in his back running down to pool on the ground beneath him. She swallowed the horror that wanted to flood her and took a steadying breath. As soon as she did, the anger seared through her.

Wattin spoke at her side, reporting to her like he always had as their shield's healer. "I dare not move him; that's a spinal hit. He's still breathing, but we need to find something to staunch the bleeding right now, otherwise he'll bleed out before anyone can do anything. We also need to get a proper healer here, fast."

By now Raiders were converging on the scene. They'd heard Arya, knew an archer was on the roofs, but came anyway. For their general.

"Someone give me their jerkin, right now!" she bellowed.

"Here, Captain!" a woman called out, and a quilted Raider jerkin was pushed into her hands, smelling faintly of sweat. Wattin snatched it from her and leaned over Desomer, doing his best to pack the jerkin around the wound and staunch the blood flow.

"No, no, no." Arken dropped beside Arya, looking genuinely grief-stricken at the sight of the fallen general. "What *happened*?"

Arya reached out, took hold of his arm and shook it. "Shooter was on the roof, he headed west. Stay with the general. I'm going to hunt the bastard down."

He swallowed, eyes glazed.

"Captain." Wattin looked at her, shot a meaningful gaze between Arken and the general. "We need you here."

She swore. Glanced up at the roof. Pictured that mocking look. Fury burned through her, hotter and hotter. She wasn't going to let Leanir get away this time. He would pay for touching her family.

"Someone get my horse!" she shouted, then looked frantically around, gaze going back to Wattin. He was hunched over the general, holding the now blood-soaked Raider jerkin to his back.

Shit. Shit. Shit.

Arya swallowed, warring with herself. She literally trembled with the fierceness of the urge to hunt Leanir down and wipe that smirk from his face. "We can't leave him out on the street like this. There could be another archer, or a follow up ambush." Mind made up, she dove into her risky gamble with confidence. "Wattin, if we can move him without jostling, would that be okay?"

"We'd have to go slowly. No sharp movements at all or it could kill him."

"Laskin!" She rose to her feet, searching him out next. Raiders were crowded around them in a group, but he appeared at her side a moment later, and she asked in an undertone. "The Arms is close by, isn't it?"

He didn't waste time asking why. "One level up from here, two or three blocks over."

"Send someone straight there. Tell them to find Tiya, let her know what happened and that we're bringing General Desomer to her—the story is that we just need to get him out of the open and somewhere safe while a healer looks at him."

"Done." He turned away and gestured at one of the nearest Raiders hovering.

Arya surveyed the rest of them. They were clearly shocked, unsettled, and uncertain.

"Listen up!" she snapped, loudly enough to grab their wavering attention. "We're going to move General Desomer somewhere safe, quickly but without jostling him. Five of you—the strongest—get over here and do everything Wattin tells you. Allicen, run for the healer in Fisher Street, tell her to get to The Ruined Arms as quick as she can. Arken, take your shield and go to every Raider post. Tell them to shift position under cover so they're not open targets, and be on alert." She clapped her hands. "GO!"

They went.

One of the Raiders had brought Zeke, and she ran to him, swinging into the saddle.

"Arya." Laskin came after her. "We need you with the general, you can't—"

"I'm going to get him, Laskin." Arya set her heels to Zeke before Laskin could finish his protest. "And I'm going to make him pay."

Chapter 39

Arya had only just turned Zeke down the street running alongside Trader's Hall, eyes focused on the roof, looking for any sign of Leanir, when she almost collided with one of Derrin's Raiders coming in the opposite direction.

"What?" she snapped, impatient at being held up.

"Captain Derrin sent me. The two Raiders guarding the intersection of Dregs End and Weasal's Corner—between levels five and six—are dead. Shot from above. Witnesses nearby say they saw movement on the roofs heading west towards the higher levels," he reported, words falling over themselves he spoke so quickly.

Satisfaction flushed through her—now she knew where Leanir was heading. "Thanks, Gosen." She set her heels to Zeke and ignored the Raider calling after her.

She pushed the horse into a reckless gallop along the city streets, winding upwards to the intersection of Dregs End and Weasal's Corner. She reined Zeke in by the fallen Raiders, making sure there wasn't anything that could be done to help them. A small group of terrified-looking residents peered out of a window across the street.

One Raider lay sprawled on the ground beside her partner, her sword fallen nearby, arrow embedded in her throat. He was facedown nearby, a pool of blood leaking from the arrow in his back. Neither had a pulse when Arya pressed her fingers to their necks.

Her jaw clenched, and she nursed the anger roaring inside her so loudly it was like white noise in her ears. Her mouth curled in a silent snarl. Her fists clenched at her sides. She rose to her feet and studied the buildings around, calculating where Leanir must have been to make the kill shots. It didn't take her long.

A voice in the back of her mind warned her that she should have backup, but the murderous heat of her anger drove her ever forward. Leanir had shot down a man she respected and admired, left him dying in a pool of blood in the street. *After* trying to hurt Rorin.

She was going to tear him limb from limb.

Getting onto the roof of the right building was easy enough, and once there, a quick canvass revealed two adjoining roofs Leanir could have taken, but only one led west towards the upper city entrance. Arya leaped across and scrambled over that roof.

Adrenaline and anger flooded her, masking the pain of her injures, allowing her to run and jump and swing herself along the path Leanir had taken. Most roofs only had one or two options for getting across to another roof, and in most cases only one led upwards.

Red hazed her vision. Lungs burning, sweat trickling down her back, she made her way from level five, to six, and then the seventh.

Here the options forced her north, and she leaped across a narrow gap between two buildings, boots pounding as she sprinted around a small storage shed on the second roof...

...only to slide to a rapid halt.

Leanir stood balanced on the opposite edge of the roof. He held a drawn bow, the arrow knocked and pointed right at her chest. "Good afternoon, Raider."

Arya's hand fell to her sword hilt, the desire to leap across the intervening space and strike him down close to overwhelming. Only the knowledge that he'd fill her with arrows before she got anywhere close stopped her. Even so, she took a step forward, a snarl curling at her mouth.

"I wouldn't," he advised. "By the time you got to me, I'd have three arrows buried in that pretty chest of yours. Not that the first wouldn't kill you."

His smug grin was too much. "I'm going to bury you for what you've done today."

He merely smirked. "That threat is becoming laughable. How many more people do you think I can kill before you *do* catch me? Shall we take a small wager?"

"I bested you, last night," she said. She was panting, and she wasn't sure whether it was from exertion or frustrated fury. "I'll do it again."

"You didn't get close to besting me. I merely chose to retreat. Your bluster is tiresome, Raider." He looked at her speculatively. "But I *am* starting to enjoy killing people while you stand by and do nothing. So I'll leave you alive for now."

"Who contracted you?" she demanded.

His eyes flashed with something unnameable. And then, for the first time since she'd met him, he became truly angry. It was a dark, quiet anger, and his words seethed with it. "You think someone contracted me?"

"You're a Shadeweaver contract assassin. Why else would you—"

"Because you deserve it," he snarled.

"Wait ... this is about *revenge*?" she asked, incredulous.

"Your warlord needs to know what it's like to never be able to feel safe, to never be able to feel like her family is safe. You thwarted me getting her son, but it was easy enough to then draw your general out. The man running her army, the army systemically hunting and killing us or handing our magic-wielders over to Andahar to be killed. Who in her household shall I choose next, do you think?"

With a final, mocking laugh, he turned and stepped off the roof. By the time Arya had crossed the rooftop to reach the edge, the street below was empty. She scrambled down the drainpipe, dropping as far as she dared and landing with a force that shuddered through her bones. She glanced left and right, began sprinting in the direction of the city exit gates.

But after two blocks, it was clear she'd lost him. When she reached the gates, they stood closed, the Raiders on guard alert but calm. By then everything hurt and she fought hard not to limp up to them.

"We haven't seen him, Captain."

She nodded. "He will try and get out of the city at some point, so keep a close watch."

They saluted and she turned and began making her way back to Zeke, shaking with frustrated rage and the fading remnants of adrenaline. Leanir could have killed her just then, and she'd have been utterly helpless to stop him. Not to mention she'd completely failed to catch him.

She hated that with a fierceness that rocked her.

Leanir was going to die at her hands one day. Slowly. No matter how long it took, she'd make it happen.

***

When Arya arrived at The Arms, Desomer had been settled in a private room on the first floor. The door was closed, Raiders lining the hall outside. Laskin spotted her and immediately came over. He looked grim.

"What's going on?" she asked. "Is the general—"

"The healer is in there with him."

She looked over his shoulder, spotted Tiya hovering among the Raiders.

Laskin caught the direction of her gaze. "You weren't here to give any orders, and the healer got here before your friend could see the general alone."

Arya stiffened at his disapproving tone. "Laskin, I—"

"Did you capture Leanir?"

"No. He got away." His disapproving look turned to disgust. "What's the situation?"

"I don't know. I've been here with the general," he said pointedly. "Has anyone informed the warlord and Commander Randin what happened?"

"Arken—"

"I haven't seen him since you sent him to alert the Raiders on the city gates."

"I'm not the only shield captain here, Laskin," she snapped, exhausted, still angry, and thoroughly fed up with his disapproval.

"You are the general's apprentice!"

Bootsteps thudded up the stairs, announcing Derrin's arrival. "I heard the news. What do you want me to do?"

Arya didn't look at Laskin as she spoke. "Will you send two of your shield to Heathrock to let Commander Randin and the warlord know what's happened?"

Shock flared in his grey eyes. "Nobody's done that yet?"

"I wouldn't ask it if it had been," she said tersely. "Also, we shouldn't continue interviews while Raiders are still potentially in danger—can you make sure they're stopped. Leanir clearly drew us into the city on purpose, and we can't rule out more attacks are planned."

"Agreed. We'll hold here for now." He made his way back down the stairs to inform his shield.

Arya had no desire to hear any more from Laskin, and she headed down the hall to where Tiya stood. There was something in Tiya's gaze as she watched Arya, reproach, maybe, or anger. Or both. Arya didn't have to ask to understand that look. Someone who could probably save Desomer's life stood inches from his bedside, yet they couldn't let her near him. Dunidaen's terror of magic could mean a man losing his life.

"Thank you for letting us use your inn," she said loudly enough for all to hear. "We needed a safe place nearby to bring him."

"You're welcome, of course. If there's anything else we can do, just let me know. My father said I should put myself at your disposal." But Tiya's eyes glittered with repressed frustration.

Arya turned to the Raiders lining the hall. "Let's get some space up here. Just Laskin and me on the door for now. The rest of you go downstairs—make sure there are at least two of you posted at the bottom of the stairs leading up, then split yourselves between the front and back doors."

Raiders saluted and shuffled off. Once the steady thumping of their boots on the stairs faded from hearing, Arya turned back to Tiya and lowered her voice. "Is he going to be okay?"

"I've no idea," Tiya said testily.

"Don't screw around with me," Arya hissed. "I know what you did for that girl the other night."

Her mouth thinned. "I can't do anything unless I can touch him. That's how it works. And the longer it is before I can touch him, the less I can do."

"Captain?"

Arya straightened as the healer called out from the now open doorway. Drying blood covered her hands and spattered her tunic. "Is he okay?"

The woman's face was grim. "The arrow lodged in his spine. It caused irreparable damage. I don't think he's going to wake up."

Those words sent all the breath flooding out of her. Even though part of Arya had known it was bad, hearing it aloud like that… Desomer couldn't be dying. Not the crusty, full-of-life general she'd come to respect and admire. It wasn't possible. "Can you remove the arrow?"

"I've done that, but it can't reverse the damage already done." She hesitated. "I'm sorry, I know it's not what you want to hear."

"He's still breathing," Arya said with an edge. "Surely you can do something?"

"I can make him comfortable."

"I could help with that," Tiya offered before Arya could protest further. "I have some experience cleaning and dressing wounds, and it would give you a chance to clean up and have a short break, Healer Kalen."

"That would be appreciated, thank you."

"I'll show you downstairs." Arya stepped forward, steering the healer away and giving Laskin a meaningful glance as they left. He nodded in return, then closed the door behind Tiya and took up guard position in front of it.

Downstairs, Arya hovered in the doorway of the kitchens, watching as the healer scrubbed her hands and forearms clean of blood, then sat wearily to sip at a pint of ale one of the cooks had drawn for her. Arya tried to keep from glancing upstairs, hoping against hope Tiya would have enough time to do what she needed to do.

Guilt already gnawed at her. She should have been here with the general instead of chasing Leanir. She'd had the authority to make sure Tiya saw him before the healer could.

The sound of galloping hooves and shouts broke her from her worrying, and a few moments later Commander Randin strode inside, catching her gaze from across the hall. "Report, Captain, and start with the status of General Desomer!"

She did, as quickly and succinctly as she could.

He gave her a look of disapproval. "You didn't take a shield with you as backup?"

"No, sir. I didn't think there was time to wait for one. I feared losing his trail." But she should have. If she had, she'd have had Raiders lining the bottom of that building before she went up after him. They could have captured Leanir as he'd come down.

Still, Randin seemed to accept her explanation. "Why did the assassin return to the city last night rather than disappearing into the forest where we'd never have come close to catching him? It doesn't make any sense."

"He wanted to draw the general into the city so he could take him out." Arya was still furious at herself for not working that out faster. "General Desomer was his target after Lord Rorin."

"Why?" Randin looked completely baffled.

"He told me it was because of the increased Raider attacks on Shadeweaver encampments, and the arrest of magic-wielders to send to Andahar. They're angry, sir," she said.

Randin scowled. The man looked completely out of his depth. He was a solid second for Desomer but had never been a candidate to take over from him. He rubbed a hand over his face. "The warlord wants the city to remain on lockdown, but I'd best go and report your news to her. Follow me back to Heathrock—she'll no doubt have questions for you."

She saluted. "Yes, sir."

Once he was gone, she took a quick look inside the kitchens—Healer Kalen was still there, sipping her ale—then went straight up to Desomer's room. Laskin remained on guard outside. He opened the door for her to go in.

Tiya was putting the finishing touches on clean bandaging. Desomer sprawled facedown on the bed, looking too pale and very old.

Arya bit her lip, almost afraid to ask the question. "Could you do anything?"

"Yes and no." Tiya sighed. "He'll live, Arya, but his recovery is going to be a long one, and he'll never walk again."

Arya sat heavily in a chair near the bed, stunned. Never walk again? For a war general like Desomer, that was as good as a death sentence.

"If I'd been given access to him sooner, I probably could have done more for him, probably saved his ability to walk. But by the time Kalen finished rooting around in there and yanking the arrow out, it was far too late."

Arya flinched at the remonstration in Tiya's voice, then lowered her face into her hands. "I should have been here. I should've taken backup with me. He couldn't have cornered me like he did if I had. Fool of an idiot!" She'd allowed her temper to get the best of her, like Desomer had always warned her about. She'd failed him.

Tiya reached out to squeeze her shoulder. "You brought your general here deliberately, didn't you? Because of what I did the other night."

"I should have stayed with him, made sure you had access to him straight away," Arya said bitterly. "I'm sorry I didn't."

But Tiya didn't look angry. "You don't hate me, then, for having magic? I've been waiting since that night, you know, for the Raiders to show up and arrest me. When they came clomping in here earlier, I thought..."

Arya sucked a breath in. "I should have thought of that, I'm sorry. I'm not going to tell anyone what you did, and neither will Essa or Darmanin."

"Why not?"

She expelled a breath, wishing she didn't have to have this conversation now. She was too tired and heartsore to think straight. "You saved that girl's life—there was nothing wrong or hateful in that. I hate Shadeweavers because of what they do to my shield-mates, not because some have magic."

"Then why do you help your warlord round them up and send them off to their deaths?"

"I don't..." Exhaustion washed over Arya. "I don't have any level of influence with her, Tiya. And that policy keeps Dunidaen safe from the Nightstalker." But the argument had already been weak to her ears, and it was growing weaker with every day, with every magic-wielder she brought into her life.

"It's wrong," Tiya said flatly.

"I know," she whispered. Then she forced herself to stand. "I have to get back to Heathrock. Thank you, Tiya, for helping the general."

Tiya walked her to the door. "I'll make sure that Healer Kalen does the right thing with General Desomer while he's here."

"I know you must feel conflicted about that, so thank you." Arya squeezed her hand. "I'll come and see you when I can."

***

Arya found Heathrock castle a hive of activity, despite night having fallen. One of the Raiders on the gates called out as she passed, letting her know the warlord wanted to see her straight away.

"Thanks, Riter."

"Captain, is he ... the general, I mean ...?" A few others near Riter drifted closer, so they could hear her answer.

"I'm sorry, I don't know for sure. He's going to live, but the injury is a bad one, so he probably won't walk again."

His face fell, but he offered her a smile. "Thanks, Captain. I heard it was your quick thinking that got him out of harm's way and to a healer so fast. Appreciate that."

She concealed a wince. If they knew she'd let a magic-wielder near him, would they be so appreciative? "I only wish I could have caught the bastard who did it."

"It's just a matter of time," Riter said confidently.

Commander Randin was in the warlord's office, as was Magen, and two shield captains were just leaving as Arya walked in. The sight of Magen abruptly reminded her of Nain's visit. She blinked. Was she still so sure it had been him she'd seen that night in the city?

"Good, you're here." Thiara Ravenstrike looked up. "Commander Randin informs me that the healer's early assessment is that General Desomer may not survive. Do you have an update?"

"Yes, Warlord. I spoke to the healer again before leaving the city, and she confirmed that he will live, but he's facing a long recovery and likely will never walk again."

Something flashed over the warlord's face. Arya thought it might be grief. Or disappointment. But it was gone so quickly, buried so deeply, that she wasn't even sure she'd seen anything.

"I will go and see him as soon as things are under control here." Thiara Ravenstrike looked between all three of them. "Commander Randin relayed your report, that this was a revenge attack on my household—to take out my heir, and my war leader. I understand that you, also, were a target, Arya?"

Arya started in surprise, but she was right. It was a detail she hadn't paid attention to in the chaos of everything that had happened afterwards. And Leanir had only missed hitting her because she'd somehow sensed his arrow coming. "That's what Leanir told me, Warlord, but I can't confirm he was telling the truth."

"Either way, I have to ensure we are stronger, going forward." Regret edged the warlord's voice, quickly erased. "To that end, I have sent a messenger bird recalling Commander Lerin from Icecliff immediately. He will be Ravenstrike's general now that General Desomer can no longer carry out those duties."

It was a neat solution. Put in place an immediate replacement for a badly injured and weakened general, and at the same time shore up support with her vicelords by promoting the brother of her most restive vicelord.

But Arya's world dropped out from under her. "Warlord, I—"

"You made multiple mistakes today, Arya, let's not gloss over that fact. As General Desomer's apprentice, your responsibility was to control the scene, ensure the general's immediate safety, and immediately notify me. Instead you went after the assassin in a temper, without backup, and lost him in the process."

Arya felt each word as a blow, sensed Magen's disapproval, Randin's agreement.

"You are not ready to be general of my army," the warlord finished. "Today has amply demonstrated that fact."

Arya couldn't swallow around the lump in her throat, but she somehow managed to rasp out, "I understand."

Thiara Ravenstrike held her gaze. "General Lerin will decide who becomes his apprentice."

Blow after blow. It took everything Arya had not to physically reel at those words.

"Your place here is assured, Arya," the warlord said, still brisk. "Do not worry on that score."

Sure. Her place was assured right up until Lerin found a way to get rid of her.

"Dismissed. Get some rest. You're off duty until tomorrow," the warlord said, her voice not softening at all.

"Warlord." She saluted, turned, and walked out.

She wasn't sure how she got from the office wing to her quarters, but somehow she did. As the door to her room closed behind her, she simply stood and stared at the walls of the dark room.

A single day, and it had all gone so terribly wrong. Her general was seriously wounded, an assassin was coming for her family, and Arya had lost what little influence or power she'd had to protect them.

She slid down the wall, head resting back against stone, and closed her eyes, biting her lip to hold back the tears that wanted to trickle down her cheeks.

How had she messed everything up so badly?

Chapter 40

Lerin arrived at Heathrock the following morning and immediately summoned Randin and all Heathrock-based shield captains together in General Desomer's office.

Now *his* office.

Arya's mentor still infused every inch of the space, from the hint of his cigar smoke in the air, to the messy piles of parchment scattered all over the desk, and his winter cloak hanging by the door. A wave of grief swamped her at the realisation that her hours with Desomer in this place were over. Only now that they were gone did she realise how deeply she'd loved her time with the cranky old general.

Lerin, with his florid face and whiskery beard, didn't fit at all. Not that he seemed to notice. He was barely making any effort to hide his ebullience over his sudden promotion. Arya hated him for it.

Arken entered and took the seat beside Arya at the table by the windows, even though there were plenty of others free. When she glanced at him in surprise, he leaned in. "The general's spot should have been mine, but if it went to anyone else, I'd take you over Lerin any day."

Taken aback, she held his gaze and said, "I feel the same way about you."

It might have been the first time ever she and Arken had ever been on common ground. And she'd meant her words too—she'd be far happier reporting to Arken than Lerin. At least she knew Arken was a competent soldier and leader. He wasn't better than her. But he was good.

"I'm sorry I failed yesterday." Arken's mouth was tight. "I wasn't prepared for what happened ... you were right all those years ago, about us at Heathrock not having combat experience."

"I screwed up too." Arya detested admitting to failing anything, but her spirits were heavy. "I should have taken backup with me instead of going after Leanir on my own."

"What did the old man always say? Don't make the same mistake twice. Let's make sure we hold to that, right?" Arken said.

"Right." She held his gaze. "Never again."

Laskin took the seat by Arya's other side when he entered, and when Derrin arrived, he went straight to the chair next to Arken. He glanced at them, muttered, "You three look as thrilled about this as I do."

Arya rubbed at the throbbing in her forehead. Arken's jaw tensed. Laskin scratched at his beard. Lerin's gaze settled on the four of them as others filed in and sat down, until everyone was there. There was speculation in that gaze. And dislike.

"Commander Randin, give us an update on the situation please," Lerin ordered, sans pleasantries. He seemed oblivious to the grief and shock that radiated from his shield captains, men and women who'd worked under General Desomer for a long time and loved and respected the man.

The lockdown on Heathrock city had been lifted, but multiple shields, including some from Icecliff and SheerRock, were combing the Diamond-fang and Wraith Forest for any trace of the Shadeweaver assassin and his potential accomplice. Randin gave a quick explanation of how the search was operating, then provided a summary of the content of the interviews they'd undertaken before the attack on Desomer.

It was a depressing report. None of the citizens the Raiders had spoken to had noticed anybody unusual or out of place. Summer was a busy time for visitors to the city, so there were a myriad of strangers around. Those working at the inns were run off their feet with work and had had little time to pay attention to their customers or guests. Residents who'd been questioned had mostly shrugged and said they'd noticed nothing but the usual drunk travellers passing by after nightfall.

"Thank you, Commander," Lerin said once Randin was done. "Starting today, we'll increase the frequency of patrols into the Wraith Forest and Diamondfang with the aim of destroying any Shadeweaver camp we find.

Yesterday's incident made clear that it's time to focus on the threats *inside* our border and deploy our army appropriately. Derrin, Laskin, Arken, your shields will bolster the forces we'll deploy from the three forts for this initiative."

Arya sent all three captains a dirty look when they simply nodded assent and then turned to Lerin. "Sir, who will respond to alerts from SheerRock, Windfall, or Icecliff if the specialised shields are already deployed hunting Shadeweavers?"

"That system is unnecessary and a waste of resources. As of today, we'll revert to monthly check-ins, and shields based at the forts can ride out if check-ins fail."

"Sir." Arya cleared her throat and genuinely tried to be as deferential as possible. "You might not be aware of the missive that Warlord Ravenstrike received from the High Warlord several days ago—that the Nightstalker is becoming unhappy we haven't found those he's searching for. Given that, increasing the border checks might be worthwhile, at least until the Nightstalker's new concerns can be allayed."

Lerin's eyes narrowed. "Be assured the warlord has briefed me on everything I need to know, Nameless," he said coldly, then looked around the table. "I want every Shadeweaver campsite, tent, shack, firepit, and shithole in this State destroyed, is that clear?"

The resounding agreement he'd clearly expected to get didn't come, and his face flushed with anger. Arya internally applauded Derrin when he spoke into the tense silence.

"Sir, not all Shadeweaver encampments are armed. Some house families, children, or the elderly," he said. "I assume you only want us to go after the criminal networks?"

"Also, sir," Arken added. "Back to Captain Nameless' point, what of Dunidaen's agreement with King Lucius to arrest and send Shadeweaver magic-wielders to Andahar? If we kill them instead, don't we risk reneging on that agreement?"

Lerin's mouth curled in contempt. "I want you to take them all out, Captains. Every single one. They are a blight on our society. They just attacked our general, and they're coming for more blood. We need to destroy them before they can hurt any more of ours. Appeasing a foreign king does not come before the security of our State."

Clothing rustled as captains shifted in their chairs, looked at each other. Most of them glanced at Arya, as if expecting her to say something.

It wasn't like she needed any encouragement. Her conversation with Tiya the previous day had made things starkly clear. She could no longer pretend that Dunidaen's policies regarding magic-wielders were right, let alone agree with Lerin's extreme interpretation of them.

"Sir," she said as politely as she could manage. "If we start killing innocents, it will give Shadeweavers licence to go after innocent Ravenstrike citizens, not just us Raiders. Not to mention, it's murder, what you're suggesting."

"A Shadeweaver assassin just *murdered* two of ours and tried to do the same to our general and future warlord," Lerin said evenly. "I'm no more interested in your opinions now than I was four years ago, Captain Nameless. Is that clear?"

A few glances darted Arya's way, but nobody protested Lerin's orders any further. Her heart sank. This was it. The day part of her had always dreaded was coming.

She was done here.

That knowledge hit hard, something akin to a fist slamming into her solar plexus. It left her momentarily winded, which probably saved her from saying or doing something she'd regret.

Lerin wrapped up the meeting soon after, and Arya filed out with the others, not saying anything, barely hearing their chatter. Much like the night before, after the warlord had delivered the news about Lerin, she was in a daze, so she went looking for her truest source of comfort in this world.

The future heir to Ravenstrike was out in the horse yards. Horsemanship was something he dedicated hours to, refusing to allow his need to use his hands to communicate prevent him from mastering a skill any other warlord's son could. Although he'd never been able to hold his focus or interest long enough to become a skilled swordsman, he had become an elite rider.

The moment he saw Arya, a smile lit up his face and he swung out of the saddle, leaving his horse with the groom. *"You're not usually free this time of day."*

"I've not yet been given any orders and decided not to point that out to Lerin," she said sourly. "Where's Taze?"

"Off duty." Rorin gave her a considering look. *"You're in one of your moods. Come on."*

He slipped his arm through hers and led her straight to the kitchens. Servants bustled around the space cleaning up after lunch and beginning early preparations for dinner. Peemla was there too. The smile that lit up *her* face at the sight of Rorin and Arya reminded Arya that not everything was bad. She was loved, here, irrespective of her position in the Raiders.

"Peemla, we need an Arya special." Rorin signed, his smile for her bright.

Rorin and Arya took a seat at an empty end of the kitchen table, where they weren't in the way, and within minutes a pot of Arya's favourite tea—orange pekoe—appeared before them, along with a plate of ginger-bread cookies.

"Sit with us, Peemla." Rorin encouraged.

"I'd love to, but I'm baking General Desomer's favourite pie to send him, and the filling gets tricky if I don't keep a close eye on it while it simmers. Enjoy." Peemla smiled and bustled off to one of the cookfires.

Rorin watched patiently while Arya sipped tea and scarfed down two cookies. She'd skipped breakfast earlier and hadn't realised how hungry she was. He waited until her attention was back on him before signing. *"First, let me be clear. If Lerin's still here when I become warlord, I'm going to post him to the coldest depths of Icecliff and ensure he's on privy duty for the rest of his career."*

Arya laughed, almost spitting biscuit crumbs everywhere. "You don't even know him."

"But you do. And you don't respect him. That's enough for me to know I don't want him as my general."

"It shouldn't be. You'll need to judge people for yourself when you're warlord," she said seriously.

"*In every other situation, yes. But not when it comes to you.*" He held her gaze. "*You will be my general, Arya Nameless. I know that's a long way off. But it's my promise to you.*"

She couldn't lie to him. "I wish that could be enough. But Rorin, I don't think…"

"*I know,*" he said sadly.

They didn't speak any further after that. Just sipped tea and wordlessly fought over the last cookie. Content to be together.

The contentment didn't last. Essa appeared, clearly looking for them. "We need to talk," she said, unusually sober.

Arya let out a sigh and drained the remnants of her tea.

Yes, they did.

Chapter 41

Taze and Darmanin waited in Rorin's rooms, sitting at opposite ends of the long sofa. Taze was off duty and out of uniform, and the oddness of it made her blink. "How did it go with General Lerin?" he asked immediately.

She waved a hand. "Tell you later. I don't have the heart to talk about it right now."

Essa touched her elbow briefly. "I'm sorry."

"I think the hardest part is that I was so certain I *would* be general one day," she murmured. "Laskin warned me, but I really thought she meant it."

"Warlord Ravenstrike made the right strategic decision in bringing Lerin here," Darmanin said in his usual grave tones. "She couldn't do anything else."

"Thanks, Dar, that's a real help." Arya dropped to one of the chairs.

"I just meant—"

"I don't want to talk about Lerin." Arya looked at Essa once she and Rorin had settled themselves into chairs too. "You wanted to talk?"

"Rorin told us what you reported to his mother. Leanir is going to keep coming," Essa said immediately. "And it seems clear now that he *was* after Rorin, and General Desomer, and *you*, Arya."

"Well, if it makes you feel better, Leanir won't be coming after me anymore. I'm no longer apprentice to the general. I'm just a mere Nameless shield captain." Arya tried for joking, landed somewhere around petulant, and winced at the sound of it.

Essa's hands were clasped in her lap, and she wrung them. "We still have to worry about the man watching us that night. We can't be certain he was working with Leanir. And if the Nightstalker is truly hunting the three of us, he's not going to stop."

Arya opened her mouth. Closed it. Hesitated.

"*What?*" Rorin signed, looking at Arya in suspicion.

"I..." she sighed. "I saw Nain when he arrived yesterday. He reminded me of the man watching us that night."

"He *reminded* you?" Darmanin said, leaning forward in his chair.

"I think it was him," she admitted. "I know how that sounds, and I can't explain why I'm so sure."

Essa glanced between Darmanin and Arya. "If it was Nain, then ... he was spying on Darmanin, wasn't he, looking for anything he could use to help his warlord against Rorin's mother? He knew Darmanin would be hidden from sight once he arrived in Heathrock, and so he arrived early to spy. And he saw what probably looked like Darmanin and his companions using magic."

The room went quiet. It felt like the walls were closing in. The Nightstalker wasn't going away as a threat, and despite the distraction of the assassination attempt, she hadn't forgotten Salyarin's warnings of him sending dangerous hunters after them. Now, she didn't dare tell her warlord that Nain had probably seen them all aiding and abetting magic use because she couldn't afford for her to find out it had happened. Because she'd sworn to protect both Darmanin and Essa. And, at the worst time, she'd just lost what little influence and authority she had at Heathrock.

Rorin stared between them in consternation. "*What could Warlord Crowtalon do—*"

A knock came at the door, interrupting. Arya rose to open it—caution an instinct now—but it was a Raider standing there. "Captain." He saluted. "The warlord would like to see you."

"Be nice, Arya," Darmanin warned.

Arya shot him a deathly scowl and left. She understood completely why Thiara Ravenstrike had made the decision to bring in Lerin. But still ... it had crushed Arya. Not to mention the secrets she'd been keeping all these years seemed dangerously close to being revealed.

All these thoughts roiled in her head for the walk from the residential wing to Thiara Ravenstrike's office. At her knock, the woman herself came to open the door, rather than just calling out for her to enter. "Come in, Arya."

She was alone, and waved Arya to a pair of comfortable chairs by the window. This wasn't an official meeting, then. Arya lowered herself carefully into one of the chairs—the long walk had her knee and ribs aching—and the warlord sat opposite, her sharp gaze not missing Arya's faint wince. "You look sore."

"I'm fine, Warlord."

The woman snorted but didn't pursue it. "I asked to see you because our meeting yesterday was quite rushed, given the circumstances, and I realised later I'd been abrupt with you. I imagine you are very unhappy with me."

"You did what was right for your State." The words were difficult for Arya to say, but she forced them out anyway.

"You don't believe that."

No, Arya didn't. As sensible and logical as the warlord's decision had been, it was the wrong one. She might be young, still inexperienced even, but she'd do a better job as general of Ravenstrike than Lerin would ever do. And now she'd never hold that position, despite Rorin's promises. Too much could happen between now and when he became warlord—*if* he became warlord. "It was your decision to make, Warlord."

"Yes, it was. I don't believe you're ready to be general, Arya, even if I could give the job to you without weakening my own position. Your actions yesterday proved that." The warlord held her gaze. "That doesn't mean I don't believe you *will* be ready, one day."

Arya stiffened. All she heard was empty promises.

The silence between them drew out, grew heavier. Then, the warlord suddenly let out a sigh, sinking back into her chair and allowing some of the weariness in her gaze to fill her expression. "What Rorin did the other night, placing himself at risk to protect Darmanin, and the courage he displayed in doing so, it makes me proud. Yet, he's my son ... and he was so close to ... if you hadn't been there, Rorin would likely be dead. Darmanin too. And now I've lost my trusted general."

Arya had never experienced such raw honesty from her cool-as-ice warlord, and it compelled her to speak equally honestly. "I'd do anything to protect Rorin, Warlord. He will never come to harm while I am with him."

"I know," she said, all coolness gone for a moment. "And I thank you for it."

Arya glanced away, feeling awkward. Outside, the surface of the lake had been whipped up into thousands of tiny wavelets by a brisk wind.

"Down to business." When Thiara spoke again, her brusqueness had returned. Arya relaxed. "I assume you understand that while Lerin cannot demote you without my approval, he will sideline you, insult you, and do everything he can to force you to either leave of your own accord or provoke you into doing something that will compel me to expel you from the Raiders. If he succeeds, I will not intervene to save you."

"I understand." Arya hesitated. "But warlord, I worry about the decisions he will—"

"For now you are a shield captain, and you have no say in the decisions he makes," the warlord cut over her. "Perhaps you could trust me to ensure he does not make any grievous mistakes."

Arya flushed. "Yes, Warlord."

"I expect you not to let him provoke you or rile you. I expect you to give him *no* reason to have you expelled or censured. Is that clear?"

"Yes, Warlord." She wasn't sure that Thiara Ravenstrike knew what she was asking.

"If I see any suggestion that you are attempting to undermine him in any way, you ever becoming general here in Ravenstrike will be off the table."

Her jaw tightened. She was being chastened like a child after doing nothing wrong. "I understand," she bit the words out, unable to keep the edge from them.

"Watch that temper, Arya," the warlord cautioned her. "If you cannot learn to control it, it will be your downfall."

To this she merely nodded. It took everything she had not to snap something back. What helped was the knowledge that Thiara was right, and General Desomer would never walk again because of it. Her temper guttered to ashes.

"Good. Now that's sorted, I'd like your advice on something."

Thiara rose and walked over to her desk. She ruffled among the papers lying atop it, picked up one, and brought it back to the small table sitting between their two chairs. Arya's ribs protested as she leaned forward to look at the paper. It had a list of names on it.

"Ravenstrike, Crowtalon, Eaglesoar, Hawkesdale, Falconcrest, and SparrowWing," Thiara read them out. "The six States of Dunidaen, each with its own warlord. Then there are each State's complement of vicelords, and all of these lords together make up the full State Council. I'm sure you've learned by now that on some matters only the six warlords and High Warlord will vote, and on others, a full Council vote is required."

Arya nodded. "In Dunidae law, a full State Council vote is required to choose a new leader when a High Warlord dies or retires."

"Yet it is only the smaller Council of warlords that confirms the heir to each State." Thiara sat back. "So at the next State Council—in just over a year—we have two goals."

"Having Rorin and Darmanin confirmed as heirs to Ravenstrike and Crowtalon and you voted in as High Warlord," Arya said.

Thiara nodded. "If we can get Darmanin confirmed as heir, we will strike a blow against Mathas *and* gain ourselves a powerful ally. But we cannot rely upon Crowtalon's vote in either matter. Falconcrest is a staunch ally of Crowtalon, and will vote with Mathas. Eaglesoar is a weak house, and Darien will be retiring as High Warlord. He'll step down gracefully and align himself with whoever gets in his ear, which Mathas will already be doing. SparrowWing and Hawkesdale will vote independently on whoever they think is best for the job."

Arya knew this already from Desomer's painstaking strategy lessons, though more from the perspective of the warlords' likely tendencies in battle. "It seems to me your best option is to get Hawkesdale and SparrowWing's votes in support of Darmanin and Rorin, and then you, War-lord."

"It will be easier said than done, but you are correct. Both warlords are older men steeped in years of tradition. It's going to take a lot to convince them to vote for a second son to be heir, let alone support the idea of a female High Warlord, but at least they have minds of their own and can be convinced on merit."

Arya wasn't sure it would be possible to do either of the two things the warlord wanted, given the obstacles in their way, but didn't dare say that. "What is it you'd like my advice on, Warlord? Does it have something to do with Nain's visit?"

"Not directly, but it has brought all of this front of mind. You know Rorin and Darmanin, probably better than I do. I'd like you to think about how we might use their strengths and hide their weaknesses to help win the other warlords to our side." The warlord rolled up the paper. "That's all for now. Dismissed, Arya."

Arya rose and saluted, her glance falling on one of the Raiders up on the battlements—one of them was shrugging off his cloak in the unseasonably warm sun. It sparked a memory of a conversation she'd had a week earlier with Laskin in the mess after dinner, and like a spark jumping from flint to kindling, her mind chased that thought to a potential solution to all their current problems. A temporary one, but one that would give her time and breathing space to come up with something more permanent.

"Is there something else?" The warlord's voice broke into her thoughts.

"I'm sorry, Warlord." She blinked. "I think I already have an idea on how to help win Warlord SparrowWing's support."

Thiara Ravenstrike arched an eyebrow but waved Arya back to the chair. "I have a few minutes before Magen will be in here nagging me that I'm late for our afternoon meeting with Nain."

"You sent Rorin and Darmanin to foster at Hawkesdale because you wanted the warlord to get to know both young men, so that when it comes time to vote, Hawkesdale already knows and likes the prospects in question and thinks well of them, yes?"

Thiara smiled slightly. "Exactly."

"You might be able to do something similar with Warlord SparrowWing," Arya said. "There was chatter in the mess recently that the seasonal fires in SparrowWing are worse than usual, even though summer ended recently. Some villages are in real danger, and there aren't enough Firemen to cope."

"I'm aware of it." Thiara nodded. "What has this got to do with winning SparrowWing's vote?"

"It's simple, Warlord," Arya said, and strangely enough, it was. "What if Rorin were to take a force of Raiders to help SparrowWing with the fires? He'll be well protected at all times by Taze and the Raiders, and Ravenstrike will be seen as offering a helping hand when it doesn't need to. We have no firefighting expertise, but plenty of strong arms and backs to help dig trenches, clear brush, or escort villagers to safer locations."

Thiara sat back in her chair. She was silent for a long moment as she thought through Arya's proposal. "I'm not comfortable with the idea of sending Rorin away from Heathrock after what just happened."

"If you sent enough Raiders with him, Warlord, it would serve two purposes. Keep Rorin safe *and* provide genuine help to Warlord SparrowWing. It was a Shadeweaver assassin who came after Rorin. Here, Leanir has the advantage of knowing the territory and being able to vanish into the mountains. Out on the open plains of SparrowWing, he'd find it a lot harder to go unnoticed."

"Those fires are burning close to the Crowtalon border—we'd be sending Darmanin dangerously close to his father."

"Then we won't announce Darmanin's presence with us, and we'll disguise him as a Raider when we go so Nain won't see him. But I still think it better that Warlord SparrowWing gets an opportunity to be impressed by both Rorin and Dar, and surely Warlord Crowtalon won't try anything outside his own State." Arya froze in the midst of scrambling for justifications to get Rorin and Darmanin away from Heathrock.

What about Essa?

She cursed inwardly. Once again, she'd spoken without thinking, verbalised a plan without proper consideration. If the elder was right about a nazal hunting them, sensing their magic, it was *Essa* who'd used her magic in the market, yet Arya's plan left her alone and vulnerable at Heathrock.

"What?" Thiara said.

"Sorry, Warlord, I was just thinking. It might be best if Essa came too. It would ensure she's not seen while Chief Adviser Nain is here."

"Not necessary. She would have no use on such an expedition, and it's easy enough to keep her out of sight for a few more days."

"I…" Arya scrambled, but she'd dug herself into a hole she couldn't see a way out of.

"And you're right. Mathas Crowtalon would never publicly attack or harm his son in another State. The other warlords would remove him from his position at once," Thiara said thoughtfully. "All right. We'll do it."

Arya's eyebrows shot up. "Just like that?"

"Your thinking is sound. I'll send Rorin as the Ravenstrike representative to SparrowWing, with you as the leader of the assistance force. That will ensure I have someone competent in charge who will prioritise Rorin's safety." Thiara gave her a sidelong glance. "Not to mention it will also get you out of Lerin's way for a while."

Arya swallowed. "Yes, Warlord."

"You look like you've eaten bad fish all of a sudden," Thiara snapped. "This was your idea! I'll speak with Lerin today. You should ride out as soon as possible."

Arya rose. "With General Lerin's approval, I can have a battalion ready to ride out in two days."

"I'll inform the general of my plan and give him instructions that he is to approve the list of shields you decide to take." Thiara paused. "Rorin will remain in weekly contact with me via messenger bird. He misses one week, and I'll recall you all home instantly. Is that clear?"

"Yes, Warlord. I'll make sure he doesn't miss a single message."

"You do not, under any circumstances, step foot over the Crowtalon border," Thiara said. "Make sure my son stays safe. If anything happens, I'll hold you accountable."

Arya closed the door behind her, temples throbbing with a worsening headache. She was going to get Dar and Rorin safely away from Leanir and Heathrock—that was something, wasn't it?

Essa was relatively unimportant in the household. Leanir would have no reason to target her. Besides, the security in Heathrock would be incredibly tight after recent events.

Still, she couldn't help but worry.

Chapter 42

The future heir to Ravenstrike was an energetic bundle of excitement at the news of their impending trip, and as they ate a late dinner together that night—in his private room, well away from the guest wing where Nain slept—he made repeated thanks to Arya for suggesting it. She tried to match his excitement and hide how troubled she was, not wanting to make them unnecessarily worried. Essa would be okay.

Darmanin didn't say much at all. After he finished eating, he just sat there, toying with the piece of flint he always carried on him while Essa and Rorin debated border tariffs—the subject of his mother's discussion with Nain that afternoon. While Arya was bored silly by that topic, Darmanin's fidgeting was a clear sign that he had something on his mind, so she went with him when he left early.

As they walked, she asked, "You didn't say much about the trip. Are you okay with it?"

"Are *you*?" He cast a look her way, suggesting he knew full well she'd been pretending to be enthused about the trip.

She sighed. "I worry about leaving Essa here alone."

"And you didn't think of that before raising your idea with the warlord?"

She stiffened. "I was trying to get *you* somewhere safe. You and Rorin."

"It isn't your responsibility to look after me, Arya," Darmanin said as they approached his door.

"While you are a member of the Heathrock household it is most certainly my responsibility."

"No," he said firmly, turning to look at her. "It's not."

Having practically grown up among soldiers, Arya had heard them posturing hundreds of times before. She had always smiled and rolled her eyes when it happened. For the first time, hearing the words from someone who wasn't even of age yet, she believed them. "Maybe you can look after yourself without help," she said. "But that doesn't mean you have to."

"It does. I refuse to put others in danger because of me, especially those I care about."

"Are you chiding me?" She stared at him in astonishment. "Dar, I didn't ask for the Nightstalker to come for me, I didn't—"

"That's not what I meant." His face softened. "You were right, all those years ago, Arya. We've found ourselves a family here. You, me, Rorin, Essa … even Taze and Peemla. Do you think you're the only one who will do anything to protect that?"

She stilled, meeting his grey gaze. "You mean that, Dar?"

"With everything I am," he said. "Essa was not wrong in what she accused me of the other day. I have ambition. I *will* be Warlord Crowtalon one day. But my family is of equal importance to me. *This* family. Do you understand?"

She let out a shaky breath. Maybe this wasn't all on her shoulders. Darmanin saw things clearly in a way Rorin often did not, and the knowledge he was as invested as she was … that felt good.

He stepped closer, voice dropping to a murmur. "Even if everything the Etherean told you is true, we should leave Andahar to itself. We don't owe that place anything. This is our home."

Darmanin's words echoed those Arya had repeated to herself over and over, but she still couldn't help asking. "Do you think that's wise? I hoped three years ago that if I, if *we*, did nothing, the Nightstalker would give up and leave us alone, but that hasn't happened."

"It will. If we forget about Andahar, it will forget about us," he said, finality ringing in his voice.

Arya wasn't so sure. Not anymore.

A knock came at Arya's door as midnight closed in. She was still awake, working at the desk in her room, making a final note of things that needed to be done the following day if they were to depart on time the morning after. She'd sent Lerin a list of the shields she wanted to take, and he'd written a terse note back approving it.

Rubbing at her blurry eyes, Arya limped over to open the door. She blinked in surprise to see Essa standing there. "You could have come though the passageways. The warlord hasn't had time to do anything about them yet, although I suspect she'll leave it alone once she satisfies herself there are no external entries."

"I'm not staying. I just wanted to…" Essa let out a breath. "Warlord Ravenstrike asked to see me this afternoon. Now that I'm of age, she offered me a position in her household, as an aide to Magen."

Arya smiled and ignored the misgivings that clustered in the pit of her stomach. Surely Ranier hadn't placed his daughter in the Ravenstrike household simply so that she'd be an aide to a chief adviser one day. "Rorin will be thrilled that you're not leaving Heathrock. And you deserve that position. The warlord is lucky to have you."

Essa didn't smile. "She must have asked you what you thought, before she offered it to me."

Arya didn't answer. It hadn't been a question. The warlord *had* asked, and even though it had been before learning of Essa's magic, Arya hadn't walked back the advice she'd given. Essa was clever and shrewd, more so than any of them, and would be an asset to Magen's staff.

"I rode into the city today to visit my old nursemaid."

Essa stopped there, but Arya waited her out. She knew Essa regularly visited the woman, taking her food or other essentials now she was old and struggling to manage by herself.

"Just down the street from where she lives, a couple of city watch were hauling a man into a prison wagon." Her breath caught. "His cheek was freshly branded."

"That's not you, Essa," Arya said gently.

"It should be. But you've protected me." Essa frowned, eyes on the floor, as if she didn't quite understand that. "Thank you."

"You're my family," Arya said simply. Whatever Ranier's intentions might be, her heart no longer accepted that Essa meant any harm.

Essa's gaze flew to hers, held it without hesitation. "I feel the same. But…"

"But what?"

"Things need to change. If I'm going to be a member of Warlord Raven-strike's staff, I'm going to do what's right. I'm going to try and change things."

Arya stifled a sigh. "I supported the warlord in giving you that position, but I can't stop her removing you if you cause problems."

"I wouldn't want you to," Essa said indignantly. "But don't *you* think things need to change?"

"I'm just a soldier. That's not my job." The response was rote, but she heard the lie even as she spoke it. Her feelings on that subject had shifted too much.

"You don't really feel that way. You can't, or you would never have kept my secret, and Dar's."

Arya opened her door wider. "Are you sure you don't want to come in to talk? I'm just finishing off a pot of tea before bed, but there's enough left for both of us."

Essa glanced into the room, hesitated, then shook her head. "I think I'm just going to turn in. Night, Arya."

"Essa?" Arya called out when she was a few steps away.

The woman turned, eyebrow raised.

"Anything happens while we're gone that makes you uncomfortable? Even if it's just the faintest of instincts. You get those knives of yours out and you use them."

"Are you worried about me, Arya Nameless?"

Arya shrugged. "Salyarin went to great efforts to impress upon me how dangerous these hunters of the Nightstalker are. I don't like the idea of you here alone."

Essa gave her a sad smile. "I'm no killer, Arya. But rest assured, I will use my knives if I have to."

"Essa?" she called softly, and Essa turned around once more. "I *am* worried about you. And I will do everything I can to keep protecting you. My word on it."

There was a moment's silence, then, "It is a momentous thing, having the protection of Arya Nameless," Essa said, and she didn't make it sound like a rebuke, or something amusing or laughable.

But like she'd been given something precious.

***

As soon as Arya made sure that preparations for departure were in full train the following morning, she rode into Heathrock city, where General Desomer was still recovering at The Ruined Arms. The advice from the healer was that he shouldn't be moved until he woke up and more healing had taken place.

When she entered the inn, Tiya was lining up freshly cleaned glasses underneath the bar. The woman waved Arya over. "You look tired. Is that pie you're carrying?"

"Haven't slept much," Arya admitted. "And yes, the general's favourite, from our chamberlain. Has he woken up?"

"Not yet." Tiya lowered her voice, then waved her through to the back. "It will be soon, I think. He's fine to be moved, but of course I can't tell the healer that it's because I've already fixed what damage I can."

Inside Desomer's room, Arya placed the pie on the small table by his bed, then steeled herself to look down at him. He seemed so vulnerable lying there, eyes closed, breathing softly. Arya couldn't bear the thought of her blunt, full-of-life general waking up to find his life so dramatically changed. A hand slid into hers, and she glanced at Tiya, realising from the sting in her lip that she'd almost bitten through it.

"I'm going away for a while." Arya explained the trip. "I feel bad that I won't be here when he wakes up."

"You'll come back," Tiya told her. "And I'll make sure he's okay in the meantime."

"He's going to be alive and mostly healthy. But I don't think he's going to be all right. Not for a long time." If ever. Arya was certain she wouldn't be, not waking up having lost her ability to walk and her job as general of an army.

"If you think that way, he will too," Tiya said sharply, letting go of her hand. "He will still have a life, Arya, and you can help him with that. The other Raiders can too."

Arya shook her head. She didn't even know where to start. And even though it sent guilt writhing through the pit of her stomach, a large part of her was glad she was going away, so she *wouldn't* be there when he woke up.

"Any chance I could have a slice of that pie? I've heard stories of your chamberlain's cooking."

"You have?" Arya lifted an eyebrow in amusement, at the same time glad for Peemla. "How about I bring you a whole one for yourself next time I visit?"

"You have yourself a deal." Tiya leaned in for a lingering kiss.

Arya tugged her closer, allowing herself to escape into that kiss, even if only for a short time. Eventually she pulled back and cleared her throat, glanced around to make sure they were alone. "You should know, we're certain now the attack on Lord Rorin and the general had nothing to do with what happened in the square the other night. You should be safe, but Tiya, you need to be careful using your magic."

"You think I don't already know that?" Bitterness laced her voice. "Trust me, I wouldn't even be here in this magic-hating hole unless I had to be."

"What does that mean?" Arya asked, startled.

"Nothing." Tiya shook her head. "I'd best get back to the bar, we're opening soon. Stay safe on your trip."

The woman was gone before Arya could even thank her.

Chapter 43

Just over three weeks later, Arya found herself sprawled by the campfire, weary to the bone and reeking of smoke. Tents, horses, and firepits dotted the sparse trees around them where her Raiders were encamped.

After travelling to Melbin, the seat of SparrowWing, and offering their services to an astonished yet grateful Warlord SparrowWing, the Ravenstrike entourage had spent the past fortnight fighting bitterly to keep the out-of-control fire in southern SparrowWing from damaging more towns and villages.

The work was hot and intensive. Over and over, they'd dug trenches, cleared brush, and cut grass. The fire was never far away. Depending on which way the wind blew, the air could be thick with smoke and ash, making it hard to breathe. Their clothes, skin, and bedding smelled of stale smoke no matter how often they washed.

Despite it all, the mood was high. Every new day brought a fresh challenge; whether it was to clear the ground fast enough to stymie or shift the direction of the fire, or finish digging trenches around a village before the flames got too close. Often, they would clear their designated area just in time, only to receive a message from a Fireman scout that they were needed at another vulnerable spot where a section of the fire tried to break towards a village or town.

The sound of laughter reached her ears, and she looked up to see Taze, Darmanin, and Rorin approach. They'd been washing in a nearby stream and were soaking wet and bare-chested. As they came closer, they pulled on shirts and slumped down around the fire as wearily as Arya had.

"I could happily sleep for a year," Rorin announced.

Arya chuckled. Taze and his shield kept a close eye on Rorin's safety, but he'd been working just as hard as everyone else. Tiredness did nothing to dampen his merry spirits. This was the first time in Rorin's life he'd been away from the watchful eye of his parents or another warlord, and he was clearly having the time of his life.

"*This work is exhausting,*" Rorin signed as if reading her thoughts. "*But for the first time ever, I feel like I'm actually doing something important.*"

Arya couldn't have agreed more. She'd been trained to kill to defend her State and her warlord. But here she was helping to save lives rather than take them. It was a nice change, and the work was intense enough that it allowed her to ignore all her uncertainty over the fact she was no longer apprentice to Desomer or would have to return to Lerin's command. So far from the Diamondfang, the Nightstalker seemed a distant concern. If it wasn't for her lingering worry about Essa, Arya would have been perfectly content.

"This is what it means to be a warlord," Darmanin said quietly. "To have the power to take action when it's needed."

"Eyes up!" Taze said suddenly, pointing to an approaching Fireman. His brown and gold uniform was marred by soot and even a couple of patches of charring.

Arya recognised him as the captain of the shield that had been working alongside her Raiders for the past two days. He looked grim, and she sat up straighter.

"Captain." He acknowledged Arya with a crisp nod as he hunkered down by their fire.

"*Taze, get the captain a mug of cold cider,*" Rorin signed. "*He looks hot and exhausted.*"

Taze signed agreement and headed over to where the battalion had their mess tent erected.

"You don't look happy, Captain Ranald," Arya said. "What is it?"

"The winds are changing direction and strengthening," the Fireman replied. "The fire will reach Seelan by tomorrow morning. There's no way we can guarantee stopping it. The city will have to be evacuated."

For a moment, shocked silence filled the space. Rorin's tutor had once described SparrowWing as the hub of the spoked wheel that made trade inside Dunidaen run smoothly. Situated where the SparrowWing, Crowtalon, and Hawkesdale borders intersected, Seelan was the most critical element of that network. Losing it to fire would have serious implications for Dunidaen, and a terrible economic impact on SparrowWing.

"Are you sure?" Arya managed. "I thought the fire was slowly coming under control."

Ranald looked grim. "If the wind had held in its current direction, Seelan would have been fine. But the fire is now burning directly towards it. We don't have enough time to finish digging trenches, and even if we did, a fire of this strength is likely to just jump them. We'll do our best, but we need to make sure everyone is out safely in case we fail."

"What can we do?" Arya said.

"I know you're all tired, but we could really use your help evacuating the city. We need the expertise of every Fireman we've got to do everything we can to hold the fire back."

She hesitated; that would be a challenging task and more dangerous than what they'd been doing. Crowds could riot in a panic, not to mention they risked being caught in the fire themselves if they lingered in the city too long. How much danger was Warlord Ravenstrike willing to place her Raiders in?

"I'd like to stay and help," Rorin signed, clearly reading her hesitation. *"I will do everything you say as regards my safety, I promise. But we should do this."*

Taze returned with the cider, and Ranald drank gratefully while Arya considered. In the end, it wasn't hard. They'd come to SparrowWing to help, and abandoning them now wasn't in her. Not to mention if Seelan was destroyed, it would impact on Ravenstrike State too.

"We'll do as you ask, Captain," she said. "Taze, would you gather the shield captains so we can tell them about the change of plans? We'll have to ride out tonight to maximise the time we have in Seelan."

Ranald's face crumpled in relief. "We have a relief camp set up five miles west of Seelan, just outside the village of Miteran and well out of the fire's path. Help us get everyone out of the city, and I promise I'll have a mug of cold ale for each of you when you arrive."

"We'll take that deal and hold you to it, Captain." Arya shook his hand.

Sometime in the early hours after midnight, they arrived at the outskirts of Seelan. The fires were a bright orange glow to the northeast—and even as inexperienced as she was with fire, Arya could tell it was frighteningly close to the city.

The plains northeast of the city teemed with shields of Firemen working desperately to dig trenches and clear brush, but a single glance told Arya how impossible their task was—there was far too much space to cover.

Ranald rode with them into the city, where he introduced Arya and Rorin to the mayor. The mayor looked rumpled, like he hadn't slept properly for days. His brisk practicality on meeting them only barely concealed his fear at receiving the direction to evacuate.

"You know this city far better than us, sir, so we'd appreciate your advice on the best way to approach the evacuation," Arya told him, keeping her tone brisk and dispensing with small talk. She didn't want to give him time to dwell on the approaching danger.

"Right." He nodded, cleared his throat, then gestured them over to a map unrolled on a nearby table. For all his fear, the man had clearly been preparing for this. "A grid-style approach is my recommendation. Starting with the northern districts closest to the approaching fires and working methodically back from there. The residents know this might be coming, so some of them will be prepared. Others won't want to leave their homes." He glanced up. "You won't find this easy."

"We can only do our best," Arya said. "Let me get my shield captains in here and we'll start assigning grids. How many exits from the city can we safely use? And Captain Ranald, you said there was a relief centre nearby?"

"That's right, you can direct people here." Ranald stabbed on the map. "I'd advise against using the city exits anywhere in this area." He drew a light circle in charcoal. "Anyone fleeing this way would be in danger of getting caught up in fire."

"I'll start marking up all the other exits if that will help you, Captain Nameless?" the mayor asked.

"Please." She nodded. "And if you've got any copies of that map you can mark up, that would also be helpful. I'll be back in a few moments with my captains."

By the time morning came, the wind had firmly changed direction, proving the Firemen's predication correct. Arya was consulting with the mayor about the progress of the evacuation when a Fireman rode in to report that the winds were stronger than they'd expected, and they no longer held any hope of diverting the fire's course away from the city.

The mayor rubbed wearily at his forehead. "What are the chances of you holding it off?"

"We're fighting hard, sir," the Fireman said, smoke-streaked but determined. "If nothing else, we'll make sure we delay it until everyone is out."

Arya saw his determination, had seen the way the Firemen operated these past weeks, and gave him a bracing smile. "For what it's worth, my money's on you Firemen to beat this."

He straightened imperceptibly. "Thanks, Captain. I'd best get back to it."

Arya followed him out, mounting Zeke so she could ride out to the northern outskirts of town. She wanted to see the situation for herself. The orange glow in the distance she'd seen hours earlier was now a visible furnace, heading directly for them. The Firemen out on the plains were retreating, looking so small in the face of nature's fury. Still, they weren't giving up.

She shifted in the saddle, planning to go and check on Rorin—who was working with Taze's shield—when Darmanin rode up. Loose hair had escaped his braid, soot stained his fair skin, and sweat dampened his jerkin.

"Where's your guard?" she asked him.

"Helping with the evacuation, which is far more important than watching my back," he replied, light eyes studying the fire. "That's getting uncomfortably close.

"At what point does it become too dangerous for us to stay?" The question was more to herself than Darmanin, but he answered anyway.

"That depends on your threshold for risk."

Arya nodded, considering. "We keep going as long as we can."

"What will you do if we can't get everyone out in time?"

Arya glanced at Darmanin's unreadable expression. "We will."

"If not? Will you keep the Raiders here and risk their safety?"

"It won't come to that," she said, with more confidence than she felt. "Come on, let's go and keep helping. If you won't stay with Taze's shield, then stick with me."

Arya lifted the reins, but Darmanin suddenly stiffened at her side, pointing. "Did you see that?"

"What?"

"Part of the fire just went out." He was staring intently. "Look, there, just to the west of that copse of trees where the Firemen were retreating a moment ago."

Arya stared in the direction Darmanin was pointing, seeing nothing but flames and scrambling Firemen. About to ask him in irritation what he was talking about, she saw it. A section of trees that had been aflame suddenly was fire-free. She blinked, sure she'd imagined it, but there ... again. A section of fire abruptly gone.

"That's impossible," she muttered.

"It's not natural, Arya, and look where it's happening—the fire was about to break through the Firemen lines right there."

"They don't seem to have noticed anything."

"That's because they're either scrambling desperately away or focusing on their own sections of the fire."

He was right. "Magic?" she asked, frowning.

"What else could it be?"

Arya continued watching carefully. At the rate they were doing it, whatever was killing the flames wouldn't be able to stop the fire by themselves, but it was certainly helping the Firemen slow it down. Beside her, Darmanin reached into his pocket, pulling out a piece of flint and toying with it distractedly; a habit of his when he was thinking.

But seeing that piece of flint triggered a memory...

"Dar, Seelan is the biggest trading city in SparrowWing, right?"

"Yes. We might be saving lives by evacuating, but if the city burns down, it's going to hit the State hard economically. Dunidaen, too."

"That's not what I mean. If you were a musician travelling through SparrowWing, this is the place you'd come for the biggest crowds, where you'd make the most money?"

"Probably." His eyes narrowed. "Arya, what are you thinking?"

"Follow me," she said, turning Zeke and setting off at a gallop. The first line of evacuating citizens she reached, she reined in and asked them where the most popular inns were. All of the ones suggested were clustered in the same block in the southern side of the city. After another helpful soul gave clear directions on the fastest way to get there, she set off towards it, Darmanin following closely.

"Do you have a musician playing here at the moment?" she asked at the first inn they came to. "Red-headed fellow, name's Chiarn?"

"No." He shook his head, looking puzzled by her question. "Chiarn's at The Fireman's Ditch."

"Where's that?"

"Across the street and a block down. Hey, what's Chiarn got to do with—"

She turned and ran, colliding into Darmanin, who was still following her inside.

"Arya—" he started, but she untangled herself from him and broke into another run down the block.

Inside The Fireman's Ditch, the innkeeper was carrying a heavy travelling bag down the stairs to add to a pile at the bottom. Some of the inn's guests were in the main bar, their own bags at their feet, waiting to be escorted out of the city. Arya scanned their faces, but none of them were Chiarn. Darmanin was a silent presence at her back.

"The musician Chiarn—where is he?" she demanded of the innkeeper.

The man shrugged. "He's around here somewhere."

As the innkeeper spoke, the front door opened and Chiarn's familiar tall figure stepped through. He took one look at Arya, and his eyes widened in shock. A second later, he was turning and sprinting out of the inn.

Arya set off after him, ignoring the innkeeper's shouted questions. She burst through the door and scanned the street outside … Chiarn was already half a block down and clambering over the top of a wall, vanishing from sight just as she spotted him. Arya ran for the wall, scrambling up over the top into a narrow alley between buildings.

The singer was a short distance ahead, fleeing down the alley. Arya pushed herself, sprinting after him as fast as she could, boots rapping on the hard ground, ignoring the soreness that began throbbing in her knee. A glance over her shoulder at the sound of running boots behind her revealed Darmanin in pursuit too.

For a musician, the man was *fast*.

Halfway along, Chiarn had to slow to dodge a pile of empty crates lined up behind the buildings. Instead of doing the same, Arya simply leaped up onto the first crate and then swung herself over, making up ground. Chiarn was faster, but Arya had the stamina to run all day and the stubbornness to ignore her aching knee and ribs.

Putting on another spurt of speed, she caught the tail end of his shirt and yanked hard. He stumbled, off balance, and she used her momentum to shove him hard against the alley wall, forearm across his throat to stop him from struggling.

Darmanin slid into her peripheral vision, one hand settling on the hilt of his sword.

Chiarn's chest heaved with exertion as he stared at her, his face flushed and dripping, fear written in his bright blue eyes. Dark patches of sweat spread from his underarms and down from his collar.

"What are you doing?" he demanded. His gaze shifted nervously between her and Darmanin. "I haven't done anything wrong."

"Then why did you run?"

"I…" He opened his mouth, closed it.

"You have magical ability. You were extinguishing the fire earlier, weren't you?"

"That's … ridiculous." He choked on the words, face turning redder.

Arya removed her arm and took a step back, confident that she and Darmanin could contain him if he tried to run again. "That night outside The Ruined Arms, I caught you in the yard. Lighting your cigar without a flint. And later … you pushed through the crowd to see what was going on with the injured girl. You felt something, didn't you? I could tell by the look on your face."

"You're imagining things." Chiarn's glance flicked to Darmanin, trying for a laugh but failing. Terror exuded from him. "And you're crazy. There's a fire about to engulf this city and you're wasting your time chasing down–"

"A fire you can help stop," Arya snapped. "I'm not going to hurt you or tell anyone about your ability. But I need to know."

He licked his lips. "There's nothing to know," he said stubbornly.

"I have magic," Darmanin said quietly, stepping closer again. Arya's eyes widened at his admission, but she didn't say anything. "And Arya has always protected me. She can protect you too."

"I can protect myself. I haven't done anything wrong and I don't have magic. You can't hold me here."

"We need your help with the fires. What you were doing before was working—why did you stop?"

Panic closed over his expression. He took a step forward and stopped when both Arya and Darmanin shifted to close of his escape. "Please just let me go. I can't do anything."

"Just tell me—"

"I've seen the branded people begging on the streets, Arya Nameless. And I've seen the Shadeweavers put into carts and shipped off to Andahar." His voice was high and panicked. "Nothing is worth that."

"You can help the Firemen contain the fire before it hits the city."

Chiarn laughed. "The fire is too close and I'm no hero. I have no desire to risk myself. You can't force me to do anything."

Shit. He wasn't budging, not even a little bit. And they were wasting so much time here in this alley.

She tried once more. "What if I promise to keep you safe if you stay and keep working on the fire? I'll make sure nobody sees it."

"I don't have magic," he said stubbornly. "There's nothing I can do."

Darmanin stepped away, urgency filling his tone. "Arya, we have to go."

"You're a coward," she spat at Chiarn. "Get out of here."

The musician pushed off the wall, his confidence reasserting itself when he realised they weren't going to force the issue. "Lose the crazy theories before you come talk to me again, Raider. They make you far less attractive."

Tired and annoyed, Arya and Darmanin found the nearest Raider shield, joining them to help direct people towards the safe exits from the city. The heat of the day increased, sun beating down on them and smoke filling their noses and mouths. Even stripped down to their uniform's undershirts, they sweated endlessly.

Arya kept glancing at the haze of smoke to the north, trying to tell how close the fire was getting. Anxiety over how slowly they were moving set her temper on a short fuse, and Darmanin had to pull her aside after she started yelling at a tailor who stubbornly refused to leave his business behind.

"I know, I know!" she told him before he had to say anything. "I'm not helping."

"Why don't you take a break?"

She gave him a scornful look. "Thanks for the condescension, but I don't think so."

His mouth set. "I wasn't—"

Cries from the shield around them cut off Darmanin's reply. Still bad-tempered, Arya spun around to demand what they were shouting about when she felt it.

A breeze gusting up, strong and decisive. And from the completely opposite direction than it had been blowing.

Minutes later, a Fireman came galloping up to them, making straight for Arya. "Captain. The wind's changed. We're pretty sure we can stop the fire reaching the city now—if we can get some reinforcements to the north. Will you bring your battalion?"

Arya grinned, temper disappearing in a flash. "Roger that. One battalion of reinforcements coming right up!"

Arya could see the weariness sloughing off her Raiders' shoulders as she rounded each shield up one by one and led them out of the city. Even so, they came to a halt outside the gates, eyes widening. The fire still looked like a monster, loud and orange and angry. The heat from it was palpable, causing fresh sweat to slick her skin.

"*Wow.*" Rorin signed, blue eyes bright in a face covered with soot.

"You don't get too close," she warned him. "And don't leave your shield."

A handful of Firemen converged on them, and Arya put her shields at their disposal, conceding to their expertise.

Darmanin looked at her before she spurred Zeke after the shield Rorin had joined. "Do you think Chiarn did end up helping?"

"No," she said after a moment. "It was the unexpected wind that turned things around. He probably bought Seelan just enough time for that wind to arrive though."

Once again, magic had been used to help, not hurt.

Chapter 44

"*What are we going to do about him?*" Rorin signed.

After hours of back-breaking work, the fire was finally contained by nightfall, and Seelan's citizens were given the all-clear to return to their homes. Firemen remained out on the plains around the city, making sure the fire didn't break back towards them, but Arya, Rorin, and their Raiders were finally able to rest.

They'd been welcomed—albeit wearily—with open arms at the Firemen encampment west of the city, and most of the battalion were soon passed out asleep on the ground, not having even bothered setting up their tents.

The four of them had sunk down around the unlit firepit outside Rorin's tent, and from there had been too tired to get back up and move somewhere to sleep. So they stayed sprawled amidst their saddlebags and blankets, and Arya explained what she and Darmanin had learned about Chiarn. They kept their voices low.

"There's nothing we *can* do," Darmanin said.

"Dar, he's another magic-wielder," Arya said without thinking. "We can't leave him roaming about out there unprotected."

"Why not?" he sounded genuinely puzzled.

She opened her mouth to reply, then realised he had a point. Chiarn was no more her responsibility than any other magic-wielder in Dunidaen. So why had she said that?

"Dar's right," Taze agreed. "Chiarn has survived this long on his own. It sounds like he only risked using his magic today to save his own hide."

"*I'm not so sure. Arya said she caught Chiarn using his magic to light a cigar in Heathrock—that sounds pretty careless to me,*" Rorin said.

Silence fell for a moment, then Arya continued, "He sensed Essa and Tiya that night, I'm sure of it. The timing of that incident in the square ... it nags at me."

She suddenly wished Essa were with them, or at least that she'd talked about this more with her before leaving Heathrock. Essa would have untangled her unease and pointed out the clear path. Not to mention her uncanny knack of easing Arya's anxieties simply by talking with her.

Darmanin said, "Chiarn has no interest in coming to us. Leave him to his business, Arya."

"*You say that so easily.*" Rorin was staring at his foster brother, aghast. "*You, who knows what it's like to be a magic-wielder. Like it's a choice that anyone would ever want to make. Like being a known magic-wielder in Dunidaen isn't practically a death sentence.*"

Arya looked between them, startled to hear that coming from Rorin. And uneasy.

"You've been talking with Essa too much, but as usual you see things in black and white," Darmanin said. "I say nothing easily, Rorin, but Chiarn is a man and can make his own choices."

"Don't forget your mother's policies on magic-wielders," Taze warned. "You can't afford to be overheard speaking in support of them."

"*My mother's policies are wrong, and you all know it, even if you won't say it out loud. When I am warlord, I will make sure it stops.*"

Arya cleared her throat in an attempt to dispel the tense silence. "We'll leave Chiarn for now. But I will find him again."

"Why?" Darmanin asked flatly.

She didn't know why, she just ... Arya sat up abruptly, weariness forgotten as shock reverberated through her. "Oh, raven's balls!"

"What is it?" Taze straightened, hand dropping to the hilt of his sword, as if readying for an attack.

Part of her had known Chiarn was watching that night in the city square *before* she'd seen him. She'd *known* he hadn't had a flint when lighting that cigar despite not having really seen anything. And she'd guessed far too quickly what was going on when Darmanin had noticed the fires being affected by magic earlier that day. She rubbed at her suddenly throbbing temples, energy fading as quickly as it had come. "He's one of them."

Darmanin sat up too, animated. "Do you *want* this ridiculous story the Etherean elder fed you about Andahar to be true? Do you want to *make* it true?"

"Of course not," she snapped. "But the elder said I would know, like instinct, and that's what it's like with Chiarn, like I have to protect him. It's the same with you, and Essa. I've ignored that, and pretended it wasn't there, but I can't change it."

"Then keep ignoring it."

"*Darmanin, calm,*" Rorin signed, then turned to Arya, eyes wide. "*Are you saying Chiarn is one of the four other Sky Lord potentials the elder told you about?*"

Arya groaned, slumped back down. "Laskin even told me once that one of the Sky Lord Houses was named Flamewielder—and look what Chiarn can do."

"It's nonsense, all of it," Darmanin snapped.

"*Why is this upsetting you so much, Dar?*" Rorin asked.

"Arya has already put herself in too much danger for us." Darmanin stood abruptly. "I don't want to see her get hurt again because of a useless idiot of a musician. He is worth nothing and doesn't deserve our attention."

With that, he stalked away, leaving them sitting there staring after him, stunned by his outburst.

"It's not nonsense," Arya murmured sadly. "I wish it was, but it's not."

"He's worried about you, Arya," Taze said.

"He's being a stubborn fool." She sighed. "And he's as exhausted as we are. We should all get some sleep."

"*I'll agree to that!*" Rorin signed with feeling. "*I feel like I could sleep for a week.*"

Arya curled up on the ground, more sympathetic to Darmanin's words than she'd let on. She was so physically exhausted that she fell asleep quickly, but her dreams were full of crackling flames and a musician with copper hair who laughed in her face when she asked him to help stop a fire threatening a city.

***

The following morning they woke to a haze-filled sky, smoke and ash everywhere. Arya, having let her battalion sleep as long as they'd like, was just returning to Rorin's tent after a makeshift wash when two horses, trailed by a shield of Firemen, rode up.

"Warlord!" She saluted as soon as she recognised Warlord Helden SparrowWing; he was a tall man with short-cropped greying hair and a ramrod straight posture, even in the saddle. Captain Ranald rode with him, and he seemed cheerful, despite being filthy and having dark shadows under his eyes. Both men dismounted and made their way over.

"Captain Nameless." SparrowWing greeted her, and at his side Captain Ranald gave her a warm smile. "I rode in late last night, wanting to help where I could. You will be pleased to know that the fire's almost out. We're confident there's no further threat to Seelan or any other villages."

"That's excellent news, Warlord," Arya said in relief.

The tent flap rustled and Rorin appeared, blinking away sleep and coming to stand beside Arya. "*Warlord SparrowWing. A pleasure to see you again, and an even greater pleasure to hear your news.*"

Arya stifled a smile. Rorin was good at this, being the charming and polite warlord's son. If nothing else, the trip had given him ample opportunity to impress SparrowWing.

"I'm told your battalion was instrumental to our efforts, and so I wanted to come and personally thank you, Lord Rorin," SparrowWing said, then smiled slightly, an impish smile. "And also to ask another favour. I am already deeply in debt to Ravenstrike, so why not double down."

"There is no debt, Warlord. Our help was freely given," Arya translated for Rorin, then asked, "There aren't more fires, are there?"

"No," said SparrowWing. "But many villages along our southern border were badly damaged by this season's fires. I hoped you would consider remaining another few weeks to lend your Raiders' strong arms to a little rebuilding? I will ensure your battalion is supplied with enough provisions for as long as you stay—tents too, if you need them."

"We'd love to stay, Warlord. I'll write to my mother this morning."

Arya shot Rorin a pointed glance, but she couldn't undermine him by hesitating to translate in front of the warlord, so she did so.

"Thank you, Lord Rorin." SparrowWing brightened. "I will leave Captain Ranald at your disposal. He and his shield will escort you to the villages and ensure you have everything you need."

"Thank you, Warlord. I'm truly glad we've been able to help."

Arya waited until the warlord had gone before turning on Rorin, scowling. "You couldn't have considered his request before agreeing to it so quickly?"

"What reason would we have for saying no? Mother sent me here to win SparrowWing's support, and building some houses will be less dangerous than firefighting."

"I would have preferred if you discussed it with me first. General Desomer taught me to always think things through properly before making a decision."

"Next time I will," he promised. *"I'll write to Mother now and let her know of our plans."* He hesitated. *"What are you going to do about Chiarn?"*

"He'll be long gone from Seelan by now." Arya sighed. "Darmanin wasn't wrong last night."

Rorin frowned. *"I don't like that Dar told Chiarn about his magical ability. If he tells anyone…"*

"I think we can assume Chiarn's self-preservation instinct will prevent that, but you're right to worry," Arya said. "You need to be careful in what you say too, Rorin. You can't afford to step wrong; you know that."

"I know. But I won't have to be silent forever."

✶✶✶

Two days later found the Ravenstrike entourage approaching the southern SparrowWing border where it crossed over into Crowtalon. Smoke still hung in the air, giving the light a brownish quality. Rorin's battalion looked a rough, travel-stained bunch, a far cry from the snappy red-and-black-clad Raiders who'd ridden out from Heathrock a month earlier.

Captain Ranald rode with them, lifting his hand to point to where a smaller road branched off ahead. "We'll turn off there. This road eventually crosses into Crowtalon, and we don't want that. The Lances aren't always friendly about us crossing the border, even when we need to get to the fires."

"Agreed, let's keep well away from Crowtalon," Arya said, glancing over to where Darmanin rode with Rorin at the head of Taze's shield. A little shiver ran down her spine. He ignored her look, his attention ahead of them. Since their argument the other night, Darmanin had been even more taciturn than usual.

Ranald continued, "Dorin is a couple miles along the road. Almost all their homes were destroyed in the fires, and the villagers are living in tents while they try and rebuild before winter hits."

They'd just reached the turnoff when Taze suddenly called out, "Something approaches!"

Arya stared where he was pointing—there *was* something moving along the road in their direction.

"*Crowtalon Lances?*" Rorin asked.

"Or a merchant train?" Arya said. "Travellers even."

But in a few moments, it was clear there was a column of riders in military formation approaching, no carts or wagons to be seen.

"What's your advice, Captain?" Arya asked Ranald.

"It's a shield of Lances," he confirmed. "We should halt and wait for them to reach us. While they don't like us stepping on their toes, they don't have any compunctions crossing onto our side of the border to make sure we're not up to anything."

She lifted an eyebrow. "And your warlord allows that?" She couldn't imagine Thiara Ravenstrike doing so.

Ranald looked uncomfortable. "Warlord SparrowWing picks his battles when it comes to Crowtalon."

Arya turned and called the halt. A twinge went through her at the sight of how smoothly the battalion responded to her order. She'd initially been wary of riding out of Ravenstrike without her three specialised shields, unsure how much she could rely on a battalion of Heathrock Raiders, but at some point along the way, she'd realised that they responded to her directions without complaint or hesitation or muttering, even though she technically didn't outrank any of the other shield captains.

It was both a warm feeling and frustrating too. Desomer had given her the backing she needed to improve upon what he'd already built. But what would happen now Lerin was in charge? She feared Desomer's sharp army would lose its edge. And with the Nightstalker once again stirring, it was the worst time for that to happen.

Taze brought his shield forward to line up behind Arya, Rorin, and Ranald. His hand rested on the hilt of his sword. Arya raised an eyebrow at him over her shoulder. "You think that's necessary?"

"Lances are a twitchy lot, I've heard."

"He's not wrong," Ranald muttered.

"Even so, we need to make a good first impression. Take your hands off your swords and try not to scowl so heavily," she told them. "Darmanin?"

After a moment, he looked over at her, his expression unreadable. He'd remained with Taze's shield but sat his horse at the head of their column. "Don't reveal yourself. Is that clear?"

He gave a stiff nod. "Fine."

Arya sighed and turned her gaze to the approaching force. Rorin reached over to tap her shoulder. *"What about me?"*

"These are soldiers, so it might be best if I take the lead. If I need you, I'll bring you in. Are you comfortable with that?"

"I trust you."

The approaching party soon resolved itself into a large group of mounted warriors—Arya counted a full shield plus two extra riders. They wore plate armour under tabards in the black and violet Crowtalon colours. The horses, too, wore light armour, and their riders carried deadly-looking lances.

The Lances halted in perfect formation some distance ahead, while three riders continued on. The lead rider pulled his horse in rather showily, then reached up to pull off his helmet. "Blasted thing's too hot to wear in this unseasonable weather," he said cheerfully, flicking back sweat-soaked brown hair as he ran his gaze over their group. "I'm Andrian Crowtalon, and I'm ... *Darmanin?*"

Arya looked back at Darmanin, whose remote expression had frozen. "Andrian," he said, then faltered. His hands clenched then unclenched on the reins.

Andrian stared at his brother in absolute astonishment. Then, in a sudden move, he jumped down from his horse and strode across the intervening space, passing right by Rorin and Arya to the line of Raiders behind them.

"Well?" Andrian stopped by Darmanin's horse and grinned up at him. "Stop staring like a stunned fool and get down here!"

Darmanin blinked, gave himself a little shake, then warily swung himself out of the saddle. Andrian immediately drew him into a fierce hug. "I can't believe it's you. You've been gone so long ... we never heard any word from you. I didn't even know if you were still alive."

"I..." Darmanin cleared his throat and finally managed words. "Ravenstrike took me in. Father didn't tell you?"

"Yes, he did, but ... you never wrote or anything."

"I didn't think he'd let any message from me through." Though he didn't give any outward expression of joy, Arya could tell from his almost non-existent smile that Darmanin was pleased to have such a reception from his elder brother.

"You're probably right." Andrian shook his head, smiling. "I can't tell you how good it is to see you. Since you left it's just been me and Father, and ... well, you remember what he's like."

Darmanin swallowed, saying quietly, "I remember."

Andrian finally looked away from his brother to take in the Ravenstrike party. "Will you introduce me to your companions?"

Rorin dismounted immediately, so Arya sighed and followed suit. She saw nothing threatening or malicious in Andrian's easy manner, but she didn't like that Darmanin's presence among them had been revealed so quickly.

"This is my foster brother, Lord Rorin Ravenstrike," Darmanin said.

Andrian shook his hand warmly. "It's a pleasure to meet you, Lord Rorin."

Rorin began signing vigorously, and Andrian waited, seemingly unbothered by the sign language. Darmanin translated, that little smile still on his face. "He thanks you and says he's thrilled to meet my brother."

"Lord Andrian, this is Shield Captain Arya Nameless. She and I lead a battalion of Raiders helping with the fire near Seelan. We're on our way to assist with rebuilding a village nearby damaged in the fire."

As Darmanin translated Rorin's introduction, Andrian turned to Arya, eyes widening. A moment later, a boyish smile broke across his face. "I know you. Long time no see!"

"Lord Andrian." She smiled back. "It *has* been a while."

His smiled widened. "I'm dying to know how you went from the young hellcat I knew at Icecliff to a shield captain alongside the future heir to Ravenstrike."

She chuckled. "I'll tell you over an ale one day."

"I'll hold you to that." Andrian winked and turned his attention back to his brother and Rorin. "You've come to help villages, you say? I admit we were a little wary when a scout told us a battalion of Raiders was approaching our border."

"Warlord Ravenstrike sent us to help SparrowWing with their bushfires, but we have no intention of crossing into Crowtalon," Darmanin explained. "Is that why you're here, to keep an eye on the fires?"

One of the men who'd ridden forward with Andrian suddenly urged his horse closer. "Our purpose here is not your business."

All gazes swung towards him.

Arya froze, instantly recognising the narrow face and short-cropped blonde hair. A slight shiver run down the back of her spine as his eyes met hers briefly. There was nothing warm there.

Andrian waved an arm. "Allow me to introduce my father's chief adviser, Nain. He's rude at the best of times, so don't let him rile you. In answer to your question, our presence here has nothing to do with the fires, though I wish it did."

Nain's face tightened, and his voice came out cold and cutting. "Warlord Crowtalon does not wish to risk his only son fighting fires that will do nothing more serious than destroy a couple of rural villages."

"His only son?" Rorin signed so angrily that Arya could barely read him. *"A couple of rural villages?"*

Andrian looked curiously between Arya and Darmanin when both chose not to interpret Rorin's signing, and he eventually continued. "Father sent us out to patrol the borders and make sure no SparrowWing refugees try to cross over and tax our emergency relief supplies."

Arya kept a firm grasp on her temper and deliberately didn't look in Rorin's direction. "Lord Rorin gives his word that his Raiders are only here in an assistance capacity. We will not cross the border into Crowtalon."

Nain reached out to place a hand on Andrian's arm. Andrian, who'd been about to say something, immediately fell silent. Arya's gaze narrowed—the Crowtalon son seemed almost cowed.

When Nain spoke, it was with that officious tone Magen sometimes used. "You will be granted permission to remain in close proximity to our border on the condition your Raiders surrender their weapons to us until such time as you leave."

Rorin flushed red with an anger that leaped bright and hot in Arya too. Behind, she heard Taze suck in a breath. Even Andrian looked surprised. Nain had just insulted the honour of Ravenstrike by implying that Rorin's word wasn't to be trusted.

"Tell him we will not surrender our weapons. I have given my word that we will not cross into his State." Rorin signed. *"He has no authority here anyway."*

Arya translated Rorin's words, then added a few of her own. "I'd think very carefully before suggesting that you're not willing to trust the word of Warlord Ravenstrike's son, Adviser Nain."

"Warlord Ravenstrike's son has two hundred armed warriors at his back," Nain said evenly. "And he's a stripling boy who hasn't been confirmed as heir to anything. His word is worthless."

Rorin went even redder. Even his angry signing faltered.

Arya had no such hesitation. "We aren't going anywhere unless Warlord SparrowWing or Warlord Ravenstrike requests it, nor are we giving up our weapons." She made her voice as cold as the winter snows in the Diamondfang. "And if any of your Lances merely breathe in the direction of one of my Raiders, you're going to find out very quickly how useless those shiny lances are against real soldiers."

"Arya!" Darmanin's soft but steel tone told her she'd gone too far, and even Rorin reached out to touch her arm, but she didn't care.

Nain turned on her. "You have *no* right to speak to me—"

"Enough, Nain." Andrian stepped in as the chief adviser urged his horse closer to Arya. "Warlord Ravenstrike isn't invading us with a single battalion of Raiders. It's clear they've been helping with the fires up north, just look at them."

Nain's face tightened. "Lord Andrian, your father would not—"

"If it all goes wrong and Ravenstrike starts rampaging through our State unchecked," Andrian said, "I'll take the blame with Father."

Nain's expression twisted sourly with distaste, but he gave a jerky nod. "Very good, Lord Andrian." With that, he levelled a single look at Arya before kicking his horse away. In that look, she saw a promise: he wasn't going to forget this little exchange.

Once he was out of earshot, Andrian's shoulders relaxed and he smiled. "Ignore Nain. He's stuffy and overly paranoid. I avoid him as much as I possibly can."

Arya hesitated as the heat of her temper faded and she realised she was letting it get the best of her. "We truly are just here to help, but if it's going to cause problems between our States..."

"I'm Warlord Crowtalon's son." Andrian shrugged. "Nain can bluster all he likes, but this is my personal shield. We accept your word, Lord Rorin. The SparrowWing villages are lucky to have you here to help."

"Thank you, Lord Andrian."

"Darmanin, will you come with me?" Andrian asked hopefully. "I'm sure I could convince Father to—"

"Never," Darmanin spat the word so fiercely Andrian almost took a step back. "It was good to see you, Andrian, but I will never return to that man's house. The moment he has me under his power again, he will kill me."

"He wouldn't—"

"He will," Darmanin said quietly.

Arya wondered at his certainty. She'd detested Mathas Crowtalon on sight, recognised him as a powerful threat to her warlord's ambitions. But a man willing to murder his son in cold blood and risk his position in the process? No, she'd read him as too rational for that.

Andrian stepped forward and hugged his brother for a long moment. "I can see that I won't be able to change your mind. Good luck, Darmanin. I hope to see you again soon."

With that, he tugged his helmet back on and strode away. At his order, the column of Lances wheeled as one and galloped down the road, back towards Crowtalon. Arya waited until they were out of sight before giving the order for her Raiders to continue. Ranald rode on ahead, leading the way.

"If I did not like Warlord Crowtalon before, then my dislike is certain now," Rorin told Arya privately, his horse close to hers as they rode. *"He is not fit to be High Warlord."*

"I don't disagree," she said. "But I advise you to follow your mother's lead on that; she is far wiser than either of us."

He smiled at her. *"You are right. But I think you are going to be just like my mother one day."*

Arya smiled, surprised. "Thank you, Rorin."

He shrugged, a teasing glint appearing in his eye. *"That's of course if you don't let that blasted temper of yours get the better of you. For a moment there I thought I was going to see firsthand what a battle between Raiders and Lances would look like."*

She shoved him affectionately, and he feinted shoving back but instead slung a long arm around her shoulders in a warm hug before letting go to sign, *"Thanks for suggesting this trip, Arya. It's going to be hard to go back home."*

Arya sighed again and nodded. Home ... back to Lerin and Heathrock in the winter and years and years before she'd have any kind of autonomy again, if ever. And she still didn't have a solution for the Nightstalker, or how to keep Essa and Darmanin—and now Chiarn—safe.

Maybe she should think more seriously about what Salyarin wanted. He'd told her that if she took up her heritage as an Andahari Sky Lord, she might be able to counter the Nightstalker.

She expelled a frustrated breath, glancing over at Rorin as he signed something to Darmanin that made the pensive young man smile. To do what the elder wanted meant leaving her family, her home. It meant no longer being a Raider. And even though that future looked much bleaker since Desomer's injury ... the Nightstalker was so powerful, how could she ever counter that, no matter what she did?

Surely it was better to help Dunidaen contain him, not provoke him into outright war by declaring herself and becoming an actual threat to his rule?

Darmanin's gaze met hers then, reaching past Rorin between them. He seemed to sense what she was thinking because he looked as troubled as she felt. She cleared her expression and smiled at him.

She'd figure it out. And she'd keep them all safe.

Chapter 45

Arya flicked a stray strand of hair from her eyes as she focused on hammering a plank of wood into position, trying to push her distracted thoughts aside. The nail had been going in straight, right up until the contents of Thiara Ravenstrike's letter—received that morning—floated into her mind.

"I think these people want a solid roof, Captain, not one full of gaps," Taze called out from where he perched just above her, working on a higher section of roof. "It does rain here on occasion."

She scowled. "It sounds to me like you want privy duty for a month."

Across from them, Rorin put down his hammer. *"A person shouldn't be scolded for being brave enough to speak the truth."*

"You may be taller than me now, Rorin, but I can still kick your behind without breaking a sweat," she grumbled, cursing as her next hammer blow landed on her thumb.

"A least I can manage to hammer in a piece of wood straight," Rorin shot back smugly, balancing precariously as he used both hands to sign.

Taze laughed, his amusement only growing when he caught Arya's glare. Clearing his throat, he went studiously back to hammering, mouth still twitching.

"Here, I'll show you a better way."

Surprised by Darmanin's voice, she spun, almost overbalancing herself, as he moved gracefully across the half-built roof to crouch beside her. "If you position the nail like this, you can hammer in the last blow without needing to hold it, so you don't catch your finger. When you give it a final hit, use a bit more finesse."

She raised a dubious eyebrow. "Finesse?"

"I shall demonstrate." He took the nail and hammer from her hands and knocked the next plank perfectly into place. After the final blow, he sat back, holding the hammer out to her.

"What a wonderful demonstration," she noted dryly. "That's exactly what I've been trying to do."

"You all right?" he asked quietly. "You've been distracted all morning. Was it the letter Rorin received?"

She nodded. "Let's focus on work today. We can talk about it tonight."

A small smile crept across his face. "Keep practising, then. You'll never be a master roof-builder if you don't."

"Oh, get away with you." She shoved him, laughing. His eyes gleamed as he rose and returned to where he'd been working. She was pleased to see it—his mood had been up and down since they'd run into Andrian two weeks earlier. Clearly, he'd been thrilled to see his brother, but it had no doubt also reminded him that he could never go home.

The flicker of Rorin's hands in her peripheral vision caught her attention and she looked up to see what he was saying. *"If you can't get roofing right, maybe you should go down and help cook our dinner instead?"*

Arya forgot all about roof-building and threw her box of nails at the smirking boy. He ducked to avoid them, slipped, and almost fell sideways off the edge of the roof frame. Just in time, he managed to reach out and grip the edge. After a brief moment of panic, both Arya and Taze burst into laughter while Rorin hung there, his face red. Even Darmanin smiled in amusement.

"Hey!" Etan's voice called across from the nearest half-built house. "I thought we'd decided to stay longer in SparrowWing to help rebuild these people's homes, not to practice our gymnastics."

"Raider Etan, I've already threatened to punish somebody for insubordination today, and I'm not above doing it again," Arya called back.

"Threaten all you like, Captain, but we're going to get this house finished before yours, which means we get dinner first."

"There's no way they're going to beat us," Taze declared.

"Damn right," Arya agreed, reached for her nails, and remembered she'd thrown them. "Lord Rorin, get back up this instant. And bring my nails with you!"

They all laughed.

***

They worked until dusk, taunts and challenges flying thick and fast between the teams of Raiders. It had been the same every day since they'd begun work in Dorin. Two hundred workers—all competing to make more progress than the others—had meant that new homes had gone up at a remarkable rate.

The villagers helped as much as they could, cooking communal meals every night from the supplies Warlord SparrowWing sent and making sure they had plenty of water to drink during the day. Those versed in building spent the days supervising, giving advice, and making sure what the Raiders constructed wouldn't fall over in the first stiff wind that came through.

It was a wonderful thing to be a part of.

As they finished up that day, Rorin joined Arya on their way to the long trestle tables where the villagers had laid out food for them. "*I take it Mother's latest letter was the reason you were so distracted today?*"

She nodded, her good mood fading.

"*Which bothers you more? The Nightstalker's latest official communication to High Warlord Eaglesoar, or the fact Mother has ordered us to return home?*" Rorin looked as troubled as she felt. "*Personally, I can't decide.*"

Thiara Ravenstrike's message hadn't elaborated on the contents of the Nightstalker's most recent missive to Dunidaen but *had* informed them that High Warlord Darian Eaglesoar was convening an impromptu Council of warlords to discuss a response—which told Arya the message had been a concerning one. Rorin's mother wanted them back at Heathrock before she had to travel for the Council.

"Me either," she said wryly, then gave him an apologetic glance. "We'll have to leave by the end of the week."

Rorin's face fell, and she understood why. He'd worked among his Raiders as one of them; he ate and slept among them and worked as hard as they did. His every movement wasn't carefully planned between lessons and riding and weapons with Laskin, and though both Taze and Arya kept a close eye on him, he'd been able to live for the first time in his life as if he were just an ordinary young man.

"We've still got a little more time," she said, trying to cheer him. "It's not over yet."

"*Things are going to change when we're back home, Arya. You know that, right?*" He sought her gaze. "*I'm only a year off being confirmed heir at the next State Council, and it is time I start taking more of an active role in Ravenstrike's affairs.*"

Arya blinked, realising she'd never really spoken to Rorin about how he felt about being a warlord's heir, that his path was already chosen for him. Whether he'd ever wanted to do anything different. "Does that bother you?"

"*I want to be warlord, don't doubt that.*" He caught the drift of her thoughts. "*But I will be* my *kind of warlord. That will very likely bother others.*"

"Including your mother," she said with a flash of insight.

"*We'll see.*" He offered her his sweet smile, then wandered over to the food table to join Darmanin.

Arya huffed a surprised breath as she watched him go. She wondered whether, in all her warlord's complex planning to be High Warlord and neutralise the Crowtalon threat through Darmanin, Thiara Ravenstrike had given any thought at all to how her son might want to do things.

She suspected not.

***

The following morning, Arya perched near the top of a roof frame, hammering in the last few slats, glad that the overnight rainfall had stopped. It meant they'd probably finish this house today.

"Captain!"

Taze's warning shout startled Arya, and she looked over. He was pointing down the road leading into the village, where a shield of Crowtalon Lances approached. She couldn't tell if Andrian was among them, not with their helmets on. But one man in civilian clothing rode with those at the head of the column—Nain.

Unease shivered through her. What were they doing across the border in SparrowWing? Movement caught her eye; Darmanin swinging down off the roof and striding towards the Lances.

"Rorin!" Arya shouted.

He glanced up, looked over at the Lances, then leaped to his feet and began climbing down off the roof. Arya followed suit. Taze met her as she landed in the mud. "With me!" she snapped, straightening her jerkin and sword belt and striding towards the centre of the village.

Spread across the roofs, her Raiders saw the Lances and began scrambling towards the ground. The column had halted in the village square, three men sitting their horses at the front, all taking their helmets off. Nain was on the left, but it was the man in the centre that drew her immediate attention.

Warlord Mathas Crowtalon.

She swore under her breath—what was he doing here? Darmanin reached the Lances ahead of Arya, but she wasn't far behind, stepping up next to him, hand instinctively hovering near the hilt of her sword. "Dar?" she asked.

He didn't respond, his stare fixated with blind intensity on his father.

At Arya's softly spoken word, the warlord's gaze switched from his son to her, quick as a striking snake. "Who are you, and what are you doing with my son?" he demanded with all the easy arrogance of a warlord.

Mathas Crowtalon hadn't changed at all since she'd first seen him at Windfall Fort three years earlier. She could now see a clear resemblance to Andrian in the warlord's colouring and features, but all she saw of Darmanin in him were the hard lines of his expression. Of all that though, it was the man's air of self-assuredness, so strong it was palpable, that was the thing she marked about him.

"This is Lord Rorin Ravenstrike," Arya spoke as deferentially as she would to any warlord. "I am Captain Arya Nameless. We're here with Warlord SparrowWing's permission to help rebuild after the damage wrought by the summer fires."

Mathas Crowtalon eyed Rorin with an amused glance. "I've heard of you, boy. I don't know how your mother ever imagines a mute will be confirmed as heir to her State. There is no question my nephew will do a better job."

"Are you here for a reason, Warlord?" Arya was careful to keep her tone and words non-confrontational; they had to be very, very, careful here. "I assume your scouts have reported that we've held to our word and remained firmly on the SparrowWing side of the border." It was on the tip of her tongue to ask whether *he'd* sought permission to cross into SparrowWing, but she thought better of it.

"I've come to retrieve my son." Mathas' gaze returned to her, rich with bored disinterest. "Nain advised me of his presence here. You can tell your warlord she is lucky I do not take offence at her kidnap of him these past years."

Arya stilled. She hadn't envisioned this could be a consequence of running into Andrian. *Why* hadn't she envisioned it? Because Crowtalon had thrown Darmanin out in disgust. She'd never imagined he'd ever want him back, not knowing he was a magic-wielder.

Which meant there could be only one reason he wanted him back now.

To remove any taint on the Crowtalon name before he made his bid for High Warlord at the next State Council. She cursed herself for not thinking of that. For being so cavalier about Darmanin's belief his father wanted him dead.

A chill closed over her chest. She couldn't let him have Darmanin, but she was unsure that there *was* a way to prevent a warlord doing what he wanted. Rorin wasn't yet of age and he held no power or influence. She was a mere shield captain and had no authority outside Ravenstrike. Darmanin had not yet reached his majority and, under Dunidae law, remained under the legal control of his father.

Darmanin spoke before Arya could think of what to do, bitterness threading his voice. "You threw me out. Where I went from there was my choice."

"Warlord Ravenstrike had no right to interfere in Crowtalon family affairs," Nain said smoothly, that smug superciliousness in his expression unchanged from their last encounter. "There is no Dunidae law that supports it."

"And none that prevent it either," Darmanin said coolly, without looking at Nain.

"Even so," Mathas Crowtalon murmured. "She has been clever, your warlord, to keep you away from me. But I won't forget the liberties Ravenstrike has taken. You will come with me now, Darmanin."

"*Refuse!*" Rorin signed to Arya.

"*We can't,*" Arya signed back. "*He is a warlord, Darmanin is his son, and we are not in Ravenstrike. We have no authority here.*"

"*Mathas will kill him! We can't let them take him.*"

"*Rorin, I doubt even your mother could countermand Mathas' authority over Darmanin. It is law. Besides, he can't murder his son in cold blood—the other warlords would mutiny over it.*" But there were ways, she knew, that deaths could appear accidental. She tried to fight back panic.

"*Then why does he want him back?*"

Mathas initially appeared amused by this signed exchange, but eventually his smile faded into impatience, and he gestured to the shield behind him. "If he won't come willingly, then take him."

There was a rustling, a blur of movement, and within seconds, a line of Raiders appeared between the Lances and Darmanin. They had their hands placed warningly on their swords.

The moment froze, tension suddenly descending on the square. Arya hid her surprise. Clearly it wasn't just Rorin who'd won the liking and respect of this battalion of Raiders in living and working alongside them.

"We could take them. Two shields have flanked them from east and west. They're contained inside our net," Taze murmured, stepping up to Arya's shoulder, reporting like a captain to his general. "And they're not in their home territory."

The urge to do exactly that was powerful. The Lances were armoured but outnumbered. With the skills and training she knew her Raiders had, they *would* win, especially in the more cramped confines of a village square. One word from her, and she could wield a battalion to protect Darmanin and wipe that smug look off Nain's face.

She *wanted* that power. Wanted to take it and use it. More than anything else in that moment, she wanted to let her Raiders loose.

But Desomer had taught her over and over to stop and think instead of reacting with her temper. And if she'd done that back in Heathrock, he might not have lost the use of his legs. They might have captured his attacker. So she took a breath and thought it through.

And immediately realised that if she did what her anger demanded now, it might start a war with Crowtalon, not to mention place the villagers' lives, and Rorin's, at risk. But she couldn't let Darmanin go, either.

"Do nothing." Darmanin turned before she could make a decision, speaking for Arya's ears alone. "This is not Ravenstrike's fight. I will handle this."

"I can't just leave you to him," she said.

He stepped closer. "I told you I could look after myself, and I meant it. This is not your fight."

She looked Darmanin in the eye. "And would you say the same, if our positions were reversed?"

He didn't flinch. "They are not reversed."

"Captain Nameless, stand down your Raiders, or I will take my son by force." Mathas' voice rang out. "And if you make a single threatening move towards us, I will consider it an offence for which there will be severe consequences for your State and warlord."

Arya gritted her teeth, hands curling into fists in her gloves. Her pride refused to back down to this man, even as he smiled in triumph at the war no doubt playing out in her expression.

She had no choice.

"Stand down," she ordered the Raiders, keeping her voice firm, but hating herself for the words.

The Raiders returned to their positions behind her as quickly as they'd moved forward, hands dropping from their swords. Without any further hesitation, Darmanin strode over to the column of Lances and swung himself into the saddle of a spare horse that was offered.

"*Arya!*" Rorin gestured frantically, but she ignored him. She had to.

"A pleasure, young Rorin." Mathas nodded, smirked, and wheeled his horse around. Within moments, the entire shield was galloping away.

Arya swore explosively and kicked hard at the ground with her booted foot. Taze went to say something, but she shoved past him and stalked off down the path. She didn't trust herself not to lash out.

Mathas Crowtalon had Darmanin, and everything inside her screamed that she needed to get him back. The sensation clawed at her chest, tugging hard, as if to repeat *wrong, wrong, wrong* over and over. But she couldn't. Arya Nameless held no power in this world.

She could do nothing.

Chapter 46

*"Y**ou shouldn't have let them take him!"* Rorin signed angrily as he paced up and down inside his tent. Rain had started to fall again, and it tapped out a steady rhythm on the canvas overhead.

"There was nothing either of us could have done." Arya tried to be patient, but it was hard when she felt as impotent and angry as Rorin did.

"We could have taken them!"

"Rorin, be sensible."

He flushed an angry red. *"I'm not a child, Arya."*

"Only a child would insist that we start a war with Crowtalon," she snapped.

"Arya is right, Rorin," Taze said.

Rorin rounded on them both. *"We have to do something. I'm not going to stand by while Warlord Crowtalon hurts Dar, maybe even worse. I refuse, do you understand me?"*

She was barely holding on to the shredding remnants of her temper, and Arya fought to come up with a reasoned response. But as she closed her eyes to take a steadying breath, her grip on consciousness blurred frighteningly, and the Etherean elder's voice sounded in her head. *"Arya, I'm sorry to do this, but we need to talk urgently ... what has happened? I sense your turmoil."*

"I can't ..." Nausea heaved in her stomach as her vision and senses continued to experience dizzying dissonance.

"Sorry. Wait."

A moment longer and then everything steadied, and Arya opened her eyes into the familiar dream hallway. *"You can do this while I'm awake?"*

"*It's risky for both of us and I can't hold it for long,*" he said tersely, the strain evident in his voice. "*Tell me what's wrong.*"

Arya didn't prevaricate, and the Etherean was a welcome target for her anger. "*Darmanin's father has taken him. Dammit, Elder, you've had me running about worried about the Nightstalker and his monster hunters, and this whole time Mathas Crowtalon was the one I should have been watching for. He's the threat to Dar, not Andahar.*"

In the heavy silence that followed, Arya realised what she'd done, but it was too late to take it back.

"*Darmanin is the one you told me about. The one who can shapeshift. Isn't he?*"

"*Are you going to pretend you didn't already know that?*" she asked bitterly. "*You've known this whole time, haven't you, even though I refused to confirm it.*"

He didn't argue. "*You must get him back!*" Salyarin sounded as upset as she was.

Arya inwardly rolled her eyes. Hard. "*Darmanin's father is a warlord and has legal right over his son,*" she explained with what she felt was admirable patience. "*I have no authority when it comes to him.*"

"*You would do, if you had just listened to me and accepted who and what you are! Darmanin cannot be left at the mercy of his father. I cannot emphasise how important that is!*" The elder's voice had turned from anger to fear, its tone soaked in urgency. The hallway began to blur at the edges, a clear sign the elder's strength was fading.

She put further arguing aside in the interests of time. "*What is your urgent news?*"

"*The nazal are in Dunidaen, Arya. I do not know what form they take, but they are on the hunt. They will find you eventually—you cannot hide from them forever, not without your wyvern and proper training in your Sky Lord magic. That is what the Nightstalker fears most, it is why he is so desperate to find you while you are still vulnerable.*" He spoke quickly, as if trying to get his entire message out before his strength faded. She could almost feel the strain in his voice.

"*How do you know they're here? How can I identify one?*"

"*The blight, you will—*"

The elder lost the contact abruptly, and Arya underwent that scary shifting of consciousness again until her eyes flew open, skull pounding. She sank forward with a groan, rubbing at her temples until the throbbing faded to a manageable level. When she finally looked up, she found Taze looking at her with concern and Rorin hovering a pace away, a bucket of water hefted in his hands.

"What happened?" Taze spoke over Rorin's signing. "You've just been standing there for ages with a blank face. Rorin was about to throw water all over you."

"The Etherean elder reached out," she said, stretching. She felt sore, wrung out, prickly. Her head continued to thump mercilessly. "He's never done it while I was awake before. I don't recommend the experience."

"*What did he want?*" Rorin asked.

Wincing, Arya relayed a quick accounting of the conversation. It was only when she saw the look on Rorin's face she realised she'd only given him further ammunition.

"*Whatever his motives, the Etherean is right. Dar must be recovered. I command you to get him back, Arya.*" Rorin crossed his arms once he'd finished signing, trying to appear stern but too young to pull it off. It came across as petulant and was the final straw for Arya's fraying temper.

"I am sworn to your mother, Rorin, not you. Only the warlord of Ravenstrike has the authority to order me to start a war."

Angry silence descended on the barn. Rorin stayed where he was, mutinous, arms still crossed. Arya paced, trying to focus enough through her pounding headache to come up with a way forward.

"Arya—" Taze eventually tried breaking the silence, but she waved him off.

There had to be something. Some middle ground between starting a war and leaving Darmanin at the mercy of his father. She forced herself to calm, to think the way General Desomer had always taught her to. *Think*, not react.

Maybe there was one thing...

"There is an option," she said. "We help Darmanin escape his father, but we make sure it can't be linked to us in any way. And that means once he's free, Dar can't come back to Heathrock. At least not until we're home and your mother decides what's best to do, Rorin."

Taze rubbed wearily at his face.

Rorin sat down on a hay bale, looking sullen. Arya gathered this was the first time in his life his wishes had been countermanded so thoroughly. *"We can't just leave him on his own."*

"If we free him, Crowtalon's Lances will come straight to us looking for him. It's what I'd do. If he finds Dar with us, Mathas will have grounds to attack." Arya sighed, then urged, "Think of your mother's letter, Rorin. Dunidaen cannot afford to have Ravenstrike and Crowtalon at each other's throats while the Nightstalker is getting restless again."

"Why don't we rescue Dar tonight and flee north as quickly as possible? Their horses and riders are weighed down with armour. We could easily make it back to Ravenstrike before they catch up."

"If we did that, Crowtalon will know for certain that we rescued Darmanin, and the consequences would be the same," Arya pointed out, hating that she had to argue against him like this. She wanted to do exactly as he commanded her.

Rorin's jaw tightened at her words, and he looked away, blue eyes bright with anger.

Taze stood. "They'll be back over the border by now, which means crossing into Crowtalon to effect a rescue. If you get caught, Arya, Rorin will have to disavow all knowledge of it. He'll have to cut you loose, pretend you went rogue."

Rorin's head shot up. *"I won't do that."*

She held his gaze. "And I won't do this unless you promise me you will."

"Arya, I don't care what you say or what order you give. I am future warlord of Ravenstrike, and I will never sell out one of my own, no matter the circumstances."

"Foolish idealism," she snapped.

"Call it whatever you like. It's not changing."

Their silent battle of wills waged for several long moments. Eventually Arya gave in, but not because she agreed with Rorin. She had to help Darmanin some way, had to protect him, even if it risked Ravenstrike. She would just have to make sure she didn't get caught.

His shoulders relaxed in relief when she nodded, and he conceded in return, "*I know it's best if I stay here in camp in case anyone comes looking. Crowtalon might even have watchers nearby. I'll make myself visible, and stay close to all the other Raiders, but I want Taze to go with you to watch your back.*"

Arya nodded. "If we go now, we can be back by dawn."

"*I'll let the battalion know I plan to leave in the morning, after we give some kind of formal farewell to the village,*" Rorin suggested. "*That way if Lances come after us tomorrow, all they'll hear from the villagers is that we left in a relaxed fashion and didn't appear to be running away in undue haste.*"

"That's good thinking, Rorin. Do that."

He nodded and stepped forward to hug her tightly. "*Be safe, Arya. I don't want to lose you too.*"

***

The rain had faded to a light drizzle as Taze and Arya rode out, dressed in Rorin's spare clothes to avoid being recognised as Raiders by anyone who happened to catch sight of them. They headed in the direction the Lances had gone, Arya banking on the fact they'd have no reason to leave the road and guessing they'd probably make camp to get out of the rain as soon as they'd crossed the border into Crowtalon.

Both assumptions turned out to be correct, and at a swift canter, they were travelling barely an hour before Arya glimpsed the pinpricks of firelight in the distance that likely denoted a camp.

They turned their horses off the road and went deep inside the cover of the trees before dismounting and leaving the horses loosely tethered. Pulling the hoods of their cloaks up over their heads, they slipped through the dripping canopy, using the shadows of night to keep them hidden.

But they'd only gone a short distance before the strident call of a sentry rang through the night. Arya immediately stilled, Taze at her shoulder, and they listened intently.

Into the echoes of the alarm call came the sounds of men shouting and horses whinnying. The cadence of soldiers giving and receiving orders was familiar—no panic, just a practiced response to an alarm being raised.

"Is someone attacking the camp?" Taze murmured in confusion.

"No." Arya shook her head, realising what those sounds meant. "Darmanin's managed to escape on his own." She didn't know how she knew that, but she did.

"What should we do?"

She wavered. The night was alive with sound now, joined by the thunder of hooves as horses were mounted and set off at a gallop. Mathas would make sure his Lances chased Darmanin down. Not enough time had passed for him to have gotten a clean getaway.

Protect him.

Arya made the decision in a blink. "We follow. We help if we can, but we don't let the Lances spot us."

She turned and sprinted back to Zeke, swinging up and onto his back and urging him after the sounds of galloping Lances. Taze followed in her shadow.

It was a reckless ride through the dark trees, Arya trusting fully in Zeke's eyesight and footing as soaking branches slapped into her face and arms. She angled around to the east of the Lances, doing her best to keep her and Taze out of earshot, and pushed Zeke hard, trying to get ahead. Her spirited stallion gamely took up the challenge.

And then, abruptly, the tree cover ended and they burst out into an open field, spraying mud as they reined in abruptly. A single rider was galloping from the southern end of the field towards the north as Arya and Taze watched from its eastern edge.

It was Darmanin; she could tell from the way he rode his horse.

Behind the fleeing rider came six Lances—two were close behind Darmanin and closing the distance rapidly. They were almost close enough to reach out and touch his horse. Arya swore inwardly.

She spun to Taze, snapping out a quick order. "Stay hidden. If things go badly, go back to Rorin and follow his plan for tomorrow."

"Arya, no!" he protested.

But she was already urging Zeke out into the field, riding straight at the two Lances closest behind Darmanin. Un-armoured, Zeke was much faster and caught up quickly. The two Lances were so fixed on their quarry that they didn't see Arya approach until their shield-mates, farther behind, called out a warning.

Zeke shouldered into the closest horse, forcing him off course and into the rider beside him. Both Lances shouted in anger and confusion and went for their swords, but Arya had already turned Zeke and set him racing after Darmanin.

Darmanin glanced over his shoulder as she thundered up behind him. "You shouldn't be here! You're putting everything in jeopardy."

"And you were about to get caught," she snapped.

"Go, leave me," Darmanin urged. "I'll get clear."

"Not alone you won't." Arya could see that easily.

He hesitated, then, "I could shift. My shadowhound could outrun—"

"No. You can't risk anyone seeing you use magic." Arya fixed Darmanin with a look. She used that reasoning, knowing it would be an argument he'd heed, but what she really worried about was the Etherean elder's warning—that they not touch their magic lest these hunting nazal find them.

"Then what? Peel away now before they get a good look at you."

There was no time for thinking this decision through, so she made it. "Ride, Dar, as far and fast as you can. I'll slow them up so you can get clear."

His expression tensed.

"Go!" she shouted. "I'll give you as much time as I can."

With that spoken, she reined Zeke in, his hooves spraying mud as he wheeled to face the Lances galloping towards them. She reached for the bow on the back of her saddle, drew an arrow … loosed it.

It slammed into the chest plate of the closest Lance with enough unexpected force to unbalance him in the saddle and send him tumbling off, even though it didn't penetrate the armour. Then she loosed her second arrow. The next Lance, prepared now, dived away just in time, but it sent his horse veering off course.

She fired again and again, a steady stream of arrows that sent the Lances wheeling away out of arrow range. Arya judged the moment when they were most in disarray, before one of them started thinking and bringing a defensive manoeuvre into play.

She was just about to turn Zeke and ride, flee into the darkness, when a stentorian shout rang through the night—it came from the direction Darmanin had ridden in.

Raven's balls. Had they been outflanked?

More shouts followed it. Instinct had her tossing her bow as far into the trees as she could, her quiver of remaining arrows following suit. Then she urged Zeke into a gallop, only to burst into a large clearing in the trees where Darmanin had reined in. His jaw was tight with frustration as he faced four Lances sitting their horses directly ahead of him. It was too late for Arya to turn Zeke. She'd been seen.

Shit.

Something approaching despair flitted over Darmanin's face at the sight of her, but she quickly turned her attention to the Lances. They'd cut off any exit from the clearing, and one held a crossbow pointed at Darmanin's chest while the others had their lances levelled right at him.

An ambush. They'd expected Darmanin to flee and had waited for him here. And now they'd caught her too.

Dread inched through her. This was very bad.

"Dismount!" one of them ordered. "Both of you, on the ground now."

When neither instantly moved, the man with the crossbow lifted it threateningly. "On the ground!"

Arya slowly dismounted. She stood still as two Lances came over to yank her sword and dagger from her weapons belt, then tied her wrists behind her back and sent Zeke galloping from the clearing with a slap to his rump. Then they dragged her over to stand beside a similarly bound Darmanin.

She scanned the dripping trees around them, looking for a gap they could escape through, or a Lance not playing close enough attention. There was nothing obvious. She tested her bindings, but there was no give in them either. Hoofbeats heralded the arrival of another rider, and she whipped her gaze around to the man who dismounted at the edge of the clearing and pushed up the visor of his helmet.

Arya's dread deepened. Mathas Crowtalon.

A snarl erupted from Darmanin, quiet enough only she could hear it, but she glanced at him, hoping his magic wasn't going to break through his control over it when there was almost a full shield of Lances to witness it. "Calm," she murmured. "Let me do the talking."

Darmanin glanced at her. Looked away. There'd been a gleam in his fey eyes she didn't like, but he seemed in control for the moment.

Crowtalon's glance raked over Arya and Darmanin with triumph, then he lifted his voice. "Captain Tiner, send your shield back to camp. You and two of your men will stay here with us."

The hoofbeats of departing Lances faded into the distance.

Arya tried, "Warlord Crowtalon, how dare you capture a Ravenstrike shield captain—"

"How dare I?" Crowtalon lifted an amused eyebrow. "How dare you fire on my Lances unprovoked and aid in the escape of *my* prisoner?"

"I did no such thing," she said evenly. "Do you see a bow and arrows anywhere on my person?"

"Don't bother, Arya." Darmanin said. "It's obvious he's set this up to kill me. I should have seen it coming."

"A father would never want to kill his own child, of course, even a wayward one," Crowtalon said with false solemnity. "But when that child escaped his bonds and tried to attack his own father, as well as the Lances that tried to protect their warlord … well, I had to do what I could to defend myself."

There was no movement from the three remaining Lances. Arya guessed these were trusted men who knew their warlord's plans. No doubt they'd carry this tale of attempted escape and the unfortunate death of Darmanin back to their shield-mates at the camp.

Arya cursed under her breath. She was an idiot. Both she *and* Darmanin were fools. Mathas Crowtalon couldn't let the fact his son was a magic-wielder ever get out, and he couldn't kill him in cold blood for the same reasons. Either would kill his hopes of becoming High Warlord. But if Darmanin attacked him during an escape … well that was just self-defence. And the threat would be forever gone.

She cleared her throat, stalling for time while she tried to figure out how to get them out of this. "If you kill me, Warlord Ravenstrike—"

"Who would know?" Crowtalon snorted. "The fact you are here alone and without your battalion means you sneaked away to do this. A smart move given we both know Thiara Ravenstrike would never sanction it. All your Raiders will know is that you disappeared from camp. And even if your warlord becomes suspicious and gets it into her head to accuse me, well, I'll just show her the Raider arrows my Lances are collecting from that field. *I* can level accusations too." He paused, considered. "I might do that anyway."

Darmanin shifted at her side, rolling his neck, hands flexing in his bonds.

Shit. Arya was beginning to panic. She didn't know how to get out of this.

"Kill them, Captain." Crowtalon gave the order as if he were telling his cook what he wanted for dinner. "Dagger straight through the heart will do it. No need to fuss around or your shield might question why we took so long."

The Lance captain walked towards them without hesitation, leaving his lance leaning against the saddle and drawing the dagger at his waist, while his two men moved to restrain Darmanin and Arya for the killing blow. Arya prepared herself to jump at the man closing on her—she wasn't going down without a fight, bound hands or no—but before the captain got halfway across the clearing, an arrow hissed out of the darkness and buried itself in his throat, the only gap in his armour.

Mathas spun to yell something at the remaining Lances, but before he could get the words out, another arrow took the Lance restraining Darmanin in the same place, his blood spraying and splattering across Arya's cheek and jaw.

Before she could process that, a terrifying snarl ripped through the night. Darmanin's shape blurred at her side and then a shadowhound leaped at the remaining Lance, even as he'd let go of Arya and started backing towards his warlord, fumbling for his dagger. Arya had only just started desperately trying to get loose of the rope binding her wrists when Darmanin brought the Lance to the ground and tore out his throat with horrifying quickness. Then, before Arya could blink, Darmanin leaped again.

He crashed into his father, sending him crashing to the mud. The shadowhound howled his fury into the night, claws scrabbling for purchase against his father's chest and screeching against the metal armour, fangs snapping at the warlord's throat.

Fury rippled over Mathas Crowtalon's face as he buried his hands in the fur around Darmanin's neck, sheer strength and will holding his son back. But it was a losing battle. Darmanin growled, pushed through his father's grip, his full body weight pressing down against Mathas' desperate hold. Darmanin's shadowhound was full grown now, a fearsome sight to behold.

"Filth!" Mathas spat, his face a rictus of disgust and fury, even as his grip slipped and a snap of Darmanin's fangs came close enough to graze the skin of his neck. "Get off me."

"Darmanin, no!" Arya gave up on freeing her bound wrists and ran across the clearing to throw herself at the shadowhound. She collided with him and sent them both rolling off the warlord. She struggled to get on top of him, to use her body weight to pin him down, but this was a much bigger shadowhound than the one she'd stopped back in Heathrock all those years ago when he'd lost control fighting Warn.

He threw her off with a growl, tried to lunge at his father, and she managed to crash into him again, grunting as her bad knee hit the ground. "Darmanin, please, stop!"

He snarled, snapped half-heartedly at her. By now, Crowtalon had gotten to his feet and drawn his sword. The shadowhound shook himself free of Arya and let out a growl so deep she felt it echo through her bones. It was a sound of pure anger and hate. She watched his hindquarters bunching as he prepared to leap, saw the fangs as his mouth opened to tear...

"Darmanin, STOP"! Arya roared at him with everything inside her, every bit of her will, everything she had. Without thinking about it or knowing how, at the same time she tugged on that thread in her chest that had always bound them. "STOP NOW!"

And the shadowhound stopped mid-gather, whining in protest. He shuddered but stayed where he was. For now.

Arya looked up at Crowtalon. "Get on your horse and go, now. If you don't, he will kill you."

"You're done, you and your warlord both." Mathas shook his head, face mottled with fury. "When I tell the High Warlord—"

"You'll tell him *nothing*," she shouted him down, then bluffed like she'd never bluffed before. "I wasn't here alone. My battalion is in these woods—two hundred soldiers that just heard you order the murder of your own son. Not to mention what they saw him do. You say a word about any of this, Crowtalon, and all of us will start talking too, and we're going to start with the fact that you fathered a magic-wielder."

He stilled, jaw tense, fury banking on his face. Darmanin let out a low growl. Arya shifted herself in front of him, forestalling any more leaps. He strained against whatever it was she'd done to stop him; she wasn't sure how much longer she could hold him.

"GO!" she bellowed.

"You will burn for this," Crowtalon promised. "You and that warlord are done. I'm going to make sure of it."

"We'll see."

She waited until he'd mounted his horse and vanished from sight before she turned, gaze searched the trees, looking for…

Taze stepped out a moment later, bow still drawn.

She stared at him, horrified. "You killed two Lances right in front of their warlord."

"He would have killed you if I had not." Taze bent to cut the rope binding her hands. "You are my general," he added quietly.

"What did you do to me?" Darmanin's voice cut through the clearing, shrill with affront. He'd shifted back into his human form.

"Stopped you from murdering a warlord and your own father," she roared back. "I know what it's like to feel as angry as you did, but you would never have come back from that, Darmanin."

Silence caught and held, the clearing heavy with tension.

After a moment, Darmanin hung his head, all the fight going out of him. He looked muddy and exhausted.

"We need to go." Taze had gone and come back leading Zeke's reins. "Warlord Crowtalon might bring more Lances back to chase us."

"Agreed. But first, collect your arrows from the bodies, then find my bow and quiver where I tossed it." She gave him a description. "We need to remove every trace we were here."

Taze nodded and left. Arya turned to Darmanin. "You know you can't come with us?"

"I'll be all right," he assured her. "And I'll find a way to get word to you once I'm clear."

She didn't fight the urge to reach up and hug him fiercely. After a weighted moment, his arms crept around her waist and he held her just as tightly.

"Goodbye, Arya."

Chapter 47

R orin was pacing his tent when they finally rode in close to dawn, having ranged a large distance to ensure they couldn't be tracked back to the Ravenstrike camp.

"*Something went wrong?*" he demanded, reading their expressions clearly.

Arya explained the night's events as if she were reporting to Desomer. "They would have caught him if we'd done nothing. Even so ... there is no guarantee my bluff will hold back Warlord Crowtalon."

She had just put everything at risk. She felt sick with exhaustion and worry.

"*Thank you,*" Rorin signed with genuine relief, not seeming to understand or acknowledge the consequences of what they'd done. "*Thank you, Arya.*"

"Rorin, I think we should leave immediately." Taze had been tense with anxiety the whole ride back.

Rorin considered. "*There is only Warlord Crowtalon's word on what happened. Even if he calls Arya's bluff and accuses Ravenstrike of attacking Lances, he has no proof apart from a handful of arrows that could be from anywhere. It's better that we give him no proof, not even circumstantial. We need to behave from here on out as if we had nothing to do with Dar's escape. That means we do as planned: pack up in a relaxed manner this morning and leave after I properly farewell the villagers.*"

"He's right." Arya's head came up, some of her weariness fading away now she was growing warm and dry. "When we ride out, we'll do it at a walk."

"And when the Lances come looking for Darmanin?" Taze asked. "You know they will."

Arya forced a confidence she didn't feel. "When they do, we deny every-thing. Darmanin isn't with us, and Nain won't attack us on SparrowWing territory without proof we've done anything wrong. At least, I hope he won't."

Rorin gave her a look. "*You did the right thing*," he signed.

"If we'd done the right thing for Ravenstrike, I never would have ridden after Darmanin," she said quietly as she rose to her feet, the nauseous worry returning. "Taze, get some sleep. I'm going to do the same."

Rorin caught her arm as she pushed the tent flap aside. "*I am Ravenstrike, Arya, and he is my brother.*"

She shook her head. "Not yet, you're not."

***

Come they did.

Rorin's battalion had barely been on the road a half hour when the rear of the column let out a shout of warning. Arya gave the order to halt. "Ballsy of Crowtalon, to send Lances so deep into SparrowWing territory. I bet he's not even with them."

"*How do you want me to respond? Annoyed? Indignant? Polite?*" Rorin asked.

A little smile crossed her face. "I want you to stay here at the front of the column. Let's not give whoever Crowtalon sent chasing us the satisfaction of an audience with the future heir to Ravenstrike. Taze, you're with me."

Ensuring the battalion had halted in a long, neatly formed column, Arya and Taze rode to its rear, reining in and waiting for the Lances to arrive, silently counting their numbers as they came close enough. Two shields, and led by Crowtalon's chief adviser.

"Remember," she said to Taze in an undertone, reminding herself as much as him, "we act as if we know nothing of last night's events. As far as we know, Darmanin is with his father. The charade must be flawless."

He gave a faint nod, his face fixed in a soldier's focused look, and she was glad of his presence at her side. They sat in comfortable silence as riders approached.

"What now?" she snapped at Nain when he reined in before her. "In case your scouts hadn't noticed, we're riding *away* from your border. Don't tell me you're trying to track down more of Warlord Crowtalon's family members."

Nain's gaze ran over the column, back to her. "Where is Rorin Ravenstrike?"

"Slimy advisers with nothing better to do than harass us warrant no more than a shield captain," she said bluntly. "What do you want?"

She held her breath, wondering if Mathas Crowtalon had told Nain the truth of what had happened the previous night, whether Nain had been in on the plan to arrange Darmanin's death.

"Darmanin escaped last night, and he had help. I demand to search your battalion."

Her gaze narrowed. There was nothing in those words to indicate how much he knew. "We're in SparrowWing territory and you're demanding the right to inspect another State's battalion. You sure that's a line you want to cross, Nain?" Arya crossed her arms over her chest.

"Three Lances were killed last night, Captain. You will let us search your battalion or—"

Pasting an indulgent but annoyed expression on her face, Arya waved a hand, capitulating without further protest. "Go on then, do as you wish. He's not here."

Nain blinked, taken aback, but then he called an order and four Lances urged their horses forward to ride slowly along each side of the Raider column, searching the faces of each Raider they passed.

"You lost Darmanin *and* three precious Lances?" Arya arched an eyebrow, unable to help needling. "Goodness, Warlord Crowtalon must be very displeased with you right now. Not to mention what Warlord Ravenstrike is going to think about your baseless accusations this morning."

Nain's mouth was a thin line. He wasn't buying any of this bluster. That didn't matter. He couldn't prove a thing. "If you have him—"

"We don't."

Conversation died then, Nain and Arya staring each other down until the four Lances returned, reporting no sign of Darmanin.

"These Lance shields will escort you back to Heathrock to ensure Darmanin doesn't try to re-join you along the way," Nain announced. He didn't seem overly surprised not to have found Darmanin with them. "If he does, they will escort him back to Crowtalon."

Arya felt her smug mood pop at the insolence of that demand. "Did Warlord SparrowWing give you permission to send two shields traipsing through his State?"

"That's not your concern."

She couldn't allow this but, like the day before, wasn't sure how to stop it without using force. And deep down, she knew Thiara Ravenstrike would never approve her doing that, not unless Rorin himself was under direct threat. She'd already risked too much the night before—there was no room to push any harder. "Risk SparrowWing's displeasure all you like, but your Lances won't step foot into Ravenstrike."

"Warlord Crowtalon has a right to—"

"Warlord Crowtalon has *zero* rights where Ravenstrike is concerned." Arya leaned forward in the saddle, the temper she'd been holding back finally spilling out. "You even try, and your Lances won't ever return home. We clear on that, Nain?"

Something flashed in his eyes then, something *other*. It was old, and it was calculating, and it saw her. She sat back, instinct warning her to hide, retreat, flee. But she would never back down to this slimy worm.

"If we hear word that Darmanin steps foot back in Heathrock, it will be war," Nain promised softly.

Arya merely smiled. "We'll see. Now, are you coming along with your Lances on babysitting duty, or are you going to make my day and remove your uppity self from my presence?"

Nain said nothing. He merely turned his horse and galloped back the way he'd come.

"You didn't have the authority to speak to him like that," Taze said as they watched Nain ride off, leaving the Lances behind.

"Maybe not, but he deserved it."

"Don't get me wrong, I'm glad you did it." Quiet anger flashed in Taze's eyes. "Warlord Ravenstrike has quite the battle to fight, doesn't she? Trying to become High Warlord when Mathas Crowtalon stands in her way."

"If she were a man, I'd say she's equal to that task," Arya mused. "But you and I both know it won't come down to how strong or effective a warlord she is. It will all rest on the *other* warlords' perception of her."

Arya didn't want to doubt Thiara Ravenstrike, but it was hard to picture her defeating Mathas Crowtalon. Not with Rorin as a mute, a sister with two viable heirs, and Lerin running her army.

"I wouldn't count Warlord Ravenstrike out quite yet," Taze murmured.

Their conversation broke off as the Lances broke into movement towards them, the two shield captains in the rear.

"You stay back a hundred paces or we start reaching for our bows," Arya snapped at them as soon as they were within hearing distance. "Taze, stay at the rear and make sure they comply."

***

A subdued air hung over the battalion for the almost three weeks it took for them to cross the breadth of SparrowWing and Ravenstrike and arrive at Heathrock. Arya spent the trip short-tempered and taciturn, her temper flaring every time her gaze landed on one of the Lances trailing them. Rorin kept to himself, mostly brooding, and while Taze had tried hard to cheer them, his efforts fell flat.

The Raiders didn't like the escort any more than Arya did, and even after they left the Lances behind in SparrowWing, they remained a morose group. Each felt Crowtalon had somehow bested them—first in taking Darmanin and then in escorting them like they couldn't be trusted—and that didn't sit well with any of them.

"They're reacting the same way you are," Taze noted one night.

"So? They *should* be mad."

He lifted his hands in the air in mock surrender. "Just an observation."

Warned of their arrival by a Raider Arya sent ahead, Warlord Ravenstrike and Lord Eaglesoar were waiting to meet them. The entry yard quickly became chaotic as two hundred riders clattered in, filling the space with horses and soldiers and the grooms spilling out of the stables.

Arya left orders with the shield captains to dismiss their shields to food and rest once the horses were settled, then followed Rorin to where the warlord waited at the top of the front steps. Her eyes were narrowed in a way that made Arya's stomach sink. She'd been dreading this conversation the whole way home.

"Rorin, Captain Nameless, why did a shield of Crowtalon Lances accompany you to the Ravenstrike border?"

Arya swore inwardly. Technically, it was a good thing that the Raider border scouts had noticed that and conveyed the message to Heathrock so quickly, but in this instance, she wouldn't have minded a little delay. "That's a long story, Warlord." Arya tried not to wither under the woman's icy stare. "Perhaps best explained in private."

"Where is Darmanin?"

Arya cleared her throat. "Also probably best explained in private, Warlord."

"Very well." Thiara shifted her glance to Rorin and it softened slightly. "You're well?"

"Yes, Mother."

"Good. Both of you come with me now."

***

"Where's Darmanin?" Thiara demanded as the doors of her office closed behind them. "And why did two shields of Lances accompany *my* Raiders to *my* border?"

"Warlord Crowtalon took Darmanin back," Rorin signed, mouth a tight line, still angry despite the passage of weeks since it had happened.

Thiara turned her piercing blue gaze on Arya. "Explain, Captain, and make it quick."

As clearly and succinctly as she could, Arya gave the warlord and her husband a full accounting of everything. When she got to the part about intervening to help Darmanin escape, and how Mathas had ambushed them, she left out only Darmanin's shape changing and the identity of the Raider who'd shot the Lances—Taze's actions had been her responsibility and she would take whatever consequences that came from it. The relaying wasn't easy, and she had to dig deep to find the courage to keep her shoulders straight and voice unwavering.

Thiara Ravenstrike's growing anger pulsated through the room.

Arya eventually finished with, "Nain insisted the Lances accompany us to the Ravenstrike border to make sure Darmanin did not re-join us."

"Oh he did, did he?" Thiara's words dripped ice.

"I'm sorry I failed you, Warlord," Arya said as sincerely as she could.

She cocked her head. "How so?"

"I risked Ravenstrike by attacking those Lances to help Darmanin escape," Arya admitted, her mistakes weighing heavily. "And I simply stood by and allowed Warlord Crowtalon to take Darmanin in the first place. I couldn't think what else to do, and I didn't feel we had the authority to challenge him."

"*You did nothing wrong, Arya!*" Rorin signed.

The warlord shared a heavy glance with her husband. While Rorin might not want to acknowledge it, his mother understood the full implications of what had happened. "Matte, will you please find Magen and return here with him. The three of us need to talk rather urgently. Don't hurry too much, though, I need a moment to process my thoughts."

"*Mother, I—*"

"We'll talk more once you've had a chance to settle in," Thiara said briskly. "I'm sure you're both hungry and tired. You'll find a meal is being prepared for you in the kitchens."

It was a dismissal. Rorin looked helplessly at his father, but there was no quarter there. Matte simply said, "Come on, Peemla's no doubt got a feast laid on for you. I'll walk you down before I go and find Magen."

Rorin's father shepherded them down to the kitchens where Peemla was indeed delighted at their return. Arya and Rorin sat glumly at the kitchen table, shoulders slumped, while Peemla sent a servant looking for Magen and set other staff to preparing plates of food.

"You're back!" a voice rang out.

Arya's head came up, her black mood momentarily vanishing at the sight of Essa in the doorway. Her smile was bright and infectious, and Arya couldn't help but return it. "Essa! You're a sight for sore eyes. And you're okay?"

"Absolutely fine. It has been a quiet couple of months at Heathrock. Where's Dar?" Essa stopped halfway across the room as she realised he wasn't with them.

Arya sighed. "You'd better sit down."

While Peemla placed plates of food on the table until it groaned under the weight of it all, Rorin and Arya took turns telling Essa everything that had happened. Matte stayed, waiting for Magen, and Rorin clearly took comfort from his father's presence.

Once Arya had stumbled to a halt, Essa sat with tears sheening her eyes, clearly not knowing what to say. "I'm so sorry that happened."

Rorin looked at his father. "*Did we really mess up, Papa?*"

Matte wrapped an arm around his son's shoulders. "My wife isn't one for praise, but you did the best you could in a bad situation."

"The truth is, I was helpless," Arya said bitterly, the words that had been building up inside her for weeks finally spilling out in the comfort of being home in Peemla's kitchen. "I want power like a warlord's. I want power enough that I can help those I care about when they need it. I never want to bow to that smirking man *ever* again."

Matte smiled, and there was sympathy in his eyes. "You're a soldier, Arya. You'll never have that power. Very few ever do."

"I know," she said, but in her heart, she didn't know if she'd ever be able to accept that.

When she looked up, Essa's knowing gaze saw too much for comfort, so she looked away and began eating the food she had no appetite for.

"Lord Eaglesoar?" Magen appeared in the doorway, eyes widening as he took them all in.

Matte stood with a final smile for his son. "My wife needs us. We'd best go straight there."

"*What do you think will happen?*" Rorin watched both men leaving.

"Trust your mother to figure out the best response," Essa said reassuringly.

Arya searched Essa's gaze. "You've really been okay? Nothing worried you while we were gone?"

"I missed you all," she said simply. "That was the worst that happened."

Some relief filled Arya at that. If the elder was right and the nazal were in Dunidaen, then it didn't seem they'd picked up Essa's trail. Her head started aching again. That was the next thing to face, now they were home, along with whatever the repercussions from their encounter with Crowtalon were.

Something told Arya each would be as awful as the next.

Chapter 48

Arya dreamed that night. It had a hazy, almost unreal quality about it, similar to how it felt when the elder communicated with her. But this was different. Instead of a long hallway with billowing curtains and a winged man, she kept seeing repeated flashes of the same image, something too unclear to make out. She tried to focus until her eyes burned with the effort, but she still couldn't make sense of it.

There were sounds too, soft cries, then a wavering snarl. A flash of rippling gold. A claw? Then a longer flash showing several men, dressed as farmers and holding pitchforks. Terror flashed through the dream, piercing right to Arya's soul. One man lunged in, pitchfork jabbing, and Arya instinctively reached out to help, to grab the pitchfork and hold it back. Whatever was terrified sensed her presence then, swinging to her, reaching out...

The vision vanished. Ripped away.

Rather than waking, Arya fell deeper into sleep, her dream segueing into endless darkness. She wasn't alone here. Another presence shared the darkness with her. It *hunted* her, and whatever it was, it exuded menace. When it felt Arya's presence, it snarled in triumph, and she heard snuffling.

As if it had her scent and was trying to follow it.

She sat up in her bed with a gasp, covered in sweat. Shaking, Arya stumbled out from under the covers and lit a lamp, almost burning her fingers in the process. Her hand trembled as she placed the lamp in its wall bracket, and it took many minutes for her breathing to begin to calm down. Her skin was clammy, and she had to pace out the remaining terror and adrenaline from her dream before she could sit still again.

Her palm lifted almost idly to rest against her heart, where the terror had hit in the first part of the dream. Where she'd instinctively turned to help. Even now, the echoes of it were still there. Who or what had that presence been?

Even once her heartbeat had calmed, she returned to bed with the lamp still on, unable to sleep for the rest of the night.

***

By the time Arya headed downstairs for breakfast the next morning, she was haggard and on edge. Skipping the loud mess in the barracks for a quieter meal in the castle kitchens—not to mention Peemla's reassuring presence—Arya had just sat down when Essa arrived.

She had dark circles under her eyes and her usual cheerful nature was subdued, quiet. Arya opened her mouth to ask what was wrong when Rorin came through the doors, followed by Taze, his energy as high as it had always been, eyes bright with excitement. But the light died, replaced with concern as he took in Arya and Essa.

"*What happened?*"

"I'm fine, I just had a nightmare," Arya said dismissively, far more worried about Essa.

Essa gave her a frightened look. "Same."

Arya froze.

"*Both of you had a nightmare so bad you look like you haven't slept in weeks?*" Rorin signed. "*What did you dream about?*"

Arya swallowed and haltingly explained her dream. Essa nodded as she spoke. "It was the same for me, except I didn't see all that stuff with the pitchforks, just what you said came after. I can't get that snuffling sound out of my head." Essa shuddered, hesitated. "It wasn't just a nightmare, was it?"

"No." Arya let out a sigh, rubbing her forehead as if somehow that would allow her to keep denying what she knew to be true.

"The creature you saw in the nightmare." Rorin frowned. *"Do you think it could be this nazal the elder mentioned?"*

Arya had lain in bed for hours worrying about the same thing. She'd never in her life felt such a threat, such fundamental vulnerability, and if the nazal could provoke that sort of feeling in a dream, how fearsome would it be in reality? "That's what I'm worried about."

Taze blanched. "You think it's looking for you in your sleep?"

"I fear for Darmanin," Rorin interjected quietly, looking miserable. *"Arya and Essa are well protected here, but he is alone out there."*

"He might have had the nightmare too," Essa said, then lowered her voice. "And Chiarn, if you're right about him."

Arya reached out to squeeze his arm. "Darmanin is very capable, and we can't help Chiarn if he doesn't want it," she said, though she, too, worried.

She needed to talk to the elder again; she'd leave his candle burning when she went to bed that night.

***

The warlord remained out of sight for the entire day, closeted with Magen, her husband, and Lerin. Arya worked out as much of her anxiety and frustration as she could on the drill yard with Laskin. Eventually, he'd protested at once again being battered just to soothe her temper, and invited her into the mess for an ale instead. Wattin and Etan, both off duty, had joined them, and the company of her old shield-mates had grounded her, so that by the time she left them, she no longer felt so jittery.

She shared dinner with Rorin and Essa, but they chose to eat in the kitchens where Peemla bustled around, rather than up in his rooms. All felt Darmanin's absence keenly, though Essa did her best to cheer them up. The warlord still hadn't made an appearance.

It made her itch with unease and frustration. There would be consequences for what had happened, she knew, but it was Lerin who got to be in the room to discuss the Ravenstrike response. Arya had to simply sit and wait to be told what to do.

At least she might be able to do something about the nightmare she and Essa had had. She retired early deliberately, sticking the elder's candle on her windowsill before turning in.

For the first time ever, Arya was glad when the Etherean elder came to talk to her.

"*You're home safe,*" he said in relief. "*It's taken me a long time to rebuild the strength to reach out to you again, and I've worried.*"

"*We're back in Heathrock, and I managed to get Darmanin free of his father,*" she explained quickly. "*Can you reach Darmanin's dreams and see if he is safe?*"

"*You're the only one I can reach this way.*"

"*Why?*"

"*There's a complicated answer to that, but suffice to say, it has to do with your bloodline. The ability to dream-walk is something only the elder of the Etherean has … and outside those of our own race, we can only reach those of particular Sky Lord bloodlines.*"

"*So your children have the ability to dream-walk too?*" she asked curiously.

He went quiet for long enough that she began to wonder if he'd lost the connection, but the dream corridor remained steady. No blurring at the edges. "*Only our successors are born with the ability. But my heir is lost.*"

He seemed sad about this, but it wasn't the grief she would expect if the child was dead. Still, she didn't want to pry, not to mention she had no idea how long he would be able to keep talking. "*Elder, I had a nightmare, one I shared with Essa,*" she said, and told him what she could remember of it.

Salyarin's fear shuddered through the dream. "*If the nazal are hunting you in your dreams … hiding isn't enough to keep you safe anymore, Arya.*"

His fear struck her own. "*Then what do you suggest we do?*"

"*Come to us. Learn of your heritage and find your wyvern. Take up the mantle of heir to Andahar and grow strong enough to protect yourself.*"

She was silent, and he took that as encouragement.

"*Ignoring your destiny is not a luxury you possess anymore. If you stay where you are, the Nightstalker's hunters will eventually find you and kill you. Darmanin and Essa, too.*" The elder paused, as if wanting to say something but unsure of the wisdom of saying it. "*You were born to be a queen, Arya Nameless.*"

I know you want that power. The power to change things. The power to protect those you love. That desire is in every breath you take."

She couldn't deny it.

It had only been the previous day she'd spoken that desire aloud.

"Come to us," the elder said once more. *"And grow strong enough to take everything you want."*

A distant thudding sound pulled her from the dream before she could respond, and Arya woke to realise someone was knocking on her door. Grumbling, still half-sleep, she swung it open to see Laskin standing there. His shield was on night guard, she recalled.

He grinned in response to her scowl. "Warlord sent a message to the barracks. She wants to see you."

"Now?"

"In her private sitting room, no less." Curiosity lit his face.

"Thanks for the message, Laskin." She closed the door on his smirk.

The moment Arya knocked, the warlord called for her to come in. The room was cosy and warm, a fire crackling in the hearth. Her warlord was still dressed for the day, and she stood near the flames. Her husband was there, too. Both looked weary, and grim.

Arya saluted. "You wanted to see me, Warlord?"

"Thank you for coming, Arya, I realise how late it is." The warlord sighed. "But speed is of the essence if we are to be prepared for any fallout from Crowtalon. I must leave in a few days for Melbin, where the Council is being held, and if Crowtalon plans to move against us, it will be there."

Arya swallowed. "I am sorry, Warlord, for—"

Thiara waved a hand. "Helping Darmanin was risky, but I must admit that if we'd left him to his father to be killed, my surest way of defeating Crowtalon would have been taken off the table. No, you did the best you could in the circumstances. What I admired most was not only how you recognised that you had no option but to let Crowtalon take Darmanin, but that you were able to swallow your pride and do so. My bid for High Warlord would have been over if you'd overtly acted against his Lances."

"Thank you, Warlord." But the words tasted bitter on her tongue. She would never agree that conceding to Mathas Crowtalon had been right, despite knowing it was.

The warlord paced. "We have put several things in motion. First, you must be protected. As a Nameless, Crowtalon can demand retribution that I will have limited ability to push back on." Thiara stopped. "In truth, this was already in train, Arya. Not only did you save my son's life some months ago, but I have received glowing reports from Warlord SparrowWing—both on Rorin's conduct, but also on that of all my Raiders. He told me his Firemen reported to him how professional and well-trained they were. You saved Seelan, and that will be a bargaining chip I can wield like no other."

Normally Arya drank in her warlord's rarely offered praise like it was fine wine, but tonight she was tired, heartsore, and still unconvinced she'd truly done anything right. "I was just doing my job."

Thiara Ravenstrike was silent for a moment. Then, she took a step closer to Arya, and Matte stood up from the sofa to stand at her side. "You have become a member of this family, Arya."

The lump that rose in Arya's throat was sudden and powerful, robbing her of speech, emotion so unexpected she wasn't sure what to do with it.

Thiara Ravenstrike continued, "Matte and I have instructed Magen to begin drafting up the paperwork to have you formally adopted into Ravenstrike House. Once those papers have been signed and lodged in Gateport, you will no longer be Arya Nameless. You will be Arya Ravenstrike, Rorin's adopted sister."

Arya's mouth dropped open. "I'm sorry, Warlord. You did *what*?"

"This will help protect you, Arya, but that's not the only reason we're doing it. Rorin needs allies. As a family member, you will be in a position to offer that support. Not to mention, an adopted member of our family—once she has demonstrated the relevant experience and patience—will be a far more acceptable prospect to be its general one day."

Arya's eyes filled with tears. Thiara Ravenstrike still fully intended to make her general. And she was giving her this gift now to prove it. She stared between Thiara and her husband—who beamed at her—and she still didn't know what to say.

Thiara held her gaze. "I fully expect that you will grow into a general who makes me stronger, not weaker, Arya Ravenstrike. I would not be doing this otherwise."

Her warlord didn't have a soft bone in her body. She was all ruthless determination. But she looked after those loyal to her. Arya swallowed, fiercely fighting to stop the tears from falling. To be a member of her warlord's house, to have Rorin as her family in name and law as well as spirit … it was something she'd never imagined for herself.

"Are you all right?" Matte asked gently. "If this isn't what you want…"

She looked between them. "You're truly giving me your name?"

Thiara Ravenstrike smiled at her, a blinding smile. "If you want it."

"I want it," Arya said. Pride flared hot and strong in her chest.

A knock came at the door, and Thiara called for whoever it was to enter. Rorin appeared, literally bouncing from step to step with excitement. "*Well?*"

She softened into a slight smile. "It's done."

Rorin leaped into the air with excitement. Eyes shining, he enveloped Arya in a bone-breaking hug before signing, simply, "*I am so happy.*"

"We spoke to Rorin about this first, of course," Thiara said briskly. "I don't think I've ever seen my son so excited in his life."

The tears welled again, and she scrubbed them away. "I'm happy too," she said quietly, warmth filling her.

"*Family.*" Rorin signed.

"Family," she agreed, her words taking them all in.

The warlord cleared her throat. "We'll make the announcement tomorrow. Rorin, off to bed with you. There is something else your father and I need to discuss with Arya."

Rorin gave her a final hug, then swept from the room with a cheery goodnight for his parents. Matte returned to the sofa, though his attention was focused on his wife and Arya.

Arya steadied herself, then faced her warlord. "You said you've put several things in motion. What do you need from me, Warlord?"

Thiara fixed Arya with her sharp gaze. "Tell me, what do you know about running the Dreadwater Gate?"

Arya shifted, surprised by the question. "Not much," she said, rifling through her memory for snippets she'd heard the Raiders talk about over time. "It was a rite of passage that involved sneaking into Khadini to steal a weapon made of their precious blue metal, cazaix. It's unique to the Khadini smelt mines and the method of making it is a closely guarded secret that nobody has been able to steal. I've heard that it's stronger than diamond and sharper than any blade made of normal metal, though that could be an exaggeration."

"It's true enough," Thiara said. "And the Khadini guard their supply fiercely because it gives them a clear edge in war with anyone else on the continent, particularly Andahar."

"Because cazaix inhibits their Sky Lord magic and can injure a wyvern," Arya said slowly, remembering what Laskin had told her.

"Right. There's only one Sky Lord now, but as we witnessed three years ago, the king of Andahar is powerful enough to be a threat all on his own." Thiara paused. There was something sad in her expression, which Arya found odd. Since when was her warlord sentimental about anything? She cleared her throat. "Back to the Khadini."

Arya nodded. "They guard their borders closely and kill any Dunidae who try to cross without permission. The only chance of getting into the country unseen is by travelling through a narrow gorge filled with rapids, hence the name of the ritual, passing through the Dreadwater Gate and running the Dreadwater rapids."

"All correct." Thiara laced her fingers together. "I'm going to send Rorin to run the Dreadwater."

Arya stared at the warlord for a moment, quelling her instinctive response of shock and carefully choosing her words before she responded. "Warlord, that seems ... risky. Rorin is young. I haven't heard of anybody running the rapids and surviving since—"

"Mathas Crowtalon, over thirty years ago," Thiara finished. "He was the last to survive it. The practice died out soon after because of its risks, but also because cazaix wasn't as important after the Nightstalker went to ground."

Again, Arya chose her words carefully. "As I understand it warlord, those risks have only increased in recent years with our alliance with Khadini drifting somewhat."

"Rorin is a mute, Arya. No matter how clever he is, or how suitable a candidate to be my heir—and I have no doubts about my son in that re-gard—the State Council will not see past his disability. I am in danger of one of Lanna's sons being confirmed as my heir, and I will never accept that."

"It will be a certainty, Warlord, if Rorin dies. He can handle a sword and put up a good account of himself in a fight, but he is no elite warrior. And his charm and cleverness won't do much for him in surviving a journey along dangerous rapids."

"I have to take that chance," Thiara said. "Rorin *must* be confirmed heir to Ravenstrike if I am to be High Warlord. I hadn't intended to do this so soon, but given recent events and the fact a Shadeweaver assassin is still out there, I think it best he be gone from Heathrock for a time. When he returns from this, it will be as a man with an unassailable claim to this State."

Arya opened her mouth to dispute further but had no ready argument to counter that. If Thiara Ravenstrike somehow managed to win the vote to become High Warlord in a year's time, somebody would have to take over Ravenstrike.

A knock sounded at the door. Thiara called out for whoever it was to wait, then returned her attention to Arya. "Imagine my effectiveness as High Warlord if I have an enemy sitting as warlord of my home State? Don't delude yourself, Arya, any son of my sister's is an enemy."

"I understand," Arya said. "But what you're proposing is an enormous gamble. I respect Rorin and truly believe he will grow into a strong war-lord—but ... what does Magen think of this?"

"He's horrified by every aspect of it," Thiara said dryly.

"Oh." If Magen hadn't talked her out of it, Arya wouldn't be able to. She snuck a glance at Matte, and he met her look easily. He was worried but clearly supportive of his wife's decision. She wondered what Desomer would think, and winced at the sharp stab of grief and guilt that went through her at the thought of her general.

"I will do what I can to help my son succeed," the warlord continued. "He won't have to do it alone. Darmanin will go with him—that's another reason we need to move now, before his father finds him. Andrian has not run the Dreadwater, and if Darmanin survives, he will have a distinct advantage when it comes time for the Council to confirm the Crowtalon heir. I will send Captain Nameless also."

Arya frowned. "How are *we* going to find Darmanin? I told him he couldn't come back here."

"A small obstacle only." Thiara shifted her gaze away from Arya to the door and called out. "You can come in now."

The door clicked open, someone slipped inside, then it clicked closed again. Arya was on her feet the instant she saw who it was, hand drawing her sword in one instinctive move at the same moment as she stepped protectively in front of her warlord.

"Stop, Arya!"

It was only her loyalty to Thiara Ravenstrike that held her back at the sight of Ranier, leader of the Shadeweavers, facing her across the room. "Warlord, he—"

"I know who he is. Stand down."

Ranier watched her with glittering eyes, a little smile on his scarred face.

Arya shifted so that she could see both her warlord and the Shadeweaver leader. "Why is he here?"

"He is going to train Rorin and Darmanin to run the Dreadwater."

What?

"You planned this years ago, didn't you?" Arya asked in a flash of insight. "That's why you took Essa into your household and educated her like one of your own children, gave her a position on your staff. In return, Ranier was to train Rorin to run the rapids."

"I always plan ahead, Arya. Always."

"It's an admirable trait, even for a warlord." Ranier's eyes glittered as he looked at Arya's drawn sword.

The warlord ignored him. "Essa will go with Rorin, also."

"Why?" Arya stared between them. Essa was no warrior. "I insisted on it as part of our deal." Ranier shrugged. "And my reasons are my own."Arya's mouth tightened. "Warlord, a Shadeweaver assassin tried to kill Rorin and Darmanin only a few months ago. He almost succeeded in killing your general. He said he was going to keep coming for your household. How could you even contemplate putting them under Ranier's power?"

"They will be under his protection. He has given me his word." Thiara and Ranier shared a nod that was far too comradely for Arya's liking. What was going on here? "Not even a Shadeweaver assassin can touch them while they enjoy his protection."

The warlord's tone was final, and Arya knew it would be unwise to argue any further. She took a long, steadying breath, trying to focus her racing thoughts. Her conversation with Salyarin had only been an hour or so ago, but after this meeting, it seemed an entire lifetime had passed.

She had to decide now. There was no time to think about it, weigh all her options.

If she left Heathrock to join the Etherean and let the elder teach her what he knew about being a Sky Lord, she'd be leaving Rorin to Ranier's control and a dangerous run into Khadini. If she stayed, she was choosing to let go of the power she craved.

In the end, there was no real choice.

This was her family. They'd just made it official, made it clear they thought of her the same way she thought of them.

She'd find her own power here.

After a long moment, Arya lifted her head and met her warlord's gaze. "If you're doing this, Warlord, then I insist that you send me to run the Dreadwater Gate too."

"I had already planned to send you," Thiara Ravenstrike said quietly. "If you survive and come back with a cazaix blade, I will make you general of my Raiders."

Surprise hurtled through her. "What about General Lerin?"

"Come back with Rorin and a cazaix blade, Arya, and you give me enough reason to dismiss him and put you in his place."

Arya nodded slowly, then shifted her gaze from the warlord to the leader of the Shadeweavers. "In that case, when do we leave?"

Epilogue

Arya twisted and turned. Her bedding tangled around her limbs, but she was oblivious, deep inside her dream.

It had that same hazy, unreal quality as her nightmare, but tonight there was no malicious presence, no bone-deep terror or sense of being hunted.

But she wasn't alone either. The *thing* that had been so scared before ... it was in a different place now. No men with pitchforks surrounded it. There was no imminent danger.

She felt cold air. The freedom of open space. The contentment of a full belly.

And then *it* felt her.

As soon as it did, she could feel it reaching out, almost blindly, as if it knew Arya was where it needed to be. There was a mewling cry, a soft snarl. *Where? Where? Where?* The question beat at her.

She caught a flash of rippling gold, and then she could *see* where it was. An open field, moonlit night, a sheep's carcass at its feet. The coppery tang of blood in her mouth.

It gave a haunting cry, and a pair of wings spread wide. Another glimpse of scales, talons, a reptilian tale swinging back and forth. It was smaller than she'd imagined, not much bigger than a large dog, but Arya had seen a creature like this before, etched into the stone wall of the underground road leading under the Diamondfang.

A golden wyvern.

Mine. It let out a cry—eerie and haunting, a pale echo of what it would be one day when it was fully grown. *Mine. Mine. Mine.*

And Arya whispered back, "*Mine.*"

THE END

***

The story continues in *The Dreadwater Gate* – available now

The Dock City Chronicle

·

Want to delve deeper into the Archive?
Buried in the depths of the Inkweaver Archive is a prequel novella: *The Stolen Throne: a hidden Record from the Archive.*
Set decades before *The Nameless Throne*, this story follows a dangerous escape involving the fearsome Nightstalker — and it's yours free when you sign up for my monthly newsletter, **The Dock City Chronicle**.

·

Each edition *of The Chronicle* is filled with:
Insider updates on my books
Fantasy world news and hot takes
Hilarious book memes
My book recommendations
Exclusive sneak peeks

·

Sign up for *the Chronicle* at my website: lisacassidyauthor.com

~

Become an Inkweaver?

This is your invitation.

I'd love to welcome you into my **Inkweaver Community**—a private space for readers who love epic fantasy, found family, and all the feels.

·

Whether you've read *The Inkweaver Archive*, *A Tale of Stars and Shadow*, *The Mage Chronicles*, or *Heir to the Darkmage*, you'll find fellow readers who are just as invested as you are.

Inside my Inkweaver community, you can:

Discuss characters, moments, and theories

Chat with me directly

Access behind-the-scenes insights, sneak peeks, and the occasional spoiler

·

It's also a place to talk fantasy more broadly — to share recommendations, discover new favourites, and connect with readers who speak your language.

The adventure doesn't end on the last page.

Join me in the Inkweaver Community:

(https://inkweavers.mn.co)

About me

I'm a self-published fantasy author by day and book nerd in every other spare moment I have. I'm also self-confessed coffee snob (don't try coming near her with any of that instant coffee rubbish) but I am willing to accept all other hot drink aficionados, even tea drinkers. I live in Australia's capital city, Canberra, and like all Australians, I'm in pretty much constant danger from highly poisonous spiders, crocodiles, sharks, and drop bears, to name a few. As you can see, I am also pro-Oxford comma.

A 2019 SPFBO finalist, and finalist for the 2020 ACT Writers Fiction award, I'm the author of young adult fantasy series *The Mage Chronicles* and *Heir to the Darkmage*, and epic fantasy series *A Tale of Stars and Shadow* and *The Inkweaver Archive*. I'm currently working on a sequel to *A Tale of Stars and Shadow*.

As part of my writing journey, I've partnered up with One Girl, a charity working to build a world where all girls have access to quality education. A world where all girls — no matter where they are born or how much money they have — enjoy the same rights and opportunities as boys. A percentage of all my royalties go to One Girl.

You can follow me on Facebook and Instagram. I also have a fantasy reading community – The Inkweavers - where you can jump in and talk about anything and everything relating to books and reading.

I also have an author street team. I call them the *Wolves*, after Prince Cuinn's fierce personal guard in *A Tale of Stars and Shadow*. If you'd be interested in becoming a Wolf, you can email me at wolves@tatehousebooks.com. Everyone is welcome, and I'd be more than happy to answer any questions you have.

If you want to learn more about me and my books, head on over to my website at lisacassidyauthor.com

BORROWED FROM
The Inkweaver Archive